SOVEREIGN

SOVEREIGN

Allen Paul Weaver III

SOVEREIGN. Copyright © 2024 by Allen Paul Weaver III

All rights reserved. No part of this publication may be reproduced or transmitted in any form or by any means electronic or mechanical, including photocopy, recording, or any information storage and retrieval system now known or to be invented, without permission in writing from the publisher, except by a reviewer who wishes to quote brief passages in connection with a review written for inclusion in a magazine, newspaper, website, or broadcast.

All Scripture quotations, unless otherwise indicated, are taken from the Holy Bible, New International Version®, NIV®. Copyright ©1973, 1978, 1984, 2011 by Biblica, Inc.™ Used by permission of Zondervan. All rights reserved worldwide. www.zondervan.com The "NIV" and "New International Version" are trademarks registered in the United States Patent and Trademark Office by Biblica, Inc.™

Scripture quotations marked (AMP) are taken from the Amplified Bible, Copyright © 1954, 1958, 1962, 1964, 1965, 1987 by The Lockman Foundation. Used by permission.

Emphasis added by author in Scripture references indicated by italics or all caps.

ISBN: 978-1-7360972-4-3 (Paperback)
Published by: Radiant City Studios, LLC
Cover layout and design created by Allen Paul Weaver III
Author picture taken by: Becoming Kreative Photography & Design
Books may be ordered by contacting: Allen Paul Weaver III at: www.AllenPaulWeaver3.com

Printed in the United States of America

In memory of my father...

Rev. Dr. Allen Paul Weaver, Jr.
November 30, 1947 — June 19, 2023

You cultivated within me a love for God, the Bible
and an enjoyment of superheroes, science fiction & fantasy.
I always took pleasure in sharing these things with you.

You were alive when I started writing this story...
Now, we are separated by time and space
as you are resting in the Presence of God the Father,
Jesus Christ His Son—the GREATEST HERO of all...
and the Holy Spirit.

Rest well with the saints and the angels!
Until That Day when we will see each other again
in God's Eternal Kingdom...

PART 1

THE WIND

*"The wind blows wherever it pleases.
You hear its sound, but you cannot tell where it comes from
or where it is going. So it is with everyone born of the Spirit."*

—John 3:8—

1: Are You An Angel?

DAY 8 — Pennsylvania

"God is sovereign," a preacher declares with great intensity. The 'seek' button on the vehicle's radio had just been pressed and this was the first station it found.

"Everything happens for a reason. It's not luck. It's not chance. It's not fate... It's divine providence. It's God working out everything according to the counsel of His will. God wants to get your attention so you can give your life to Jesus, before it's too late."

"Turn that off or change the station," a male voice declares. "I don't want to listen to that nonsense."

"But... what if he's right?" a female voice inquires.

"We are not talking about this again. I said, change the station or turn it off."

"Okay. I'm sorry. I don't want this to ruin our drive."

A wrinkled finger presses the 'seek' button again as the radio lands on a news station.

"Now, *that's* much better."

A white 2000 Toyota 4Runner moves at a lazy pace. It drives along a stretch of winding roads on route 80 down the side of the Appalachian mountain range. The scenery and the weather is picturesque—like it was taken straight off of a "wish you were here" postcard. Nothing but blue sky and puffy clouds for miles. Inside the vehicle sits an elderly couple—enjoying the scenery while now listening to the news. They smile at one another through wrinkled creases while rubbing each other's withered hands. The wife adjusts her glasses on her face as "breaking news" comes on the air.

"There have been scattered reports of a man, in the area, wearing some kind of superhero costume. Some have said he appears and then vanishes. Others have seen him walking for miles. One witness stated that he demonstrated superhuman abilities. While nothing illegal has been reported, authorities urge caution until they can ascertain this man's identity and motives. For all we know he is probably on his way to a comic book convention... but until we know, please be mindful of your surroundings. And if you see something... say something."

The elderly couple glance at each other with a slight shaking of their heads.

"Always something strange going on somewhere," the husband utters. Just then, he grimaces and claws at his chest! "Nancy..." He groans like a wounded bear as his eyes roll in the back of their sockets and he slumps over the steering wheel! Before his wife can react, the SUV swerves out of its lane, barrels through the guardrail for a distance—snapping the metal railing like twigs—and spins completely in the opposite direction before hurtling off the side of a cliff... For a second times seems to slow... and then like a football flipping across the field, the SUV somersaults backwards, front over rear, down a steep embankment for a few hundred yards. It finally comes to a sudden crushing stop at the bottom in an upside down tangled mess of twisted metal and shattered glass. The sound of the entire ordeal, including the crash was unimaginable. Now there is only silence and the sporadic hisses of leaking vehicle fluids and punctured pressure valves releasing smoke.

Moments pass... Increasing plumes of smoke rise into the air as a small fire kindles. Thanks to the restraints, both husband and wife are hanging upside down in their seats like bats. The wife awakens to the repeated voice of an Onstar representative.

"Can you hear me?" the voice projects with urgency. "Our system indicates you have been in a crash! Is anyone there?"

It takes her a moment to regain her bearings. "We've been in an... accident," she replies—barely over a whisper. Her mouth is dry, but she can taste her own blood in the back of her throat. She winces while trying to take a deep breath. "I-I don't know where we are..."

"Hang tight ma'am. Help is on the way. Can you see any of your surroundings?"

"I lost my glasses. Everything's blurry, but I can smell smoke... and I think the engine is on fire!"

"Okay. Don't worry. Can you move?"

"No," her hands feel for her seatbelt. She struggles to release it, but is unsuccessful. "I'm stuck!" She feels for the door handle and pulls it repeatedly. "The door won't open!"

"Okay," the voice replies calmly. "Help is on the way. What's your name?"

"Nancy."

"My name is Frank. I'm right here with you, okay?"

"Okay," Nancy grimaces.

"Is anyone else with you in the vehicle?"

"My husband..." She calls for him... "John?" He doesn't answer. Through her blurred vision she can barely make out his hanging motionless form in his chair. She tries to remove her seatbelt again, but it's still jammed! Thankfully, the airbags deployed and spared them from certain death. But, they are riddled with cuts and bruises. With barely a warning, a brief sharp static blares from the speakers as the Onstar system cuts out.

"Hello? Hello?! Frank! Are you still there? Hello?"

Silence mocks her. The only sound she hears is the fire crackling as it grows. Her tears flow freely as fear of their impending demise fills her heart and smothers her mind. Her weeping grows so intense that she can barely cry out for help. Negative thoughts bombard her mind... Words spoken in a voice so similar to her own that she easily receives them into her soul.

There's nothing you can do... You are trapped. You are too far from the road... No one is coming to save you. You and your husband will die here...

The heat from the fire can be felt now. The flames inch closer to their prey. Nancy fights her hopelessness by straining to listen for any sounds of first responders... She only hears silence, punctuated by the distant sounds of passing vehicles on the highway far above.

The hopelessness continues with increased ferocity, as if it were somehow alive. *Just give up... There's no hope... This is the end...* In all of her years, through various health scares, she has never encountered this complete and utter desire to give up. It's almost as if it's being forced on her psyche from another realm outside of her own consciousness. But again, the voice sounds so very similar to her own. Yet, she resists once more.

"God," she mumbles through her sobs. "Please help us! Don't let us die like this."

Moments of stillness follows... and then... a breeze swells nearby, washing over the vehicle as a quiet peace fills her heart and silences the fears of her mind. It is then that she sees a sudden glare out of the corner of her eye. She painfully turns her head and witnesses something she can't explain. With blurred vision she sees a red, blue and gold form descending towards her position—gracefully as if it were flying! A second later, two feet land strongly nearby, skidding to a halt, kicking up dirt, dust and pebbles.

"Hello?" Nancy whispers, somewhat frightened due to her inability to see. "Is somebody there?" Her desperation forces her to speak up. "Please help us!"

The thick sound of approaching footsteps stop next to the SUV. Red-gloved hands grab hold of her dented door at two points. Their grip tightens as the doorframe crumples under their grasp. A second later, the entire door screeches as the hinges pop and the door separates from the vehicle. In an instant, it is hurled several meters away. The strong form bends down and snaps the seatbelt free. Nancy's body falls limp as she is pulled out of the contorted heap and carried a safe distance away. As she is placed softly on the ground, she tries to look into the face of her good samaritan, but the sun serves as a blinding halo around his head.

"Are you an... angel?" she utters before remembering: "My husband!"

The strong form turns back toward the SUV. The fire has just now consumed the front half of the vehicle! He quickly moves to the driver side door, rips it off in one fluid motion and tosses it a full thirty feet away. He frees her husband just as the flames overtake the cabin and he carries him to her.

"John!" she yells while the strong form lays him by her side. "John, wake up!" She checks her husband's pulse while the strong form towers over them—watching silently.

"He's not breathing! I think he had a heart attack right before we crashed. Please... can you help him?"

She can hardly make out the details, but even with blurred vision Nancy can tell this angel is gazing up to the sky. A long moment passes as approaching sirens are heard in the distance.

"Please," She pleads. "Is there anything you can do to help him?"

The strong form looks back down at the couple, kneels beside them and places his hands on John's chest. With a sudden swift and forceful movement, he presses hard against the husband's torso. His body convulses under the blow, but remains still—seemingly lifeless.

The good samaritan stands up, turns his head towards the roadway and then heads in the opposite direction. Several vehicles arrive at the top of the embankment: an ambulance, two state trooper cruisers and a fire truck. Within minutes the first responders make their way down the embankment and approach the wreckage.

"Please help my husband" the wife calls. "His heart stopped!"

The EMT's tend to them while the firemen douse the vehicle with flame retardants. The state troopers secure the area and try to ascertain what happened.

"His pulse is strong," an EMT announces as the husband slowly regains consciousness. "He's breathing well."

"It's a miracle," Nancy shouts!

The troopers and firemen look at the wreckage, the crumpled doors several meters away and the couple as they are prepared to be hoisted up to the roadway. A trooper approaches the woman, and hands her a damaged pair of glasses.

"We found this in your vehicle."

She uses her shirt to wipe the dirt off of the crooked frames and cracked lenses. Then she places them on the bridge of her nose and blinks several times while trying to adjust her vision. "This is a little better."

The trooper smiles at the sight and makes his inquiry. "Those doors look like they were ripped off their hinges. Never seen a crash do that. What happened?"

"He saved us."

"Who saved you?"

"The angel…" Nancy smiles broadly. "It was a beautiful red, blue and gold angel…"

The trooper scans the area, but sees no indication of anyone else nearby.

"Take a look at this!" The other trooper calls him over to where the passenger door lays in the dirt.

As the first trooper approaches, he updates the other. "The lady said an angel saved her and her husband. I think she's hallucinating."

"Well," the other trooper says as she points down. "A hallucination doesn't leave two in-depth hand impressions on a metal door."

2: Who's that Clown?

DAY 9 — Pennsylvania

Route 80, near Du Bois: three men in orange jumpsuits run through the forest as fast as their chains allow. A white man with long reddish hair leads the pack. A bald black man with a thick beard follows behind him. Another white man with blond hair and a stubbly jawline takes the rear. They pass tree after tree while jumping downed logs and ducking low branches. It's been almost three hours since their escape from the penitentiary. They have done their best to conceal themselves while getting as far away as possible from the widening search perimeter of the authorities. If their calculations are correct, they would have had at least a thirty minute head start before the guards even realized they were missing. Because of this, the entire county is on high alert.

Now, as the shadows grow long under the setting sun, the three men hide in a large crevice on a high perch near the highway's overpass. From there, between boulders and foliage, they can see any who approach, while they themselves remained hidden. They can also see a neighborhood of immaculate houses nestled on the other side of a nearby field down below.

"We gotta find a way to stay ahead of the cops," the black man says.

"Here's the plan," the blond-haired man replies as he points to the nearby neighborhood. "We break into one of those houses down there."

"Yeah," the red-haired man agrees. "We can get some food, clothes and cut these chains off!"

"Then we steal a car and get out of town," the blond-haired man finishes.

"I'm down for that," agrees the black man. "Which house you want to hit?"

"Let's sit here and watch. See which one has the least people."

A car drives down the street of the neighborhood and turns into the driveway of one of the houses at the end of the block. The three men watch like vultures as a woman exits her vehicle, struggling with an armful of groceries. Even separated by a distance of several hundred meters, the men can make her out: a tall, white woman with long brown curly hair. She's wearing a long tan coat and red scarf, which do little to hide her voluptuous curves.

"Food and clothes ain't *all* we need."

The three men snicker in agreement.

"*That's* the house we hit. Only her car in the driveway. No one came out to help with her bags. She most likely lives alone."

"So, we go now?"

"No. We wait till it's good and dark and then make our move."

Hours later... lights illuminate half of the overpass as a myriad of stars punctuate the night sky. As countless cars speed down the highway, the three men, now shivering and huddled together, notice a curious sight. A colorful red, gold and blue figure walks up the highway to the nearby overpass and stops.

"Who's *that* clown?"

They eye the unknown man in silence. "Don't know," one of them whispers. "Maybe he's going to a comic book convention."

"If he is, then he has to have money on him."

They watch as he kneels on the pavement for about fifteen minutes.

"What's he doing?"

"Yoga? Meditation?"

"I think he's praying."

He then removes his boots.

"Is he wearing a footed onesie? Even his feet are covered in red."

"Look at him massaging them," they laugh. "He must have been walking for miles."

He puts his boots back on and removes his cape, folds it up and uses it as a pillow as he lays down in a corner.

"He's going to sleep?"

"And he's not taking off his helmet?"

"This makes no sense."

"Doesn't matter. Let's wait and rob him."

"What about the house... and the woman?"

"We'll get to that," the presumed leader replies. "This guy seems like an easy mark."

"And if he fights back?"

"We kill him."

An hour passes... Now, in the darkest part of the night when traffic is minimal, the predators prepare to come out of their hiding place.

"Wait!" the black convict warns as he points.

They all watch as a large muscular man, dressed in a white robe with a gold belt, enters from the farthest side of the overpass, walks over to the sleeping man in red and stands next to him.

"Is that... an angel?" the black convict stutters with a hint of trepidation.

"A *real* angel next to a guy *dressed* like a superhero?" the blond convict replies sarcastically. "Can't you see they both probably going to *the same* comic-book convention!"

"Well, why are they hanging out under the overpass?"

"How should I know? We all just saw them at the same time!"

"Maybe their car broke down and they're waiting for a tow truck."

"If it did, then it don't help us none."

"Well, who do you think *he* is?" asks the red-haired convict.

"I dunno... but I think he's standing guard."

"Maybe the guy in red paid his bodyguard to *dress like* an angel."

"Oh, then he definitely got money!"

"But, I don't know if we can take them both."

"Yeah, just look at the size of that guy. He's like Arnold Schwarzenegger in The Terminator!"

"We got knives don't we? It's three versus two. We can take them."

"Three versus one is better odds. Let's wait and see if he goes away."

"What about the woman's house?"

"Let's get this guy first, then we'll go to the house!"

Hours pass as the darkness gives way to the early morning light. The men have not moved from their perch as they are startled awake from an unexpected slumber.

"We fell asleep?"

"I don't know what happened. I got tired all of a sudden!"

"Now it's too late to hit the woman's house!"

"I was so focused on this clown!"

"You guys shut up! We'll just get this guy before it's too bright out."

They look at the red figure. He is still lying on his folded cape. And the large, muscular man still has not moved from his side.

They watch the red figure begin to move as the large man exits from the overpass and turns a blind corner as the sun crests over the horizon.

"The bodyguard's leaving," one of them points.

"Quick. Let's get ready to get this guy."

As soon as the man puts his cape back on, exits the overpass and is on a secluded path the three inmates pounce! In an instant, they corner him.

"Give us your money," they command while brandishing large knives.

The man in red silently raises his hands.

"I said give us your money," the blond-haired convict growls.

Their victim slowly shakes his head.

"What you mean, no? You want us to kill you? We know you got money."

"Yeah," the other interjects. "We saw your bodyguard last night while you were sleeping."

The man in red tilts his head.

"Don't play dumb! We saw him! He was dressed like an angel!"

"We don't have time for this," the group leader sneers. "We can check his wallet *after* we kill him!" He steps forward with a slash, but the blade doesn't penetrate. Instead, it skips across their victim's chest while barely leaving a mark.

"What the—?"

"Body armor," the man in red replies through his helmet's voice modulator.

The convicts lunge at him, but as soon as they touch his suit a powerful surge of electricity—evidenced by a bright blue flash—courses through them! In an instant their bodies stiffen and fall to the ground in a twitching heap. The colorful figure throws one convict over his shoulder and drags the two other unconscious prisoners to the side of the highway. A driver sees the sight, pulls over and jumps out of the car.

"Are those the three escaped convicts the police are looking for?"

"Yes. Do you have any rope?"

"Yeah!" The driver opens his trunk and retrieves some, which the man in red uses to restrain the them.

"Call the authorities," he says as he finishes tying them up. "And don't get too close." With that, he walks up the road.

"Wait," the driver exclaims. "Who are you?" He watches the colorful figure keep walking without a reply. "Man, the police are never going to believe this," he says while dialing 911.

Several minutes later, the man in red turns around and watches as a multitude of law enforcement vehicles quickly arrive. He then continues his trek out of sight and over the horizon.

3: What Do We Call You?

DAY 12 — Pennsylvania

There is a Pittsburg neighborhood riddled with questionable behavior. Law enforcement rarely makes an appearance here without a show of force. Guys stand on the block with their heads on a swivel while handling their illegal business. Others loudly joke around while fighting each other to test their mettle. Law abiding citizens, with no option but to live in the neighborhood, do their best to avoid these characters as much as possible. They just want to go to work, to school and make a living for their families. But, each day is like walking in a minefield. You never know which step will cause one of these boys to explode on you. If you can believe it—it wasn't always this way.

Back in the day, this and other nearby neighborhoods used to be filled with so much beauty, warmth and laughter. Neighbors looked out for one another and "helping hands" were never in short supply. The houses, though a bit on the small side, were pristine. So too were the stores, churches and school. Not a shred of garbage littered the streets. Everyone took pride in where they lived as dreams and visions—both communal and individual—abounded in their hearts. And then slowly... almost imperceptibly... things began to change.

First, new zoning laws were enacted at the city government level. Next, interest rate hikes in the financial district made it difficult for local businesses to get loans. Then taxes on commercial and residential properties increased, causing landlords to raise their rents. While businesses were closing and residents were having difficulty making their monthly payments, an influx of drugs and criminal behavior began to proliferate through the community. All the while, resources in the local school district were shifted from the schools which truly needed them... to others in the "nicer" part of town where abundance already seemed to flow.

Just over a decade later, the neighborhoods which were once bright and vibrant were now a pale shell of what they used to be. Those who could move to better pastures, did so. Those who couldn't had to settle for what the community had become and adjust accordingly. Kids could no longer go outside to play by themselves. Gunshots punctuated the air throughout the night and day as gangs became prevalent. Good citizens who tried to stand against the darkness didn't stand long... Now, everyone had grown used to there being no heroes where they live. There was no one coming to save the day. Smiles gave way to creased lines on their foreheads brought about by stress. The tragic reality of it all was that law abiding citizens and criminals alike were just trying to survive circumstances beyond their control. Hope was thin-to-non-existent. And today was like any other day... until it wasn't.

V

The noon day sun shines brightly, but due to the cold air no real warmth is felt. Even so, seven young men, wearing big coats, fitted hats and baggy jeans, stand near a street corner, laughing at coarse jokes. Each of their outfits incorporate red into the color scheme, signifying their allegiance. As if by chance, one of them glances down the block and notices a strange sight. He shoves his friend's shoulder and points.

"Aye yo, Trey, check this out!"

Everyone turns to see what he's pointing at. To their surprise, the sight is both hilarious and enraging at the same time. Walking up the block, towards them, is a figure clad from head to toe in some kind of red, gold and blue superhero suit.

"Is this fool crazy?"

They stand at the ready—bold but slightly unsure of what might happen. As the colorful figure approaches, one of them yells out.

"Who you supposed to be?"

"A Superman wannabe," a friend laughs.

"Nah," another chuckles. "He's like the Mandalorian!"

"Whoever you are," another adds, "you got to be *crazy* walking through our hood wearing blue!"

In a moment, they stand in front of him like an impenetrable wall. Each one taking in the curious sight: a masked, armored individual with a flowing cape whose suit colors include those of a rival gang.

"You must be lost *'Wannabe'*," declares Trey—the group's leader. "The red suit is hot. But the blue cape... We shoot people for disrespecting us like that. But, since you repping red, I'mma give you a pass just this once. This ain't the way to no Comic Con. So, turn your butt around and get outta here, *now*."

A moment of silence passes before the tri-colored man speaks. "I'm just passing through."

The guys laugh.

"You just passing through… Do you know who we are? Whoever you are under that helmet… you don't just *pass through* our hood. These are *our* streets."

Again, a moment of silence lingers as self-confident men and boys glare at their uninvited guest. As they stare at him, he speaks again.

"The earth is the Lord's, and everything in it, the world, and all who live in it."

"What?" Trey replies. "What's that supposed to mean?"

"He quotin' the Bible," one of them answers.

"How you know that?" another asks.

"My grandma be always reading her Bible at home and quotin' verses like that."

"I don't care about your grandmother," Trey sucks his teeth as he focuses on the man in red. "Look around… God? He don't come down here. Neither do the cops, unless they rollin' with S.W.A.T.… Where we from, there ain't no heroes. We run these streets."

"You might run them," the man in red counters, "but you don't *own* them. Psalm 24 says these streets belong to God. *All* of this land and the people on it belong to *Him*—not you."

This group, always raucous and outspoken, suddenly find themselves strangely at a loss for words. They stare at each other warily as their leader swiftly reaches into his coat, whips out his gun and points it at the red man's helmet.

"Last time, 'Wannabe.' Turn around or I'll put a bullet in your head."

Again, a moment of silence… before the man in red speaks.

"This is the path I must take to get where I need to go."

"Suit yourself," Trey replies as his friends eagerly anticipate the fallout from him pulling the trigger. To their surprise, his gun clicks but doesn't fire. He repeatedly pulls the trigger. CLICK. CLICK. CLICK. CLICK.

"What the—" the guys look at their leader as he raises his gun into the air and pulls the trigger again. BLAM! It fires easily as he lowers the gun back to its target and pulls the trigger again. CLICK! "How did you—"

"The earth is the Lord's, and everything in it, the world, and all who live in it," the man in red declares again with greater intensity.

At once, they all stumble backwards—each falling to the ground! Fear grips their hearts, but it's not the usual kind they work so hard to keep hidden. This type they have never experienced before. They do not have words to adequately describe the growing dread which now washes over them. It's as if each of them is exposed—stripped naked before an unseen force which cuts through their souls and reveals the depths of their own depravity. Whatever this force is, they *know* it emanates from the man in red, standing before them. They all cry out, unsure of what to do as they struggle to stand back on their feet.

"Yo... this is crazy!"

"This guy ain't human!"

"He's got psychic powers or somethin'!"

The red figure turns towards the young man who mentioned his grandmother and calls him by name. "Marcus..."

They all yell in disbelief!

"How'd he know your name?!"

"I dunno," Marcus replies!

The red figure continues. "Why don't you tell them *what else* your grandmother says."

They all look at the red man with wide eyes and a stunned silence before turning their attention to Marcus as he fumbles over his words.

"You m-mean what she a-always be tellin' me?"

The man in red nods slowly.

Marcus clears his throat. "Uh, I never really pay her no mind, but everyday she tells me... 'God is sovereign. He sees everything. H-He knows *everything*. Like He's everywhere at the same time. And... He doesn't like what we're doing."

"And what else does she say?"

Their heads swivel in unison to the man in red and then back to Marcus.

"She says we—we better repent. We... better stop this foolishness and give our lives to Jesus while we still got time."

The red figure presses Marcus further. "Go on."

"C-cause she says... Jesus is comin' soon—not as a lamb, but as The Lion of the Tribe of Judah. And... and one day we will stand before Him and be judged." Marcus gulps as he looks intently at the man in red. The rest of his friends do the same.

"How do you know what my grandma be tellin' me? How do you know my name? Do I know you?"

"We've never met. But God knows all about you and your friends. And He *speaks* to me."

Each young man wants to run away as fast as they can, but their bodies don't respond to their 'fight or flight' impulses. It's like their feet are glued to the pavement and their legs are frozen in place. The silence smothers them as some are barely able to catch their breath. Yet, a few manage to utter the questions burning in their hearts.

"Who... *are*... you?"

"*What*... are... you?"

"Are you an... angel?"

"Or... an alien?"

Another moment of silence passes before a reply is given...

"*What* I am is human, just like you. *Who* I am doesn't matter. What matters is that God loves each of you and He has a plan for your lives. And if you are willing... I will stay with you for a while and tell you about God's desire for you to know Him."

The group gazes at each other in a silent deliberation as the man in red adds: "You have nothing to lose and everything to gain."

The dread each of them felt, subsides as a new feeling replaces it. Again, it is something they've never experienced before... and it pervades their hearts and minds. It is a sense of overwhelming peace.

A moment later, Trey speaks.

"I dunno how you did what you did, but we'll hear what you gotta say. But first... what do we call you? Dressed like that, you must got a dope superhero handle."

Trey's friends smile and nod in agreement as their uninvited guest replies.

"You can call me... **VALOR**."

4: Encampment

DAY 13 — Pennsylvania

Valor has walked along interstate 76 for miles. Now, he follows an impression and exits at an obscure place near New Castle. Within minutes, he finds some kind of large remote tunnel system. He leaves the outside light behind at the entrance and walks into the tunnel, through periodic puddles leading into the shadows. Fortunately, his chestplate insignia illuminates the dark path before him. He doesn't know *why*... but he knows his presence is needed in this place—at this time.

The long tunnel opens into a much larger underground space. As his eyes adjust to the darkness, an entire community of homeless people come into view. Row after row of cobbled-together-huts line the perimeter. Some are *actual* tents, while others are an amalgamated array of everyday materials. People walk around, some aimlessly, others with unknown purpose. Many are huddled around numerous barrels where combustibles are being burned for heat and light.

As Valor enters this domain, his presence is quickly noticed by a lanky, toothy kid with glasses who appears to be around 10 years old. The boy runs up to him with a bright smile—which stands in stark contrast to his dirty clothes and skin.

"Wow!" He points to the center of Valor's chestplate. "That's a cool light! It's like Iron Man's arc reactor! Are you a superhero?"

"I just dress like one," Valor replies. "What's your name?"

"Everybody calls me 'CK.' It's short for Clark Kent. He's my idol. People don't think much of him, but he's got a secret identity! I know I'm not from Krypton, but I want to be strong like him, in my own way. So, what's *your* name?"

"You can call me Valor. What's your *real* name, CK?"

The boy's eyes search the ground. "My name is... Timmy. But it doesn't sound strong at all."

"I have a friend named Timmy. He has a big heart and is always helping people."

The boy looks up at Valor with a smile. "Really?"

"Hey!" a man shouts as he approaches with a few others. He clearly seems to be in charge of this motley group. "Who are you and what are you doing here?"

"His name is Valor!" the kid says.

"I'm just passing through," Valor responds. "Just need a place to stay for the night."

"Why are you dressed like that?" the leader inquires in a slightly accusatory tone. "You going to a comic book convention?"

"Actually, I am. In California."

"On foot? Why would you do a crazy thing like that?"

"Because God told me."

"God?" the leader retorts. "If God exists, He doesn't come down here."

"Except for Jonas," another interjects. "He's on the other side of the camp. For years he's been saying that he's god. But if that's true, why is he still homeless?"

Some laugh as others see this curious looking visitor and walks over.

"We all know Jonas is crazy," someone else pipes up. "You can be crazy and still walk the streets. But if you're insane, then they gotta lock you up!"

The group laughs at the joke.

"Seriously," the leader continues, "You said God *told you* to do what you're doing. So, you think God talks to you?"

"Yes. He does."

"Okay... Can you ask God, if He exists, why doesn't he help us?"

"I've met many people on my journey so far," Valor replies. "Quite a few believe just like you. They think Jesus doesn't care about what they're going through."

"Jesus is a lie," the man counters. He flashes a sarcastic expression as he imitates the cadence of stereotypical television evangelists. "Preachers say, if you give your life to Jesus and your money to the church then God will bless you with your best life now. You'll have everything you need and you'll never get sick. Everything will go in your favor. You'll be the head and not the tail... blah, blah, blah."

"You have that down really well," Valor responds.

"I used to believe it too. I had a decent life... regular problems like regular folk. But I never could seem to get ahead and reach my dreams. Then I went to church and the pastor preached about how Jesus wanted to give me everything I needed so I could be successful in life. He wanted to help me overcome my problems. He wanted to grant me the desires of my heart. So, when the time came, I walked up and gave my life to Jesus. That's when all my problems *really* began!

"A week later, I got sick, had to be rushed to the hospital and almost died. A month after that, I lost my job. Three months later I was evicted. Family and friends took me in for a while. The whole time, I was like, 'Jesus, I thought you were supposed to make my life better?' Eventually, I had no where else to stay and ended up on the streets. Tried the shelters, but many of them are dangerous. I did odd jobs in order to eat. Did some other things I'm not proud of. Eventually I ended up here. It's not a great place to be, but we look out for each other and try to police ourselves. So, the message by those preachers don't work. It isn't true. Either Jesus doesn't exist... or he exists, but doesn't care."

"Or..." Valor adds, "The preachers with that message *misrepresented* Jesus."

The man looks at him inquisitively. "What do you mean?"

"What happened to you—all the problems that came after you gave your life to Jesus—that's a common occurrence for many people all around the world. And it speaks to the fact that humanity has an unseen enemy that doesn't want people to come to the truth."

"You mean the Devil?"

"That is a major part of where our struggle lies. Satan's empire of darkness fights to keep us from God's Kingdom of Light. Part of his strategy is to cause chaos in our lives so we will turn away and reject God."

"Well, I don't believe in the Devil."

"That's too bad. Jesus spoke about him often. But if you don't believe in Jesus, I can see why you don't believe in the Devil either." Valor discerns the spiritual hunger in the hearts of many that surround him. Even so, he can tell this man's influence with the group is great, even though he's bitter.

"Do you mind if I share the true message of the gospel with you?"

"Sure!" Timmy yelps. "We don't mind. Right Mr. Thomas?"

The leader glares at Timmy for revealing his name, but the rest of the group adds their voices to young Timmy's reply. Mr. Thomas acquiesces to the approval of the group and reluctantly motions for Valor to come with them.

The crowd of people—approximately fifty in all—excitedly gather around one of the trashcan fires as Valor begins:

"Ten years ago, I met a homeless man in New York City."

"You've been wearing that costume for ten years?!" Timmy blurts out with wide eyes.

Everyone laughs at his comment as Valor raises his hands with a chuckle.

"No, Timmy. I just started wearing this suit a few weeks ago."

"Oh," Timmy responds with reddened cheeks. "Sorry."

"It's okay," Valor replies. "There are no bad questions if you honestly want to know."

Timmy's face beams with joy as he nods his head profusely.

"So," Valor continues, "the man's name was Emmanuel. He was very well educated and had been married with children. For most of his adult life he sought to follow Jesus. After a series of traumatic events, he lost his job. Then his house burned to the ground. When his money ran out and he could no longer support his family, his wife took the children and left.

"When I met him, he had been homeless for almost two years and was trying to get his life back together. I was amazed that his faith in Jesus was still intact. You know, a few traumatic events can be enough to break *any* of us. But God is always present and available to help, no matter how bad things may be... After that day, I never saw Emmanuel again. As much as I sought to encourage him... he had encouraged me.

"Maybe Emmanuel was an angel," Timmy interjects with a sense of wonder.

"Perhaps," Valor replies. "The Bible does say that we sometimes meet strangers who are in fact angels in disguise."

"Are *you* an angel?" a woman asks.

Valor looks at everyone sitting in front of him. "No. I'm just a human being, like all of you."

"I dunno," Timmy counters with a sly smile. "Why don't you take off your helmet and show us?"

"I can't just yet. So, you all will just have to take my word for it."

Valor focuses on Mr. Thomas once more. "You were right to come to Jesus all those years ago. However, you did not receive an adequate introduction. Jesus declared what the gospel is and how it applies to all of us. In Luke 4:18-19 he quotes from the book of Isaiah.

"The Spirit of the Lord is on me, because he has anointed me to proclaim good news to the poor. He has sent me to proclaim freedom for the prisoners and recovery of sight for the blind, to set the oppressed free, to proclaim the year of the Lord's favor."

"That sounds beautiful," a woman smiles deeply. "I've *never* heard that before."

Valor nods in her direction. "The good news that Jesus came to give is that through faith in Him, you can *be free* even if your physical situations never change. He promises to be with you every day of your life. Through Him your sins can be forgiven. Then, you can be reconciled to God and adopted into His eternal family. The way you think *can be different*. Your emotional wounds can be *healed*.

"And those who trust in Him will never be separated from His love, no matter what happens in this life. And when Jesus returns to this planet, He will give us brand new physical bodies which will never grow old, get sick or die. And we will reign with Him in His Kingdom of Light forever. That… is the core of the gospel: the salvation of our hearts. The renewal of our minds. Being in relationship with the God of the universe. Everything else, like the healing of our bodies and financial well-being are icing on the cake, but not the main meal."

"I would love to have a good meal right about now," one of them interjects. Everyone agrees with the sentiment.

"Right now, we are dealing with spiritual food for our souls," Valor replies. "After we finish, I'll see about getting you some food for your bodies."

Everyone cheers and then listens with *even more* attention.

"I would love to say that if you give your life to Jesus he will get you out of poverty. But the truth is many people who trust Jesus still remain in less-than-desirable situations. Yet, they *continue* to trust Jesus because they didn't come to Him so they could have 'their best life now.' They came to Jesus because He is the Way and the Truth and the Life. So, can we trust Jesus because He is truly Lord of heaven and earth? Even if we receive no major change in our circumstances? Or do we only want Jesus because we think He can make us healthy and wealthy? The rich and the arrogant may look down on you because you are homeless. But God *sees* you. And He wants you to know that His gift of eternal life is available to *anyone who will believe*—whether they be rich or poor.

"You may be rejected by the powerful and the elite. You may be marginalized by the systems of control they create. But if you trust Christ, He will make you an heir to His eternal kingdom. That is a truth no one can take from you."

Many more minutes pass as Valor answers a flurry of questions. Once done, the request arises: "What about some physical food now?"

People pipe up in agreement with the inquiry.

"Yeah, what about some actual food for our stomachs?"

"We've hardly eaten anything for the past few days."

"How are you going to get us some food?"

"Everyone hold hands," Valor declares to the group as they all look at each other in hesitant surprise.

"Why do you want us to do that?" Timmy asks loud enough for everyone to hear him.

"We're going to do what I have had to do every day on my journey. We're going to pray and ask God to provide what we need."

They all still look at each other a bit hesitantly.

"You want us to pray?"

"What do you have to lose by praying?" Valor asks rhetorically. "Absolutely nothing. But you have everything to gain. And if you don't want to hold hands, you can put your hands on the shoulder of the person standing next to you."

"Valor's right," Timmy blurts out. "Praying wouldn't hurt."

Many in the group look at young Timmy with slight smiles on their faces. Slowly, they agree to pray. Some are holding hands, others are resting their hands on the shoulders of others.

"I would like everyone to bow their heads." As those in the group respond, Valor notices that even Mr. Thomas participates.

"Heavenly Father," Valor begins, "we thank You for providing everything we need each day. You have given us our spiritual daily bread today and now I ask that You provide for our physical daily bread. We are hungry and only You can make a way for us to eat in this moment. We say 'thank you' for the blessings you have given us in the past and for what You are doing right now in our present. We also say 'thank you' in advance for what You are about to do in our future. I ask, Father, that You will make Your Son Jesus known to everyone in this place. I also ask for Your Holy Presence to reside in this space, with Your people. In Jesus' Name we pray. Amen."

They all look up with inquisitive eyes.

"So, where's the food?"

Many of them laugh at the immediate question, but also wonder how God will provide for their need.

"Follow me," Valor proclaims with a wave as he heads for the entrance to the tunnel. They all follow him out of the tunnel with much chatter and growing anticipation.

Soon, they come a nearby road. To their surprise, a food delivery truck is parked with its front hood raised and its hazard lights flashing. The driver sees the group and quickly approaches.

"Oh, you all are a sight for sore eyes!"

Everyone stares at each other, unsure of how to respond to the driver's remark.

"Are any of you hungry?"

"Yeah," several people from the group exclaims. "Real hungry!"

The driver laughs. "This must be providence! My truck broke down and the replacement truck won't get here in time to save the food. So, I either have to throw out these hot meals or give them away."

"We'll take them off your hands," someone else yells.

"Great," the truck driver claps as he scans the group. "I know I have enough for everyone to have a meal. Maybe even enough for people to get seconds."

The group cheers and gives God praise as they stand in awe at His provision. Whoever heard of a food truck breaking down near a homeless encampment? As the truck driver gets ready to hand out the meals, Mr. Thomas and Timmy look around for Valor.

"Has anyone seen Valor?" Mr. Thomas yells.

"Yeah," Timmy adds. "Has anyone seen him?"

Everyone looks around, but he is nowhere to be found.

5: Show Us Some Identification

DAY 15 — Ohio

An Akron, Ohio police officer's voice blares from a speaker system...

"Stop right there! Let me see some identification!"

Valor stops his walk—mid stride—in a nice neighborhood and slowly raises his hands. A police cruiser slows to a stop as two officers exit the vehicle with their hands on their holsters. One officer is clearly larger and more intimidating. The other officer is slender and unassuming and hangs back by a few steps.

"Good evening," Valor declares. "Did I do something wrong?"

They examine his appearance before speaking.

"You're walking through a neighborhood with a concealed identity and it's *not* Halloween."

"Is that a crime?"

"No... But we've received a couple of calls from concerned citizens about your presence."

"I'm just passing through."

"Where are you headed?"

"California."

"You're walking the entire way?"

"Yes. If you're not arresting me, may I put my hands down now?"

One officer motions in the affirmative.

"I've seen some news reports about you. No one knows who you are. So, we need you to remove your helmet and show us some identification, now."

"I'm sorry. I don't have any ID on me and I can't remove my helmet until later in my journey."

"Says who?"

"God."

"God?" The first officer rolls his eyes at his partner. "God has nothing to do with this."

"God has something to do with everything."

"We got ourselves a crazy one…" the first officer exclaims as he walks over to Valor and firmly grabs his arm. "Alright, you need to come with us to the precinct for questioning."

Valor doesn't move—neither can the officer move him no matter how hard he tries. "Have I broken any laws?"

"Excuse us for a moment," the second officer interrupts while pulling his partner a few feet away. "Why are you giving this guy a hard time? He hasn't broken any laws."

"You don't think it's strange he's got no ID and he won't take off his helmet?"

"Strange? Yeah. But we've seen stranger things without arresting anyone. So, he's an eccentric dresser. His costume *is* pretty cool." He turns around. "You got a name to go with your costume?"

"Valor."

"Like a… man or soldier of valor?"

"Yes, like a man of valor"

"He could be a criminal," the first officer quips.

"Maybe, but until we have concrete evidence, we have to let him go. You're already under review by internal affairs. So, you need to play this by the book." He turns back around. "Mr. Valor. You are free to go. Have a good day and stay out of trouble."

"Thank you, officers. You do the same."

Both officers stand next to their vehicle while watching Valor walk down the block. Meanwhile, three men, dressed in black, are watching *them* from a blue car parked half way down the street.

"Been following these two all night," the driver growls. "Waiting for the right time. Can't believe that big cop shot my brother and he's back on the job like nothin' happened. He gettin' his tonight!"

"What about his partner?" the guy in the back seat inquires. "I've seen him around. He's legit. Treats everyone with respect."

"What about him?" the driver retorts. "I don't care how much respect he got. He's still one of them. So, he's guilty by association. Let's do this."

The three men brandish their guns as their electric car silently powers up.

The driver chuckles. "They won't even hear us comin'."

They drive up the block, pull their masks over their faces and roll down the windows. The second officer notices movement out of the corner of his eye. Both barely have time to react as a hail of bullets streak past them—causing them to dive for cover behind their squad car! Pieces of the car explode all around them under the barrage! The officers have no opportunity to return fire! All they can do is stay pressed to the ground and radio for back up.

"We're sitting ducks out here!" The first officer yells—just barely —over the sounds of rapid gunshots, which suddenly stop.

The three men reload and jump out their vehicle—swiftly making their way over to the police car. The head guy motions for them to go around on both sides. Before they can split up, a strong hand grabs one of them from behind, crushes his gun with his free hand and launches him screaming into the air. The other two shooters turn around to find Valor standing firmly in front of them. As their friend hits the concrete on the other side of their car, they raise their guns and pull the triggers, but their weapons only click repeatedly!

"What the—"

The two officers jump to their feet with their guns drawn—just in time to witness Valor crushing the assailant's guns—one in each hand. Then, with one smooth motion, he grabs both shooters by their shirts and effortlessly hoists them into the air as they grab and kick at Valor, but to no avail!

"You would risk the lives of innocent bystanders for an unjust retribution?" Valor inquires. "The LORD says your brother received the consequence of his guilt. You will too unless you repent."

"Who are you? How do you know about my brother?"

"Don't know how you so strong, hero, but we willing to die for what we believe!"

One of them pulls a knife out of his pocket. But before he can use it, Valor slams their bodies to the pavement. The two trembling officers slowly step from around their damaged car. Their shaky hands can barely hold onto their firearms. Valor stands to his feet while holding both men by their shirts—unconscious.

"You—came back... and saved us," the second officer exclaims!

"Are you both okay?" Valor inquires.

"Y-yes," the first officer replies. Clearly he is shaken up. "Thank you. We'd be dead if it weren't for you!"

"All of this happened because of your unscrupulous ways, Officer. The Lord wants you to repent and get right before Him or the investigation by Internal Affairs will be the least of your problems."

"How did you know about that?! Did you overhear my partner talk about that?"

Before an answer can be given, the first man that was thrown across the street comes to, stumbles to his feet and makes a run for it. But, he stops immediately—throwing his hands up—as three police cars screech to a halt in front of him. Within seconds, he's surrounded.

The two ambushed officers handcuff the shooters and then turn around to address their hero. But, Valor is nowhere to be found.

"Where'd he go?"

"I don't know! He was just here a moment ago! It's like he pulled a Batman!"

The other officers walk over to them.

"Your cruiser looks like Swiss cheese!" an officer balks.

"How did you guys survive that?" another officer asks in astonishment.

"Even *after* we tell you, you won't believe it." The shorter officer replies while looking at his partner. "Maybe God does have something to do with everything."

6: Roadside Assistance

DAY 18 — Ohio

As Valor continues his trek, he happens upon an old grey Toyota Camry awkwardly parked on the side of Interstate 80. Black skid marks trail behind it, leading to the back right tire which is mangled, flat and hanging off the rim. Valor notices a woman crying in the driver seat. A nearby sign indicates that Norwalk is the next upcoming exit.

Okay Father. He prays silently. *What am I to do here?* He approaches the driver's side door and taps on the partially open window as cars speed past—catching his cape in the wind gusts. His sudden appearance startles her as she puts on her sunglasses and looks up with dried mascara etched down her cheeks.

"Ma'am. Are you okay?" Valor asks.

Clearly she is not, but his heroic garb—though a curious sight—puts her at ease.

"It's you..." She says as she rolls down the window a bit more. "You're the guy from the news." She tries to pull herself together. "Not sure if I should be scared or relieved. My tire blew and I'm... running late for an appointment. My spare tire and jack are missing... and my phone is dead. I tried to flag some people down, but no one wants to stop." She glances at herself in the mirror. "The way I look, people probably think I'm some crazy woman!" She breathes deeply. "I've been praying to God for help... And now, you're here."

"Do you have roadside assistance?"

"No."

"Well, let's see how I can help you. What's your name?"

"Elizabeth," she mutters.

"Nice to meet you, Elizabeth. My name is Valor."

"You on your way to a comic book convention or something?"

"That's the million dollar question. I am, actually. Still got a long way to go."

Valor notices the large sunglasses resting on her nose, even though it's overcast. He sees her luggage piled in the back seat—as if thrown there in haste. *She's running from something... or someone,* he thinks as he prays silently, *Who is she running from, LORD? What do you want me to do?*

Just then, a silver Ford F-150 pickup truck roars to a stop behind them. The engine quiets as a sizable man, wearing black jeans and a black skull t-shirt, steps out. Valor notices Elizabeth's widening eyes when she sees him. Her fear is immediate.

"Baby," the man calls out as he slowly approaches. "I've been looking for you. You okay?" He stares at Valor. "Who are you supposed to be?"

"I'm just walking," Valor replies firmly. "As you can see, her car has a flat tire. Was just about to help. Who might you be?"

"I'm her boyfriend," the man replies in a forceful tone. He looks at her still sitting in the car. "Get out the car and come get in the truck, baby. I'll take you back home, get the spare and the jack and come back with one of the guys to fix your car."

Her only response is the nervous shaking of her entire body.

"How did you know the car didn't have a spare and jack?" Valor inquires.

The man betrays a nervous look. "I just... figured since she had a flat and I didn't see the jack... Look, I don't have to explain anything to you. You're not the police!" He focuses his gaze on the woman and belts out a command. "Liz, go get in the truck!"

Valor watches as she reluctantly opens her car door and slowly steps out—slightly hunched over, shrinking back in fear.

"You don't have to go with him if you don't want to," Valor cautions. "And you don't have to hide your black eye behind those sunglasses either."

Her mouth opens in astonishment as she slowly reaches up and removes them from her face, revealing a badly bruised right eye and a cut under her left.

"Hey!" the man yells nervously. "Liz, get away from that freak and get in the truck right now!"

She remains behind Valor and looks at him with pleading eyes. "There's no place for me to go," she admits. "He *always* finds me."

"Stop talking to him," the boyfriend commands in a deeper voice, "and get in my truck, now!" For all of his size and strength, he hasn't moved an inch towards Elizabeth. Valor is a wildcard which makes the situation unpredictable. Even so, his fuse is short.

"He almost killed you before," Valor declares as Elizabeth and her abusive boyfriend stare at him in disbelief. "You won't survive if you go back again."

"How do you know that?" Elizabeth emphatically whispers.

"Yeah," her boyfriend exclaims! "Who told you that?"

"*God* told me."

"God?" She weighs his words and considers her options before making her decision. "I... I don't want to go with him."

Valor turns, squarely facing the boyfriend and speaks resolutely.

"Elizabeth doesn't want to go with you. So, I suggest you leave and let her go wherever she's going."

"You suggest?" the man erupts. "I don't take orders from no one, especially from some cosplay clown wannabe superhero. You think you some kind of hero?" He immediately rushes over and slams his palms on Valor's chest—in an attempt to push him to the ground. But, the force pushes back as Valor's body doesn't budge—like he's bolted to the earth beneath his feet.

The man stumbles backwards in a moment of surprise, especially since he's larger than Valor. He snarls as he steps in again with his strongest blow aimed straight at Valor's faceplate. In one swift move, Valor raises his arm and catches the man's fist firmly in his hand! The boyfriend yelps as he tries to retract his arm, but Valor's grip is like a vise! With each passing second Valor squeezes tighter, applying incremental crushing pressure.

"The only language you know is *force*," Valor utters with a quiet conviction as the man struggles—in vain—to retrieve his fist from Valor's grasp. "I can speak that language too... but there is another language you can *learn* how to speak." He lets go of the boyfriend's fist. "It's God's language of love and forgiveness."

The man winces in pain as he backs away, cradling his injured hand with his other arm. "You're a freak!"

"And you are a *sinner* in need of God's grace. Jesus wants to save you, if you let Him. But you must first repent of your abusive behavior."

"Save your preaching for someone who cares!" He rushes back to his truck, opens the door and retrieves his handgun. Elizabeth screams as Valor jumps in front of her.

"You may be strong, but can you stop bullets?" the man cackles as he pulls the trigger twice. The gun only clicks. He looks at his weapon in disbelief as he checks the magazine and the chamber—it's fully loaded. He aims and mashes the trigger again. CLICK.

"You don't have to do this," Valor says while slowly approaching the man.

The man raises the gun to the air and pulls the trigger. BLAM! He quickly aims it back at Valor and pulls the trigger again—still... nothing.

"What in the—?"

Just then, a passing state trooper sees the scene, screeches to a halt on the side of the road, and exits his cruiser with his firearm drawn.

"Drop your gun and get on the ground, now," He barks as he aims his firearm squarely at the boyfriend.

The man looks from Valor to the trooper and back at Elizabeth.

"This is your last warning! Drop the gun and get on your knees with your hands behind your head... now!"

The man groans as he engages the safety, drops the gun to the pavement, gets on his knees and places his hands behind his head. The trooper cautiously approaches and kicks the gun away. In one fluid move, he places his gun back in its holster while pulling out a pair of handcuffs and quickly places the man under arrest.

"Are you two alright?"

"Yes," Elizabeth yells with a smile as she hugs Valor.

"I'm going to put him in my cruiser, radio for backup and then ask you both some questions." He looks at Valor with a quizzical smirk. *"Especially* you." The trooper pulls the boyfriend to his feet and walks him to his patrol vehicle.

"I don't know how I can thank you," Elizabeth exclaims while the trooper tends to his duties. "You saved me!"

"God had me in the right place at the right time," Valor replies. "After all... you did pray to Him for help."

"And He sent you," she smiles. "I wish I could see your face so I could give you a big kiss."

"No kiss is necessary. Your thanks is enough."

"Did you mean what you said back there? About God's love and forgiveness?"

"Yes."

"I've done a lot of terrible things in my life. When I look back, I can see all the times God tried to help me... All the times He got me out of bad situations, but then I went right back into them. Do you think God ever gets tired of trying to lead us down the right path?"

"God's love, shown through His Son Jesus, covers a multitude of sins. No matter what you've done, Jesus will receive you if you are willing to yield yourself to Him."

"You seem so *sure*..."

"I know God's word to be true. Jesus can be yours... and you can be His... if you surrender your heart to Him."

"Is it just that easy?"

"Yes. It's just that easy."

"I would like that."

Around ten minutes later two state troopers and a tow truck arrive on the scene. As one of the troopers prepare to drive Elizabeth to a safe destination, a question lingers in the back of her mind.

"I don't understand it."

"What?" Valor replies as the state trooper looks at her.

"I had my phone off. How did he track me?"

The tow truck driver finishes putting the car on the lift and comes over to the group.

"I found this tracker underneath the rear bumper of her car." He hands the device to the trooper.

With that, the answer is found.

The original trooper on scene approaches Valor. "You sure you don't want a ride? It will be dark in a couple of hours."

"Thanks so much, but walking is how I must travel. I'll be staying at a guest house not too far from here."

"Suit yourself," he shrugs. "Be safe out here... whoever you are."

Elizabeth gives Valor one last hug. "You truly are a godsend."

"You take care of yourself. And do what I suggested."

"Right. I'll get a Bible right away when I get into town and I'll start reading the gospel of John." With that, she waves and gets into the cruiser.

Valor watches as everyone drives off into the distance.

"Once again, You've had me in the right place at the right time," Valor says to the LORD. "You are worthy to be praised. And Your ways are past finding out."

Valor begins walking again, continuing his journey out west... while gazing at a beautiful sunset in the distance.

7: This is a Robbery!

DAY 22 — Indiana

The butt of a gun smashes the back of the security guard's head—knocking him to the ground. He had been so focused on the man who just entered with baggy jeans and a hoodie, that he didn't pay attention to the well dressed man in a suit who just clobbered him.

Gunshots ring throughout the Fort Wayne bank, capturing everyone's attention.

"This is a robbery!" The well dressed man yells through his Covid mask.

People scream and scatter—but all exits are blocked by well-dressed robbers in masks holding guns.

"Nobody try to be a hero and nobody gets hurt!"

Two robbers ransack the cash drawers, while two others relieve the patrons of their valuables. Moments quickly pass as the men complete their scheme.

'Let's go! Cops will be here any minute!"

The men quickly exit the bank with their bounty and run for a black Suburban, which is parked around the corner. But, as they round the building, to their dismay, they find Valor standing between them and their getaway vehicle. A robber shouts as they all stop in their tracks.

"Who's that?"

"It's that superhero guy from TV!"

Valor prays silently. *"Father? What do you want me to do?"*

The Holy Spirit prompts him: ***"Stand still."***

"Guys, come on!" the getaway driver yells out the window.

The men are still hesitant as Valor literally *stands still*—only his cape billows in the wind. Approaching sirens scream in the distance.

"Get out of the way!" one robber yells while pointing his gun at the man in red.

But, Valor remains motionless.

"We don't have time for this," the leader yells as he runs past Valor. The others do the same as Valor turns and watches them jump into the SUV.

"Father?" Valor prays again. "Are you sure—"

"Stand still," the Holy Spirit replies firmly. ***"See My salvation."***

"Gun it," the lead robber yells as the tires squeal! The Suburban takes off down the street in a plume of rubberized smoke. They are barely half a block away before a large dog breaks away from its owner and runs into the street right in front of them. The driver loses control as he swerves to avoid the dog. The Suburban jumps the curve, knocks over a street lamp and then crashes into an empty bus stop.

Just then, two police cars enter the intersection in front of the SUV as the dazed robbers stumble out of their vehicle. They are immediately taken into custody. Dazed and bruised, they fume at each other as the police arrest them.

"You all should have listened to me and left when I said so!"

"It wasn't our fault. We didn't know that superhero guy would show up!"

"Yeah, he slowed us down long enough for the cops to get here."

"And where'd that dog come from? You should have just ran it over!"

"No way! I love dogs!"

"Well, you loving dogs and your bad driving got us caught!"

8: Eyes to See

DAY 25 — Illinois

The day is far spent… Valor has walked from sun up to sun down. There have been no major interactions except for a few people honking their horns as they drove by him on the Interstate. Even with boots reinforced for comfort, his feet are throbbing. Each passing step feels like hot pins and needles clawing up his legs. His usually fast pace gait has slowed down considerably. His muscles scream from exhaustion. The churning of gastric juices in his empty stomach growls and bubbles. Saliva has dried up—making his mouth feel like gravel. His breathing, through his vented helmet, is labored. His body—from head to toe—is running on empty.

"LORD, it's been three days since my last meal," he prays silently. "I know You said, 'Man shall not live by bread alone, but by every word that proceeds from the mouth of God,' but I am really hungry and tired. Please… can You provide me with some food, drink and shelter tonight? I don't know how much of this I can take."

Another minute passes before he stops on the side of the road to take a break. As he leans over and rests his hands on his thighs, the sound of running water catches his attention. He raises his gaze and spots a stream beyond the guardrail, several meters into the trees from where he's standing. A Scripture comes to mind: *"If you are thirsty come to Me and drink. If you believe on Me, as the Scripture says, out of your belly will flow rivers of living water."*

"Yes, LORD…" He mumbles through dry lips. "May I drink from Your Presence." Valor lowers his tired body and kneels in the dirt. Even as cars drive behind him, he slowly raises his hands to the heavens and begins to worship God. With each tired utterance of words of praise and worship, his body and mind are replenished with strength: His mouth moistens. His stomach quiets. A cooling sensation smothers his burning feet like a cold blast from a fire extinguisher. As strength returns to his legs, he stands to his feet. He is still hungry and tired, but the sensations have diminished greatly as a feeling of refreshment overtakes him.

"Thank you, LORD," he smiles underneath his helmet. "Thank you... So, where to now?" A moment passes as the words of Psalm 42:1 flood his heart. He smiles and repeats them out loud. *"As the deer pants for streams of water, so my soul pants for you, my God."* He gazes at the flowing water of the stream. "Ok, let's see where it goes."

With each step forward, Valor gains even more strength as an excited anticipation fills his heart. He is unsure of what he will find, but God has always answered his prayers and this time would be no different. He would be eating something *tonight*. As excited as he was about that prospect, he was even more grateful for the lesson God was teaching him through this completely unorthodox journey across America. He thinks to himself: God *truly provides for us when we work with Him to accomplish His purposes for our lives.*

The path of the stream winds through an increasingly lush forest with no apparent end in sight. The sounds of the wild can be heard all around as stars pepper the night sky. The sounds of nocturnal animals and the calls of unseen scavengers sound both near and far off in the distance. A quarter mile later, about a stone's throw away from the stream, Valor comes to a slight clearing where a log cabin sits nestled among the trees.

It is a sizable log cabin home with two stories. Light fills the windows on the lower level and smoke rises gently from the chimney. The aroma of a meal being prepared fills the night air.

"LORD, I would have never found this place on my own," Valor whispers. "I have no idea who lives here. But if You sent me, then they won't be too upset by an unannounced visitor."

He makes his way through the front yard, unable to avoid stepping on crisp dried leaves, broken twigs and branches. Suddenly, an elderly man with sunglasses appears from the side of the house with a shotgun aimed squarely at the unknown guest. Valor hears the sound of the gun cocking and he slowly raises his arms.

"Uh, hello, Sir," he says as calmly as he can. "My apologies for showing up unannounced at such a late hour."

The elderly man stands motionless for a few seconds before responding. "Oh, it's you." He slowly lowers his weapon. "I heard some noise and thought you were a coyote or some other animal. Come on in out of the cold."

The man walks up to the front door, opens it and beckons for Valor to follow. As they enter the cabin, the sound of the news is heard throughout the house.

"Do, you know who I am?" Valor asks.

"Sure. You're the hero the news has been reporting about. The LORD told me you'd be stopping by tonight. But He didn't say what time. Feel free to make yourself at home."

"You said, '*The LORD,*'" Valor calls out. "So, you are a Christian."

"I am a follower of Jesus," the elderly man replies, "…Just like you."

"How did you know?"

"I told you the LORD *told me* you were coming by… In fact, He told me three days ago to make sure I had a meal and a room prepared for you."

Valor stops in his tracks and shakes his head in amazement at the goodness of God. "Father, *You never cease to amaze me.*"

The man passes through the living room and heads for the kitchen. Valor enters the living room and notices all of the pictures of wild animals and awards arranged around the room. In some of the pictures a much younger version of the elderly man stands smiling next to various beasts. Valor notices his green uniform, tie, gold badge and brown wide brim hat.

"Are you a park ranger?" He calls to the kitchen.

"Ah, you see my photographs," the elderly man calls back. "I'm retired now. For 40 years it was the most exciting time of my life. There are 424 national park sites in these United States of America. I have seen them all and worked in 237 of them."

"That's impressive! How did you do that?"

"My speciality is wildlife migration patterns. If it has four legs, I've tracked it. And not just in the U.S., I've had the opportunity to track wildlife all around the world as well."

"I bet you have some amazing stories."

"Oh, I do. I can tell you a few as we eat. I'm pretty sure you must be hungry."

"I am. But eating together might be a problem."

"Why's that?"

"I'm not allowed to reveal my identity until God says to do so."

"So, you can't take off your helmet in my presence?"

"That's right. I'll have to eat outside or in a room by myself, if that's okay with you."

"You don't have to worry about me revealing your identity."

"How's that?"

"Look around some more while I make the plates, and tell me what you see. My name is Steve, by the way."

"I'm Valor."

"Nice to *officially* meet you, Valor."

As Steve works in the kitchen, Valor looks around the living room and the adjacent doorways.

"Bathroom's on the left if you need it," Steve yells.

Valor looks at the bathroom and notices a small grey strip with several dots on the wall next to the door. He then looks at the table in the living room. A solitary brown book sits at its center. It's an impressively thick hardcover volume—similar in size to one of those old unabridged Oxford dictionaries. Valor notices similar types of dots on its cover.

Steve hums a tune as he places the plates on the kitchen table.

"Food's ready! What do you want to drink? I've got water, root beer, orange juice, milk and hot tea."

"Surprise me," Valor calls back as he scans the room and notices the same small grey strips and dots on each doorway. He then sees the book shelf where a large collection of the same brown hardcover books rest—each around 4-5 inches thick. Each with the same type of dots on the cover. Valor then notices the television next to the bookshelf is off. The broadcasted news is coming from a nearby radio. He then notes the Hellen Keller quote on the wall:

"The worst thing in life is having sight but no vision."

Underneath the quote is another set of dots. But this time, Valor notices that all of the dots aren't flat, but raised.

"Steve?"

"Yeah?"

"Are you... blind?"

"Bingo!" Steve claps. "So, you see the braille!"

"The book on the table..."

"It's one volume of my braille Bible collection."

"So, you really *are* blind?"

"For the past two years. Now, you see why I said you don't have to worry about your identity! Your secret is safe with me. Now come... let's eat."

Valor prays for confirmation before moving toward the kitchen. A moment later, a feeling of peace floods his soul as words ring within his heart: *"I have brought you to him for such a time as this."*

Once seated at the table, Steve removes his sunglasses and prays over their meal. Valor studies Steve's face—watching as his eyes dart back and forth staring at nothing in particular.

"Checking me out to make sure, huh?" Steve chuckles.

"Yes," Valor responds as he slowly unlocks his helmet, lifts it from his head and sits it on the chair next to him. He takes a deep breath. "The food smells even better without the helmet."

Steve laughs. "Does the helmet cover your entire face?"

"Yes."

"I bet it feels good to come up for some air."

"Oh, it does!" Valor unbuckles his cape and drapes it over the back of his chair.

"Well, now that you're all relaxed, let's eat!"

Minutes pass in silence, punctuated by sounds of scraping forks, chomping mouths and gulping throats.

"This is *really good*," Valor says. "You are a *great* cook."

"I'm glad you like it!"

"So, you mentioned you've gone without your sight for the last two years. If you don't mind me asking, what happened?"

"Well, I retired five years ago and moved here. Had this house built on 10 acres of land... My own personal nature preserve. I know every inch of my property. But God has a... curious sense of humor... or is it irony? I've made my living using my keen eyesight to track wildlife of all types. I've always paid attention to details no matter how small. I had 20/20 vision for my whole life. Then one day, just over two years ago, I started noticing the details were getting a bit blurry. Then they began to get dark and muddy-like. The ophthalmologist diagnosed me with a severe case of macular degeneration.

"Within six months I went from crystal clear to complete darkness. I can still notice some gradations of light and shadows, but that's it. Now, all the details are gone from view. So, it was a tough transition... Honestly, I almost didn't survive it. I was so angry with God. But He slowly revealed that He was still *with* me.

"Someone donated those volumes of the braille Bible. Then a friend connected me to a teacher who taught me how to read Braille. It was difficult, but I learned. All the while my other senses increased to compensate for my lack of sight. I may not be able to see, but I perceive so much more of my environment now. Tell me," Steve switches subjects with a big smile, "are you ready for desert?"

The rest of the night is filled with amazing stories, warm fellowship and great tasting food and beverages.

"I have an extra bedroom set up for you. You're more than welcome to stay for a few days so you can get some rest."

V

Three days later, Valor and Steve stand outside of the log cabin house and share a strong handshake. The early morning sunlight bathes them in a warm glow.

"Thank you so much for your warm hospitality."

"You are most welcome, my friend. But I am merely being obedient to the leading of the LORD. He told me to give you time to rest so you can continue your journey."

"I certainly *feel* rested... and grateful for God's provision through you."

"Whatever the LORD is doing with your life, it is **mighty**—right out of the pages of Holy Scripture!"

"Yes," Valor agrees. "God *is* doing something unorthodox for this generation, but firmly rooted in His Word. By the way... Is there... anything I can do for you before I leave? Anything you want prayer for?"

"You mean like the obvious—*my sight*?" Steve chuckles.

"I can ask the LORD. He has given me the gift of healing."

"When I initially lost my sight, I spent months praying and fasting, asking God to restore it back to me. One day, I was feeling dejected because He had not answered my prayers. Then, in the silence, while I was weeping, the Holy Spirit spoke gently to my heart. He spoke the same words He told the apostle Paul in 2

Corinthians 12:9 after Paul had prayed three times about the removal of his physical ailment."

"*My grace is sufficient for you. For My power is made perfect in weakness.*"

"That's when I knew, like Paul, that God desired for me to trust Him at an even greater level! That He desired for me to walk terribly close to Him. And He would lovingly provide for me if I did. I'd be lying if I said I wasn't interested in seeing again... But the LORD has done so much for me during this season *without* my sight. I have had to rely on Him in so many new ways and He hasn't let me down yet. Honestly, I want to see where He is taking me, even if I can't *see* with my *natural* eyes for a while."

"So, you don't want me to ask God to return your sight?"

"Do you know why Jesus performed miracles?"

"To demonstrate He was the Son of Man, the Christ, God's Messiah."

"That's right! His greatest miracle was His crucifixion and resurrection from the dead. I already believe He is the Savior of the world and *my* Savior. So, if He never does anything else for me, He has already done enough! The Last Day is coming when Christ will reward everyone who believes in Him with new resurrection bodies. When He gives me *my* glorified body, you better believe I will be *looking at every detail* of His renewed earth!"

"I never thought about it like that."

"It took a while for me to land there myself. So, I'd rather you ask God to help me stay the course and finish the race so I can cross the finish line and hear Him say, '*Well done My good and faithful servant!*' That matters most—regardless if I can see or not."

"Well then, *that* is what I will pray!"

"And I will do the same for you, Valor. I am praying that you be obedient and faithful to the LORD, so you can finish the race He has set before you."

"Amen, brother."

Steve extends his hand and Valor meets it with his own. It's then that he notices something in Steve's hand.

"What's this?"

"This is for you."

Valor looks at the folded dollar bills.

"The LORD says you will need this soon. For what, I don't know. But, I hope you have pockets on that suit of yours."

"I do," Valor laughs as he puts the money in his suit's secret pocket. "Thank you for this."

"Just trying to play my part. It's been an honor, Brother. God's speed to you, Valor!"

"And to you as well, Brother Steve!"

With a hearty handshake and wave, Valor exits Steve's property and makes his way back through the forest as he continues his journey to the west coast.

"Thank you, LORD," Valor prays as he walks without any tiredness or discomfort of any kind. "I had a need and You provided once again! Please help both Steve and me to remain faithful to You in *every* situation."

9: Motorcycle

DAY 28 — Illinois

After about thirty minutes, Valor exits the forest at a different point from where he entered three days earlier. He makes his way to the nearest roadway. There, he finds a fork in the road. He glances to the left, down one road and then to the right, down another. There are no obvious signposts anywhere and no people nearby.

"Where to next, Father?" He prays as he looks at his options. "I'm not sure how to get back to the Interstate. I should have asked Steve for directions."

Just then, a dragonfly zooms to a stop right in front of him—at about chest height. Valor watches as it hovers up and down, back and forth in swift-but-concise-motions. He slowly raises his hand to the insect and extends his gloved index finger. A few fluttering seconds pass before the dragonfly sets down on his finder.

Valor stands motionless for a few seconds—just watching the majestic insect flutter its wings ever-so-slightly. He slowly brings it close to his visor. The entire time, it never flies away, but only tilts its head and wings as its abdomen pulses with life.

"Father," Valor prays, "You know dragonflies are my favorite insects. Thank you for this."

At once, the dragonfly takes flight and slowly pulls away. Valor instinctively follows as it heads down the road to the right. After about ten minutes, the dragonfly stops at the side of the Interstate as vehicles speed by. It then soars away—high into the sky—in a burst of speed!

"Thank you Father," Valor prays as he watches the dragonfly zoom into the heavens. With that, he sets off again, walking down the Interstate at a quick pace. By mid afternoon, he shows no signs of slowing down. A moment later, the Holy Spirit speaks to his heart with a sense of urgency: ***"Motorcycle."***

"Motorcycle?" Valor asks as he looks at the passing traffic. Two seconds later one passes him at over 80 miles per hour!

The Holy Spirit speaks again. **"Catch the motorcycle."**

Valor is completely surprised at the command! "You want me to *chase down* that motorcycle?"

The Holy Spirit responds immediately: ***"I enabled Elijah to outrun King Ahab's chariot. Now go!"***

The Presence of the Holy Spirit flows from Valor's belly like a raging river and swells up within his legs like a torrent! Valor crouches into a ready stance and then launches himself! To his surprise, he bounds down the highway with increasing speed! The sound of the rushing air as he quickly accelerates is exhilarating! A sense of awe overtakes him as—within moments, he quickly closes the distance between himself and the speeding motorcycle. Countless expressions of wonder and disbelief smother the faces of drivers and passengers as Valor races past their vehicles as if they were standing still!

The motorcycle rider is oblivious to Valor's approach as the bike weaves in and out of the sparse traffic at now more than 90 miles per hour! The rider leans into a blind curve and finds a deer standing in the middle of the highway! The rider mashes the brakes as the motorcycle swerves—missing the deer by mere inches! But the bike jackknifes—ejecting the rider—as it somersaults through the air!

Valor overtakes the bike, leaps into the air and catches the rider! He flips his body, with the rider in his arms and lands firmly on the side of the road as the bike crashes into a nearby rock face! The deer watches for a second—its ears flicking—and then runs off into the woods. Valor lowers the dazed rider to the ground as cars slow, but continue driving by as people record the incident on their cell phones.

After a brief fumbling with the straps, the rider's helmet comes off.

"It's a woman," Valor thinks to himself as she gazes at him, completely amazed.

"How did you—? Where did you—?" She inquires.

"Are you okay?" He asks.

"Y-Yes." She is clearly shaken up by the entire ordeal!

They both look over at her bike which is now a flaming heap of a mess.

"That could have been me…"

"Your bike is ruined. Do you have a cell phone?"

She nods.

"You should call for help."

"When I saw that deer and lost control of my bike... my life flashed before my eyes. I would have been dead if it weren't for you!"

"No. You would have been dead if it wasn't for Jesus. He made it possible for me to save you."

She looks away with disdain. "I don't believe in Jesus."

Valor stands and gazes at her as the Holy Spirit speaks to his spirit.

"You have a Bible in the bottom of a box in the back of your basement closet."

Her eyes widen. "How could you know that?"

He disregards her question. "You haven't read it since your father died tragically 6 years ago. Ever since then, you have blamed God and turned away from Him. But He hasn't turned away from you. You've made poor choices and put yourself in danger, but the Lord has repeatedly delivered you, including *just now*. Yet, you still refuse to give Him glory."

Tears begin to stream down her cheeks.

"The Lord says it is time for you to stop blaming Him for your father's death. It is time for you to come back to Him while you still can. He will heal your heart—if you let Him. He has a great work for you to do... but if you continue to refuse Him, both you and the work will be lost. Repent now and no longer harden your heart against the Lord."

Valor turns and walks away as the woman, is completely overcome with emotion. As she cries, the Holy Spirit convicts her of her rebellion and offers His comfort and peace which surpasses all understanding. Although difficult, she yields herself to her Creator and Christ floods her heart and mind with His Presence. Just like that... a child of God has been reclaimed! Now, the process of restoring her heart begins. Moments later, she stumbles to her feet—looking around through blurry eyes while wiping away tears. She scans the highway in both directions and to her astonishment, Valor is nowhere to be found.

10: News Reports

DAY 36

National news stations play an amalgamation of citizen footage and news reporter commentary...

An elderly lady in glasses speaks: "He saved me and my husband after our car crashed. My husband had a heart attack and he brought him back from the dead. He's an angel!"

News reporters speak:

"It has been just over a month since the first sighting of the man dressed as a superhero. We are told that his self-appointed moniker is, Valor. From what we have gathered, he actually seems to be doing acts of... well... *valor*—having saved numerous people from dangerous situations."

"But *who* is the man under the mask? Where is he from? Some have wondered if he is even human. What motivates his actions? How is he able to perform such feats of strength? Where does his alleged ability to heal others come from? Are all of his abilities the result of advance technology built into his suit? Or is this all some kind of elaborate hoax to garner attention?"

"While the authorities are well aware of his presence, since he has not broken any laws, they have yet to detain him for questioning."

"One thing is certain: this enigmatic figure who seems to be making his way across the country without making any kind of public statements is beginning to draw the attention of the entire nation."

11: Close Encounters of the Third Kind

DAY 42 — Iowa

"Hey Valor! Wait up!" a voice shouts from behind. Valor slows to a stop and turns around to see who's talking. A wide-eyed young man stands a short distance away with a man and a woman. No doubt, they are friends of his. "We know who you are. You're a vanguard for the coming alien disclosure."

Valor shakes his head, turns and continues walking. The trio watches him for a second before giving chase—following like a pack of hungry dogs happily surrounding someone dangling tasty food.

"My name is Mitch. This is Jay and Trina." They waste no time sharing their theory. Mitch begins. "You've got that suit. And the news says you got super strength and the ability to heal. I bet you can fly, too."

"And," Trina adds, "no one knows where you came from and what you look like because you're not from earth!"

"Yeah," Jay continues. "We think you're either an alien or an alien-human hybrid. Our friends are gonna flip when we tell them we saw you!"

"Yeah," Mitch continues. "We're part of a UFO watch group. Members are from all over and most of us have seen UFO's."

"We know they're called UAP's now," Trina interjects, "but we still like the term UFO. Some of us, like me, have had visitations and abductions!"

"Yeah," Jay interjects. "They're called, close encounters of the third kind."

"Right," Trina agrees. "We know they're getting humanity ready for the big disclosure!"

Mitch continues. "I don't talk about this outside the group. People think I'm crazy. The third time I was abducted by aliens they said the disclosure would be soon. And here you are! They're *coming*, right? The world is gonna know aliens are real!"

"I'm not an alien," Valor finally says as he continues to walk. "I'm human like you."

"I *can't* do what you can do," Mitch responds. "So, you can't be human *like me!*"

"What planet are you from?" Jay asks.

"Earth. Now, if you'll excuse me... I have to get going." Valor picks up his pace.

"Who's your leader?"

"Jesus."

"Jesus? As in Jesus Christ from the Bible?"

"Yes."

They stop in their tracks and look at Valor in awe.

"You are from them! We follow Jesus too! You know aliens abducted his mother, Mary. They impregnated her with him. He was definitely an alien-human hybrid, sent to earth to show us how to evolve to the next level of Christ consciousness!"

Valor stops in his tracks and slowly turns to face the trio as they continue their theory sharing.

"You know, the Bible *mentions* aliens and UFOs in the book of Ezekiel, right? He saw aliens that traveled in crafts shaped like 'a wheel within a wheel. Some think they were angels, but we know better. When the Bible talks about these *supernatural beings* humans call *angels*, it *really* is referring to aliens from another planet or even another dimension!"

Valor looks at them silently for a moment. Their anticipation of his response is almost uncontainable as they hop around like kids waiting to open presents on Christmas. He finally speaks.

"Does everyone in your group subscribe to this belief?"

"Yeah. Most of us."

"When does your group meet?"

"Tomorrow, actually... You want to come?"

"Perhaps. I am in need of shelter for the night."

"You can stay at my place tonight and then meet with our group tomorrow! My house is small, but you can sleep on the couch. If that's too much, I got a garage. It's pretty clean, as garages go."

"I will stay *there*."

V

Later that night. 3:00am

Valor awakens from sleep in an agitated state. Strange sounds punctuate the silence as an unusual light shines through the cracks of the door which connects the garage to the house.

He gets up, makes his way to the door and slowly opens it. A blue light washes through the house—shimmering as if it was somehow alive. Valor walks through the house, following the light's increasing intensity until he stands in front of a closed bedroom door. This strange blue light bursts through every crack around the doorframe. He listens as sounds of a struggle are heard from within the room. He can hear Mitch's voice weakly call out.

"No... please don't... somebody... help me..."

Valor turns the knob, opens the door and steps into the room. To his astonishment, he finds Mitch hovering on his back, four to five feet above his bed. His body is caught in a ray of intense blue light which somehow shines down through the ceiling. He shakes slightly as he tries to resist, but his attempts are futile. Three small shadowy figures with elongated heads and slender limbs stand at the foot of his bed.

They turn towards Valor and train their oversized bug-like eyes on him. Suddenly, his throat constricts as if a Sith Lord from Star Wars was using the Force to choke the life out of him! He can hardly speak as he stumbles backwards out of the room, landing hard against the hallway wall. One of the figures glides effortlessly towards him while increasing in musculature and height to over seven feet tall! As it towers over him in the doorway, Valor forces the last bit of breath out of his mouth—forming a single word... rather it's a single *Name* which he speaks barely above a whisper: "Jesus..."

Suddenly, the invisible force trying to collapse his throat relents! The towering shadow shrinks in size as it quickly retreats back to the side of its cohorts. Immediately, the three dark beings vanish in a shadowy plume of smoke. The strange blue light quickly dissipates in a matter of seconds as Mitch's body falls to his bed with a thud. All is silent as he awakens in a fright—seemingly released from a trance—his body drenched in sweat. He stares wild-eyed around the room as Valor hits the light switch. Mitch sees Valor in the doorway and weeps as he struggles to sit up in his bed.

"I don't understand…" He looks around bewildered. The aliens are *usually* nice. But this time they were… malevolent. They didn't like that you were in my house! They told me not to trust you. But when I tried to resist their pull, they became vicious. They were attacking my mind and it was hard for me to speak! And then they suddenly got scared! I couldn't open my eyes, but I could feel their emotions. They were terrified and angry—but not at me. Then they disappeared and when I came to, you were standing in my door! What does all of this mean? Am I going crazy? Please tell me you saw them!"

"I saw them with my own eyes," Valor answers. "But, they were not aliens."

"But each time they've come, they said they were from a distant planet outside of our solar system. If they weren't aliens… then what were they?"

"I believe they were inter-dimensional beings *impersonating* aliens. The Bible talks about these beings. They are fallen angels, also known as demons."

"Demons?! As in, *from hell*? I don't believe it."

"Then how do you explain that when I called on Jesus for help, they stopped attacking you and vanished. If they were really aliens from another planet, they shouldn't know anything about Jesus, let alone be afraid of Him."

"Unless…" Mitch surmises, "I told you Jesus was an alien-human hybrid. He must be from a rival alien group they know about. Maybe there's some kind of cosmic war going on and they and Jesus are from two warring factions."

"There *is* a cosmic battle going on. But it's not between aliens. Fallen angels and demons are trying to fight against God in order to deceive and destroy the souls of humanity. Jesus is not an alien/human hybrid. He is the Son of God who came to earth, not to help us evolve to Christ consciousness, but to save us from our sins which separate us from having a relationship with His Heavenly Father."

"I don't believe in all of that "god crap."

"But you believe in aliens?"

"It's easier to believe that they seeded the planet and got us started on it, then to believe that we were created by some invisible, intangible all-powerful being."

"Well, God—who is invisible, all-knowing, all-powerful and everywhere at the same time, arranged our meeting so you could know the truth."

"What truth?"

"That you are a slave in need of salvation—trapped in a prison beyond your ability to conceive. If you choose not to believe in the Jesus of the Bible... If you choose not to place your faith in His crucifixion and resurrection, so you can be saved and protected, then those demons will be back. And you will have no defense against them. You will also be lost—doomed to the eternal flames prepared for the devil and his angels—as Jesus teaches. The choice is up to you. Either believe the truth and be set free or believe your lies and continue to be deceived and manipulated by an enemy who only wants your complete and total destruction."

Valor walks out of the room and heads for the front door.

"Wait! Where are you going?" Mitch asks while giving chase.

"I'm leaving to continue my journey."

"But you can't leave me here *alone*! What if the aliens—demons—whatever they are... what if they come back? What am I supposed to do then?"

"You'll be on your own."

"But what about speaking to the group in the morning?"

Valor stops at the front door and faces Mitch.

"You just received a preview of what I will say *if* I speak to them. Do you still want me to do so?

Mitch's mind vacillates in a moment of indecision before finally arriving at his conclusion.

"Please stay... if what you say is true... then the group and I need to hear it."

12: Living Proof

DAY 50 — Nebraska

It's a late Saturday morning, just before noon. Valor stands on the corner of a block in a semi-urban area. A convenience store and a string of shops sit across the street. Cars pass by slowly as their occupants try to catch a glimpse of him. Nearby pedestrians come to a stop as well. All of them wondering, *what is he doing here?* It's been almost two months since his journey began and he has already impacted many for God's Kingdom. News coverage has increased with each exploit. The question on everyone's mind remains, who is the man beneath the helmet?

Beneath the helmet, his eyes scan the row of stores as he whispers a prayer. "Father, are you sure this is the right place?"

"Genesis 41:14," echoes in his spirit.

Valor nods his head as he recalls the Scripture and begins walking down the block.

He passes the corner store, then a beauty salon, then an empty store front, followed by a tax preparation business and then stops in front of his destination. It is almost packed to capacity. He opens the front door and enters. The Hip Hop music greets him immediately as 10-15 customers sit inside. Every eye is on him within seconds. The owner of the shop reaches for the remote to the stereo system and presses the mute button. The silence is deafening.

"You're that guy I've seen on the news," the owner declares. "What… can I do for you?"

Valor replies, *"So Pharaoh sent for Joseph, and he was quickly brought from the dungeon. When he had shaved and changed his clothes, he came before Pharaoh…"*

"Okaaayyy," the owner says. "I"m not sure what to do with that."

Valor's hands rise up to meet his helmet. All eyes widen as he releases the straps and removes it while replying: "This is a barber shop, is it not? I need a haircut."

The shouts are immediate. **"HE'S BLACK!"** Everyone reaches for their camera phone to capture this unexpected moment.

Valor holds up his hand with a smile. "I don't mind the photos and videos, but can you please wait until *after* I get a cut first." Beads of sweat drip from his forehead as he rubs his hand over his unkempt hair and beard. Both are in desperate need of grooming.

Everyone laughs. Some applaud.

"Right, says the owner. "Can't have the brother looking all rough on social media! If no one minds, I'll cut his hair next."

Everyone is in agreement.

"You do have... money somewhere on that suit of yours, right?"

Valor thinks back to the money Steve had given him and smiles. "Yes, I do."

"Well, come on in and have a seat Mr..."

"Daniel. My name is Daniel Davidson."

"Nice to meet you, Daniel. I'm Albert. Welcome to my shop!"

Conversations immediately erupt as he takes off his cape and hangs it and his helmet on the coat rack. The questions abound, quicker than he can answer as he takes a seat in the barber's chair.

"So, where are you from?" "Why are you dressed like a superhero?"

"Did you design the suit?" "Why are you doing all this?"

"Did you really rip a car door clean off its hinges?" "How strong are you?"

"Are you bullet proof?" "Where are you headed?"

"Hold up!" Albert raises his hands to get everyone's attention, while turning Daniel around in the chair. Everyone immediately lowers their voices and comes to attention.

"That's too many questions for the man," he continues. "Let me get him situated first, *then* we'll try the questions... but this time... *slower*!" Albert turns his attention to Daniel as he swivels the chair back around to face the mirror. "Alright. Let's find the *man* underneath all this ruggedness!" Albert begins by picking Daniel's thick hair.

"Ouch!" Daniel chuckles.

"I guess that's what happens when you wear a helmet for over a month. Your hair gets matted. When's the last time you got a cut?"

"Right before I started this journey."

"So, no one has seen your face since you started your walk?"

"That's right. I do take my helmet off every now and then when I'm alone. It can get stuffy inside."

"Wait, a second ago you said *'ouch.'* I thought you had super strength and were like, invulnerable."

"Only when I need to be."

"What kind of superpower is that?"

"It's not a superpower. It's more of a *supernatural ability*."

"Supernatural?" Albert chuckles. "How does *that* work?"

"Good question," Daniel replies. "But, let's get a question from the group first."

A teen boy's arm shoots up into the air like a rocket.

"Yes," Daniel smiles as he points at the boy. What's your name?"

"Isaiah."

"That's a good name, Isaiah. What's your question?"

"I've got a few," he replies while the others in the shop laugh.

"Don't we all," someone adds.

"Go ahead, Isaiah" Daniel replies. "What questions do you have?"

"Are you an alien from another planet?"

"No."

"Did you get bit by a radioactive spider?"

"No."

"Irradiated by gamma rays? Struck by lightning?"

"No and no."

"Took a super-soldier serum? No, wait, did you eat a heart-shaped herb? Are you a Bang Baby?"

Daniel laughs. "You watch a lot of movies and read a lot of comic books. But, no."

Daniel smiles while shaking his head. "I'm just a guy in a suit."

"Just a guy in a suit? Like Batman?" Isaiah replies.

"Just a guy in a suit," Daniel smiles.

"Okay. Next question. You have super strength, right?"

"No."

"Wait," Albert interjects, "so the news reports are wrong? You don't have super strength and invulnerability?"

"I haven't been following the news reports much. Too much to do… But to answer the question, I don't *generate* these abilities… They are given to me by God."

"God?!" Albert replies. "Like the 'man upstairs?' Come on... you can't be serious!"

"So, you'd believe the other options that Isaiah said, even though they are make-believe, but you won't believe God did this even though He's real?"

"But God doesn't do stuff like that," Albert responds.

"He doesn't? How do you know that?"

"Wait," a man interjects while snapping his fingers. "What about that guy from the Bible with the long hair. What's his name?"

"Samson," another man answers.

"Right! Samson," the man replies. "Didn't he have super strength?"

"Yes," Daniel replies. "And where did his strength come from?"

"...God..." Albert says hesitantly.

"I can see you didn't want to admit that."

"Wait," Isaiah interjects. "There's a story in the Bible about a super strong guy? Like how strong was he?"

"Based on what the Bible says and what scholars have researched," Daniel replies, "Samson was able to lift somewhere between ten to twenty tons."

Isaiah's eyes look like ping pong balls about to pop out of their sockets as he does the calculations in his head. "That means Samson's strength levels was between Captain America, Black Panther and the Hulk!"

"That sounds about right," Daniel smiles. "God made a covenant with Samson. He was told not to cut his hair—as a sign of that covenant. As long as his hair wasn't cut, God supernaturally empowered his body with great physical strength."

"Maybe we should stop cutting *our* hair," a man shouts. The entire group laughs.

"Now wait a minute," Albert counters with a smile while raising his hands in the air. "If you guys don't come you would put me out of business!"

Everyone laughs again.

"So," another boy asks, "If we believe in God, will He give *us* super strength too?"

"That's not the point," Daniel answers. "God *chose* to have a covenant with Samson. It wasn't Samson's idea. God decided ahead of time how he wanted to use Samson for His glory. In Samson's case, great physical strength was given to him so he could begin to deliver his people from their enemies. God has a purpose for each of us as well. And He will equip us with the skillset we need to carry out His purpose."

"So, God gave *you* super strength and you are here cutting your hair?"

"The length of my hair isn't a requirement for what God has chosen to do with my life. But yes, when I need added strength God provides it."

"So, are you as strong as Samson?"

"When God wants me to be."

"So, aren't you super strong all the time and you have to learn how to keep that power under control so you don't break things unintentionally?"

"No. I'm a regular guy with average strength. But when I'm in a tough situation which requires more strength, God provides it proportionate to the need."

"But why would God do it that way?"

"Well," Daniel thinks, "If I was super strong all the time, then I would run the risk of trusting in that strength. Since, God provides it when needed, my trust remains in Him."

"So, which God are we talking about?" a man speaks up. "The Christian, Muslim, Hindu or some other one?"

"I believe what the Bible says," Daniel replies. "Jesus Christ is Lord over all things."

Side conversations quickly sweep through the shop.

"So, God is real?" Albert asks with a new conviction.

"He is," Daniel affirms.

"And He's the one telling you to do what you do?"

"Right."

"Brother, that's the *craziest* thing I've ever heard… but I *love* it."

"So," Daniel continues, "God does do unusual things like what He did with Samson, the prophets Elijah and Elisha and the apostles of Jesus. The Bible provides accounts of them being empowered to do the miraculous and the extraordinary. But they didn't ask God for the gifts. God chose them according to His purposes."

"So, why has God chosen you?"

Daniel weighs his words as he prays silently for guidance. "God wants me to go to California to deliver a message to this nation... while we still have time."

The shop grows eerily silent... as the weight of his statement settles in.

"And," Daniel continues, "He uses me to help individual people along the way."

Again, moments of silence pass as the customers wrestle with the obvious question everyone wants to know the answer to, but nobody wants to ask.

Albert finally speaks what everyone is thinking. "Are you saying America doesn't have a lot of time left?"

Daniel breathes deeply before speaking. "All I know right now, is that this message is *time sensitive*."

"But, California?" Albert asks. "If it's for the nation, why not go to Washington D.C.?"

"The Lord has His reasons," Daniel answers. "D.C. might be the seat of political power, but California is the seat of media and entertainment power. They are intertwined, but in many respects, entertainment has a greater impact on people's lives."

"I never thought about it like that," Albert replies. "So, can you tell us anything right now?"

"Jesus Christ is the Savior, Lord and King of the universe. He is the Champion of Humanity—having defeated Satan when He died on the cross so we all can have our sins forgiven. He conquered death, so death won't conquer us in the end. God wants to have a relationship with us that will never end. But we have to humble ourselves and come to Him in the way He has provided... which is Jesus Himself."

"But what if we don't believe in God or that there's only one way to God?" a patron asks. "Look at how many different people there are on the planet and everybody believes differently and worships different deities."

"Right," Daniel agrees. "But the entire population of the planet can be traced back to one people. So, at some point, we worshiped one God... *until we didn't*. If the Bible is right—that the devil has an evil kingdom which opposes God and all that's good—then we can see how this evil would create a system of false gods and religions to deceive humanity away from worshiping the One True and Living God."

The room sits quiet as the only sound comes from the clippers in Albert's hands.

A man pipes up with a slight attitude. "If Jesus has all power, it sure don't look like it! How come he ain't destroyed evil yet and made everything right in the world? I think either he ain't strong enough, he don't care or he don't exist."

"Bro," another man answers, "God must exist," He points to Daniel. "We got living proof sitting right in that chair!"

Some nod in agreement, while others sit cautiously, waiting for Daniel to respond.

"We are *all* living proof," Daniel replies. "Whether you look at the galaxies, nature or in the mirror, proof of God's existence is all around us *and* within us. The Bible tells us in Zechariah 12:1 that God stretched out the heavens, laid the foundation of the earth, and formed the human spirit within each of us. Romans 1:20 says, *'For since the creation of the world God's invisible qualities—his eternal power and divine nature—have been clearly seen, being understood from what has been made, so that people are without excuse.'*

"So, the fact that we exist is *proof* of God's existence. And the greatest proof is Jesus coming to earth. John 3:16 says, *'For God so loved the world that he gave his one and only Son, that whoever believes in him shall not perish but have eternal life.'* So, even if I didn't have these abilities, I would still believe because God's Word has revealed the truth and human history confirms its reality. God is sovereign. He loves us. And He is involved in human history.

"To answer the brother's question about God seemingly not doing anything about evil... it's not time yet for God to eradicate it. But one day He will. Acts 17:31 says, *'For he has set a day when he will judge the world with justice by the man he has appointed. He has given proof of this to everyone by raising him from the dead.'* God is giving us time to be saved. He wants as many people as possible to come into His eternal Kingdom through His Son. And He is the only One who can bring about His good purposes, even in the midst of evil situations. But He won't wait forever. Time is winding down."

"You're talking about Jesus coming back," a man scoffs. "Christians have been saying that for hundreds of years." "My grandmother used to tell me that when I was little and she's dead and gone. It's been like 2000 years and Jesus still ain't returned."

Others nod their heads in agreement. "Yeah. So, what makes today any different?"

"That's a good observation and great question," Daniel replies. "A lot of time *has passed*. But there are at least four things which make our generation different. **One:** Israel became a nation again in 1948. That was prophesied in the Bible almost two thousand years before it came to pass. **Two:** Jesus gave a list of broad signs that would happen before He returns to earth to set up His Kingdom. He also said the generation that sees them *all happening at the same time* will be the generation that witnesses His return. Historically, before Israel became a nation in 1948, there were only a few signs happening here and there. Now, almost all of them are taking place simultaneously. **Three:** Technology. The Bible teaches that seven years before Jesus returns, the entire world will be ruled by a global government. *Our generation is the only generation* to have the technology which would make this future reality possible. There is currently a growing international consensus that a global government is necessary. We are seeing all of the pieces coming together right before our very eyes. **Four:** You said it's been 2000 years and Jesus still hasn't returned."

"Yeah," the man agrees.

"Actually," Daniel continues, "It's been 2000 years since His birth, but not since His crucifixion, resurrection and ascension."

"What you mean?"

"In the Bible, God does something major approximately every 2000 years. The 2000 year anniversary of Jesus' birth has come and gone. However, Jesus never told us to commemorate His birth. At the end of His three and a half year ministry, at the Passover supper with His disciples, Jesus told them to *always* remember what he was going to do on the cross and to look forward to the day when they would see Him in His coming kingdom. In fact, the majority of Jesus' teaching during His earthly ministry focused on pointing people to His second coming. If you examine the dates, you will discover that Jesus' crucifixion, resurrection, and ascension took place between

30-33AD. So, the 2000th anniversary would be somewhere between 2030 and 2033."

"Wait," a man shouts as he does the math. "Are you saying Jesus is coming back between 2030 and 2033? That's less than ten years from now!"

The quiet tension in the room grows exponentially as the man's comments are considered by all who are present. After a moment, Daniel answers.

"What I'm *saying* is we all have less time than we think. Whether Jesus returns in 2030 or some time further in the future or we die tomorrow. Either way, we will find ourselves standing before the King and Judge of the universe. And what will matter in *that moment*—when our eternal destiny is on the line—is what we did with God's Son. Did we receive His gift of forgiveness and salvation or did we reject it?"

Only the clippers are heard in the barbershop as each man and boy consider Daniel's words. Albert finishes the haircut and slowly directs Daniel's attention to the mirror while making an attempt at lightening the mood.

"You are now, once again, a sharp brother... thanks to *my* amazing skills."

The laughter cuts through the growing tension in the room.

"You do have some skill," Daniel agrees. "It's good to see this face again."

Albert proceeds to spray a sheen on Daniel's head and then wipes his face and neck down with rubbing alcohol.

"There you go," he declares while removing the cutting blanket from over him. He then brushes off the excess hair. "You look like a man who's ready to meet the public."

"Thanks Albert," Daniel smiles. "You did a great job."

"So, *is* Jesus coming back in just under ten years?" someone asks.

Daniel stares at the group before he speaks... "I am not trying to scare you. I'm just sharing what I know. Jesus clearly says no one can know the day or the hour of His return. So, we can't know the *exact* time. But He does let us know, if we watch for the signs He talks about in Matthew 24, Mark 13 and Luke 21, then we can know the *season* we are in.

"When I study what He teaches in these chapters and the other Scriptures in the rest of the Bible… and then I look at the state of the world today… it is clear that time is winding down. What is of *critical importance* is that you know God loves you and desires for you to be in a relationship with Him. All you have to do is admit to Him that you can't save yourself. That you are a sinner in need of His forgiveness which He provides through His Son. Declare your belief that Jesus is God's Son and that He died and rose in your place so you can receive eternal life from Him. Then surrender your hearts and live the rest of your lives in service to His will and glory."

Without the clippers being on, one could literally hear a pin drop as the silence is deafening.

"I know you probably have places to be," Albert says, "And I appreciate all the truth you've been sharing with us. But, before you go, I do have one question that has *always* bothered me."

"Sure," Daniel smiles. "What's that?"

"Christians say Jesus is God. But I read through the gospels once and didn't see where Jesus said He was God. Other people said so. What do you do with that? I mean, I believe He was a good teacher. I believe He was chosen by God to die. But *being* God and rising from the dead on the third day? That's a problem for me if He never said He *was* God."

Others in the barbershop sit up with great attention to see how Daniel will respond. It would seem they too have wondered about this very thing. Some smile slyly, as they suspect Albert has asked a question to which there is no definite answer.

"That's a good and honest admission," Daniel smiles again. "You know, God loves it when we are honest about our struggles with understanding His Word. Did Jesus ever claim to be God? *Yes.* In the gospels He declared Himself to be God over 70 times."

"He did?" Al exclaims as the shop erupts in a low chatter. "How did I miss that?"

Daniel waits for everyone to quiet down.

"The issue is *the way* He said He is God is *unfamiliar* to how we would say it in our modern context."

"Okay..." Albert concedes. "Can you explain it for me..." He looks around the shop. Everyone else is thoroughly interested. "...*for us*." Daniel faces the group while Albert leans against the wall with his arms folded.

"People called Jesus the Christ, Messiah, Son of David and Son of God a handful of times. He affirmed their usage, but only occasionally used these terms to refer to Himself. The term 'Son of God' was in common use by the Roman emperors and others to try and claim their own divinity. So, had he used the term 'Son of God' he would have been placing Himself in the same category as these other men who aren't gods at all. However, the term He **did** use—which was in a category all its own—was 'Son of Man.' He used that term **constantly** to refer to Himself."

"Wait," one of the men interjects. "I've heard that term before. Wasn't the prophet Ezekiel called 'son of man'? Doesn't it just mean a 'human being?' So, that would mean when Jesus used it, he was saying, 'I'm human just like you.'"

"You are partly correct," Daniel replies. "God does call the prophet Ezekiel, 'son of man,' and it does mean 'human being.'"

"So, that's what Jesus was saying about himself," the man counters. "Not that he was God, but that he was human."

"A lot of people think that," Daniel replies, "but it is incorrect. The term in the book of Ezekiel is written in Hebrew. When Jesus uses it, He is referencing Daniel chapter 7 which is written in Aramaic. In Daniel 7, the term essentially means, 'Divine human.' If you read that chapter, you will see that the time of final judgment has come for the earth and evil is about to be vanquished. The Ancient of Days is present on His throne.

"When you put the Old and New Testaments together you see that the Ancient of Days is God the Father. Beginning in verses 13 and onward, there is another figure who is present. This figure is called the Son of Man. And He is divine just as the Ancient of Days is divine. The context makes that absolutely clear. The Ancient of Days gives the Son of Man the eternal kingdom. The Son of Man then judges all evil. Then the inhabitants of the world worship Him. And those who belong to Him rule and reign with Him in His eternal kingdom.

"Daniel 7 is a vision of the future that is yet to come. And when Jesus walked the earth, He used *this* Son of Man title in Aramaic over

70 times to refer to Himself. No one else *anywhere* used this term. Any Jew who had read the book of Daniel would know *exactly* what Jesus meant each time He used the term. He was claiming to be God who has come in the flesh as the Savior of the world: The ultimate Judge of all evil and the Rewarder of the righteous."

"Whoa…"

"There's more…" Daniel continues. "In the book of Revelation the apostle John is given a tour of heaven. The first person he sees is Jesus in His glorified state. John used the same Aramaic term Daniel used to refer to Jesus: Son of Man. And in Matthew 24 Jesus calls the prophet Daniel by name, again pointing us back to the truth of His claim. So, by referring to Himself as the Son of Man of Daniel 7, Jesus *emphatically claimed* that He is the Son of God. We just need the cultural lenses in order to see the evidence in the appropriate light."

"That… makes sense." Albert nods his head in silent agreement. "Thank you. You cleared up a lot of my confusion. I'm going to go back and read it for myself."

"Yes," Daniel agrees. "Read it for yourself. *All* of you should. Don't just take my word for it. Always go and check it out for yourself. I did. And I came to the conclusion that it's true. Jesus… is true and I eagerly look forward to His Second Coming."

Another moment of silence…

"That sounds good, but I don't buy the whole 'Jesus Messiah' thing," another guy adds. "Christianity is the 'white man's religion.' I can't believe in the religion of my oppressors."

"That's a good point," Daniel replies. "Christianity and the Bible were used to help enforce the enslavement of our ancestors. But, you know, *people with ill intent can and will use anything good to oppress others*. What matters most isn't *how* something was twisted, but the *original intent* of the thing that was perverted. In the case of Christianity and the Bible, both originated in the middle east. Neither began with people of European descent. Jesus was not white. He was a man of color from a people of color. Also, every Scripture used to reinforce slavery was taken out of context."

"But," the man replies, "the Bible advocates slavery! Doesn't it say, 'slaves obey your masters?"

"Yes, but the *type of slavery* the Bible speaks about was more like indentured servitude where the slave could work off their debt. God also gave specific instructions for the humane treatment of slaves—which many slave masters completely ignored. Not to mention that slaves were to be set free during the year of Jubilee and all debts were to be forgiven and land was to be restored. This was to take place every 49-to-50 years.

"Slaves could also marry into the families for which they worked, if they so desired. So, God never intended for people to remain slaves indefinitely. This is one of the reasons why He sent Moses to liberate the Hebrews from Egyptian slavery. By the way, that was one story in the Bible that white slave masters did not want their black slaves to know about. That's also why they tried to stop us from learning how to read. Because then, we would have discovered the truth about what they were doing and how God did not support it.

"Also, Jesus Himself gave us the golden rule, among other teachings—telling us to treat others like we want to be treated. This was another passage many white slave masters ignored. So, saying that the Bible supported *the kind of slavery* our ancestors endured during the Trans-Atlantic Slave Period and everything that came afterwards, is **just not true.**"

Daniel stands, gets his cape from the coat rack and places it around his shoulders. He then picks up his helmet.

"I want you to understand something before I go. When God chooses someone, it does not mean that person is loved more than others. It simply means God has set them apart to carry out a specific work. Jesus said, *'Many are called, but few are chosen.'* What He means is, His call goes out to everyone, but only those who surrender to Him get to carry out His Will for their lives. God loves each of you more than you can know. He desires for you to know, love and serve Him… He wants you to *walk* with Him. He has plans for your lives and is not far from any of you… He has bridged the gap between heaven and earth to reach each one of you. What matters *now* is what you do with the truth I've presented."

After a round of photos and videos, he shakes hands with everyone.

"Feel free to post your pics and videos to social media. And when you inevitably see more news stories about me, know that God chose you to be the first group to know who I am and what I am doing. May the peace of Christ be with you all."

Everyone watches as Daniel puts his helmet back on, walks out the door and heads up the block. The men and boys return to their seats as the cutting continues in the midst of an avalanche of conversation and social media posts. Albert grabs his remote and changes the music station on his stereo.

"I think I'm in the mood for some gospel."

13: Media Coverage

DAY 51

Social media explodes at the revelation of Valor's identity as the barber shop encounter goes viral! The men and boys who were there become local celebrities as major media outlets seek out interviews—beginning with Albert. As the interviews take place, short clips and soundbites proliferate across digital space and over the airwaves.

Clip 1: "I don't know why he chose *now* to reveal his identity. I guess that will become clear as time goes on. But, it's great to see he's a brother who's trying to make a positive difference in the world."

Clip 2: "That brother is deep. When it comes to God, he's got a *ton* of insight!"

Clip 3: "He said God told him to wear the suit, but he ain't no vigilante. Still, if God is with him, you sure don't want to cross him if he finds you doing evil!"

Clip 4: "His suit looks really cool up close. I challenged him to an arm wrestling contest. He beat me. Even though I'm 10 years old, I can tell he's really strong."

Clip 5: "Daniel's a man of God trying to deliver a message of hope to the people. He helped me see things more clearly so I could get my relationship right with God."

Clip 6: "He said Jesus might be coming back around 2030. That's not that far away. If he's right, then it's time for people to get serious about what truly matters."

For every positive comment there are negative ones as well—proclaimed by people who don't even know the truth of the situation:

Clip 7: "Daniel Davidson is a charlatan out for his 15 minutes of fame!"

Clip 8: "He's doing this to deceive people! All the good deeds he has *allegedly* done were probably staged by actors."

Clip 9: "Why would God tell someone to dress up in a superhero suit anyway? That makes no sense at all! And why would God even care about superhero stories? They don't mix!"

Clip 10: "They say this guy has super strength? But I saw a show where special effects were used to fake superpowers in public. He's doing the same thing. I don't trust him."

Clip 11: "He's black? Was hoping he'd be white, or at least an alien from another planet."

Clip 12: "A guy walking around in a superhero suit claiming to speak for God? Why would God tell someone to do that? Daniel Davidson needs to be in a mental institution. At minimum, he sounds like a false prophet to me."

Clip 13: "All this nonsense about him raising a guy from the dead. Even if it *were* real, why doesn't he go into the hospitals and heal *all* the patients? If God can heal us, then why doesn't he do it?! What's his problem? That doesn't sound like a "good God" to me!"

V

Daniel's wife and 16 year old son sit in their living room, behind locked doors and darkened windows, watching the news on television.

The news anchor speaks: "As you can see, people have many different opinions about the man introduced to the world as Valor—who we now know to be Mr. Daniel Davidson. He's a native of New York, although he has been living in Atlanta, Georgia for the last 15 years or so. Now, more than ever, people want to know: What is he really up to? Are his alleged powers really supernatural in nature, technological or a complete fabrication? And *why* is he doing any of this at all? We will just have to go to the source. Still, finding him has proved difficult as recent credible sightings have been sporadic at best. In some instances, it seems that one minute he's present and the next he's gone. Is this the case because he is a master of misdirection? Or can he actually make himself disappear at will? And what about his controversial statement that the world will end in 2030? Is he another doomsday prophet?"

V

Daniel's wife turns off the television. Both she and her son look at each other in silence while shaking their heads.

"Now things have really kicked up a notch," she says.

"Dad said this would happen once he revealed his identity."

"But, I didn't think it would be this quick. These reports just came out yesterday and we already have to turn the ringers off on our phones because the calls keep coming!"

"And now," her son continues, "we are barricaded in our own home because the news reporters are on our front lawn asking a ton of questions."

The cell phone near them buzzes. They look at the screen.

"It's dad!"

His wife picks it up and answers. "Hey…" she smiles.

"Put him on speaker!" DJ urges.

She presses the speaker button. "We can both hear you now."

"Are you guys alright?" Daniel asks.

"You see what kind of trouble you caused?" She says somewhat teasingly.

"Rebecca, has it been that bad?"

"Like a madhouse!"

"Hey Dad!"

"Hey DJ. How are you holding up?"

"We're doing alright. Never thought we'd be famous though. People were going crazy at school today. I don't know if I'll go back tomorrow. May have to wait till this blows over."

"I'm really sorry you both have to go through this."

"While it is annoying," Rebecca says, "we did know this would happen. All a part of God's plan, right?"

"Yes," Daniel agrees. "This is all a part of God's plan. Speaking of plans…"

"Pastor already came by to check on us," Rebecca interjects. "We're good."

"Great. So, the rotation has started?"

"Yeah," she replies. "Church family and close friends will be checking on us regularly. Some are already stationed outside the house."

"Now that I'm in the spotlight, you both are too. I don't expect opposition to what I'm doing to reach *you*, but you can never be too careful."

"God told us to do this," his wife counters, "so He has it all under control."

"That's right Dad," DJ adds. "God's got us!"

"Thanks buddy."

"Baby, you sound tired."

"I'm only half way through this journey and sometimes it's been exhausting. But… it's absolutely amazing! Right now, my spirit is filled with the joy of the LORD, but my body and mind are exhausted. Still, God provides everything I need… *when* I need it."

"So, where are you now?" DJ asks excitedly.

"I'm near the state line between Nebraska and Kansas."

"Hey Dad. When you were a kid, did you ever think this is what you would be doing with your life?"

"You mean being married with a son?" Daniel feigns ignorance.

"Dad…" DJ shakes his head. "You know what I mean."

"Oh, you mean did I think I would be walking across the country like this?"

"Yeah."

"Not at all, Son. But I know God knew this would be the plan."

PART 2

THE CALLING

"The word of the Lord came to me, saying,
"Before I formed you in the womb I knew you,
before you were born I set you apart;
I appointed you as a prophet to the nations."

—Jeremiah 1:4-5—

14: Where it All Began

1994 — 30 Years Earlier...

Growing up in the inner city was no easy feat, even with two parents who worked hard to ensure our success in life. What made it easier was not having to grow up alone...

Daniel and his older brother, Zachariah were inseparable. They were two years apart, but you would have thought they were twins. They excelled in their studies, martial arts, track and field, and basketball. Both boys served to motivate the other as they followed the lead of their parents. Jonathan and Miriam Davidson worked hard to instill within their sons a love for God, a deep work ethic and noble character. And it paid off.

When Zachariah graduated high school, he chose to pursue a career in law enforcement. Two years later, Daniel graduated and chose to pursue engineering. Several years later, Daniel had an advanced degree in mechanical engineering and Zachariah had worked his way up the ranks to detective with the NYPD.

v

One summer night...

The two brothers exit a downtown restaurant in Brooklyn. Daniel is still wearing a party hat and Zachariah has a party blower hanging out of his mouth.

"Happy Birthday little brother," Zachariah smiles as he throws his arm around Daniel and pulls him close in a hug-like headlock. Daniel laughs as he pokes his brother hard in his side, hitting that one vulnerable spot amidst his formidable build—forcing a tickled laughter.

"No fair, Bro!" Zachariah chuckles as he pushes his brother away.

"Come on, Zach," Daniel interjects. "A big tough detective like you and a small poke can render you useless!"

"You know being tickled is my kryptonite!"

"Seriously," Daniel laughs. "forget torturing people with pain. Find their *tickle spot* and they will give up *all* their secrets!"

The two laugh as they get into Zachariah's car and drive away.

"I appreciate the early celebration, Bro. Thanks for dinner."

"I know I'm a week early, but this was the only time I had available."

"How's the case coming?" Daniel asks with both excitement and concern.

"Bigger than we expected," Zachariah breathes deeply. "That's why I took you out tonight. The next six to seven days will be very eventful."

"Really? How?"

"You know I can't tell you that."

"But I'm your partner," Daniel feigns seriousness.

"Mom and Dad would say you're my *partner in crime!*" Zachariah laughs. "But seriously, we're working with several agencies to take this group down. When we're done, it will be all over the news."

As they drive through the city, with their windows down, a sudden scream and movement to the right of the car catches their attention. Half a block away, a woman runs for her life—followed by four men. Zachariah calls dispatch, reports what he sees, and turns his car in pursuit.

"Bro," Daniel says nervously, "you're off duty."

"Crime doesn't wait until you're on duty," Zachariah replies while becoming laser focused on the task at hand. "By the time patrol gets here, that woman could be dead."

The four men chase the woman into an adjacent alley as Zachariah's car screeches to a halt. He pulls his badge out from underneath his shirt, retrieves his gun from a special lockbox beneath his chair and jumps out!

"Stay here," he commands while grabbing the flashlight from his belt.

"Maybe *you* should wait," Daniel counters.

"No time." Zachariah rushes quietly into the dark alley with his police shield visible and his gun drawn. He spots the group of men, at the end of the corridor, towering over the woman.

"NYPD!" Zachariah shouts with his gun and handheld flashlight trained on the four men. "Show me your hands!"

The men squint as the bright light temporarily blinds them. This gives Zachariah the advantage. They can't see him clearly, but he can clearly see them.

"Keep your hands where I can see them," he barks!

The men slowly raise their arms without making any sudden moves.

"Back away from the woman now." Zachariah's six foot two muscular frame is normally imposing, but the men seem... *too calm*... not nervous at all. It's like they *know* something he doesn't.

Daniel's nervous energy gets the better of him as his legs jitter uncontrollably. The silence is deafening and the police backup has yet to arrive. He strains to listen out the open window and hears no sirens in the distance. So, he quietly, but quickly exits the vehicle and carefully makes his way to the alley's entrance.

"You alone?" one of the men asks with a smirk. "Just one cop all by yourself?"

"No," Zachariah replies confidently as he studies them. "Backup's got the alley covered, so you don't escape."

"Don't see no flashing lights," the man counters—calling his bluff. "Don't hear no sirens."

"Get down on your knees—all of you—NOW!" Zachariah barks the order with increased intensity.

"Nah," another man answers. "YOU get on *your* knees."

Just then, a fifth man slithers out of the shadows behind Zachariah with his gun drawn. A split second before the man can pull the trigger, a swift kick to the back of his left knee sends him tumbling to the ground in pain. In an instant, a form jumps on him—disarming and immobilizing him with a quick succession of submission holds.

"Told you I had backup," Zachariah smiles as he keeps his eyes trained on the four men. "Let's try this again. *All* of you get on *your* knees, now!"

They comply as he calls to the woman.

"Ma'am? Are you alright?"

"Y-yes," the frightened woman replies with a nod.

"Can you stand and walk towards me as quickly as possible?"

She nods once more, stands to her feet and quickly passes her assailants to approach the detective.

"I thought I told you to stay in the car," Zachariah calls over his shoulder.

"If I did, you'd be dead," Daniel calls back.

"Right," he concedes as the woman reaches him. "Ma'am, please go with my *partner* and wait on the street so we can get your statement."

Just as the words leave his mouth, a sharp jab pierces the side of his torso. The unexpected pain is instant as Zachariah cries out while dropping his flashlight and clutching the spot on the side of his chest. To his alarm, he finds the woman's hand holding the handle of a knife—the blade fully forced in between his ribs. Daniel watches in horror as the four men jump to their feet and rush toward his brother.

Zachariah knocks the woman away and fires two quick shots as his assailants are upon him! One falls to the ground—the bullets hitting their mark. The next man slaps the gun from Zach's hand and punches him squarely in the jaw—bringing him crashing to the pavement! The man raises his foot high in the air with every intention of crushing the detective's head with his steel-toed boot, but the sudden impact from a flying side kick sends him careening through the air and into three nearby trashcans. Before the other two criminals can react, Daniel delivers a furious onslaught of well-placed punches, kicks and throws! In a matter of moments he has immobilized them. Daniel quickly scans the alley while maintaining his defensive posture. The only movement he sees is the woman running away.

"Zach," he yells as he goes to his brother and kneels beside him.

A sound like thunder erupts as his body awkwardly falls backward to the ground with a terrible thud. The first assailant slowly rises from the trash cans with his gun in his hand—smoke rising from the barrel. Distant sirens announce the approaching police, as the man walks over to Zachariah and towers over his body. Zachariah stares up at him from the pavement.

"I hate cops," the man says—matter-of-factly. "And you won't be stopping my crew." With that, the sound of thunder cracks again… and the man exits the alley with his fellow cohorts stumbling behind him.

Moments later, backup units arrive and secure the area. All they find is the detective lying motionless next to his brother who also isn't moving… both in a pool of intermingled blood.

V

Some time later…

A QUIET DARKNESS… A sudden… a string of disjointed scenes and impressions flash in rapid succession, submerged in a void of nothingness:

A dusty street… Simple buildings… Trees… Angry faces…. The taste of dirt and blood… A face… Youthful… Smiling… Radiant… Mountains… Dwellings… Blue sky… Three points of golden light merge into one… The light becomes a hand holding seven smaller points of radiance… Blood Red… Royal blue… A lone pathway winding off into the distance… An then… Darkness…

V

Nagging pain slowly drags Daniel back to consciousness. The repetitious hissing of beeping monitors reveal his location. He lays in a hospital bed. His parents sit closely by his side surrounded by the machinery. He opens his dry mouth to speak. His voice sounds like gravel.

"Where… where is Zach?"

His mother sobs as his father strains to say the words no one wants to hear.

"He… didn't make it."

In an instant his entire world is shattered.

Minutes pass as silent tears stream down Daniel's cheeks. He struggles to sit up.

"Don't," his mother cautions as she rushes to her son's side and gently pushes him back down to the bed. "Don't try to move. You need your rest. We… we thought we lost you, too."

Daniel gazes from his mother to his father with a slightly perplexed look.

"You *died*," his dad responds. "In the emergency room, while the doctors were working on you. Your heart stopped for about seven minutes…"

"Do you remember anything about what happened?" his mother asks with sad, but inquisitive eyes.

Daniel's eyes search the room as he tries to recall the timeline of events.

"How long… have I been here?"

"Two weeks," his father replies.

"Did the funeral… already happen?"

His parents look at each other before turning their attention back to their son.

"Zachariah's home-going celebration was yesterday. We waited as long as we could to see if you would wake up."

"It's okay… I know you did… what you had to do. Did a lot of people show up?"

"The church was packed," his mother smiles softly. "Almost 900 people."

"The line of people stretched out the door and down the block," his father adds with a sense of pride. "And that didn't include the police. A couple hundred of them were there to pay their respects."

"So," his mother asks again, "what do you remember?"

Daniel pauses again as he recollects his thoughts…

"An alley… maybe five men… a woman… she stabbed Zach…"

"The police think your brother was ambushed. Whoever did this most likely had been watching him for a while. Apparently, they didn't like the kind of impact he was making as a detective."

"He told me… about a case he was… working on. A big bust that was… gonna happen real soon."

"They surmised as much," his father replies. "But you were there… You *saw* something. You may be able to provide some details to catch these guys."

"I'll do whatever I can."

"An officer has been assigned outside the room. If whoever shot you finds out you're still alive… It may not be safe for you."

"For me?" Daniel replies as he looks at his parents with an increasing anger. "When I get out of here, it's not going to be *safe* for *whoever* killed my brother."

V

Some time later...

Daniel sits in his room writing in his journal.

It's been three months since my brother was killed and the authorities are no closer to solving his murder. My grief had given way to anger and I swore to solve this mystery myself. I began my own private investigation. I asked questions by day and forced answers by night. The rabbit hole drew me into a downward spiral as the darkness began to consume me. My parents just confronted me this morning when they discovered what I was doing.

V

That morning...

"This is not *God's way* son," his father protests.

"I don't care!" Daniel yells. "If God isn't going to help us find answers, then I have to do this on my own. I *will* avenge my brother's death!"

"God says, "vengeance is Mine. I will repay,'" his mother interjects. "Let the Lord handle this. If you keep going down this path, you may not make it back. What if you end up dead like your brother? We can't lose *both* of you... not like this."

Silence punctuates the room. The gravity of her words weighs on the three of them. Daniel's mind fills with a flurry of thoughts. He breathes deeply and runs his hands through his hair while closing his eyes and shaking his head slightly.

"Mom, I hear you... But, whoever did this to us *has* to be brought to justice! They *have* to pay."

"And they will," his father replies. "We've always told you that nothing escapes God's sight."

"I... I know. But you just want to sit back and let them get away with this? Zach was your son! He was *my* brother! I don't understand why you aren't fighting to get at the truth!"

"We want the truth just as badly as you do, Daniel," his father replies. "Zachariah was our flesh and blood. Our first born son. And he was *stolen* from us. Even so, God doesn't make any mistakes. If He allowed this to happen—no matter how painful it is for us—then it must be for a reason. And we just have to wait until that purpose reveals itself."

"Well, *you* can wait all you want. I'll keep doing what I am doing."

"I know we can't stop you, Son... but you must remember that God is sovereign. And He alone has the power to work all things out for our good. Not just the good things... but *all* things... including this... tragedy."

My parents had raised me to believe and trust in God... to trust the promises He made in His Word... but at this moment, trusting Him was the most difficult thing for me to do.

V

One week later...

The entire day was spent running errands. Daniel drove from one end of the Bronx to the other, then to Manhattan, over to Queens and finally into Brooklyn. *I can't believe Mom would have done all this on the bus and the train,* he thinks to himself. *Glad I could do this for her. She has so much on her mind, now that Zach's gone. We all have so much on our mind.* Finally, after about six hours of back and forth, an exhausted Daniel was on his way home.

Traffic was flowing uncharacteristically smooth on the Major Deegan Expressway for this time of day. The speed limit was 50 for trucks and 55 for cars. Most of the drivers, including Daniel, were doing at least 65 miles per hour. The window was down and his arm was hanging through, with his hand cupping the wind and directing it into his face. The constant buffeting helped to keep his drowsy eyes from closing. As he yawned, he noticed a change in the traffic up ahead, way in the distance. A sea of red brake lights strobed like a flock of birds in close formation. The flow of traffic was slowing and Daniel would have to stop in a minute. He pressed his foot on the brake and the peddle slipped straight to the floor with barely a hesitation.

Immediately his eyes opened wide as a jolt of anxious energy brought him to full awareness! His foot pumped the brake pedal several times, but the car didn't slow at all! He grabbed the emergency brake handle and yanked it up as hard as he could! But there was no deceleration! Other cars were slowing in staggered positions on the expressway, but Daniel's car barreled ahead, as he swerved past those nearest to him!

Car horns punctuated the air as he was quickly running out of drivable roadway. His knuckles almost burst through his skin from the pressure exerted on them as he gripped the steering wheel for dear life! Out of space and out of time, all he could do was swerve to the shoulder of the expressway and pray the concrete barrier would stop his vehicle. He clipped the car in front of him that had come to a complete stop! Both cars—at the point of impact—shattered as his car broke into a spin, hit a minivan and catapulted into the air before crashing on the side of the expressway, flipping once and coming to a sudden dead stop.

The concrete barrier had done its job. Now, his car—a mangled smoky mess, was wedged tightly against it. Shattered glass, crumpled metal, gas and oil were everywhere. As people got out of their cars, fearing the worst, to everyone's surprise Daniel crawled out of the wreckage with barely a scratch! Every airbag had deployed. But somehow, Daniel knew his survival, while aided by technology, had more to do with the miraculous.

"Bro! You should be dead!" a bystander yelled while looking at Daniel and his mangled car! "Your car looks like an accordion! Somebody's been praying for you!"

V

Forty-five minutes later…

Police, firetrucks, an ambulance and tow truck were on the scene. Based on his description of events, a quick assessment of Daniel's car revealed the brake line had been *cut*. This was no accident… it was *intentional*. Daniel put two-and-two together real quick. *Whoever killed my brother was sending me a message. Or maybe, they were trying to kill me?*

V

Four hours later...

Daniel walked in the door of his parent's house. Both his mother and father greeted him with nervous-but-relieved bear hugs.

"When the police officer called us and said you had been in an accident," his mother began with tears in her eyes, "I expected the worst. It was like my heart stopped beating!"

His dad held his son by the shoulders and smiled deeply. "We were grateful that the Lord had spared your life."

"He did *more* than just spare me..." Daniel replied in a hush.

"What do you mean?"

"I... don't know how to explain it," Daniel continues as he extends his arms out so his parents can get a good view. "I don't have a scratch on me. You should see the car. There's no way I should have walked out of there alive. Somebody even said that on the scene. He told me... someone had prayed for me."

"We did," his mother smiles broadly with a twinkle in her eyes.

"You did? When?"

"What time did you get into that accident?" she asks.

"I dunno," Daniel tries to recollect the event. "I left the last store around 3pm... Was on the expressway for about twenty minutes or so... So, maybe around 3:40-ish?"

Both his parents clap their hands with a shout: "Hallelujah!"

"I don't get it..."

"Of course you don't," his dad laughs, "not without all of the pieces to the puzzle God is putting together!"

His mom continues. "Your dad and I were sitting in the living room reading when a sudden feeling of danger came over us! It was *heavy*..."

"It *smothered* us," his dad interjected.

"We felt like we had to pray *immediately*," his mother continues.

"So, we started praying," his dad says. "but we didn't know where the danger was nor *who* was in danger."

"So," his mom interjects, "we asked the Lord."

"Then we *knew*," his dad urged, "that you were in great danger! And we began to intercede to the Lord on your behalf."

"We asked the Lord to put his angels around you," his mom continues, "to cover you, to protect you from *all* danger seen and unseen."

"We asked the Lord," his dad continues, "to bring you back home to us safe and in one piece."

"Do you know what time that was?" his mom smiled.

Daniel looked at them speechless while slightly shaking his head.

"It was exactly at 3:30pm! Right as you were about to have that accident!"

They both shout again. "Hallelujah!"

"Anyone who says God doesn't exist has no idea what they're talking about!" His dad claps. "He may not show up when we want Him, but He's *always* right on time!"

Daniel gazes at his gleeful parents as they worship the Lord with uplifted hands. "You know," he begins, "I didn't say this to the first responders…"

They quiet down to listen.

"But right when I crashed into the first car, a split second before the airbag deployed, I felt… I felt something like… *strong hands*… resting on my chest and my head. Then the car catapulted into the air and I don't remember feeling… *anything*… no inertia… no centripetal force… and when the car landed and flipped and the glass shattered all around me… I felt like there was this… invisible… barrier… like I was inside of a protective bubble which kept the glass from cutting me."

Parents and son stare at each other in a stunned silence.

"But that's crazy… right?" Daniel asks with wide eyes.

"You're standing here right now, without a scratch," his dad replies.

"We know in our hearts that if God had not intervened, you would probably be dead right now… or at least close to it."

"God spared your life," his mother adds.

"I know," Daniel replies. "But why? That's what I can't figure out. *Why* did He spare my life?"

His parents stare at their son and then at each other.

"Miriam. It's time," his father says with an air of quiet conviction.

"Time for what?" Daniel asks.

"Yes," his mother nods while taking a deep breath. "It is time for you to know why God has preserved you."

"You *know*?" Daniel replies—his eyes wide. "How could you know?"

His father takes his mother's hand. Her eyes wrinkle a somber look as she speaks.

"I became pregnant with your brother right after your father and I were married."

"We were on our honeymoon, actually," his father says proudly.

"We wanted a child," his mother smiles, "so we started trying right away. When it came time for Zachariah to be born… childbirth was… difficult."

"There were so many complications," his dad interjects.

"Yes," his mom admits. "I almost *died*. That was such a terrifying experience, that when I accidentally became pregnant with you I chose to have an abortion."

"An abortion," Daniel blurts out! "You were going to *abort* me?!"

"Son, I know this is shocking," his father replies. "We are not proud of this. But we want you to understand what happened *then* so you can comprehend what is happening *now*."

"Okay…" Daniel huffs. "Why didn't you tell me about this before?"

His mother gazes at him with an air of shame. "What child would want to know they were going to be aborted? And what mother would want to admit to their child that they would have done so?"

Silence…

V

Before Daniel was born…

In a sparsely furnished apartment, Jonathan sits on the bed holding his one year old restless son, Zachariah, on his chest. Zachariah is fighting a nap, but as the father rubs his son's back, he slowly closes his eyes and falls asleep. The sound of flushing water echoes through the apartment as the bathroom door opens a moment later. Miriam walks out—her face a bit flustered as she looks at her husband and firstborn son.

"He's finally asleep," Jonathan whispers as she sits down next to him on the bed. His eyebrows wrinkle as he looks at his wife. "That's the third time you've vomited today. Do I need to take you to the doctor?"

"I'm pregnant," she responds flatly as her eyes swell with tears.

"But we took precautions…"

"Well, they didn't work."

Jonathan takes Miriam's hand, but she pulls it away and turns from him.

"I can't go through that again," she whispers.

He can see that she is shaking slightly.

"Maybe the second pregnancy won't be like the first," Jonathan utters soothingly.

"It's too much." Miriam turns back towards her husband and pulls her shirt up, revealing her scarred belly. "I will not go through *this* again," she points. "The doctors said—"

"I know what the doctors said." He cuts her off, but not in a rude way. "I was there with you, remember?"

"But it's not *your* body," she replies.

"What are you saying?"

"I'm saying…" she hesitates to say the words, "I'm saying… that I want to get an abortion."

"You can't be serious."

"I am… serious." Her eyes plead with his. "If we go through with the pregnancy… and I *die*, then *you* will have to raise our son *alone*. Is that what you want?"

"You know that's *not* what I want."

"Then this is the *only* way. We already have one son. Yes, we wanted two, but the risk is too great. And we're already struggling to make ends meet as it is."

"What about your mother?"

"I know she won't understand. She'll say we are going against the Bible. She'll tell us to just trust God to get us through this. She'll remind us of our relationship with Jesus... but Jesus wants us to be happy... to be together... to live."

"So, we don't tell her?"

"Right. We don't tell her. We don't tell anyone."

"Ok," Jonathan reluctantly agrees. "I will support whatever decision you want to make."

V

The present...

A few days later we drove to the clinic. The whole time I felt like we were making a mistake, but I didn't know what else to do. So, I asked God to give us a sign if He didn't want me to go through with it."

"What happened?" Daniel whispers, hanging on his parents' every word.

"My mother showed up."

"At the abortion clinic?" Daniel's eyes almost pop out of his head!

"Yes. She drove her car right between us and the entrance."

"We were horrified," his father adds. "She told us to get in her car."

"What did you do?"

"We got in the car."

V

Outside the abortion clinic...

Miriam, Jonathan and her mother Esther sit in the quiet car.

Miriam doesn't even look up from her lap. "How... did you know we were here?"

"The Lord told me to come," Esther says softly but firmly. "You know He sees everything."

Miriam bursts into tears as her mother and husband quietly look on. Minutes pass as she weeps uncontrollably. Then Esther softly places her hands on her daughter's belly.

"Look at me."

Miriam slowly looks up in her mother's direction. Her mother cracks a warm, knowing smile as she gazes into her daughter's brown eyes.

"The Lord sent me because He knows all about your fears and how you believe you won't survive another pregnancy. He understands how you feel. And so do I... God understands why you've made this choice. But, He wants *you both* to know He has ordained this baby, that is in your womb, for a unique task. And He promises to be with you on this journey... if you will trust Him. The choice is yours."

V

The present...

There is silence once again as they gaze at their son... and he stares at them.

"Aside from our shame, we kept this from you because we didn't want to burden you. We knew God would reveal when it was time for you to know."

"And that time is now?" Daniel surmises.

"Yes," his father confirms.

"And so, we kept you," his mother replies. "And God has provided for us."

"From the time your grandmother uttered those words," his father adds, "we have covered you and your brother in prayer tried and tried to keep you hidden."

"Hidden? From who?"

"From the enemy,"

"You mean the devil?"

"Yes. That is why we have never shared that prophecy with anyone. We did not want Satan to catch on. But, somehow he has. That is why these tragic things have been happening to you. It is time for you to fulfill your calling and the enemy is trying to thwart it."

"What about Zachariah? What about his purpose?"

"We have to trust in God's sovereignty," his father replies. "We have to believe that your brother has played the part God wanted him to play."

Silence once again…

"I can't believe I almost wasn't born," Daniel thinks out loud. "If it wasn't for grandma…"

"Many times she followed God's leading and ended up helping a lot of people. She had a gift for discerning God's will."

"But if she hadn't listened and you ended up aborting me, what do you think would have happened?"

"Well," his mother thinks, "whatever purpose God determined for you to accomplish would not come to pass."

"Do you think He would just raise up someone else to do it?"

"Perhaps… Or maybe not. Even if He did, there would be a chance that time and lives would have been lost in the meantime."

"When your grandmother stopped us," his dad adds, "and we chose to go through with the pregnancy, God provided everything we needed. That entire experience made us keenly aware of His provision and of the sanctity of life."

"That's right," his mother continues. "If God ordained *your* purpose before you were born, just like He did with the prophet Jeremiah in the Bible, then that means He ordains *all* of our purposes. Sadly, our free will makes it possible to abort God's purposes both in the womb and in our lives. And we are left with the repercussions of our actions. Even so, through Christ, forgiveness and restoration can be found. Then, whatever aspects of God's vision for us which remain, may still be fulfilled."

The three of them sit in silence once again.

"There's something I never told you guys," Daniel whispers. His parents silently wait for him to continue.

"I had this… *vision* after I was shot. I don't know if it was when I died or when I was in a coma."

"A vision of what?"

"I was in some kind of void... it felt... like I was outside of time and space. It was dark... but I wasn't scared at all. I could see myself... my hands and feet. I was clothed in white. And I had all of my thoughts and memories. There was this... invisible sense of overwhelming peace and I *felt* like I wasn't alone."

"Did you see God?" His father interrupts.

"I didn't... *see* Him. But somehow I knew He was there."

"Then what happened?"

"A bunch of images flashed before my eyes. I don't know what they mean, but when they ended, I woke up in the hospital with you both sitting in the room."

They stare at each other in silence once again.

His mother speaks: "We didn't tell you the whole story either."

"About what?"

"When you died on the operating table the doctors tried to resuscitate you, but they were unsuccessful. After four minutes they called your time of death and covered your body with a white sheet. We were in the waiting room when they informed us. We asked to see your body and they escorted us to the operating room."

His father picks up the story. "We stood next to your body as one of the doctors pulled back the sheet. We cried for a moment and then we thought about what your grandmother had said. There was nothing unique about your life up to that point that would indicate God had used you in the way she declared. So, I took your mother's hand and placed it on your chest right above your heart."

"And," his mother continues, "we asked the Lord to send you back to us so you could fulfill His purpose for your life."

"A few moments after that prayer... you came back!" His dad smiles with great delight!

Daniel stares at his parents in silence. "I... don't know what to say..."

"Four attempts have been made on your life," his mother continues, "but you are still here. So, God has a specific work for you to do."

"The devil knows this," his dad adds. "He's been trying to take you out!"

"Do you think he knows why I've been chosen?" Daniel asks.

"Highly unlikely," his dad replies. "*We don't even know the specifics*, so why should the devil know more than you do? God will make sure *you* know your calling before the enemy is made aware of it. We believe now is that time. Any child of God who answers their call is dangerous to the devil's dark empire."

Another moment of silence passes before things grow somber. Daniel notices the change almost immediately.

"You guys were just smiling," he utters in a perplexed tone, "why are you looking serious all of a sudden?"

"We've already decided," his dad says with finality. "If this car crash wasn't an accident, then whoever killed your brother is trying to kill you."

"I thought about that," Daniel agrees.

"So, the only *logical* thing to do, is send you away."

"Wait," Daniel tries to register his father's words. "What are you saying? You're kicking me out?!"

"You need to lay low until all of this blows over."

"We need to fight them!" Daniel's anger is apparent.

"What you need," his mother replies, "is to *live* so you can carry out whatever purpose God has for you."

Daniel stares at his parents for a moment. "Fine. Send me down south or out west."

"No," his dad counters. "They will find you."

"So, what then?" Daniel chuckles. "You want me to leave the country?" His parents stare at him solemnly. The pain of their decision suddenly becoming evident on their faces. "Wait. You *really* want me to leave the country?"

"We don't *want* you to leave," his dad replies, "But, if that's what it takes to keep you safe, then that's what it takes. We're getting you a plane ticket first thing in the morning."

"A plane ticket? To where?"

"If you have to go out the country," his mother answers, "then you might as well go somewhere you've always wanted to visit."

"And," his dad adds, "since you've already been to Ghana, the only other location is—"

"China?" Daniel cuts his dad off. "You're sending me to China?"

"Like your mother said, you have always wanted to visit."

"Yeah, but not like this!"

"Don't worry, Son. We'll give you enough money. Stay for a few months or a year. While you're gone, the police can do their job. And when they're done you can come home."

"What about you? What if these guys come after you?"

"We're going down south to our hometown," his dad answers.

"We'll stay at my sister's place," his mom adds. "Her house is more than big enough. And as you know, her husband is retired law enforcement."

"Besides," his father adds, "the town is a close-knit community. So, it will be *real difficult* for anyone from the outside to try something without encountering interference."

"How long will you stay there?"

"As long as it takes," his mother replies.

Daniel didn't want to admit it, but his parents were right. They couldn't stay in New York, and he… he needed to leave the country.

15: A Lasting Legacy

Two days later... Daniel sat on a 12 hour international flight to the other side of the world. Little did he know that this one move would change the trajectory of his entire life. He had only been in the air for two hours before he pulled his brand new journal out of his bag and wrote his very first entry.

Entry #1. July 27, 2005
It hasn't even been a full year since Zach's murder... So much has happened. So much has changed. And now, I'm on a plane to China! Life is not going any way near like I had hoped or imagined. Why did God allow my brother to die? I miss him so much! And why did God preserve my life? What's the purpose in all of this? And what about that vision? What does this all mean?

Daniel sits, sifting through his thoughts as the roar of the jet engines fill the cabin. He smiles slightly as he continues to write.

I always had an unexplainable attraction to China and its people. I guess it started with watching those old Kung-fu movies with my dad when I was a kid. I can remember those Shaolin monks being powerful and honorable warriors. And every now and then one would say, "God's name be praised," when expressing thanks for a blessing. I wasn't sure if they meant the God of the Bible or some other deity within their own belief system, but that phrase stuck with me.
Then one day, as a teen, my father handed me a small book. It was the biography of Hudson Taylor, a famous British missionary. I had no idea who he was. Yes, I was a Christian, but at that age, I could care less about missionary work and about the past. My issues, my likes and my friends were my world. But there was something about the look on my dad's face that day. His expression teased that this biography was some kind of buried treasure waiting to be discovered.
And so, I read... and couldn't put it down! Here was a man who was not much older than me when he became a missionary. I couldn't believe the major impact he made sharing the gospel in China' in the 1800's! At a time

when other missionaries would stay on the coast in their mission compounds for safety, Hudson would venture into China's interior forging new ground for the name of Jesus. And while other missionaries maintained their own definitive culture and expected the Chinese to convert not only to Christ, but also to European ways of doing things, Hudson took a different approach. He embodied the mindset of the apostle Paul, in 1 Corinthians 9, who said, "I have become all things to all people so that by all possible means I might save some."

Hudson took on those cultural norms of the Chinese which did not go against the Bible. He learned their language. He wore their clothes. He adopted the common hairstyle of the men. He ate their food. And these decisions served to open up unique opportunities to share Jesus in places and to people who would have otherwise been closed to the message. Many of the Chinese favored his efforts to honor them in these ways. Meanwhile, some of the other missionaries who stayed on the coast viewed his efforts with disdain. But he focused on reaching the people of China, no matter the personal cost to himself. His example paved the way for a wave of new missionaries being inspired to join his pursuit. They pledged themselves to his type of service to the Chinese people on behalf of Christ. He eventually organized his efforts and founded the China Inland Mission. And God blessed him to take the gospel into many Chinese provinces.

Sadly, the Boxer rebellion happened in 1900. A massive group of indigenous Chinese fought to expel foreign missionaries and Chinese Christians from the country. Many Christians were killed... Five years later, Hudson died after having spent 54 years in China! Hudson Taylor left everything he knew to follow Jesus. And Jesus had led him to give his all in China. Reading that biography, about how God used this man to create a lasting legacy to Christ, inspired me. Not only did I have a general interest in the country, but I now had a genuine desire to see her people come to know Jesus. That's why I minored in Chinese while in college, so I could learn the language. I barely use it now—mostly when I'm at the Chinese restaurant. So, my Mandarin is a little rusty.

But, now, here I am... on a plane to China. I know China is a communist country and Christianity—true Christianity is illegal. There are state-sanctioned churches, but they are monitored and censored by the government. Many genuine Christians quite possibly number in millions. Yet, they have to worship in secret or risk being imprisoned or killed. So, I *will have to be careful as well. But it would be amazing if I could track down someone who had a direct connection to Hudson Taylor's ministry.*

V

10 hours later…

The plane lands in Beijing, China early in the morning around 8:00am (China Standard Time). The sound of a guzheng— a stringed instrument which looks like a horizontal harp—greet the passengers as they disembark. The airport is bright and spacious. Once through customs with his book bag, duffel bag and satchel, Daniel enters a new world he has only seen on television, in the movies and read about in books.

The sights and sounds of modern-day Chinese culture assaults his senses: the sheer number of people, the active busyness, the smog… caused by the immense number of vehicles throughout the city.

"I thought downtown Manhattan was *crowded*," he mumbles to himself with a smile as his excitement completely overwhelms his jet-lag.

After a pre-arranged early check-in, Daniel spends the day traversing through Beijing: trying new foods, visiting the Forbidden City, walking through Tiananmen Square and observing the new stadium being constructed for the 2008 Olympic games. All the while he talks to people—many of whom are surprised at his command of their language—even though he's a bit rusty. By evening, thoroughly tired, he heads back to his hotel. The first day is done… many more are still to come.

By the end of the week, he has visited every major tourist attraction in Beijing, including the world-renowned Great Wall of China. Now, that he has given himself time to adjust, he is ready for the real work to begin.

V

3 weeks later…

Daniel has ventured further and further from Beijing with each passing day—making his way through several cities in a variety of provinces. One of his favorite modes of travel in local areas is the Chinese rickshaw—the carriages that are pulled by men who either run, bike or ride a scooter. He also enjoys the wide variety of food choices. Although on one occasion what he ate did not agree with him. Thankfully, he had a hotel stay which lasted for two days, which was enough time for his stomach to settle. And so, he continued his quest to find anyone directly impacted by the work and legacy of Hudson Taylor. After several more days of travel—further and further into the interior of the country—the legacy he searches for... finds him.

Daniel walks through a semi-remote village... that is situated in a great valley surrounded by majestic mountains. Within minutes after walking down a somewhat crowded street, he exits from the marketplace and finds himself on the outskirts of the village. Daniel notices the foot traffic has suddenly become sparse. As he follows the path away from the village, he immediately feels that something is not right. His pulse quickens as he picks up the pace. The simple buildings and the empty and dusty road are now eerily quiet.

"This... seems *familiar* somehow..." he mumbles to himself, while trying to recollect his thoughts.

Daniel stops. Even the wind does not blow. Everything is still. His eyes scan the nearby buildings and tree lines. His ears listen intently in the silence. Somehow, he knows he is being watched.

"Lord, what is happening here?" He whispers.

It is then that he sees them: four men exit from the tree line. All of them dressed in dark clothing and wearing masks to hide their identity. They approach with body language that screams *obvious ill intent*. Daniel turns to retreat, but two more men block his path—having appeared from behind a nearby building some meters away. He recalls a warning from one of the locals a few villages back. "Watch out for bandits."

The men now surround him. Some brandish weapons: one has a knife. Another has a metal pipe. A third wears a pair of brass knuckles. Who knows what the others have? Daniel drops his duffel bag and satchel to the ground.

⟨*I want no trouble,*⟩ he says in Mandarin Chinese while raising his hands in a non-threatening manner. ⟨*I'm just passing through. Will you kindly allow me to pass?*⟩ He bows slightly to them in an act of deference: not that they *deserve* to be submitted to... but so he may potential pass unscathed.

They say nothing as they slowly circle him like a pack of wolves ready to pounce on their prey.

"Okay, then," Daniel says in English. "This is how we are doing this?" He closes his open hands into fists and assumes a defensive posture. "Lord, help me."

In an instant they rush him! In a flurry of moves Daniel ducks, dodges, parries and strikes. The bandit with the knife is the first to go down! A metal blow lands on Daniel's back. His bookbag absorbs most of the impact as he stumbles forward. Another blow lands across his jaw! Fortunately, it wasn't from the guy wearing the brass knuckles! He's next! The punch comes fast and furious! Daniel parries, traps the arm and sends the bandit flying into the air. Another blow strikes his leg! He falls on all fours to the ground. A blow hits his arm. He crumples to the dust and curls up like a ball as a hail of blows hammer his body. He covers his head as the onslaught increases like a jackhammer! His world spins as the edges of his vision dim to black. He can taste blood in his mouth as his arms slowly drop from exhaustion. A blow lands across his face—breaking his jaw—and a boot stomp cracks his ribs in several places. He slumps to the ground—motionless—covered in cuts and bruises. The bandits cease their attack, standing over him with heaving bodies, as they take a moment to catch their breath.

Before they can rummage through his pockets and his bags, a sound behind them draws their attention. They turn to find a young monk, wearing traditional garb colored in red, blue and gold. The edges of his garments are lined with Chinese characters. He is standing several feet away with his hands behind his back. They recognize the design of the monk's robe and immediately grow fearful as they read the Chinese characters on his clothing.

⟨*He's one of them,*⟩ a mugger says to the group with anxiety rising in his voice.

⟨*A son of thunder,*⟩ another confirms as he backs away from the fallen body on the ground. Following his lead, they all back away slowly, immediately becoming immensely aware of their rebellion against an unseen holy force. The monk stands motionless for a moment, with his eyes closed, seemingly in prayer. The wind kicks up in the distance, as a breeze descends upon them all and centralizes around the young monk—as if it is responding to his presence. He opens his eyes and looks intently at them.

⟨*My friends,*⟩ the monk utters confidently in Mandarin Chinese, ⟨*you have allowed the devil to use you for his foul purposes. Repent of your ways. Surrender your hearts to Yeshua, the LORD of Hosts and He will receive you. You do not have to remain on this path of destruction just to find a way to take care of your needs. The LORD has another path for you to walk. But if you refuse, you will face His wrath which is to come. The choice is yours.*⟩

The bandits turn and run back to their den of thieves. The monk watches them leave as he slowly approaches Daniel's body. He can see the bruises, his swelling and broken face and multiple cuts and gashes.

Daniel teeters back and forth between consciousness and darkness. As he looks up from the dusty earth, his blurred vision becomes clear for an instant. In that moment, he sees the monk's face looking down on him with a radiance surrounding his head like the sun. Then he passes out cold.

The monk gazes down on him with pity as his shadow passes over Daniel's body. He then prays in Mandarin. ⟨*Heavenly Father, what would You have me to do?*⟩

16: Monastery

2005 — The Inner Sanctum of the Holy

A voice utters the Scriptures in Mandarin Chinese: ⟨*He who dwells in the secret place of the Most High, shall abide under the shadow of the Almighty.*⟩ It is as if these words are being spoken as a prayer to God and as a covering over another. ⟨*I will say of the LORD, 'He is my refuge and my fortress, my God, in whom I trust.'*⟩

Daniel's eyes open slowly as a blurred form asks: "What are you doing here, American?"

Daniel slowly scans the room, trying to gain his bearings. Sunlight streams through the openings in the walls... openings which appear to be in the form of a written *language*... Mandarin characters? He can't be sure, but they seem to be carved right into the wood paneling in such a way that the sunlight illuminates them like tongues of fire. His gaze shifts from them as he tries to recollect the recent past. The last thing he remembers was being in the street, outside of a village. Then... the bandits.

"Where am I?" Daniel utters in response to the unknown form. "How... how did you know I was American? Wait. You speak English?"

"I speak many languages," the figure replies.

"Are you... an angel?" Daniel asks, while squinting, trying to get his eyes to clear. Just then he looks across the small room and the young monk comes into focus. "Wait..." he says as he slowly sits up in the bed. "I've... seen you before... in a dream. But it was only flashes of different scenes... 5 or 6 angry faces... a fight... darkness... the mountains... some kind of monastery... and *you*. You were looking down at me... there was blinding light all around you."

"It was the sun," the monk replies.

"What?"

"The blinding light around me. It was the sun. You were laying on the ground after the bandits attacked you on the roadway and I was standing over you. The sun was to my back and it cast my shadow over you... and you were healed from your injuries by the LORD of Hosts."

"Healed? You mean like when God used Peter's shadow to heal people?"

"Yes. You had several major injuries."

Daniel feels over his face and body... everything seems normal. He thinks about the dream and then what *actually* happened to him...

"If you hadn't shown up... I could have been dead by now."

"The LORD sent me to you. He has a great work for you to do."

"How... how could you know that?"

"Because," the monk smiles. "I had the same dream just over three months ago. Except I saw it with greater clarity and with a date... the date when you were attacked just outside of the village in the valley below."

"Below? Where are we?"

"In the monastery you saw in your dream. High in the mountains."

"But how is that possible?!"

"The Lord works in mysterious ways."

"I don't remember walking... How did we get here if I was unconscious?"

"I carried you and your bags," the monk smiles.

"You *carried me*?" Daniel balks. "Up a *mountain*?"

"It was not difficult. The joy of the LORD is *my* strength."

"How old are you?"

"I am 18 years old."

"Okay... Wait... my dream... I had it about three months ago while I was in the hospital. It was on—"

"March 23rd," the monk replies.

"How did you know—"

"That was the same day I had *my* dream. And in it, you cried out for me to come and help you."

"I... I don't understand," Daniel stares at the monk stupefied. "Why would God do this?"

"You are a believer in The Way are you not?"

"You mean in Jesus?"

"Yes. Yeshua is the Way, the Truth and the Life."

"Yes. I believe in Him."

"Have you not read when Paul tried to discern where the LORD wanted him to travel on his missionary journey? He had a dream in which a man from Macedonia called to him to help them. So, Paul headed there, knowing that was where God wanted him to minister. What has happened with *us* is no different. The LORD has ordained our meeting for His purposes. And you arrived in that village on the very day I was traveling through the area—which I only do one day each month."

Daniel sits in quiet, taking it all in.

"So, I ask you again, Daniel Davidson. What is it that you seek?"
"How do you know my name?"
The young monk smiles and motions to a small table next to the bed Daniel is lying on. Daniel turns toward it and sees his open passport on the tabletop and his bags with his other personal items leaning next to it.
"I… I was trying to find anyone who knew the founder of an old missionary group called the China Inland Mission. His name was Hudson Taylor."
"I know of him well."
"You do?"
The monk nods with a smile. "Come with me."
"Wait," Daniel hesitates. "You know my name. What's yours?"
"I'm Brother Léi. And you are now Brother Dàiwéisēn."
"What do these names mean?"
"My name, Léi, means Thunder. The name I gave you, is simply your last name in Mandarin." The monk smiles as he motions towards the doorway.

They rise and exit the humble dormitory abode and walk the grounds of the monastery. Men, women, boys and girls—all wearing similar red, blue and gold, garb—are engaged in various activities: cleaning, gardening, cooking, carrying supplies… Some stop and take note of Daniel's presence, smiling as he and Brother Léi walk by, before resuming their duties.

Daniel notices that exotic plants are everywhere, along with a variety of vegetable gardens. A giant wall, overgrown with plants and foliage, stands in the distance connected to a strong-looking gate. In the other direction are a series of small buildings—each distinct in their architecture, yet sharing a common theme. Behind them is the edge of the grounds which lead to a cliff—with a sheer drop almost two thousand feet down to a raging river below. Looking up, the mountain curves over the majority of the grounds before rising even higher into the air. Above the area not covered with the overhang, there is nothing but blue sky and clouds. From a distance, it would look as if a portion of the mountain was excavated—scooped out—in order to nestle the monastery into its side.

The beauty of the sight takes Daniel's breath away. But there is more. Daniel senses… a great unseen holiness which seems to permeate every square inch of the grounds.

"It is the palpable Presence of the Lord that you discern with your Spirit," Brother Léi says, answering Daniel's unasked question.

"How did you know what I was thinking?"

"There is not much which is not revealed to us in this place. Our hearts and minds, by the Holy Spirit, are laid bare before the LORD and each other. As they will be in heaven."

"I have… *never* felt God's Presence like this before. So heavy. It is… beautiful and yet… overwhelming."

"*He* is surely both," the monk replies. "This is because the Holy Spirit purifies us for Himself. However, to your quest for Hudson Taylor's legacy. All of us you see here are the result of Brother Hudson's faithful efforts. I am much too young to have known him, but several of our elders are direct descendants of those who lived and worked with him in the late 1800's."

"That… is amazing! The elders must be old!"

"Yes, there are three of them. Each over 100 years old. Brother Hudson made great strides for God's kingdom here in China. Many were coming to Christ and finding freedom from the idolatry and superstition of our ancestors. It was a wonderful time of joy in the LORD. The parents of our elders came to the LORD through Brother Hudson's ministry and worked with him to reach other communities.

"However, unknown to us at the time, there was growing animosity and opposition gathering in secret. Then, in 1900, the Boxer Rebellion unleashed its fury on our country. All who hated religion in general, and Christianity specifically, took to the streets in the organized expulsion of religion from our country. Hundreds of

Christian converts were killed. Foreign missionaries were expelled. Within the China Inland Mission, 58 missionaries and 21 children lost their lives.

"The tribulation of that time was great. The fear was immense. Brother Hudson had been out of the country, but news of the rebellion distressed him to great lengths. In the midst of the turmoil our elders were separated from the rest of the mission. To save their lives, they felt compelled to *flee to the mountains*, inspired by what Jesus said to His disciples in Matthew 24.

"It was a journey of several days to reach this place. It had once been a Buddhist temple, but was abandoned. Our elders swept this place clean of all previous relics and dedicated these grounds to Yahweh, the God of the Bible Who is the Sovereign Ruler of the universe. They petitioned God for His protection, and vowed to serve Him in every generation until the return of His Son Jesus to the earth. God honored their prayer with an outpouring of His Holy Spirit unlike anything before witnessed, except on the day of Pentecost.

"The LORD commanded each of them to develop their spirit, soul and body according to His Word. They were to raise their families here and build a monastic community, yet without restricting marriage. And they were to venture into the valley only at the times He would determine for them... Now, here we are... carrying the mandate forward into our day. Sadly, our elders were never able to reconnect with Brother Hudson. And several years later, in 1905, they learned of his death in the city of Changsha in Hunan Province. But, they will see him in heaven. We all will."

"Amen," Daniel nods in agreement. "So, all of this time, you have been shut up here?"

"We do not look at it as being 'shut up.' Rather, we are 'set apart' for the LORD's purposes. At the set times we go into the valley to get needed supplies and to share the gospel. Those who give their allegiance to Christ are given the opportunity to return here with us, if they so desire."

"But how have you stayed hidden for over a hundred years? How has no one found this place either by foot or by airplane or satellite? You do... *know*... what an airplane and satellite are, right?"

The young monk laughs as they enter a building that has large wall maps on every wall and several old radios sitting in each corner.

Each map covers a different part of the world and is filled with different color pushpins.

"Living in seclusion does not mean we are unaware of what is happening in our country and the world," he points. "But, to answer your question, we employ multiple techniques to hide ourselves. Even so, the LORD Himself keeps us hidden on every side by His Holy Spirit and His mighty angels."

"Angels?"

"Yes. They are posted throughout our grounds."

"You say that like you've seen them."

"We have," the young monk smiles. "Seeing them has been one of the LORD's wonderful mercies towards us."

Daniel's eyes almost pop out of their sockets as his mouth drops open.

"Do not think this strange. The supernatural is a natural occurrence in this place. And did not many servants of God in both the Old and New Testaments visibly encounter angels? Even the Apostle Paul states that we can encounter angels unawares."

"Do you... talk to them?"

"Only when directed by the LORD to do so. Or when they initiate the conversation at our LORD's command. Mostly, we are just made aware of their almost constant presence."

"Almost?"

"At times, as we pray, they are sent on other assignments. However, the Holy Spirit abides with us unceasingly."

"This is all so... amazing! I have had a couple of encounters with God back in America at church, but *never* on this level and magnitude!"

"It is easier to encounter God—and for God to encounter us—when there are less distractions to draw our attention away."

"I see... so, what about those who you bring here? What if they left and divulged your location to the authorities?"

"Very few know the winding paths through the mountains to arrive here. And by God's grace and mercy, no one has ever left to return to their former lives. It helps that we only bring those whom the LORD points out to us."

"What about the rest of your Chinese brothers and sisters? Those who are part of the underground church? They are facing immense persecution from the government."

"We are keenly aware of what our brothers and sisters in Christ are facing. It breaks our heart when we see and hear of their maltreatment at the hands of those who do not believe. So, we intercede for them that their faith may not fail—no matter the amount of difficulty they face. And we help those we can when our paths cross. However, the LORD has given us a very specific mandate, which must be carried out. That command requires us to maintain our position—*here*—on this mountain."

Daniel considers the young monk's words as they exit the building. He scans the surrounding area once more. "So, what is it that you all do here?"

"We live in communion with the LORD and with each other. We prepare ourselves spiritually, mentally and physically for Christ's second coming. And we intercede through prayer, at all times, for God's purposes to be done on earth as it is in heaven. There are great forces of darkness at work in the world, bent on enslaving and destroying humanity. God has assigned us to help keep those forces at bay, wherever they may be at work in the world. We do this primarily through intense prayer and fasting. The bad things which do happen are what the Lord allows for His purposes. However, there are other levels of evil our Heavenly Father does not at this time permit. He uses us and other saints around the world to stand in the gap as watchmen on the wall. We participate with the LORD in being a barrier of light against the darkness which desires to consume the world and all who are in it."

Daniel stops and looks at the young monk. "That is a serious level of responsibility."

"Yes, it is," the monk replies as they enter another building with a dome roof. Inside, two sizable telescopes rest next to a large open window. The domed ceiling carries an intricate three-dimensional chart of the night sky, accurately depicting the solar system. Daniel gapes in awe of the sight before returning to his train of thought.

"Wait. You said, *'there are other levels of evil God does not at this time permit.'* Are you saying there *will be* a time when He allows more evil to happen?"

"Have you not read the Scriptures?" Brother Léi raises his hand to the ceiling and slowly lowers it. "As we draw closer to Yeshua's 2nd Coming, evil will be allowed to flourish... for a time... to test the inhabitants of the world. This is one of the reasons why we have this room and these telescopes. Yeshua taught that there will be unique signs in the sun, moon and stars as we draw closer to His return. So, we study them in similar fashion to the Magi who studied the sky and discovered the star which led them to our Messiah when He was a young child."

Daniel looks at him perplexed. "Okay. I get that. You want to be prepared for Jesus' return. But, why would God allow evil to increase before He comes back?"

"This is one reason why I believe the LORD has sent you to us," the young monk replies. "Time is short. And there is much you must learn." With that, Brother Léi exits the building and begins to walk once more as Daniel follows closely behind him. They both step into the next nearest structure. Once again, Daniel's eyes and mouth are wide open. The entire room, from floor to ceiling, is filled with well-ordered rows of books.

One entire wall is filled with a multiplicity of Bibles in various translations and languages. The rest of the room is filled with books on almost every conceivable subject matter. Daniel scans some of the labeled sections: Philosophy. Physics. Natural Sciences. Medicine. Poetry. World History. Robotics. Artificial Intelligence...

"I did not expect to see all of these books on all of these subjects here at a monastery on the side of a high mountain," Daniel utters in disbelief and wonder. "I figured you all would only have Bibles here."

"The Bible is the primary source text for our lives. It serves as the lens through which we view the world and is the foundation for all of our studies. It encourages the study of the natural world, the celestial heavens and the supernatural realm. It tells of the makeup of human beings—that we each have a spirit, soul and body. It also reveals the nature of God's original intent for humanity and our fallen human condition due to sin. It tells us that the causes of suffering are physical in some instances and spiritual in others. It reveals our past, present and future. God has given us the revelation of His Word so we can be fully equipped to live a life that is pleasing to Him through His Son, Jesus. Sadly, many do not make the time to discover this truth for themselves. Instead, they pursue their own interests without take God into account. But, what good is it to become everything you want to be, if you never become all God meant for you to be?"

Brother Léi turns and exits the building, with Daniel following close behind him. A moment later, both of them turn a corner and come upon a large open square where close to thirty men, women and children stand in formation. Daniel stops in his tracks and watches as they execute various stances, kicks, punches and blocks in unison.

"I've studied a couple of martial arts styles," Daniel admits. "and I've seen many others. This... has similar elements to Tai Chi and Wing Chun Kung-fu, but it seems to be... completely unique. What style is it?"

"It is a fighting style developed under the direction of the Holy Spirit," the young monk replies.

"Really?" Daniel looks amazed. "*God* taught you this?"

"He did."

"Many Christians in America are taught to turn the other cheek and refrain from fighting. Then there are others who believe Christians should have the right to bear arms and defend themselves."

"Yes, as followers of Yeshua, we are to turn the other cheek when faced with violence. But how many cheeks did God give us?"

Daniel smirks as he counts silently.

"From Genesis to Revelation, the Bible is full of warriors. God Himself is a Warrior. He is not a pacifist, although He always seeks the peace of His people—of those who surrender to Him. Violence is often not the answer. However, there are times when an enemy will be so determined to cause destruction that peace will only come through the meeting of physical and spiritual force. The problem is that men often resort *first and foremost* to force. And they use it for the destruction of their opponent.

"While turning the other cheek *is* the sure command of the LORD, He is not advocating pacifism. Rather, He desires us to bring our power to retaliate under the control of the Holy Spirit. Jesus calls us to be peacemakers and teaches that we should treat others as we want to be treated. If I am out of control, and physical force is necessary to bring me under control, then I would hope someone would do what was necessary to help restore me to where I *should* be. This is at the center of our fighting style. We fight only when necessary and only to help bring restoration. This allows an adversary to see the truth, witness the error of their ways and realize their need for surrender to Christ."

They continue their walk as Daniel takes everything in…

"So, what about me? What am I to do?"

"You are to remain here until it is safe for you to return home."

"You know about my… situation?"

"I told you," Brother Léi smiles, "there is not much that is hidden from us. The Holy Spirit is the revealer of truth and shows us things to come. The men who seek your life will be brought to justice. Your parents will be safe. And you will return to America to complete the purpose the LORD has assigned for you."

"So… what do I do in the meantime while I'm here?"

Brother Léi smiles again. "You *learn* how to draw closer to Christ. And it begins right now." The monk places one hand on Daniel's shoulder and the other over Daniel's heart and utters these words with a quiet boldness:

"Receive the Holy Spirit!"

17: Returning Home

2008 — Three years later...

It is the realm between time and eternity... Darkness gives way to light and then bright flashes of color: CRIMSON! BLUE! GOLD! Three points of magnificent illumination converge into ONE with the brilliance of ten thousand suns... The singular light transforms into a mighty hand holding seven points of lesser lights—like stars. These seven lights morph into seven flaming golden lamp stands. A winding road appears beneath them and stretches off into the distance... Words are uttered with a Voice sounding like a multitude of oceans: "Follow Me!"

Daniel awakes in his bed with a jump! Somewhat startled, he gazes at the sunbeams piercing into the room through the ornately engraved lettering on the walls. He turns to find Brother Léi kneeling in prayer in the corner. A moment of silence passes as the monk stirs and opens his eyes. They both look at one another.

"You had another vision from the LORD," Brother Léi declares.

Daniel nods his head in agreement. "Yes, but I am not quite sure what it means."

"Brother Dàiwéisēn," the monk replies, "it is time for you to return home."

Daniel looks away as he considers things.

"Take no thought for your life," the monk's soft assurance preempts Daniel's anxious thoughts. "The LORD has shown me that those who want you dead can no longer do you any harm."

Daniel smiles and breathes a sigh of relief. "I've been here with you all for three years and *that* never gets old."

"The LORD knows exactly what we need," the monk smiles. "Until now, you have received visions from the LORD in pieces. Each one builds on the previous. Know that they are leading you to a culmination. The day will come when the Holy Spirit will speak in no uncertain terms about the way you will glorify Him in the earth. However, the vision will tarry for a number of years as the LORD prepares every aspect of what must take place. But when He is ready, things will happen quickly. In the meantime, live your life. Be faithful to the LORD in everything. Get married. Have a son."

"Get married?" Daniel asks in surprise. "Have a son? Brother Léi, *what* are you talking about? I don't even have a girlfriend!"

"The LORD is sovereign. What He has declared will come to pass very quickly. What He has called you to do requires you to be part of a family unit."

"But what does that even mean?"

"The LORD will reveal all at the proper time. You must remember what you have learned during your time here. Hold tight to each lesson. Do not let them go. The past three years will serve as the foundation for your mission."

As Daniel replays the past few years in his mind, a question rises within his heart.

"Will we… ever meet again?"

Brother Léi smiles. "If not in this life, then we will meet in Christ's heavenly kingdom. But know there is no distance in the Spirit. Whenever God places you on my heart, I will pray and fast for you intently."

Daniel smiles as he replies, "And I will do the same for you. Thank you."

The two shake hands and embrace as brothers.

That evening, a great celebration is held in honor of the LORD's purpose being done in Daniel's life. The next morning, Daniel—now wearing his regular clothing—makes his way with the monk, down the mountain to the valley below.

"This is where it all began," Daniel smiles as they stand just outside the village at the very spot where their lives intersected.

"It is," Brother Léi nods in agreement.

"Thanks for allowing me to keep the uniform," Daniel nods as he pats his bookbag.

"I know you will take good care of it. It will also serve as inspiration for you."

The two embrace once more before parting.

"Take care Daniel Davidson," the young monk waves with a broad smile as he watches Daniel walk away.

"You too, Brother Léi," Daniel shouts as he waves in return.

"May the Name of the LORD Jesus *always* be praised!" The monk shouts. "May the LORD be with you!"

"And also with *you*," Daniel shouts back. "May the Name of the LORD Jesus *always* be praised!"

V

Two weeks later... Beijing Capital International Airport.

Daniel boards his plane bound for America. It is a full flight. After several minutes of making his way towards the back, he finds his aisle seat, stores his bag, ducks his head to avoid hitting the overhead compartment and sits down. He notices the empty middle seat next to him and an overweight man sitting at the window. He buckles his seatbelt, leans his head back and closes his eyes—ready for a nap. For some unknown reason, he opens his eyes and glances to the front of the plane. That is when, to his surprise, he sees a beautiful black woman who has just stepped on board.

His tiredness instantly vanishes like a puff of smoke! He watches her intently, barely able to breathe, as she carries two bags while looking back and forth from her ticket to the overhead seat numbers. When she gets six rows from him, he quickly turns his head, grabs the magazine in the seat pocket, flips it open and tries to look preoccupied. A moment later, he notices out the corner of his eye that her shoes have stopped right next to him.

"Excuse me," she says in a voice that practically melts him like butter. "The seat next to you is mine."

He looks up at her and smiles. Their eyes lock in a gaze. He tries to get up, but is snapped back down by the seatbelt. She giggles as he fumbles to press the release button and stands up so quickly that he forgets about the low height of the overhead baggage compartment.

"CRACK!"

He grabs his head with a slight whimper as she cringes at the sight.

"Oooh..." She blurts out with an empathetic chuckle. "That had to hurt."

Even though he's seeing stars, Daniel plays it off as he steps into the aisle to let her get to her seat. "I'm okay..."

"Good. Can you help me with my bag?" She asks coyly.

"Sure," he smiles nervously as she hands him her compact suitcase and he hoists it up into the overhead compartment.

She sits down and stores her second bag underneath the seat in front of her. He sits back down as well. Both buckle up at the same time and then discreetly scan each others' left hand. *No wedding ring*, they think to themselves.

"Thanks for helping me with my bag."

"Thanks for asking me."

"I'm Rebecca."

"My name is Daniel. Nice to meet you."

They shake hands—both holding the other's hand a bit longer than is casually customary before slowly letting go.

"So, were you in China on vacation?" Daniel asks.

"No," Rebecca replies. "I'm an educator. I've been here for three years teaching English to elementary school children. What about you?"

Daniel looks at her with slightly wide eyes.

"You may not believe this, but I've been here for three years too."

"Get out," Rebecca says in a hushed shout while smacking his arm. "Really? What did you do?"

Daniel searches for a way to explain, "I was...," he lowers his voice and glances around. "I was... researching the legacy of a British missionary from the 1800's."

Her eyes grow wide as *she* lowers her voice as well. "Are you talking about Hudson Taylor?"

Daniel's eyes widen again as he whispers, "You've heard of Hudson Taylor?"

Rebecca nods furiously. "His biography is one of my favorites. I know all about his China Inland Mission."

Daniel looks at her quietly, thinking this is almost too good to be true. "Are you a..." he hesitates, "...follower of The Way?"

She smiles warmly with a nod. "Yes. The Way, the Truth and the Life."

Twelve hours later...

Rebecca and Daniel have talked non-stop for the duration of the flight! Even as the plane lands at New York's JFK airport and taxis to the gate, their conversation shows no sign of slowing down. They have talked about everything, from the trivial to the heart-felt. And their time together has proved to both of them that this unexpected encounter is in fact a God-ordained happening. They stand on the other side of baggage claim: both prepared to go their separate ways —neither wanting to leave the other.

"So, what do we do now?" Rebecca asks a bit shyly.

"I was thinking we should share phone numbers and emails," Daniel replies.

"And then what?" Rebecca presses. "Do we just… stay in touch?"

"Okay," Daniel breathes deeply. "I'm just going to state the obvious… I have *never* met anyone like you. And… how we met… and all of the things we have in common—first being our love for Jesus. If this is not God, then I don't know what is!"

"I *completely* agree," Rebecca nods. "So, what does it *mean*?"

"I don't want you to think I'm crazy, but God told me… that when I left China, I would meet my wife. *And* that it would happen very quickly."

"Is this… soon enough?" Rebecca replies. "Or is it too soon?"

"As far as I'm concerned," Daniel gazes at her intently and smiles deeply, "This is *right on time.*"

"So," she perks up, "we exchange information. We talk *every* day. We get our parents to meet. I'm a daddy's girl… so you will have to ask my father for my hand in marriage. And when he says *yes*, we make it official! And once we get married… wherever the Lord leads us, we will support each other… as a family."

18: Follow Me

15 years later. Atlanta, Georgia. May 5, 2023. 3:00pm.

"Can you say that *again*?" Rebecca asks with a rise in her voice as she stops chopping celery with her knife and turns to face her husband. "I know I didn't *hear* what I think I heard."

"You heard correctly," Daniel stammers, a bit embarrassed, as he shrugs. "I think—No, I *know* God wants me to walk from New York to California in a superhero suit."

Rebecca's expression says it all. She is dumbfounded and at a loss for words—something that happens *very rarely*. What her husband said just doesn't compute. Her eyelids flicker as she tries to processes potential meanings.

"…Do you mean like… cosplay?"

"No," Daniel replies. "Not exactly. Although, God does want me to deliver His message at the San Diego Comic Con."

"Okay!" She yells while throwing up her hands. "None of this makes *any* sense! Why would God tell you to do that? Wait. Just go back to the beginning." She breathes heavily. "How do you know God wants you to do this?"

"Remember, I told you about the visions the Lord gave me while in China?"

"Yeah. They started when you were in the hospital before you went to China."

"Right. Each one has been building on the previous. Well, last night, around 3:00am, He gave me another vision—the most detailed one of them all!"

Rebecca looks into her husband's eyes. "You're serious, aren't you?"

Daniel nods his head as his eyes moisten. "Why would I play about this?"

She wipes her hands with a towel, grabs her husband's arm and pulls him to the couch.

"Okay, Daniel," she declares with intention as they sit down. "Tell me about the vision. Tell me *everything*."

V

Earlier that morning… 3:00am

Both Daniel and Rebecca are lying asleep in bed—oblivious to their surroundings. They are completely motionless, except for the rhythmic rising and falling of their torsos as they breathe. Everything is silent and dark, except for the illumination of the nightlight in the hallway. And then…

V

In a flash, Daniel was standing in the monastery back in China! In front of him was Brother Léi, the young monk whose smile shone like the sun. The monk spoke: 'It is time…" And then a blinding light burst forth! Daniel threw up his arm to cover his eyes! When the radiance dissipated and he lowered his arm, he was back in America, on a busy New York City street, surrounded by people engrossed in their own lives. The sky was dark.

A voice thundered: *"DANIEL!!!"* He turned around to see who it was. Suddenly the people were gone and he could see a hazy figure approaching in the distance wearing deep red highlighted with gold and what seemed to be a flowing blue cape. Three points of light converged into one, at the center of the suit. As the figure approached, it became clearer, but its face was obscured by a dark cloud. The figure walked past, allowing him to see many of its design details, and continued down the street.

Daniel followed the figure through a large crowd of people and… locations. It seemed one moment the two of them were in New York, then they were in New Jersey and then a host of other cities and states followed. With each location came varied groups of individuals— some happy, many saddened, others filled with hate and anger, all in different situations. This red, gold and blue figure laid a hand on them all. And when he did, their countenance changed, as light began to shine upon them and then from within them.

Suddenly, he and the figure stood in California before a large assembly of people. Daniel heard the thundering words once again: *"FOLLOW ME!!!"* As the figure stood still, Daniel approached from behind. It then turned and faced him. The dark cloud which covered the front of its head dissipated revealing first a helmet. A moment passes as the face became apparent. Daniel was now staring at himself!

He no longer stood apart from the figure, but had become him! Daniel turned back around and walked through the midst of the large crowd, touching some. Once through the crowd, he turned to address the people. He opened his mouth and the same voice which had thundered—now flowed through him to the crowd—*"FOLLOW ME!!!"*

In an instant, Daniel finds himself standing in front of Jesus. All other surroundings vanish into the radiant Presence of the LORD. Jesus smiles tenderly and then speaks: *"You are to make this suit according to the pattern you have seen. Then... Come and follow Me."*

The LORD turns around as the air in front of him ripples. A portal of light opens up before them both. Jesus turns his head toward Daniel and motions with his hand for him to follow. Both he and Jesus walk through the shimmering portal of light... and then...

V

Daniel wakes up in his bed! But he and his wife are not alone. An invisible wave of the Presence of the LORD flows over Daniel—similar to what he experienced while at the monastery. It increases in intensity as golden ribbons of light materialize in the room, swaying like reflections of water. His eyes are drawn to a corner of the room where a bright human-like being stands. The being looks very much like a man—yet is 7 feet tall with a musculature which conveys strength and authority. His body is draped in a white linen robe, where the very fibers burst forth with glory! Around his waist rests a shimmering golden belt. His eyes pulsate like flames of fire—filled with power. His head and hair radiate like a star. Daniel sits up in his bed—backing towards the headrest—as a holy fear grips his soul. The being speaks with a voice which reverberates through the very atmosphere of the room.

"Do not be afraid, Daniel. I—who stand before the LORD of Hosts—am Gabriel."

Daniel looks at his wife, who is still lying on her belly, motionless. He then returns his gaze to the angel.

"The time has come for you to glorify God in a most unique way which has not been witnessed since ancient times."

"What... does the Lord want me to do?"

"The people of this generation have turned away from truth, in favor of myths and legends which cannot save... The LORD will use you to draw those who will believe back to Him while there is yet still time."

"How... does the Lord want me to do this?" Daniel responds.

"He, who alone is sovereign, has given you the vision of what He desires. I have been sent to explain it to you."

V

3:45pm that afternoon.

Rebecca and Daniel are still sitting on the couch.

"Wait," Rebecca interjects. "All of that happened while I was asleep?"

"Yeah."

"How did I miss that?" she exclaims. "I've never seen an angel before!"

"I guess the encounter was for me first," Daniel replies softly. "Who knows what God may do in the future..."

"Fine," she nods. "I guess you're right. Okay. Back to your encounter."

"So, the angel Gabriel said to build the suit I saw in the vision. Then I'm to walk across the country, going through the states God will reveal to us."

"So, everything has been leading to this," Rebecca replies in astonishment.

"Right," Daniel agrees. "It has."

"But do you *realize* what God has been up to?"

"What do you mean?"

"*Us* as a *family unit*. Didn't Brother Léi say that would be a crucial part to God's plan? Think about it. You are an engineer who works with exotic materials and can build anything. And our 15 year old son has been building costumes since he was 5 years old! And we never had to introduce that desire to him! It's like the Lord put it in him from birth! And we gave him his own workshop down in the basement last year."

"You're right," Daniel replies as he sees the connections. "And now he has his own YouTube channel where he builds his favorite Marvel and DC superhero suits. And they look really good!"

"Right," Rebecca agrees. "He's always wanted to make props and wardrobes for movies, but what if God gave him that desire, not for movies... but for *this*?

Rebecca and Daniel stare at each other in stunned silence as the magnificence of God's calculating and arrangements begin to come into view. Rebecca continues...

"And just a few weeks ago he said he's gotten good enough to make his own custom suit, but he wasn't sure what to design. Well, God *already* gave *you* the *blueprint*, so if you and Daniel Jr. work together, I'm sure you'll come up with something amazing!"

Daniel nods his head with a broad smile as he considers his wife's words. "I'm sure we will too! But, what about you? What role would you play?"

Rebecca looks at her husband with an *as-if-you-had-to-ask* expression. "Me? I'm *just* your R&D department! Your research and development! Lifelong educator and *queen* of logistics and multi-tasking! Who else is going to help you with all the different facets that need to come together to pull this off? Just off the top of my head you need to determine suit design materials, a travel itinerary, put together a support group to assist you at key points along the journey. Ooh! Maybe we can talk with pastor about this."

Her speaking rate increases as her ideas begin to flow freely.

"Maybe, once we determine the route, he can get a network of churches to offer you room and board. And we definitely need to set up a prayer ministry, *just for this*, so you're bathed in prayer from the time you start walking until when you complete the assignment. There's sure to be many unknown situations and variables. And God has given *me* to you to help manage all of these things as they happen in real time. So, don't think *you boys* are going to have all the fun! If you're doing this, then I'm going to be right there with you doing my part!"

Daniel chuckles. "Okay, take a breath... You just said a mouthful!"

Rebecca laughs as she proceeds to take a few deep breaths. "That was a lot, right?"

They both laugh for a moment.

As they quiet down, Daniel speaks. "You know, I didn't expect you to be so... *accepting* of this—at least not this quickly."

"Well..." his wife replies with a rise in her voice. "At first I thought you lost your mind!" She breathes deeply again. "But, we have been known to move pretty quickly in the realm of the unexpected, when the Lord says, 'Go!'"

Daniel gazes at his wife with a grin. "You know you're beautiful right?"

"Oh, *I know*," she smiles knowingly.

"Even more beautiful when that mind of yours starts calculating."

They share a touchy-feely giggle.

"So," Daniel asks, "we're doing this?"

"First," Rebecca replies. "The *Lord told you* to do this. So, we *have* to say yes. *Second*, you've got one more person to convince."

"Well," Daniel smirks, "I don't think that'll be *too* difficult."

V

An hour later...

"YES!" Daniel Jr. shouts with a huge smile as he plants his hands on the kitchen countertop. "YES! YES! YES! I'm in! 100 percent!"

Rebecca and Daniel look at each other and then back at their son, who is grinning from ear-to-ear.

"DJ, you just came in from school 15 minutes ago and haven't even heard everything yet," his mother says.

"I've heard enough," Daniel Jr. beams. "Dad just said, God gave him a vision and said He wants us to build a custom superhero suit so dad can walk across the country spreading the gospel! How cool is that? This is gonna put us on the map! When do we start?"

Rebecca shakes her head with a sigh, while Daniel looks at her and points to their son.

"And you thought I would have to convince him?"

Rebecca chuckles before speaking to her son. "Look, I know you're excited, but there will be no 'starting anything' until you sit down and listen to *everything* your father has to say. As cool as *you think this is*, it is also very serious and we all have to approach this with the right mental and spiritual disposition. So, you need to let your father bring you up to speed, so you know everything I do."

Daniel glances at his wife and son with an awkward expression. His wife and son immediately take notice.

"I know that look," she says with a somewhat serious tone. "What is it?"

"Yeah Dad," DJ chimes in.

Daniel breathes deeply. "Well, there's still… something else about the vision that I haven't told you yet."

"What is it?" Rebecca asks.

"I think we should all sit down first before I tell you."

Thirty minutes later…

DJ is caught up on the vision—up to what Rebecca already knows.

"You *actually saw* an angel?" DJ exclaims. "And not just any angel. You saw Gabriel?"

"Yes."

"What did he look like? Oh, I know he must look dope!"

"DJ," Rebecca interjects. "Stay focused."

"Okay. Okay." He raises his hands. "I'm just excited."

"We know," Rebecca and Daniel chuckle in unison.

"Okay," Rebecca sighs as she turns her attention to her husband. "So, what *haven't* you told us?"

Daniel looks back and forth between his wife and son before speaking.

"If you thought what I already said was… *unusual*, then what I'm about to say is going to knock your socks off."

V

The 3:00am vision…

The angel Gabriel continues his explanation.

"No one outside of your immediate family is to know your identity until the appointed time, except for the one the LORD reveals who will help you on your journey. You are also not to take any food or money with you. The LORD will provide what you need, at the moment in time when you need it."

"And what if I run into some kind of danger?" Daniel questions. "Like if I'm attacked. Or I'm in an accident or have to help someone in an unpredictable situation? How... will I know what to do?"

The radiant bands of golden light surrounding Gabriel increase in glory as he answers Daniel's questions.

"To accomplish this calling, the LORD will be with you as He was with Moses and Joshua. He will, by His Holy Spirit, give you: The WISDOM of Solomon. The STRENGTH of Samson. The DECISIVENESS of Deborah. The WONDERS of the Prophets. The ACTS of the Apostles. And the LOVE of Christ."

V

"Wait!" DJ interjects with a shout as he jumps up from his chair. "Are you saying God gave you superhuman abilities?"

"DJ," Rebecca chides, "Don't interrupt your father! He wasn't done!"

DJ counters. "But, Mom... this is huge! Dad just said he's got super strength like Samson!"

Rebecca turns from her son to her husband. "You *did* just say that..."

"And," DJ continues, "he said he can do miracles like the prophets and the apostles! Some of them controlled the weather! Others could heal the sick, raise the dead, see into the spiritual realm and cast out demons!"

"I'm sure your father realizes these things," Rebecca interjects as she turns from her son to her husband. "You... *do* realize these things, right?"

DJ continues without hesitation, "Do you know what this means?"

"What it means," Daniel interjects with a bit of hesitancy, "is that I don't know how any of this works or when it will start."

"Well, that's easy to figure out," DJ smiles while pointing across the room. "Go see if you can lift the refrigerator!"

Daniel shakes his head while Rebecca chuckles slightly.

"Well, that is a good way to check," she concedes.

"I don't think that's how it works."

"What do you mean?"

"I don't think Samson was super strong all the time. When you read the text it seems to infer that God only gave him added strength when he needed it."

"Well, *we need* to see if this works," DJ replies.

"No," Daniel responds while throwing his hands up. "What we need is for me to finish telling you what the angel said."

V

The end of the 3:00am vision…

"The LORD will reveal how much you must suffer on behalf of His Name. You must walk terribly close with Him, trust in His Word and obey His leading in all things. Only then will you be victorious. He will give you what to say and will tell you what to do. To the level of your obedience, will be the level of your effectiveness for His kingdom.

"The forces of darkness will flood against you and many will oppose you on account of Christ. Do not be dismayed by their unbelief and hatred for the truth. Do not allow the darkness to overcome the light of Christ that is within you. Those who believe the message the LORD will give you will be delivered from their sins and made righteous in His sight forever.

"The time of the Son of Man's appearing draws near, but is not yet. Therefore work while it is yet day, because night comes when no one can work. These last days will soon come to an end. The LORD has and will continue to pour out His Holy Spirit on all who trust in Him right up to the end of this age. He has poured out His Spirit within you and upon your flesh. This is how He has chosen to use you

and your family for such a time as this. Do you accept this burden from the LORD?"

Daniel gazes at the angel and considers all he has uttered. "May it be to me and my family as you have said."

The angel Gabriel nods in approval before speaking one last command.

"Pray about everything. Leave nothing to chance."

In a flash of brilliance the room is dark again.

However, the palpable fear of the Lord still lingers. Daniel pulls back the covers and kneels at the foot of the bed in worship and prayer to the Lord. Before he knows it, the sun has risen and the busyness of the day is about to begin.

V

Daniel sits in the living room with his family. Both his wife and son are quiet.

He breaks the silence, "So, this is a *serious* matter. We cannot tell anyone. Not our parents. Not relatives. No friends at school or work. No neighbors. We can only talk to the one God reveals. I believe it will be pastor, but we'll have to wait until Sunday to see if I'm right. So, this is a top secret assignment given to us by the Lord. And if we are going to do this, we must agree to do so... *as a family.*"

Rebecca and DJ stare at Daniel with determination as they render their response: "Let's do it."

Daniel gazes at them for another moment as a smile slowly rises to his lips. "So, we are in agreement. Any questions?"

"Yeah," DJ answers. "I get you having wisdom, decisiveness, strength and power, but why the love of Christ?"

"Well," Daniel surmises, "the Bible does say that faith, hope and love are important. And God's love is most important. It is what holds everything else together."

"And," Rebecca adds, "Everything Jesus did was motivated by His love for His Heavenly Father and for people—even His enemies. So, it makes sense that your father would need that same kind of love to deal with the different kind of people he's going to encounter—especially any enemies."

V

That Sunday. Radiant City Church.

Worship service has just ended as Daniel and his family prepare to leave. One of the church workers makes his way through the large crowd and walks up to the Davidsons as they head for the exit.

"Hey Daniel, Rebecca, DJ!"

They turn to see who called their names. "Hey Harrison," Daniel replies. "What's up?"

"Pastor Mike wants to see you guys before you leave."

"Okay. Did he say what he wanted?"

"Yeah," Harrison smiles. "He wants you guys to come to his office right now."

A few minutes later…

The door closes as they sit down in their pastor's office. Pastor Mike, who is six foot four, muscular, wearing jeans and a rugged long-sleeved shirt, locks the door and sits at his desk. Daniel and Rebecca notice immediately that he seems a bit nervous—which is not like his usual temperament at all.

"I appreciate you coming to see me so quickly," Pastor Mike says.

"Harrison made it seem urgent," Daniel replies.

"Are you alright?" Rebecca asks while watching Pastor Mike fumble with his pen.

The pastor takes a deep breath before continuing. "This is not the first time God has asked me to do something unusual…"

Daniel, Rebecca and DJ glance at each other.

"I was praying last night and this morning and strongly felt the Holy Spirit… wants me to help you with some kind of… major undertaking. When I saw you at the beginning of service the Holy Spirit told me to meet with you privately after service. Then… during offering time, while everyone brought their tithes and offerings to the front, you all walked up and... for about 3 seconds I saw Daniel..." his voice trails off while he shakes his head.

"What is it?" Rebecca presses.

"You are going to think this is crazy," Pastor Mike balks. "But..." He takes another deep breath. "I'm just going to say it." He looks at them resolutely. "Daniel, for three seconds, I saw you dressed in a red... superhero suit with gold accents and a blue cape." He looks at Daniel and his family for any kind of expression that says he's crazy, but he finds them quietly looking at one another with serious faces.

"Why... do you not seem surprised by what I just said?"

Daniel looks at his wife and son. They all nod to each other and turn their gaze back to their pastor.

"You're not crazy," Daniel replies. "God has revealed that He wants me to walk across the country in a custom superhero suit and share His gospel."

"And," Rebecca interjects, "the Lord said He would send someone to help us accomplish this."

"And since God gave you that vision during the offering," DJ smiles, "I guess that *someone* is *you*."

The three of them smile and nod in unison as Pastor Mike takes a deep breath before responding.

"I wonder what kind of adventure this will turn out to be."

19: More Than Cosplay

June 2023 — One Month Later

Back in elementary and middle school, DJ's friends and other kids laughed at him when he built costumes. It used to bother him, but his parents encouraged him to pursue his passion, and so he used the laughter from others as fuel for his dream. While his friends were busy playing video games and hanging out, he spent most of his time —when not at school or church—following tutorial videos on prop and wardrobe fabrication. By the time he entered high school, DJ won 2nd place in a city-wide costume competition. That win earned him a summer internship with industry professionals which allowed him to improve his craft. Now, the other kids don't laugh at him anymore.

A year ago, his parents officially gave him the house's sizable basement. They also gave him an initial investment of cash, which he used to turn the basement into a workshop. He bought mannequins, EVA foam in a variety of sizes and thickness, a sewing machine, various kinds of fabric, paint and other needed accessories. He has since made money from paying cosplay customers for custom suit and prop builds. Within a year, DJ transformed a hobby that he loved into a growing business that pays for itself and allows him to contribute to household expenses.

His business name is: *More Than Cosplay*. And the sign greets everyone who enters the basement. The main wall displays *his own collection* of finished suits: Iron Man, Batman, Captain America, Black Panther and Falcon. A series of containers sit on a shorter wall, which house the majority of his fabrics, foams and accessories used to build each suit. Along the other short wall sits several pieces of equipment: a sewing machine, computer, 3D printer and metal shaping tools. In the center of the room sits two large work tables. Next to them are two bare mannequins.

The other long wall is for conceptual design. On it rests three full color life-sized drawings of the suit he and his father plan to build: a front, side and back view. They display many details, including the bodysuit and the armored pieces. Each piece corresponds to the elements seen in the vision, which correlate with the Armor of God description found in Ephesians 6. Both he and his father stand at the primary work table.

"So, what capabilities do you want to build into the suit?" DJ asks.

"I don't know if it needs any," Daniel replies.

"Why not?"

"If God wants me to trust Him, then I shouldn't need any enhancements. I think it should just be a basic suit."

"That's *one way* to look at it. But, the world is a tough place. Having the suit be more than just colorful pajamas is a resource God can use. Enhancements isn't the issue… trusting in *them* instead of God *is*."

"So," Daniel smiles as he looks at his son, "the student has become the teacher."

"I have a great teacher, Dad," DJ smiles back. "You've taught me a lot about the Bible over the years."

"I've tried my best," he nods as he smiles at his son. "So, the costume—"

"Wait," DJ interjects. "It's *not* a costume, Dad. "It's a *uniform*."

"You're right," Daniel agrees. "God is calling me into battle. Those in battle don't wear costumes. They wear uniforms."

"Exactly," DJ affirms.

"Okay. So, what capabilities were you thinking about adding into my… *uniform*?"

"Well, the obvious ones are protection from sharp objects like knives and dog teeth. Random fact, but did you know more than 5,000 postal workers get bit by dogs every year?"

"I… did not."

"Crazy right? I also think you should have padding to give protection against blunt force trauma caused by bats and metal rods."

"Do you think I'm going into a war zone?" Daniel laughs.

"You never know *where* you'll be. The suit also needs protection from small caliber rounds, fire and extreme weather. And maybe even some kind of electric stun feature or a sonic deterrent. *And*, it also needs a way to keep you cool while wearing it!"

"That's a lot of things the suit needs to do!" Daniel replies. "Don't forget it needs to be *comfortable to wear* and *lightweight*. With all of the walking I'll be doing, it can't be cumbersome."

"You need to start working out," DJ says matter-of-factly. "You're in decent shape already, but you need to prepare like you were going to run a marathon. So you can build up your endurance."

"You're giving me a lot of work to do."

"You and mom did say to take this seriously," DJ smiles. "By the way, I'm reading this really cool 5 book series called *Speedsuit Powers*. In the fourth book, called *Flight*, the main character designs a cape that actually functions like a wing which enables her to glide through the air like Batman. I think the design could actually work."

"And... you want to work it into our suit."

"You *do* have a *cape*," DJ agrees. "Might as well make it do more than look good!"

"It's a good thing you and I have gone hang gliding a few times."

"And don't forget vertical wind tunnel flying! All of that will come in handy if we can get the cape to actually work like a glider."

"I have to stop talking to you," Daniel laughs. "This just gets crazier by the minute."

"Does it though?" DJ replies.

"You know, all of this is sounding a bit expensive."

"Oh, it's definitely going to cost you, Dad. I'm still working on the supply list, but at minimum we'll need to buy or make a lightweight padded bodysuit. Then we'll need kevlar, flame resistant fabric, carbon fiber plating, polycarbonate for the helmet and faceplate, a LED light system and a hundred other things.... Good thing you have a great paying job. We're going to need a lot of cash."

"Good thing you have your cosplay business. You can contribute towards the costs too. I hope you're not charging me for labor."

V

Three months later...

Daniel stands in the basement workshop wearing the full version of the suit. DJ, Rebecca and Pastor Mike examine him from head-to-toe and provide their critique.

"This looks amazing," Pastor Mike declares.

"How does it feel?" Rebecca asks.

Daniel walks around in the suit while assuming a number of postures. "It's pretty flexible," he says through the helmet with a hint of surprise. He leans from side to side as the torso armor plating slides with him. I feel... supported in all the right places, yet it's easy to move around." He squats and bends over, encountering minimum resistance.

"It does make you stand up straight though."

"How's the helmet?" DJ asks.

"Easy to breathe through. Not too heavy."

"Try retracting the faceplate."

Daniel pushes a small button on the side of the helmet and the faceplate lifts up and slides back over the top.

"It's spring-loaded." DJ continues. "To lower it, just use your hand to press it back into position until it locks."

Daniel does so and the faceplate lowers smoothly back into place with a click.

"Didn't you say the suit lights up?" Rebecca asks.

"I was saving that for last," DJ smiles from ear to ear. "Go ahead Dad. Press the button on the belt buckle."

With the press of the button, the cross insignia at the center of the chestplate illuminates.

"Dad wired the LEDs so they can cycle through different intensity settings and illumination patterns."

Daniel quickly demonstrates the low, medium, high and strobe settings.

"Does the suit run on batteries?" Pastor Mike asks.

"Yeah," Daniel replies as he removes the helmet. "Several rechargeable flat battery packs are built into the belt and hip pods. All of the electrical elements are wired to them and connected to piezoelectric sensors in the boots. Since I'll be walking, every step I take will generate electricity, which will charge the batteries in order to keep the suit powered up."

"Nice! But, I have one serious question," Pastor Mike inquires. "How do you go to the bathroom when you're in the suit?"

V

One month later...

The group meets to finalize the plan and address last minute details, as the day to begin the journey is less than a week away.

"Well, leave tomorrow to drive up to New York," Rebecca says. "We'll use Daniel's parent's house as the staging area. They're visiting relatives down south."

"And the network of churches is all set up," Pastor Mike adds. "Several churches are on standby to offer assistance along the way should you need it. I've explained everything to them, *without* giving away your identity."

"And," DJ adds, "I'm building a backup suit, in case you have a major suit failure and we need to switch it out."

"But I wanted to ask," Pastor Mike inquires. "Why did you choose this particular route? There's a more direct way to get from New York to California. The one you'll be walking is quite a bit out of the way."

"Like I always say," Daniel replies, "God loves the scenic route... After much prayer, this is what we settled on. To your point, I tried to change it twice, but the Lord kept bringing me back to this."

"God must have specific people He wants you to meet," DJ surmises. All of the adults look at him with surprised expressions.

"Now, *that* makes perfect sense," Rebecca agrees as she gazes at her son with a sense of warmth. "Very good observation." She then looks over the checklist. "Well, it seems like we are just about ready. Everything's packed. So, all that's left to do is get some rest... You're going to need it."

"We all will," Daniel smiles.

"More than rest," Pastor Mike adds, "you'll need prayer." He looks at his watch. "Can we pray now? I have to pick up my wife soon."

"It's always a good time for prayer," Daniel replies.

The group stands in a circle and holds hands as Pastor Mike takes the lead. About a minute into the prayer, he stands in front of Daniel and places his hand on his stomach. Compelled by the Holy Spirit, he presses forcefully and shouts: "Jesus said, if anyone believes in Me, as the Scriptures have declared, out of his belly will flow rivers of living water!" At that moment, Daniel falls backwards to the floor as the Presence of the Holy Spirit fills his entire being!

As Daniel lays somewhat unconscious, Pastor Mike places his hands on Daniel's head and chest and shouts: "The LORD will be with you as He was with Moses and Joshua! He will give you, by His Holy Spirit—The *WISDOM* of Solomon! The *STRENGTH* of Samson! The *DECISIVENESS* of Deborah! The *WONDERS* of the Prophets! The *ACTS* of the Apostles! And the *LOVE* of Christ!"

Rebecca and DJ stare at each other in amazement. Neither they, nor Daniel had ever told Pastor Mike about that specific declaration.

An hour later, Pastor Mike is still in their living room—having never left. The Presence of the Holy Spirit fills the house to such an extent that no one moves nor pays attention to the time. Pastor Mike, Rebecca and DJ worship in awe, as the Lord works on Daniel, who is still lying on the floor. They can't see into the spiritual realm, but if they could, what they would witness would be glorious.

"I don't know what happened," Pastor Mike says in a hushed tone to Rebecca and DJ. "After your husband fell to the floor, I... felt the need to place my hands on him. As soon as I did, these words just started flowing from my belly, up to my throat and out my mouth. I didn't even know what I was saying!"

"It was confirmation from the Holy Spirit," Rebecca replies in a whisper. "Those were the *same exact words* spoken to Daniel when God called him to this task."

"My dad said, he didn't know when those words would come to pass," DJ adds—also in a hushed tone. "Maybe when God had you say them, they were being activated somehow."

A few minutes later, Daniel opens his eyes. DJ is the first to notice. "Dad!"

"Are you okay?" Rebecca asks while kneeling at his side as Pastor Mike stands towering over them.

Daniel smiles and sits up. "I... don't know how to explain this," he says while looking around at everything. "I can feel this... *river of living water*...flowing from within my belly... and out through my entire body. I feel... more alive than I've ever felt before—like my body is being *quickened* by the Holy Spirit. And I feel this... overwhelming love... beyond anything I've ever experienced before. God's love for me and *that love* being poured out through me for you and others. And I... have access to the Scriptures... in a way that carries more... depth and breath."

"What do you mean?" Pastor Mike asks.

"Name a Scripture verse," Daniel replies. "*Any* Scripture verse."

Pastor Mike opens his Bible and flips to a series of random passages and calls out chapter and verse. Without hesitation, Daniel is able to recall each passage with perfect clarity.

"It's like what Jesus taught," Pastor Mike says as he closes the Bible. "The Holy Spirit is bringing to your remembrance everything Jesus has said. And since He is the Living Word of God, that includes the entire Old and New Testaments!"

"And didn't you read through the Bible last year?" Rebecca asks.

"That's right," Daniel remembers. "I felt this overriding desire to read through the entire Bible last year. So, that's what I did."

"And now," Rebecca concludes, "it seems you can recall all of it!"

"Absolutely amazing," Pastor Mike adds.

"What about the strength of Samson?" DJ asks while hopping up and down—barely able to restrain himself. "Can you try to lift the fridge now?"

Daniel smiles as he stands to his feet and walks from the living room to the kitchen. DJ, Rebecca and Pastor Mike follow close behind him. He stands in front of the refrigerator, places both hands on either side and then hesitates.

"What's wrong?" his wife asks.

"We should probably take everything out of the fridge first… just in case the doors open. I wouldn't want to make a mess."

She agrees.

5 minutes later…

The refrigerator is unplugged and all of its contents are stacked high and wide on the nearby countertop. Pastor Mike pulls the appliance away from the wall out into the middle of the kitchen floor where there is more space. Daniel kneels down and places his right hand under the refrigerator and his left on the doors. DJ, Rebecca and Pastor Mike watch eagerly as Daniel takes a deep breath. Then, in one fluid motion, he stands to his feet… effortlessly holding the refrigerator above his head!

"Wow!" DJ shouts! "You have the strength of Samson! How heavy does the refrigerator feel?"

"It feels," Daniel replies as he raises it up and down several times, "like I'm lifting a pillow. It doesn't feel heavy at all!"

They are all amazed as Daniel lowers the appliance back to its position and stares at them while he looks at his hands. Just then, Daniel gasps as he suddenly looks all around the room.

"What is it?" Rebecca asks. "What do you see?"

"The Presence of the Lord... I can see His glory... and I can see... angels."

His family and Pastor Mike look around, but see nothing.

"That must be awesome! I wish we could see what you see, Dad," DJ says with a slight disappointment.

Just then, a thought occurs to Daniel. He prays. "Lord, open their eyes to the unseen realm so they can *see*."

In a flash, the fabric of reality is pulled back as their eyes are opened to the spiritual realm! Rebecca, Daniel Jr. and Pastor Mike stand in awe as they witness the glory of the LORD all around them... flowing through them.... And they can feel God's glory nourishing them... They also see eight angels standing guard in the corners of the kitchen and living room. Each as tall as the nine foot ceilings of the first floor of the house. Four of them are clad in a shining metallic-like armor.

In another flash, reality is clothed again with the mundane realm of human existence. The four of them look at each other with tears of joy in their eyes and smiles playing on their lips. The fear of the LORD causes them to silently worship the God of heaven and earth in humble submission. Several more moments pass. Then Pastor Mike whispers:

"In all my years of ministry, I have *never* witnessed anything like this. What we experienced was just like what happened with the prophet Elisha and his servant when they were surrounded by the Syrian army. Elisha prayed for the Lord to open the eyes of his servant so he could see into the unseen realm. The Lord answered Elisha's prayer. Daniel, you really have been given the wonders of the prophets!"

Daniel softly declares in return: "All I can say is... Praise God from whom all blessings flow. Blessed be the Name of the LORD!"

20: Launch Out Into the Deep

DAY 1 — New York

Tuesday March 5, 2024. New York City. 6:30am. In the heart of Manhattan, a minivan with slightly tinted windows, is parked on a side street. It is several blocks from Times Square. Rebecca sits in the driver's seat. Daniel Jr. sits on the front passenger side. Daniel sits on the second row. The three watch and pray. Daniel is wearing the full suit—minus the helmet which rests next to him. Several minutes pass before they run through their final checklist. By 7:00am, the sun sits just below the horizon—minutes away from making its brilliant appearance.

"It's time for me to go," Daniel says with a bit of anxiety in his voice.

"Dad, are you nervous?"

"A little."

"Me too," DJ admits. "I know God wants us to do this, but now it's about to get *real*. Once you step out that door..." his voice trails off.

"There's no coming back," Rebecca finishes. She starts the car. "Well, we've done everything we could. We've prayed every step of the way. We've quadruple checked everything—your suit, the route, the network of people who will assist you."

"Being nervous is normal when you do something new," Daniel muses. "Even Pastor Mike says he gets a little nervous each time he has to preach... and he's been preaching for over twenty years!"

They all chuckle slightly.

"It's the nervousness that can help you keep your focus on Christ," Rebecca adds. "This is only going to work if you... if *all* of us keep our eyes on Jesus. Hebrews 12 does say, He's the Author and Finisher of our faith!"

"That's what it says," Daniel smiles as he takes a deep breath. "Time to head to the drop off point."

Rebecca puts the minivan in gear and begins to slowly drive the four blocks. The streets and sidewalks are slowly filling up, as rush hour has just begun. Within the hour though, the roads will be packed with vehicles and pedestrians.

"Remember Dad," DJ speaks with confidence, "you got the strength of Samson and all the other gifts. And your suit should protect you from knives and blunt force trauma. So, *no one* can hurt you."

"They won't necessarily be able to hurt me *physically*," Daniel replies. "But, no doubt, people are going to oppose me. They will laugh and make fun. And when people find out who I am, they might even try to make life difficult for *all* of us."

"Didn't you say the angel asked if you accepted the *burden from the Lord?*" Rebecca inquires.

"That's what he asked."

"And you accepted it. And when you told us, we accept it too. So, here we are. Remember, God hasn't given us a spirit of fear, but of power, love and a sound mind."

"That's right Dad," DJ adds. "God's got you. *He's* got all of us."

"Amen to that," Daniel agrees as he dons his helmet and retracts the visor. "Remember, I'll try to call you every three days."

"And we'll be praying for you *every* day," Rebecca smiles.

"As soon as I get out and close the door, drive away. Don't wait."

The van arrives at the drop off point.

"One more thing," DJ says. "I've been doing some research. The biggest thing Samson lifted were the gates of Gaza. Some scholars believe the gates could have weighed anywhere from 10,700 to 21,400 pounds! That's approximately 4 to 8 tons! If that's true, you could easily lift 3 or 4 large SUV's!"

"I will keep that in mind," Daniel chuckles.

"That's not all," DJ continues. "We often think about Samson using his strength to lift things. But his entire body would have been strong. So, your super strength may translate into being able to run incredibly fast. If that's true, then you should *also* be able to jump large distances."

"Like the Hulk," Daniel replies.

"Exactly!" DJ beams from ear to ear. "And…" DJ utters with a rise in his voice as he pulls out his cell phone and quickly types on the screen. "ChatGPT 3 says, 'the Hulk's leaping ability varies in the comics and movies, but he can leap several miles at a time, depending on the specific iteration…' Just something for you to keep in mind."

"Do you ever *not* think about superheroes?" Rebecca chuckles while gazing at her son in disbelief.

"Nope!" DJ laughs before growing quiet. "But… I do know they're just fiction. What we're doing now… what Dad is *about to do*… all of *this* is based on *truth*."

"Well said," Daniel and Rebecca state in unison as she hugs her son and Daniel ruffles his hair from the back seat.

"There you guys go," DJ laughs, "responding in stereo again."

"Well, we are married," they both say together with a laugh.

After a moment, DJ starts filming with his cell phone. "Remember Dad. No matter what anyone else says, you're wearing a uniform… not a costume."

"Right. Daniel agrees as he pulls down his helmet's visor—which hides his identity. "This suit is my uniform. From this point forward, my codename… is Valor." He opens the side door, steps out the minivan and closes the door behind him. The van slowly drives away as Valor watches for a moment.

"It's time to launch out into the deep," he says to himself as he begins walking.

DJ records the entire time until they have driven out of sight.

The sun crests over the horizon—its light bathing the red suit with its gold accents and blue cape in a beautiful glow. As Valor makes his way through Times Square, towards Central Park, he notices the stares of people as they pass by him. But, no one says anything, while others try to discreetly take his picture.

V

Several hours later, around 10:45am, Valor finds himself in New Jersey, walking down a street as a sports car screeches to a halt next to him. Five teens are in the vehicle. Three of them hang out the windows.

"Who you supposed to be?" one of them yells.

"Do not engage," the Holy Spirit speaks. Valor remains silent as he continues to walk.

The car slowly coasts by his side as the engine revs loudly.

"Hey," another shouts. "You hear us in that helmet?"

"Nice costume! You going to a comic con?"

After a few more moments of non-engagement, their amusement morphs into anger.

"You ain't talking? Forget you then!"

They cackle as one of them throws an unopened soda can at Valor. It bounces off his shoulder pad as the car speeds off in a squealing plume of smoke. *Good thing my suit has extra padding.* He thinks to himself as he watches the car run the red light at the end of the block. *Getting hit with that soda can would have hurt.*

Suddenly, a bus immediately slams into the car! The sound of the massive crash mixed with the screams of the teenagers create a terrifying sonic dissonance in the air. Somehow, four of the teens are injured, but alive. The fifth teen ejected from the car and lay a good twenty to thirty feet away sprawled awkwardly on his stomach, on the pavement.

The bus driver and other bystanders rush to help. One assesses the lone teen in the street and quickly determines that he is deceased. Those with cell phones begin to record. The bus driver radios for assistance as Valor arrives on the scene. He quietly sees that the teens in the car are alive, so he focuses on the lone victim in the street.

Everyone—including the teens in the car—watch as this man in a crimson superhero suit approaches the dead body. "It's too late," a woman says as Valor walks right past him, undeterred. "I'm a doctor. That boy is dead."

Bystanders and pedestrians watch as this unknown man slowly turns the boy's body over onto his back. The boy's fatal injury—a broken neck—quickly becomes apparent. Valor looks at the boy's painfully contorted expression and recognizes him as the one who threw the soda can. Sirens are heard in the distance as Valor kneels down over the body, reaches out with both hands and places them on either side of the boy's crooked neck. He lowers his helmeted head and remains motionless. Every person watching refuses to move as well. Many of them hold their breath in unknown anticipation as they stare at this unusual site.

"What's he doing?"

"I don't know?"

"Is he trying to heal the boy?"

"Should we stop him?"

Just as the ambulance and police cars arrive, Valor stands to his feet and starts walking down the street. Before anyone can call out to stop him, their attention is drawn to the body—once motionless—now moving. Those nearest to the boy gasp as they see his neck is no longer broken. The boy coughs as he opens his eyes and slowly sits up. His body is still scarred from the accident, but he is now alive! And to everyone's surprise, when they turn their attention back in the direction of the unknown man in red, gold and blue, he is nowhere to be found.

PART 3

THE GOOD

*"**1** We who are strong ought to bear with the failings of the weak and not to please ourselves.
2 Each of us should please our neighbors for their good, to build them up."*

—Romans 15:1-2—

21: Give 'Em Heaven!

DAY 54 — Kansas

"What in the sam hill do you mean?" the sheriff asked while his mind tried to register the words he just heard.

"It turned!" the bearded man exclaimed with an awed laugh while removing his ball cap and rubbing his hand through his messy hair.

"It turned?" the sheriff replied with disbelief. "Jeff, what do you mean *it turned*?"

"Just what I *said* Sheriff Johnson! The tornado *turned*! It was coming straight for us—bearing down fast and hard—tearing up everything in its path—and then that superhero guy showed up and stood in between us and the twister! He raised his hand at it and shouted something, but the winds were too loud for me to hear what he said. And then... the tornado stopped right in front of him... and turned into the field! A few seconds later, it just dissolved into thin air! I been living here for 40 years and *never* seen anything like that! And when we turned around to thank the guy, he was gone! What happened... it was... *biblical*! He saved us... He saved our house. He saved... the whole neighborhood!"

"You know which direction he went?"

"I have no idea."

"Well, wherever he is, we could use all the help we can get. Weather man says a supercell has formed and tornados might keep coming for the next 8 hours."

V

4 hours later...

Warning sirens blare as a 3rd tornado drops from the dark clouds. Within seconds of touching down, the EF-2 twister begins tearing up everything in its path with winds of 134 miles per hour!

A family of six, plus their dog, rush out of their home, into the windstorm, taking only what they can carry. They descend the front steps as the wind pummels them—making it difficult to stay on their feet. As they run across the yard to their storm shelter a large piece of wooden debris breaks off from a nearby highway billboard and somersaults through the air right for them! With barely time to react, they scream just as Valor runs in front of them and bodychecks the giant slab of wood! His boots dig into the ground as the impact slows the wood just enough for him to redirect it *away* from the family. A split second later—unharmed—they watch as the debris is taken up high into the sky by the wind.

The father's nod expresses his gratefulness as they resume running for the storm shelter while the tornado barrels across the neighbor's property. One child slips and falls, only to be quickly picked up by Valor's strong grip as he follows the family to the double doors protruding out from the ground in front of them. The father turns the knobs and swings the doors wide open as he pushes his family down the steps. Valor hands the child to the father and pushes them both down the stairs as he slams the doors behind them.

The tornado—now so close that the winds feel like a thousand cuts—catapults Valor into the air! He swirls head-over-heals for several hundred feet, wrapped in his cape, as the winds buffet his body. The roaring monster quickly changes direction, causing the winds to die down just enough for Valor's cape to unfurl and catch the air. The sudden additional surface area aids in his safe landing, but he slams into the ground hard—knocking him unconscious. As the tornado rides off into the distance, Valor lays motionless.

V

2005 Chinese Christian Monastery...

Brother Léi and Daniel walk along a path. They stop at a cliff, which overlooks the vast countryside.

"This is a lesson we must learn," the young monk says. "God is sovereign."

"Right," Daniel agrees. "He's in control."

"But what does that mean?" the young monk replies.

"Well," Daniel thinks, "it means nothing happens that's outside of God's will. Either He has caused it or allows it."

"And," Brother Léi presses.

"And…" Daniel continues his line of logic. "…If God causes or allows something, then He has a reason for doing so."

"You are correct," the young monk replies. "Romans 8:28 assures us that we can have full confidence in knowing that God, who is deeply concerned about us, causes all things in our lives to work together for good, if we love Him and have been called according to His plan *and* purpose. Ephesians 1:11 assures us that, we who believe have been chosen in Him. We have been predestined according to His plan. And He works *every* situation out in conformity with the purpose of His will."

"Right," Daniel agrees. "I know this already."

"On the surface, you do," Brother Léi replies. "But you must *internalize* it. There is no waste in the kingdom of God. Our LORD uses everything for *His purposes*: success, failure, trauma, disaster, good, evil. All of these serve a purpose in the hands of The Sovereign One. We may not understand the purpose in the moment, just like we do not understand the direction of the wind which we cannot always see. But we can trust that God's heart towards us is good and pure and right. And given enough time, His purpose, in *any* given situation, will become clear."

V

Present Day…

It's been 12 hours since Daniel's encounter with the tornado, which left him unconscious… Now his eyes flutter as he slowly becomes aware of his surroundings. His mind is groggy, but the repetitious beeping indicates his location. His vision slowly clears and he sees the white hospital sheet which is pulled up to his neck. He turns to the left and notices his suit and helmet hanging on the other side of the room.

"You're awake," a voice speaks from his right."

Daniel swivels his head to the right to find a doctor standing next to his bed with a digital tablet in his hand.

"My name is Dr. Finkelstein." He motions to the hanging super-suit. "If it wasn't for *that*, you'd probably be in worse shape than you already are. Your suit has some really good padding and structural supports built into it. And boy did we have a hard time getting you out of it."

Daniel winces in pain as he tries to sit up.

"You are pretty battered and bruised," the doctor continues, "but no major injuries except a slight concussion."

Daniel tries to moisten his dry lips. "…Water…"

The doctor grabs a nearby pitcher of water, fills a cup and hands it to Daniel—who slowly swallows the cool liquid in a few satisfying gulps.

"You know, eye witnesses said the tornado sucked you right up in the air as high as two hundred feet and then threw you a good three hundred feet away. They said you looked like a rag doll fumbling through the air. So, you're really lucky to be alive."

"Blessed…" Daniel replies softly.

"I'm sorry," Dr. Finkelstein leans in slightly. "Did you say you were *stressed*?"

"*Blessed*," Daniel repeats with a bit more force. "I'm not lucky… God *protected* me. So, I'm *blessed*."

The doctor shakes his head in slight pity. "I almost forgot you're the guy who's been walking around telling people about God. Well, I hate to burst your bubble—and I don't mean to be offensive—but God doesn't exist."

Daniel stares at the doctor for a moment and then speaks. "Why do you say that?"

"Because," the doctor replies, "I've seen too much for me to believe that God exists, let alone that he actually *cares* about us—if he exists."

"What do you mean?"

"Working in hospitals," the doctor continues. "I've seen enough trauma to last a few lifetimes. The types of destruction that happens to the human body and mind… The accidents, the bladed attacks, the gunshot wounds, the ravaging illnesses and diseases that are too many to name. The impact of Covid-19. I've seen too much death and too many crying families for me to believe… *If* God exists, then *why* does he allow humanity to suffer to such immense proportions? If he exists, then he could stop all of this with a *snap* of his fingers. So, my conclusion is that there is no God... there's just *us*. As a result, I do the best I can to make as much of a difference as *I* can."

"How do you cope?" Daniel asks. "With all the trauma you've seen. What do you do to hold everything together?"

The doctor chuckles while making a wild-eyed sarcastic expression. "How do I cope?" He mulls the question over in his mind. "You're the one in bed... why do I suddenly feel like I'm the one on the *couch*." He chuckles again. "Well, I exercise regularly, try to eat right, get what *little* rest I can with my schedule. I like to read, travel once or twice a year. Periodic sessions with a therapist. I'm not married, so I don't have the stress or responsibility of a family to hold me back. So, that's how I cope."

Daniel lays in the bed quietly.

"Well, you asked," continues the doctor. "What do you think?"

"You didn't mention that you were *divorced*," Daniel replies.

The doctor stares at him dumbfounded. "How-how did you know that?"

Daniel continues without missing a beat. "...And it was a messy divorce because you cheated on your wife with one of your resident doctors."

The doctor backs away from Daniel and presses his body up against the wall.

"That *decision* destroyed, not only your marriage, but also the relationship you had with your three children."

"Stop," the doctor whispers. "Please... stop."

"And you didn't mention the illicit activities you do to try and numb the pain of the trauma you *have* experienced—both here at the hospital and in your own personal life."

Dr. Finkelstein can barely breathe as he looks like a deer in headlights before the inevitable collision with a speeding car.

"This is how I *know* I am not lucky," Daniel continues, "but I am blessed by *God*. More specifically, I am blessed by Jesus Christ, the Son of the Living God. He is the one who allowed me to be thrown, *like a rag doll*, by the tornado. He allowed me to be knocked unconscious... so I would be brought here in order to deliver this message to *you*."

The doctor gulps as he tries to think of a logical reason for this most *illogical* situation, "Let's say I believed you—*which I don't*—what message… does… God have for me?"

"At one point in your life, when you were young, you believed in God. You willingly went with your parents to synagogue. You were proud of your Jewish heritage and the Old Testament Scriptures. But the lures of this world pulled you away. And once you left home for college, you left the spiritual roots of your Jewishness at home as well. Do you know of the prophet Isaiah?"

The doctor nods his head silently. "…Yes…"

"This is what he says in chapter 53 verse 5 as he talks of the coming messiah who would save the world: *'But he was pierced for our transgressions; he was crushed for our iniquities; upon him was the chastisement that brought us peace, and with his wounds we are healed.'* The Messiah would sacrifice Himself in order to save us. Have you heard of Jesus?"

He nods again. "…Yes…"

"Jesus died on the cross in fulfillment of Isaiah's prophecy. But, He did not stay dead. He rose from the grave on the 3rd day. And in the gospel of Mark chapter 2 verse 17, Jesus declared: 'Those who are well have no need of a physician, but those who are sick. I came not to call the righteous, but sinners.'"

Daniel stares at the doctor intently.

"Look at the life decisions you've made. You've brought yourself pain and heartache. So, do you consider yourself to be a sinner?"

The doctor glances from Daniel to the floor and back again. He thinks back over every conscious decision he has ever made and the resulting fallout of many of them. He doesn't want to admit the truth. After all, who would want to admit they are guilty and deserve punishment? He fights against the truth in his mind, but the Holy Spirit speaks to the sliver of conscience he has left and whispers the truth in his heart. Moisture swells up in his eyes as he blinks rapidly, trying to hold back tears, but it is too late. The sudden gush of tears reveals his broken heart and all of his pain testifies to the truth.

"Yes…" the doctor admits. "I am a sinner." He whimpers as the tears flow freely. "I know I've done wrong… Now, this is the part where you tell me God's going to send me to hell."

Rivers of living water swell up from Daniel's belly, as the Holy Spirit quickens him. The pain from his injuries diminishes greatly as he forces his hospital-gown-covered body to sit up in the bed. He then pulls back the covers, turns and places his feet on the cold floor. Dr. Finkelstein watches, but doesn't make a move to stop him. A moment later Daniel is up. He walks around the bed, pulling the beeping heart-rate monitor and IV pouch with him, and stands in front of the crying doctor.

"It is true that we all deserve hell for our rebellion against God. But God loved us so much that He sent His Son Jesus to save us. You heard Jesus' words... He came to save sinners. That means anyone who realizes they are a sinner *can* be saved if they come to Him. That means *you* can be saved *if* you come to Jesus."

"But," the doctor stammers, "everything I've *done*..." The full weight of his transgressions overwhelm him, "Everything I've *said*... Everything I've *thought*! Everything I *refused* to do!" His tears burst forth even more.

Daniel places his hand on the doctor's shoulders and stares into his eyes. "You heard what the prophet Isaiah said. The messiah was pierced for *your* transgressions; He was crushed for *your* iniquities; upon Him was the chastisement that can bring *you* peace, and with His wounds *you* can be healed. Jesus has paid the price to cover *all* of your sins. Now, He wants you to believe in Him and give Him your heart. You work to bring healing to others... but you can only deal with the physical. God wants to bring the *ultimate healing* to you. He wants to cleanse you from the corruption of sin so you can be free and live with Him forever in His kingdom. *This* is why He has sent me to you. Do you want to receive the LORD into your life?"

Another moment of crying passes before the doctor can pull himself together enough to answer. "...Yes... I want to receive Jesus as my Messiah. I want Him to forgive me. I want Him to *save* me."

Daniel smiles broadly. "You told me... now tell *Him*. Just like you're talking to me, *ask* Him to save you."

The doctor nods in agreement as his eyes blink rapidly. He gathers his thoughts, takes a deep breath and closes his eyes.

"Uh... Jesus? I... I really messed up my life. I admit... *everything*... to You. I'm *guilty* of so much! But... this man You have sent... Daniel... he says You can save me. And he showed me... from Your

Scriptures... that You *want*... to save me. So, please... save me. I am *so*... tired. I believe in You. I... I *trust* in You. I want to know more about You... I want to be *with* You. Uh... Thank you? Amen."

"Welcome to God's family," Daniel declares with great delight!

In that instant, a river of joy floods the doctor's soul, as his tears of sorrow and guilt transform into tears of gratefulness and freedom!

Minutes pass as the doctor cries these new tears which swell up from his heart.

"It's like," the doctor exclaims while grabbing Daniel on both shoulders, "It's like a giant weight has been lifted off of me! A weight I didn't even know was there until a few minutes ago!"

Both he and Daniel laugh heartily.

"Praise the Lord," Daniel shouts.

"Yes," the doctor agrees. "Praise the Lord!"

"In the Bible, Jesus says that all of heaven rejoices when one sinner is saved. So, right now, there's a party happening up in heaven over you!"

The doctor hugs Daniel tightly, which causes him to grimace ever so slightly.

"Oh, sorry!" the doctor laughs. "I'm so excited... I forgot you have bruises."

"No worries," Daniel chuckles while in a bit of pain. "This makes it all worth it."

The doctor helps Daniel get back in bed.

"Now that you are a believer in Jesus, this makes us brothers in Christ."

The doctor stares at Daniel, practically overcome with gratitude. "I have so many questions."

"I will do my best to answer them and to get you some resources by the time I'm discharged."

"Yes," the doctor agrees. "Let's keep you for observation for one more day. If everything looks good, then I see no reason why you couldn't be discharged tomorrow afternoon. And since we're brothers now. My first name is Ezra. My shift ends in a few hours. I'll come back by and see you then."

V

The next afternoon...

The nurse enters Daniel's hospital room.

"Okay, Mr. Davidson. You've been cleared to leave. Your discharge papers are being prepared now."

She removes all of the sensors.

"You can get... dressed." She blushes while looking at his super-suit hanging in the corner.

"Thank you," Daniel smiles. "Where's Dr. Finkelstein?"

"He's on another floor dealing with a patient. He said he'll try to meet you by the time you are ready to leave."

"And what about... the fees for the hospital stay? I can call home and get my insurance information."

"Oh, that's already been taken care of." The nurse smiles and turns to leave. "I'll let you get dressed."

V

30 Minutes later...

Daniel stands outside of the hospital with the doctor. His helmet is held under his arm.

A crowd slowly builds as curious onlookers take in the sight of a black man wearing a superhero suit.

"Daniel, thank you for everything and for answering all of my questions last night," Dr. Finkelstein smiles. "I truly owe you my life."

"Ezra," Daniel replies, "we owe Jesus our lives."

The doctor nods in agreement. "Right."

"Don't forget, God will help you handle the traumas you experience here at work."

"Yes, I am grateful for that. Do you think He can help repair my relationship with my ex-wife and kids?"

"With God, all things are possible," Daniel answers. "You will have to make amends to build their trust again. It will take time, but *trust Him* in the process."

"Yes. Okay. I am ready to do *whatever* the Lord tells me."

"Good. And don't forget to read the passages I suggested."

"Already started. *And* I put the number for Pastor Mike in my phone."

"Great!"

A minute passes as they both look at the crowd and the arriving ambulances.

"You asked why God allows so much trauma," Daniel says.

"Yeah… I did. But honestly, I used that as an excuse for me not to believe."

"True. But it is a valid question. The Bible reveals it is our sinful natures and desires to live life apart from God that results in many of the traumas we experience. It also reveals God brings healing through Christ. And we who belong to Him, will be *used by Him* to bring healing as well. And on that day, when Jesus finally returns to earth to set up his eternal kingdom, *He* will bring complete and ultimate healing for us all."

"Amen to that. Thank you… So, will we ever see each other again?"

"If not in this life… then definitely when we get to God's kingdom."

Daniel and Ezra shake hands heartily.

"One more thing," Daniel adds. "The nurse said the hospital fees were already covered. Were you able to get in touch with my wife?"

"No. I got a call from someone who wanted to cover the fees. So, it's already been paid in full."

"Really?" Daniel is surprised. "Who called?"

The doctor glances up to the sky and smiles.

"So…" Daniel asks curiously, "who paid?"

The doctor tilts his head with a smile. "You said Jesus paid it all. Besides, I've got more money than I know what to do with. I imagine God has some plans for how I should use it from now on."

"Thank you," Daniel smiles as they hug. "I really appreciate you."

"Until we meet again," the doctor declares.

"Yes," Daniel agrees. "Until we meet again."

Dr. Finkelstein and curious onlookers watch as Daniel dons his helmet and begins his journey once more.

"Godspeed, Valor!" He shouts. "And whoever you run into along the way… give 'em heaven!"

22: Hands in the Dirt

DAY 55 — KANSAS

Daniel finds himself standing in front of a farmer's home. Fields of crops can be seen for miles. However, the crops on this farmer's property seem to be a bit *unusual* for this time of year.

"Can I help you?" the head of household approaches in dungarees, a hat and holding a pitchfork with both hands. He appears to be about 50 years old with a sturdy, muscular physique.

"Hello," Daniel answers while taking off his helmet. "I'm just passing through and felt compelled to stop here at your property."

"You're that superhero guy we've seen on the news."

"I'm just a guy like you," Daniel replies.

"Well, you sure don't dress like me," the farmer answers.

"I can't argue with you there," Daniel laughs.

"The news says different things about you—depending on which outlet we watch."

"Which do you watch?"

"All the major ones," the farmer replies. "One of the only ways to get at the truth."

"So, what do you think the truth is?" Daniel inquires.

"Some news folks say you're a crackpot. Others say you're the real deal… a man sent from God. Others don't know what to make of you. But, the way I figure it, truth is like a sandwich. There's two sides to every story and then there's the truth somewhere in between."

"So. what's the truth—as *you* see it?"

"Well," he looks around at his property for a moment. "The way I see it, we could really use a *miracle* right about now. So, if you *are* the real deal, I would be grateful if you could put in a good word with the Lord. I've been praying and praying, but nothing has changed. If God is listening, I don't know why He's waiting so long."

"Perhaps," Daniel answers, "God is waiting for the *right moment*."

The man smiles with a nod. "Perhaps He *is*."

Daniel steps forward and extends his hand. "I'm Daniel Davidson, also known as Valor."

The farmer lowers his pitchfork, steps forward and extends his hand. They both share a hearty handshake.

"My name is Norman Berkshire. Nice to meet you."

"So, what's the issue here?" Daniel inquires.

"Our crops are dying. We lost them last season. If we lose them again, I won't be able to provide for my family and the few employees we got left."

"What's the source of the issue?"

"As far as I can tell, the main culprit is the extreme weather conditions."

"Well, you mind if we go take a look?" Daniel asks.

They both go and examine the acres of farmland behind the house.

After a few hours, they arrive back at the front.

"So, what do you think?" The farmer inquires.

"Farming is not my expertise at all. But, what I do know is that God can do anything He desires. And the more time I spend here on your farm, the more I am convinced that God *wants* to restore your crops. Can you bring your entire family outside?"

Fifteen minutes later, Daniel stands at the edge of the fields with the Berkshire family: father, mother, three sons and two daughters. The children's ages ranging from fifteen to thirty-two. He gazes at them while praying silently. *Heavenly Father, what do you want to say to this family?* A moment passes while the family waits in silence.

"Dad," one of the sons speaks up, "is he going to say anything?"

"Son, we will wait here *as long* as it takes." The father is resolute as faith rises within his heart.

Another moment of silence passes as a breeze slowly begins to blow around them. It is then that the Holy Spirit gives Daniel a word of knowledge. And so, he speaks:

"Over the years you have sought to give God your best and you have been blessed with abundance. So, much so, that the notion of crops failing never even entered your mind. Then, two years ago, it seemed that God's blessing on your farm began to dry up. You've done everything you could. You mixed your faith with grit and determination. Yet, with each passing month, things have gone from bad to worse."

The family stares at one another in astonishment.

"Dad," one of the older daughters interjects, "how does he know all of this? Did you tell him?"

"Nope," her father replies. "He is getting all of this from the Lord!"

"What else do you know?" his wife asks.

"Well, Mrs. Berkshire, you've drained both your checking and savings accounts. You've cried out to the Lord, trying to understand why all of this is happening to you. You give your tithes and offerings to your local church and you bless others with the bounty from your land. And yet, it seems as if your prayers have not been heard.

"But how would we know that God is a great deliverer if there is nothing for us to be delivered from? How would we *know* God is faithful and able to work all things out for the good of those who love Him? This time has tested your faith. In many ways it has been the process God uses to purify your faith—to make it *stronger*. These past two years has caused you to seek God like never before through prayer, Bible study and worship. Even with all of the unknowns, you have grown closer as a family. Most importantly, you have made the decision—as a family—that no matter the outcome, even if you lose everything, you will not give up on your relationship with Jesus.

"God has ordained this entire experience for His glory and for your good and the good of those around you. So, now, we are going to pray and ask the Lord to *bless your crops*."

With that, the family holds hands and as Daniel instructs them, Norman and his wife Luna place their hands on his shoulders. He then kneels to the ground and places his hands into the dirt of the field. As they all begin to pray, the sweet and powerful Presence of the Holy Spirit envelops them. With each passing second, God's Presence intensifies. When they finish their time of prayer, each of them are able to discern God's blessed assurance. Their request has been heard... and it has been answered.

V

Later that night...

The Berkshire family prepares a wonderful meal for their invited guest and provides him with a room in which to sleep.

The next morning...

At the crack of dawn, Daniel and Norman are awake, ready to tackle the new day: Norman in his dungarees and Daniel in his uniform. A contagious excitement fills Norman's heart as he waits at the front door for Daniel. Minutes later, both walk out to the fields together.

As the sunlight crests over the fields, Norman stops in his tracks, his eyes widened in wonder. In less than a day, the fields have changed in color and stature! Yesterday, the crops were devoid of moisture and carried a brownish hue. Now, they were a vibrant green, full and bright! Norman turns toward Daniel in astonishment, but Daniel is no longer standing next to him. The farmer squints as he searches the horizon and just at the edge of his vision he sees the flowing movement of a blue cape and red figure.

"How did he get that far so quickly?" Norman doesn't ponder long as he runs back to the house and calls for his entire family to come outside. For the next 30 minutes, as the sun rises into the sky, they worship God in unbridled adoration and thanks. Norman then leads his family in a prayer. As they—with smiling faces and moistened eyes—hold one another's hands, he offers up these words to the Lord:

"Heavenly Father, thank you for hearing our prayers. Thank you for sending Daniel. Thank you for restoring our crops. Thank you for being with us through this whole ordeal. Thank you for *seeing* us! Whatever you desire for us to do with these crops, we will do. And we don't know what your ultimate purpose is for Daniel, but may he complete it to Your full pleasure. In Jesus' Name. Amen!"

23: I Almost Died!

DAY 57 — Kansas

A crowd has gathered on the street in front of a high-rise building. All of them are in a frenzy as they point towards the sky. A man and woman stand on a ledge twenty-six stories up. They hold hands, with their backs facing the building and stare into the open air through tear-filled eyes. Their feet slowly move toward the ledge's edge. One more step and they will fall into the open air and... face certain death. A voice rings out behind them.

"You are not an accident!"

They stop and turn around, finding Valor standing behind them. His cape blowing in the wind.

"How'd you get up here?" the man asks perplexed as he points behind the unwanted guest to the roof's blocked entrance. "We barricaded the door!"

"That's not important," Valor responds. "What matters is that we're all here... *together*."

"I've heard about you on the news," the man replies. "The things you've done. The people you've helped. But, you *don't* know us!"

"I don't need to," Valor responds as he takes a few steps towards the couple. "God knows all about you."

"Don't you move," the man barks. "Or we'll jump!"

Valor stops immediately and raises his hands. "Okay. I will stay right here. And you can share why you want to do this."

The man and woman stare at each other, unsure of what to do. But then the man speaks up.

"You mention God, but he *doesn't* exist! We have *no* souls. We're all here by a cosmic rolling of the dice! And when we die, there's nothing. So, why even live anymore?"

The woman interjects. We're... tired."

Valor slowly raises his visor so they can see his face. "Is that what you both believe?"

The woman looks at her friend and then back to Valor.

"My name is Daniel? What are your names?"

"I'm... Vanessa."

"Don't tell him your name," the man replies. "Don't you see what he's trying to do? He's trying to get us to connect with him so we won't jump!"

"Yes," Daniel admits. "That's *exactly* what I'm doing. Is it wrong for me to want both of you to live?"

"...No..." Vanessa admits. "It's not. We... tried to get people to *listen*, but nobody's taking us seriously."

"*I'm* taking you seriously."

"Why?"

"Because your life matters to God. And I can promise both of you that if you jump to your deaths, you will find yourselves greeted—not by a restful nothingness—but by the fires of hell. Is *that* what you want? You are tired and want life to end... but ending your life *on your own terms* will only lead to unimaginable suffering for eternity."

The woman hesitates. "H-how can you be so sure?"

"Because Jesus taught in the Bible that hell and its torments are *very real*. He also taught that hell was not made for humans, but was created as a place of eternal punishment for the devil and the fallen angels. It has been *enlarged* for humanity because of our sinful rebellion. But God sent Jesus to earth to save us from hell. And if we place our belief and trust in Him, we can spend eternity with Him in His kingdom."

"I don't believe it," the man balks. "You can't prove that God, heaven *or hell* exists."

"Can you prove they don't?"

The man hesitates... "You're twisting my words."

"No. I'm trying to get you to see reality for what it *really* is," Daniel replies. "Tell me, if proof exists, would you *really* want to know?"

"I would want to know," Vanessa replies while the man remains silent.

"Jesus is the proof. He proved God is real by dying on the cross to secure our forgiveness and then rising from the dead three days later. Because He rose, those who believe in Him will be raised from death when He returns to earth to set up His eternal kingdom. Even if there's a ten percent chance that what I'm saying is true, wouldn't you want to find out? But if you refuse and jump, you will be taking a permanent action which can't be reversed and there will be no hope for either of you. But, God does not want you to go to hell. He wants you both to come to Him through His Son, Jesus."

"We're just... so tired..." the man moans. "You don't know how hard life has been for us these past few years. We've lost... everything. Our jobs, homes, family... There's nothing left to live for."

"I know what it feels like to have nothing left to live for."

"You do?" the man stammers in slight disbelief. "Look at you! Standing there in a shiny red suit. What could you possibly know?"

"Can I be honest with you?"

They both slowly nod.

Daniel completely removes his helmet and sits it down on the floor.

"When I was seventeen, I attempted suicide."

Vanessa and the man stare at Daniel. "You're making this up—telling us what you think we want to hear."

"No," Daniel shakes his head without looking away. "I'm telling you the truth. It was a month after I graduated from high school. I was already accepted to college. Both my parents were in my life. I had... an older brother. I had friends. All of the adults in my life—at least those who invested in me—said I would do something great when I grew up. But, I couldn't *see* what they saw. I hated my life... I had a long list of things I didn't like about myself. So, one night in July, I tried to end it all."

V

Many years earlier... 1:30am.

An argument with his father forced a young Daniel's emotional dams to their breaking point. As they crumbled, years of insecurity and self-hatred spilled over into his consciousness like a raging river! Daniel ran out of his house and into the dark night—without looking back! He now stood in the middle of a one-way street, just on the other side of a blind curve. There were no nearby street lamps to warn drivers of his distraught intentions. He desperately waited to welcome the blinding headlights which would herald his impending departure from this life. Tears poured down his cheeks as mucus streamed from his nose. His body heaved with each sob. He didn't even try to wipe his blurry eyes. All Daniel wanted was to be put out of his misery.

He picked this street because of the numerous accidents that have occurred when drivers speed through the area. He figured ending his life this way will be painful, but quick—hopefully instantaneous. Even at this hour, a steady stream of speeding vehicles are usually present. However, on this fateful night, there were no cars at all.

Daniel was so overwhelmed with an onslaught of depression and suicidal thoughts that he couldn't speak. All he could do was cry... and groan. He stood motionless in the center of the one-way street. Five minutes passed... Then ten minutes... Then fifteen minutes... Finally *twenty minutes*... and still not a single vehicle!

Daniel stumbled his way back home and collapsed in the driveway. He looked up at the night sky with a shout. "Why did you make me God? You did such a terrible job! All I want to do is die... I've got *nothing* to live for."

V

The present...

Daniel looks at Vanessa and the man in silence.

"Why did you stop?" Vanessa asks.

Daniel hesitates. "If I tell you what happened next, you may not believe it."

The man says nothing—but he doesn't move toward the edge of the ledge.

"You can't start a story like that and not finish," Vanessa replies. "How did you make it through that?"

V

Many years earlier... the conclusion of Daniel's suicide attempt.

"Daniel," his dad yelled from the window. "Come back inside!"

Moments later, Daniel did something he had never done before: he stood toe to toe with his father while his mother watched.

"There can't be two men trying to run this house," his father declared. "You either follow the rules or you leave!"

They don't even know what I just tried to do, Daniel thought to himself. *I don't need this... I am out of here!*

Just when Daniel opened his mouth to tell his parents that he was leaving and would never come back, the unthinkable happens.

TIME... STOPPED.

At least for him. Everything... slowed... to... a... halt as his parents froze in place. Before Daniel fully comprehended what was happening... a Voice spoke. It came from both outside of him and from within him at the same time.

"You don't want to do that," the Voice said.

Daniel immediately knew it was not *his* voice. It was not his *conscience*. Nor was it his *imagination*. It was clearly *another* Voice... a Voice with sovereign authority.

"Yes, I do," Daniel responded.

"Where will you go?" The Voice inquired. **"Your father took the keys to your car."**

"I will walk to my godmother's house," Daniel replied. "It will take me a couple of hours, but I can get there."

The Voice spoke again, **"You don't want to do that."**

Then... TIME... BEGAN TO FLOW... ONCE MORE.

Immediately his father asked, "So, what are you going to do?"

Daniel looked at his parents and thought about what just occurred... *Did God just stop time in order to have a conversation with me? Did God really hear me when I cried out to him in anger in the driveway? Did God actually see me standing in the middle of the street that is usually filled with speeding cars? Was God responsible for there being no cars on the road for twenty minutes? And was God right when He said I really didn't want to throw my life away?* Daniel pondered all of this and then responded to his father. "I'll stay." He then went to bed.

Later that morning...

Daniel awakened, in his bed. He threw on some clothes and headed outside. He stood in the driveway—at the very spot where he cried out to God early that morning while it was still dark. He lifted his eyes skyward and gazed at the beautiful clear blue sky. It looked so different from just a few hours ago...

"God," he whispered, "You didn't let me die last night... I guess that means You have a plan for my life. I don't know what it is. But, whatever it is... *I want it.*"

V

The present.

Daniel shares with Vanessa and the man. "All I wanted was the pain to stop. I thought suicide was the only way out. That was over twenty-five years ago. Now, I'm living the future I never knew existed. My life hasn't been perfect. I've had low points, but never as low as *that* night. Now, I know without a shadow of a doubt that God is with me...helping me... working all things out, according to *His* plans, for my good. And He brought me to both of you, so I know He wants to help you, too."

"We've tried everything..." the man admits. "Drugs, counseling, meditation..."

"But have you tried Jesus?" Daniel replies. "Have you read the Bible to see what He says? Have you asked Him to help you?"

"...No... we haven't."

"Then you haven't tried *everything*. Jesus invites us: 'Come to Me, all you who are weary and burdened, and I will give you rest. Take My yoke upon you and learn from Me, for I am gentle and humble in heart, and you will find rest for your souls. For My yoke is easy and My burden is light.' Jesus wants us to give Him *our* weariness and He will give us joy, peace and rest for our souls. But, we must *first* come to Him."

Vanessa, with a slight smile and tears in her eyes, lowers herself from the ledge.

The man gawks at her in disbelief. "What are you doing?"

"He's right," she counters. "We *haven't* tried everything. What if ending it all is the wrong thing to do?"

"There's no other way," he barks! "Vanessa, we talked about this! You can't back out now!"

Vanessa stares at her friend. "When we came here—before we climbed up on this ledge—I asked God, if He were real, to send us help. Then Daniel showed up," she points. "And all he's been doing is talking to us about God. So, I think him being here is also proof that God exists." She now looks up at her friend as he stands on the ledge alone. "Brian... please come down."

"Don't say my name!"

Suddenly a burst of wind whips past the building—knocking Brian off balance—toppling him over the ledge.

"No!" Vanessa yells.

Daniel moves with blinding speed—catching Brian's shirt a split second before he would have fallen beyond reach! The large man dangles in midair as Daniel easily hoists him back up and over the ledge. As soon as Brian is placed back on solid ground he crumbles to the floor in a wide-eyed hyperventilating heap.

"I almost died!" he grasps his heaving chest as Vanessa hugs him through her tears. He looks at her intently. "As soon as I started to fall I thought, *I don't want to die!* I thought it was all over!"

Vanessa smiles through her tears. "Now you have a second chance. We both do. Thanks to—" She turns in Valor's direction, but he's gone. "Where did he go?"

They both notice the door is no longer barricaded. It flies open as several first responders burst onto the roof and proceed to help them.

"Did you see the superhero guy?" Brian asks them.

"What are you talking about?" the police officer replies.

"You know," Brian continues, "the guy from the news! He was just here!"

The officers and EMT's look at Brian incredulously and then addresses Vanessa. "Did he hit his head?"

"He's telling the truth," Vanessa adds. "Did you see him? He was wearing a red, gold and blue super-suit."

"No," the officer answers. "There was nobody fitting that description in the elevators or in the stairwell."

Vanessa and Brian stare at each other.

"Did we just hallucinate this whole thing?"

"No," Vanessa replies firmly. "He was real."

"If he didn't take the stairs or the elevator..." Brian muses. "Do you think he just flew away?"

"I don't know," Vanessa replies as they both look up to the sky.

"Well," Brian says sheepishly as the first responders continue to check their vitals, "you did ask God for help... Maybe we should look into this Jesus thing."

Vanessa smiles warmly, "I think... that's a *great* idea."

24: Help Him

DAY 59 — Kansas

A man, wearing unique orthodox clothing which identifies him as Jewish, merrily makes his way through the streets of his city with several packages in tow. It has been a busy day of shopping and now he eagerly looks forward to making it home to a nice warm meal, prepared by his wife. As he thinks of her and their children, he says a quiet prayer to God thanking Him for all of the many blessings that have been bestowed upon his life. His prayer is barely finished before his wonderful mood is tragically interrupted by a fist which swiftly comes from behind him and lands squarely on his jaw.

Down he crumbles as his packages tumble hard to the ground. Before his mind can register the attack, a furry of fists assault his head and body—knocking off his glasses and his hat.

Valor comes upon the scene of five young men pummeling the man with their fists and stomping him with their feet as they shout anti-semitic slurs.

The Holy Spirit speaks immediately to his spirit. *"Help him."*

In an instant, the five young men are pulled off—each thrown in different directions. They land with a thud as the Jewish man, now balled up in the fetus position, slowly looks up. His face is bloodied and his body bruised, but he is bewildered by the sight of this hero standing before him... standing between him and those who would do him harm.

The five men stumble to their feet to find the same unexpected sight. Their hatred-fueled fight drains from them as fear grips their hearts. They look at each other warily, motioning for someone to take the lead in an attack. But none do. Instead, they all run away.

Valor turns to find the Jewish man still on the ground. He extends his hand and helps him up.

"T-thank you," the man utters with a sense of awe. "I don't know who you are... but thank you." He pulls a handkerchief out of his black coat and begins wiping blood off of his face.

"Do you not watch the news?" Valor asks.

"Vary rarely. Too much propaganda. Why? Have you been on it?"

Valor nods.

"If not for you, I might be dead right now. How can I repay you? I know! Come to my home for a meal. My wife is a good cook!"

Valor takes off his helmet, which shocks the man.

"Y-you're... black!"

"I am. My name is Daniel... My parents named me after the prophet in your Old Testament—the Tanakh."

Daniel's remark puts the man at ease.

"Do you know our holy book?"

"I do."

"Well then, praise the Name of HaShem. You *must* come to my house for a meal. I insist!"

V

Hours later...

The meal has ended and Daniel has become acquainted with Mordecai, his wife Miriam and their two children Caleb and Leah. They have all been fascinated by Daniel's account of his journey thus far. Although, he has been very careful to only share with them certain details.

"You're knowledge of our holy Scriptures is impressive," Mordecai admits.

"So, do you really have the strength of Samson?" his son Caleb asks while leaning forward in excitement.

"Yes. The Lord gives me the strength when needed."

The boy turns to his father. "What do you think father?"

"Well," Mordecai replies, "all that you said is highly unusual... but since HaShem did these things once, as recorded in our Tanakh, it is *possible* that He would do so again if He desired. And I did see Daniel fling five men off of me as if they weighed nothing!"

"But why are you doing all of this?" Caleb inquires. "You still haven't told us."

"Because," Daniel hesitates but then continues. "God wants people to know about His Son, Yeshua, who we call Jesus."

All of the family members freeze in their place as their eyes widen. Mordecai quickly stands to his feet—his countenance changed.

"We do not say *that name* in this house. It is anathema!" He points to the door with such force that his body shudders. "You must leave at once!"

Daniel slowly pushes his chair back and rises to his feet. "I am sorry to have offended you. But what I have said is the truth."

"No more of this!" Mordecai shouts as he covers his ears. "Leave now!"

A soft hand presses firmly on his shoulder. He turns to find his wife staring intently at him with soft-yet-determined eyes.

"I know you have spoken," Miriam says, "but since this man has saved your life from certain harm and possibly death, should we not... *at least* hear him out?"

"He speaks the forbidden name!" Mordecai responds. "Our rabbis have always told us to never entertain even the *thought* of that name!"

"But, here we are," she responds softly, "at *this* moment... We should at least hear him out. Then, we can refuse him if we so desire."

"*If...*" Mordecai looks at his wife warily.

"He speaks of Adonai," She continues. "He speaks of the same Scriptures as we do. You said it yourself."

Mordecai hesitates, but then begrudgingly motions for Daniel to sit back down. The rest of his family sits back down at the table as well.

"I will only entertain you now, because of the bidding of my wife. Say what you want, but be brief about it."

Daniel prays silently within his heart to the LORD... asking for the words to say. Wisdom begins to rise up within him from the Holy Spirit.

"With your *permission*, I would like you to read aloud from the Tanakh."

The man's hands close into fists, but he nods slowly.

"Read from the prophet Isaiah. The 53rd chapter."

The man opens to the chapter and clears his throat. "The rabbi usually skips over this chapter..." But he begins reading aloud. As he reads, several verses jump off the page in his mind:

3 He was despised and rejected by mankind, a man of suffering, and familiar with pain.

Like one from whom people hide their faces he was despised, and we held him in low esteem.

4 Surely he took up our pain and bore our suffering, yet we considered him punished by God, stricken by him, and afflicted.

5 But he was pierced for our transgressions, he was crushed for our iniquities; the punishment that brought us peace was on him, and by his wounds we are healed.

6 We all, like sheep, have gone astray, each of us has turned to our own way; and the Lord has laid on him the iniquity of us all.

10 Yet it was the Lord's will to crush him and cause him to suffer, and though the Lord makes his life an offering for sin, he will see his offspring and prolong his days, and the will of the Lord will prosper in his hand.

11 After he has suffered, he will see the light of life and be satisfied; by his knowledge my righteous servant will justify many, and he will bear their iniquities.

12 Therefore I will give him a portion among the great, and he will divide the spoils with the strong, because he poured out his life unto death, and was numbered with the transgressors. For he bore the sin of many, and made intercession for the transgressors.

As he finishes, his wife nudges him softly. Daniel notices and asks the question.

"Who does this sound like in human history... in *Jewish* history?"

The husband refuses to answer as his wife nudges him again.

"It sounds like Jesus," Leah replies sheepishly as her parents look at her. Her father glares with disapproval, but her mother gazes with soft eyes and a warm smile.

"I don't know what your rabbis have told you," Daniel continues, "but did you know Jesus was Jewish? *All* of His disciples were Jewish. According to the New Testament Scriptures, He followed *all* of the Jewish customs of His day as prescribed in the Tanakh."

Daniel stops for a moment to let that information set in...

"And He is *the only one* who has fulfilled what you just read in Isaiah 53. Through His death on the cross at a place called Golgotha, just outside of Jerusalem.

"I know you have not read the accounts of Jesus' life and ministry as found in the gospels—the New Testament, but in one account Jesus says that all of the writings of Moses, the prophets and the Psalms point to Him. He actually took His disciples through the Tanakh to help them see that what He said was in fact true. If you have eyes to see and ears to hear, *you* can research this as well to determine if what He says is true."

Silence…

"And where," Mordecai mutters, "would you recommend we begin *if* we were to study this for ourselves?"

"In addition to Isaiah 53, I would suggest the prophet Daniel: specifically, the 7th chapter. It is the chapter of the Tanakh Jesus referenced the most because it encapsulates the entire message He taught during His earthly ministry for just over 3 years."

"May I share something?" Miriam asks a bit cautiously while holding onto her husband's arm. Her husband slowly nods in agreement.

"I have not mentioned this to anyone… not even my husband. But three nights ago, while I was sleeping, I had a dream. It was the most vivid dream I have ever experienced. I was standing in a beautiful field with the most perfect flowers and colors beyond anything I've seen on earth. A soft breeze was blowing. Then I saw a blinding light in the sky that was much brighter than the sun! I shielded my eyes, but as I squinted I could see the form of a man *within* the light. Suddenly, a voice from the light, spoke my name. The voice said: "You have been in darkness, but I am coming to free both you and your family. Then you will know Me and I will know you." I asked, 'Who… are you?' A moment passed and then the voice said, 'I am the One who died and rose from the dead for you. I am Yeshua, your Messiah… The King of the Jews. The Son of Man as found in the writings of My prophet Daniel.'

"Then the dream ended and I woke up. I have never read about Yeshua. I did not even know he was Jewish. And here you are. You saved my husband from an attack and you are sharing about the same One who came to me in a dream. This cannot be a coincidence."

"Your time is up," Mordecai declares curtly. "We have heard enough. You may leave now."

Miriam opens her mouth to object, but her husband cuts her off.

"I have spoken."

Daniel picks his helmet up off the floor next to him. He stands to his feet as the family does the same.

"Thank you for your kind hospitality," he smiles.

They lead him to the door and bid him farewell. He exits their home in the cool of the evening and takes a few steps toward their walkway's front gate.

"Daniel," Mordecai calls.

Daniel stops and turns around in quiet response.

"To do what you ask... to give our lives to... *him*... do you understand what that would mean? We would be ostracized from our community, from our synagogue... from our relatives."

Daniel thinks for a moment before responding.

"If I'm right and He is your *true* Messiah who came to forgive your sins and give you eternal life, then wouldn't *any sacrifice* on your part be worth it to follow Him? Any loss you incur He would replace. And who knows if your decision for Him, right now at this very moment, is *for such a time as this* so you can share the truth with your family, your community, your synagogue and beyond?"

His remarks are met with silence.

"I know you have many questions. If you are willing, read the gospel of Matthew. It is the first book of the New Testament and is written specifically for a Jewish audience. It highlights Yeshua's Jewishness."

Mordecai takes in Daniel's words before speaking.

"I... will search out these things which you have shared to see whether or not they are true." With that, the door is closed.

Daniel breathes a deep sigh as he turns and exits their front yard. He places his hands on the gate and prays.

"Father, as You have desired, the seeds have been planted and watered. May You give the increase. In Jesus' Name. Amen."

With that, Daniel puts on his helmet and continues his trek westward.

25: Carrots

DAY 76 — Colorado

Valor has walked over one thousand miles so far. Fortunately, the planned support along the way has been incredibly helpful to his physical, mental and spiritual well-being. Still, there are stretches of the journey—like this—where the distance between the last scheduled stop and the upcoming one is vast and food is scarce. He takes off his helmet and licks his dry lips while trying to summon moisture in his parched mouth.

"Lord, I know You said when You were in the wildness being tempted by the Devil, *'Man shall not live by bread alone, but by every word which proceeds out of the mouth of God.'* And I know You have been sustaining me these past few days without food... but right now... I'm *really* hungry and could use a burger, fries and a giant glass of water, or maybe a lemonade or sweet tea." He smiles at the thought of the meal. "Please show me what to do."

Ten minutes later, as he continues to follow his current route on I-25, a sign reveals that a diner and a gas station can be found at the next exit. At the sight of the sign, a gentle prompting swells up within him. A few minutes later, he takes the exit and follows the meandering roads to the diner. As he sees the small restaurant in the distance, he notices a few cars sit in the parking lot. The lot is more of a dusty gravel field than anything else. All of the cars, but one, are empty. The occupied car, with a driver in the front seat, is idling near the entrance.

"Must be waiting on an order," Daniel smiles to himself as he walks past the car, ascends a couple of steps and opens the door to the diner.

He steps into the establishment, with the ring of the bell which hangs over the door. Everyone looks at him as he smiles and nods at the onlookers. Nobody smiles back, but resume what they were doing. He notes he is the only person of color in the room. He approaches the unattended counter, rings the bell, takes a seat at the counter and places his helmet on the stool next to him. The relief to his legs and back is immediate as he lets out a sigh. A moment later, the waitress—blond with red lipstick and slightly running mascara—appears from the back and sees the unexpected sight of Daniel in his uniform. She hesitates for a moment before forcing a smile, wiping her eyes and fixing her uniform.

"Hello," she welcomes with a slight twang in her voice. "What can I do for you?"

"Hi. Judging by your expression, you don't often see people dressed like this."

"No, I don't," she replies with a nervous smile.

"I know this is unusual, but I am really hungry. I don't have any money, but I am willing to do any kind of manual labor for my meal. Can we work something out?"

The waitress looks around the room and then back at Daniel. "I'm sorry, we can't help you. Food is so expensive these days."

"I understand," Daniel replies. "Can I at least get a glass of water before I leave?"

The waitress smiles rather curtly and then gets him the water. As he slowly drinks and savors every drop, he spins in the chair scanning the dinner again. With one last gulp, he stands up, grabs his helmet and thanks the waitress before heading for the door. Again, everyone present watches him with great interest, but no smiles. He exits the diner and begins walking across the lot.

"Okay Lord," Daniel frowns, "what's the deal? You lead me here... only to be rejected?"

An uneasy feeling begins to swell up within him as his mind recollects the experience. Images flash before him, causing him to pay more attention to what he saw. Everyone's expressions when he entered and when he left... he thought it was just due to what he was wearing or maybe because he was a black man in a primarily white area. As he focused on each person he saw, more information rises to the forefront of his mind. No one was smiling *at all*... No one laughed... No one suddenly made quiet remarks or had any side conversations. And where were their cell phones? No one tried to take a picture of him. Suddenly, this seemed unusual. In every previous encounter, where he showed up in his uniform, people *always* had a reaction of some kind. But not *here*.

The more steps he took away from the diner, the more this realization began to pull on him. It was as if the Holy Spirit was a fishing rod which had hooked Daniel and was reeling him backwards. As he thought about things a moment longer, it suddenly dawned on him that all of the people seemed nervous... perhaps even scared. All, except two gentlemen sitting near the door. They seemed to be watching him like a hawk. Then the waitress replayed in his mind, how she came from the back, adjusting her slightly disheveled clothes, wiping her eyes. She forced a smile... but he didn't pay attention to the fact that her forehead was covered in sweat and her mascara was smudged. And then there was another detail he saw, but it didn't register... he could hear the sizzling of food, but when he glanced into the kitchen, the cook was nowhere to be found.

Suddenly a new image floods his mind as one word is spoken to his spirit.

"Carrots."

"Carrots? What does that mean, Lord?" The compulsion to return to the diner overwhelms him as a bold confidence swells up within him. Daniel can feel his *"fight or flight"* response trigger as the voice of the Lord speaks again.

"Do not fear. I have given them into your hands. You must speak for Me in California."

Daniel still does not completely understand, but he stops walking away and turns around in the gravel lot. With every step towards the diner, his famished weakness diminishes as strength rises up from within his belly and courses throughout his entire body. Within seconds he is completely alert! As he passes the idling car, he catches a glimpse of the license plate and the driver, who clearly looks worried. Decisiveness rises within him as he dons his helmet, closes the visor and ascends the steps once more. He then opens the door and crosses the threshold of the diner's entrance. As the hanging bell signals his return, he is fully aware and completely confident in God's control of the situation.

Again, all eyes are on him. The counter is unattended and smoke now rises heavily from the grill in the kitchen. Clearly, the food on it is burnt to a crisp. Nobody moves as Valor crosses the room and rings the bell at the counter. The waitress hurries back out, surprised to see him, but this time, when she smiles nervously, her expression seems a bit more relieved.

"Back again?" She utters as her eyes silently plead with him.

"Yes," Valor replies. "I'm here to help you."

Before she can answer, Valor speaks boldly for all who are present. "Perhaps the guy in the back is having issues trying to open the safe since the cook is unconscious and you can't remember the combination."

The two men sitting by the door jump to their feet and whip out their guns from underneath their jackets.

"Don't move!" One of them yells.

Several patrons cry out in horror as Valor raises his arms in a slow, calm manner. A second later, the third man—who was in the back—walks out with his gun drawn.

"This was *supposed* to be quick," the second man says!

"Nothing has gone according to plan,"the third man replies in a huff.

"We should just leave before the cops show up."

"Not an option!"

"But the safe—"

"We'll *take it* with us."

"But it's bolted to the floor! We don't have enough time."

The leader looks at Valor. "You're that superhero guy from the news… Some people say you can rip a car door clear off its hinges. If its true, then you've got super strength. Go rip the safe off the floor and put it in our car outside or else we start shooting people."

"You know, this is the second robbery I've been able to stop while on my journey."

The three men laugh even in the midst of their nervousness.

"Stop?" the leader replies. "You ain't stopped nothing! Now go get that safe!"

"I'm sorry, but it doesn't work like that."

"So, *how* does it work?"

"My abilities come from God. He gives them as I need them. And since one of His ten commandments is that we shouldn't steal… I'm sure He won't provide strength for me to do it."

"So, you talk to God?" the leader scoffs.

"Yes."

"And He talks back?"
"Yes."
"Prove it."
"Carrots."

The leader's eyes widen as he tries to process what he just heard. "What did you say?"

"You. Like. Carrots."

The two other men look at each other with an uneasy nervousness as Valor continues.

"You like carrots so much that since you were *eight years old*, you've been stealing them from grocery stores."

"H-how could you know that?" The leader replies just barely over a whisper.

"It's one of your... *many* fetishes." Valor replies.

"Who told you that!" He yells while angrily pointing his weapon at him and then at his two accomplices. "Did you guys tell him?"

"No," they yell—unsure of what to do. "We didn't tell him! And stop pointing your gun at us!"

"I already told you," Valor interjects. "God tells me things when I need to know them."

"We need to get out of here," one of the robbers urge.

The leader ignores him as he keeps his eyes on Valor. "I'm going to kill you and be done with this."

"You can't kill me."

"Why not?"

"Because God said I have to speak on His behalf in California."

The man sucks his teeth. "Let's see if God can stop a bullet." He pulls the trigger several times, but his gun jams.

"Shoot him," he yells to his accomplices. They pull *their* triggers and their guns do the same—nothing.

The man grabs the waitress and puts the gun to her head.

"We're leaving! Don't try to stop us!"

"Father," Valor whispers, "Don't let them leave. Do for me what you did for Elisha and Paul. Take away the sight of my enemies."

Suddenly, the three men drop their weapons and scream as they claw at their eyes.

"I can't see," they exclaim as they stumble and collapse to the floor. "I can't see!"

Valor grabs their guns, removes the bullets and puts them on the counter.

Outside, the driver witnesses the commotion and opens his door to jump out of his car, but notices movement out the corner of his eye. To his horror he sees a police car entering the far side of the lot. In a heartbeat, he closes the door and drives off, trying to look as calm as possible as the police car parks and a sheriff and deputy exit the vehicle.

"It's the cops," a patron yells.

"We're saved!" Others cheer.

The sheriff and deputy enter the diner and find the strange scene of three men floundering on the floor like fish out of water.

"Dottie," the sheriff asks, "what in the sam hill is going on here?"

"Arrest these guys Sheriff," she points. "They tried to rob us!"

Both sheriff and deputy jump into action and restrain the three.

"A fourth guy in a car drove off when you pulled up," a patron yells.

"Dang it," the deputy utters.

"Don't worry," Valor replies as he raises his visor. "I know the license plate number."

"And just who are you?" the sheriff asks.

"He's a mighty man of God," the waitress replies. "And he saved us all!"

Everybody claps and cheers for him.

"I only did what the Lord told me to do," Daniel responds. "It was *Jesus* who orchestrated your rescue. Speaking of that... how's the cook?"

"Jimmy!" Dottie exclaims as she turns around and runs to the back. The sheriff follows her as the deputy radios headquarters. They find Jimmy sitting up on the floor, rubbing his head.

"You're awake!" Dottie smiles as she and the sheriff help him to his feet. "The robber hit you over the head real good. knocked you right out!"

"It *still* hurts," he winces, "but I'm glad to be alive. Aw, man the food is burning."

"Food can be replaced," she smiles. "But you can't."

"What happened while I was out?"

"You won't believe me when I tell you. Come see for yourself."

As they make their way to the counter, they find Valor addressing the patrons.

"...If you want to have a relationship with Jesus, then let me introduce you to Him."

"Tell me more," a patron says as he gets up from his booth with a broad smile.

"*This* guy stopped them?" Jimmy asks.

"Yep!" Dottie smiles. "I'll fill you in. It was incredible! Never seen anything like it except in the Bible."

"Well, ask him if he's hungry," Jimmy replies, "Because lunch is on the house!"

An hour later... everyone present has heard the gospel, including the sheriff and deputy. Many of them place their faith in Jesus. The rest would consider it.

Daniel then eats a wonderful meal—the best hamburger, fries and lemonade he's had in a long time. And the fourth robber was captured on the interstate a few exits down in a neighboring town.

As Daniel says his goodbyes and exits the diner, he prays:

"Lord, thank you for Your mercy and patience with me. I was a bit upset after I first arrived and received nothing but a glass of water. I did't understand what was happening. But You worked with me. You... taught me to trust You even more. I see that even with everything You've already shown me, there's still a lot more I need to learn. Please... don't stop teaching me how to walk closely with You. Amen."

With that, he crosses the gravel lot and continues his walk to San Diego, California.

26: What Did You Say?

DAY 78 — Colorado

Valor walks down a long stretch of I-25. A biker gang—of 15-20 members—all take note of him as they ride by on their loud Harley Davidson motorcycles. The sound is deafening as they pass by and ride off into the distance. About an hour later, Daniel follows one of the highway exits and comes across a bar. The bikers are parked outside laughing and talking when they see him approaching in the distance. In an instant, the command is given. They all mount their rides and head for this lone walker. Everyone laughs as they encircle Daniel while revving their engines. He stands still in the center of the display as several bikers come within inches of hitting him. After 5-10 minutes of showboating, the bikes come to a halt and each rider dismounts. Several of them approach Valor as he removes his helmet.

"That was absolutely amazing," Daniel claps! "I have never seen motorcycles up close and personal like that! Thank you!"

The approaching leaders of the gang look bewildered by the unexpected response.

"You weren't scared?" one of them asks.

"Why should I be?" Daniel smiles

"Cause we didn't do that for your entertainment," another barks.

"Oh, I know you didn't." Daniel holds his smile. "But I'm on a mission from God. Jesus told me I have to deliver a message in California. So, since I'm not yet *in* California, why should I worry about anything?"

"We saw you on TV," the main leader of the gang declares. "We don't like no Jesus talk."

"I'm sorry to hear that," Daniel replies. "I'll just be on my way then—"

The leader forcefully puts his hand on Daniel's chest plate.

"We didn't say you could go."

"So… you want to keep talking?"

The leader—clearly a gruff persona—studies Daniel's face for a moment before speaking through gritted teeth. "Prove to me that God exists and maybe we'll let you walk out of here in one piece."

The other bikers cackle while slapping each other around.

"That's the million dollar question everyone wants an answer to. But, I don't have to prove His existence to *you*," Daniel replies confidently. "You *already* know He's real. Every time you look in the mirror you see the evidence. There's proof all around you in creation. That's why you fight and resist and rebel so much. You already know. You can't get away from it. That's why *you* don't like it."

Daniel's words are paralyzing to everyone who hears them. The bikers no longer snicker. But their leader persists in his affront by grabbing Daniel's shoulders with both hands.

"Even with your fancy suit, I could crush you!"

"You could," Daniel agrees. "After all, you are much bigger than me. But if you did, you'd never get the answer to the question that's been burning in your heart for the last 48 years."

The leader's eyes widen in disbelief as he releases his grip and stumbles back a step.

"What did you say?"

Daniel steps forward. "You want an answer to the question that's haunted you for the last 48 years. It's the reason why you've thrown yourself headlong into rebellion."

"Shut up," the leader utters while stumbling back again. The other bikers watch in confusion as Daniel takes another step forward.

"It's why you barely sleep at night… Why you give yourself over to the dark thoughts which enter your mind."

"I said—shut up!" The leader falls backwards to the ground as Daniel steps forward.

"You asked for proof, Trevor. Here it is." Daniel towers over the biker as the two bikers nearest to him suddenly come out of their stupor and step in between their leader and Daniel.

"You crazy," one of them says. "His name's not Trevor. You don't know what you talking about!"

Daniel never takes his eyes off of the leader. "You never told them your real name?"

"What's he talking about ST?"

175

Daniel motions for them to move out of his way and somehow, against their will, they take a few steps to the side. They watch as Daniel kneels down in front of their leader.

"They don't know how you started life in church. You loved reading the Bible *and* singing in the choir. And you *wanted* to be a preacher of the gospel... until that fateful day when you were ten and everything changed."

"H-How—?" Trevor can't even get the words up out of his throat as Daniel continues.

"Just because you experienced an unimaginable tragedy that day doesn't mean God isn't real. He didn't turn away from you. *That day*, you turned your back on Him. But even to this very day, He's the One who has been holding you together. He still calls out for you to come back to Him. This is *why* we're talking right now. When your group rode by me on the highway, God told me to come here *specifically* to give you this message: Repent... And turn back to Jesus while you still have time. All of these people who follow you... don't lead them into darkness and damnation. Lead them to God's light and His eternal salvation!"

The eyes of both men lock in a silent gaze as the entire gang slowly encircles them to see what the outcome will be. They've always been ready for a fight. They've stood toe to toe with law enforcement without breaking a sweat. Yet, at this moment, they find themselves fearful and held at bay—as if by some invisible, otherworldly Presence which seems to be in their midst.

"You're mother prayed for you every day of your life until the day she died. I know her death caused you great pain, but there's One who knows your pain even more than you."

Trevor tries to resist vocalizing the truth, but the words swell up within him and flow from his lips. "J-Jesus..." It takes all of his strength to hold back the tears swelling up in his eyes.

"*Jesus,*" Daniel agrees with a strong breath of authority.

The Name that is above all other names washes over Trevor like a mighty river; causing him to burst into an agonizing wail of a cry! The whole while, Daniel watches and prays. After Trevor's agony subsides to a manageable level, Daniel speaks once more.

"Jesus is the door by which you can see her again," he comforts. "Even more important, Jesus is the door by which *you* can see *Him* face to face for all eternity! But you *must* make the decision. You can keep running or you can surrender your pain to Jesus so He can heal your heart and mind."

Daniel stands up, looks at everyone else and then gazes down at Trevor. He then turns and takes a step back towards the highway. As he walks, the circle of bikers separate before him like the Red Sea parted before Moses.

"Wait!" Trevor utters while wiping his eyes. "You can't leave."

"I have to keep heading for California," Daniel replies as he prepares to put on his helmet. "You already know what you need to do."

"But..." Trevor's eyes dart back and forth as his lips tremble. "Can you *stay* for a few hours and... talk with us?"

The other bikers look around at each other with confused expressions.

"Is that what you want?" Daniel inquires.

"...Yes..." Trevor admits unashamedly.

"What about everyone else?"

Trevor gathers his strength and stands to his feet. He wipes his eyes, looks at his fellow bikers, clears his throat and address the group.

"You all have followed me across the country and into a whole heap of trouble. I *still* want you to follow me—right here and right now. So stay. Let's listen to what this man has to say. And then you can make whatever decision you want to make."

For three hours they listen, ask questions, discuss issues and eventually pray. By the time Daniel leaves, Trevor has returned to his Heavenly Father and many of his fellow bikers have found eternal life in Christ. Those who have yet to receive Jesus... have had seeds of truth planted within the soil of their hearts. Both Daniel and Trevor know that one person plants the seed of truth. Another waters it. And it's God who gives the fruitful increase.

27: Up in the Sky!

DAY 80 — Colorado

The roadway ascends to well over 2,800 feet above sea level, winding along the twists and turns of a mountain range. For the past few hours, gravity has been working against Valor with every step on this leg of the journey. Finally, the highway crests, revealing a sizable rest stop on the side of the road. It overlooks an awe inspiring view of the expansive valley below. Valor stands at its entrance and can see the surrounding countryside for miles. The view above is just as breathtaking as the one below. It is a clear-blue-sky of a day as white puffy clouds float across parts of the atmosphere. Right where the rest stop is, the clouds are so low that it looks like you could reach out and touch them.

As Valor stands at the entrance to the rest area, a caravan of three cars drive past him and slows to a stop. The doors of all three vehicles burst open as family and friends jump out in a flurry of excited conversation and stretching. In a hurry, the man leading the pack leaves his car running as he exits. Due to the car resting on a slight incline—enough to keep it from moving forward—he absentmindedly neglects to put his vehicle in 'Park.' As he jumps out, his 12 year old son, jumps from the back seat into the front to play with the steering wheel. The rest of the group takes in the amazing view of the expansive countryside.

A moment later, the son mashes the gas pedal to the floor and with a roar, the car lurches forward out of the rest area! That sudden, forceful movement causes an already misplaced water bottle to fall from the arm rest to the floor. Before anyone can react, the car begins rolling down the hill. Valor watches as the group members scream while the father runs after the car, yelling, "Tommy! Hit the brakes!" But he can't catch up, loses his balance and takes a tumble! The son slams his feet on the brake pedal, but it doesn't move! The fallen water bottle is wedged tightly between it and the floorboard.

Valor, seeing this terrible turn of events, scans the mountainside highway down to the bottom. Vehicles pepper the road, but a traffic jam rests firmly at the end!

"Father!" Valor prays. "If that car doesn't stop before it reaches the bottom—"

The reply to his spirit comes before he finishes his sentence.

"FLY!"

As the group members jump into their remaining cars to give chase, Valor sprints perpendicular to the mountainside—towards the edge of the cliff—and without thought for his own safety launches himself up and over the metal guardrails into the air! His body arcs through space with his arms outstretched like an expert diver. He plummets under the pull of gravity for a few seconds and then, amazingly, arcs upward and banks to the left towards the mountain like a falcon on the hunt! His eyes train on the swerving car as it descends the steep roadway with increasing speed.

Tommy screams—knowing he can't stop the car! He can barely keep the car on the road as he swerves to avoid other vehicles! The two cars from the caravan quickly approach from behind, but they can't get next to him due to his wild side-to-side swerving! Time is quickly running out! The traffic backup at the bottom of the roadway fast approaches. Without some kind of miracle, the car will crash and the boy will most likely die.

"Look!" The mother points out her passenger side window. "Up in the sky!"

Everyone watches as Valor dives from the air like a fighter jet. In an instant he's in between the three vehicles, banks hard to the right and overtakes the out-of-control car. He flares his cape like a parachute, slowing himself down enough to land on top of the car while grabbing both sides of the roof. The boy glances up at the open sun roof as Valor sticks his head inside and shouts.

"Pull the emergency brake lever by your right leg!"

The boy looks down, sees the lever and yanks it up as hard as he can! The tires lock with a screech as large plumes of smoke trail behind them. The group watches as the car slows in an awkward skid.

"Oh, thank God," the father yells as everyone shouts in celebration!

Just then, the car hits a sharp dip in the road. In response, the boy turns the steering wheel hard as the car bounces, catches the pavement, spins and launches uncontrollably toward the guardrails! Family and friends scream, watching helplessly as the car—in an instant—careens off the roadway, crumbles the railing like aluminum foil and rolls over the side embankment! But it stops suddenly before it can fall off the cliff!

All nearby cars screech to a halt as passengers gaze in awe at the sight of Valor grasping the front of the car. His boots are dug deep into the dirt, acting as anchor points for him as he supports the car's weight. The middle of the car sits on the cliff's edge like a seesaw, while its rear dangles in the open air.

Valor yells to the boy as he grips the car's fender like a vice. "Do not move!" His muscles flex as he prays and pulls with all of his might. The bottom of the car screeches against the ground as Valor, step-by-step, pulls it back onto the roadway. Once the car is completely stabilized, the father rushes to the driver side door, yanks it open and retrieves his son—who practically jumps into his father's arms.

"Dad!"

"Tommy," the father replies as he hugs his son tightly. "I thought I lost you!"

They embrace for several long moments as family, friends and bystanders crowd around them.

"Are you alright?"

"Yes."

"Let me look at you."

"I'm sorry, Dad!"

"It wasn't your fault, Son. *I'm* sorry. I got out in such a hurry, I forgot to put the car in Park."

"Did you see the superhero?" Tommy smiles widely.

"I did," the father laughs.

"That was the guy from the news, right?"

"Yes. If it wasn't for him—" He turns around and scans the crowd, but doesn't see him anywhere. "Where'd he go?"

Everyone turns and looks up and down the mountainside highway. But he is gone.

"I don't know where he went," one of the family members exclaim with glee, "But, I caught the whole thing on my phone!"

People gather around him to see the footage.

"We're going to be rich!"

They all just look at each other in amazement, unsure of what to say.

"Money or no money," the father concludes, "I just thank God he was here."

28: Speak My Word

DAY 81 — Colorado

In the middle of the night, near the Rocky Mountains… Daniel has found a comfortable spot in a field to lay down to rest. Exhausted, it only takes a minute before he is soundly asleep—in his full suit.

V

"Come. Follow Me…" The Voice echoes… causing Daniel to open his eyes. A man stands in front of him, wearing a glorious white robe that barely touches the ground, with a robust golden sash across his torso. His bronze feet are visible and just at the point where they meet His ankles, two scars are evident. His hands radiate with power as two scars are visible at the point where his palms and wrists join together. His eyes blaze with fire, yet His kindness is evident through them. His face and hair shine like the sun, yet the brilliance is somehow tolerable.

A holy fear, awe and reverence envelopes Daniel at once as he immediately realizes the man's identity. Daniel quickly sits up, retracts his helmet's visor and kneels, while lowering his head to the ground. "My Lord, Jesus!"

The Lord steps forward and places His strong right hand on Daniel's shoulder. *"Sit up My child."* Daniel sits up and glances at his Lord's hand, noticing the wound made by the nail which had pierced His flesh. Even it—a cause of great pain—emanates unsurpassed glory! *"These scars will be an eternal reminder of the price I paid for all who belong to Me."* Daniel lifts his head and gazes into the face of his Savior. With an incomparable smile Jesus speaks once more: *"Your uniform represents the armor I give to all My children. Yet, you lack weapons for the coming battle. Follow Me… and you will learn how to walk in the strength of My mighty power."*

Jesus turns and begins walking. Daniel stands to his feet and just as suddenly the entire environment changes! The field has become an expansive road which stretches into the distance. The more they walk, the further away Jesus gets. Daniel quickens his pace, but the distance between them does not lessen.

Weeds sprout on the path, quickly becoming a large barrier between them, which Daniel cannot pass.

"Jesus," Daniel calls out as he can barely see through the growing barrier, "Wait!"

But Jesus keeps walking. *"I have given you My Word,"* He replies. *"You must follow Me."*

The weeds continue to spread, as some spiral around him, twisting and turning their way up his legs eventually restraining his entire body. Daniel tries to break free, but he has no added strength. A sinister fear grips his heart as the weeds cover his face.

These weeds have a mind of their own, Daniel thinks fearfully as a voice speaks in his tenor—as if from his own heart. "I will never get free from these weeds!"

Daniel agrees with the voice that he believes to be his own. But then another voice speaks with bold authority. *"You have been given My Word!"*

Fear grips even tighter as the weeds squeeze and restrict to the point of cutting into his skin. He prays within his mind, "Lord, help me!" Words flood his soul as he is compelled to repeat them in his thoughts: *God has not given me a spirit of fear, but of power, love and a sound mind.*

As soon as he thinks this thought, the weeds restricting his mouth ease their tension *ever-so-slightly*. He repeats the words again in his mind with a bit more conviction. The weeds over his entire body suddenly constrict, but the ones around his mouth ease up even more—now drooping slightly from his lips. Daniel musters up increased conviction and repeats the words—this time verbally from his lips.

"God has not given me a spirit of fear, but of power, love and a sound mind!"

A burst of light explodes from his mouth—slicing through the weeds around his lips! He turns his head down towards his right hand—the light still emanating from his mouth slices through the weeds which bound his hand. He looks to his left and the same happens for his other hand!

Daniel utters the verse once more with even greater conviction than before!

"God has not given me a spirit of fear, but of power, love and a sound mind!!!"

The light intensifies to blinding levels as a high-pitched hum radiates from its brilliance! Daniel, compelled, grabs hold of the shaft of light which flows from his mouth and it becomes a shining sword in his hands! The voice of the Holy Spirit declares from within him:

"The Sword of the Spirit, which is the Word of God!"

In an instant, Daniel quotes the verse with ever-increasing faith as he slices at every weed in sight! Within moments he is free from the claw-like grasp of the weeds! A few moments later, he has cut his way through the barrier of weeds which prevented him from following on the path Jesus had laid out before him.

A lesson was learned... the Word of God was not just for *comfort*, not just for *guidance*, not just for *sustenance*, but it was also a *weapon* which could slice through the restrictive lies of the enemy! Daniel raises the sword to this lips and it transforms back into a shaft of light which disappears into his open mouth.

Still, the journey was not over. Even with this being some kind of dream or vision, Daniel felt *tired*... exhausted. He strains to scan the distance for any sight of his Lord. But, he sees no sign of Jesus.

The Holy Spirit speaks, reverberating from within Daniel's belly and echoes up through his chest: ***"You have My Word."***

This prompts him to take a few steps forward, but his feet feels like they are pressing through sludge. Words flood his soul once more. He wastes no time in repeating them out loud as he stands still. "I can do all things through Christ who strengthens me." As soon as the words leave his lips he realizes what God had already demonstrated—*everything* God has *called* him to do, He would also *empower* him to do.

"Yes, Lord..." Daniel utters with a tired smile. "I believe Your Word." He takes several more steps... this time the Presence of the Holy Spirit rises up within him like a river swelling in his belly and flowing down to his feet. With each step, strength quickens his body. He then bolts up the road like a race horse released from the starting gates of the Kentucky Derby!

Somehow, he was running as fast as the wind would propel him! A radiant dot in the distance soon took on human form as it became apparent that Jesus was once again in sight! Minutes later, Daniel was several meters behind Jesus. Overjoyed, he slowed his pace to rest a moment. At once the distance between them began to spread!

"Lord! Please wait!"

"Follow Me," was the only reply as Jesus continued His walk.

Just then, a flaming arrow struck the ground right in front of Daniel's foot. He looks in the direction from where it came, but sees no one. The air buzzes as another flaming arrow just misses his head—the heat from the flame easily felt. Again, he searches, but sees no one. A third arrow streaks towards him! He barely dodges it! Now, he begins to run as several more flaming arrows barrel through the sky towards his position! He runs off the road and hides behind a large boulder that rests among the brown, dying grass. The arrows ricochet off of the rock—the sounds of their impact is deafening!

"Jesus! Help me!" Daniel panics as he looks around wildly.

"Return to the path," the Holy Spirit speaks.

"But the arrows!" Daniel counters. "I can't see the enemy!"

"You have My Word. You must return to the path."

Daniel quiets his thoughts and focuses his mind on God's Word. As he does, the thundering impacts of the flaming arrows diminishes as Ephesians 6:16 rises up within his spirit. Immediately, he speaks: "In addition to all this, take up the shield of faith, with which you can extinguish all the flaming arrows of the evil one."

Light emanates from his mouth once more! This time, as he raises his hand to grab it, the light wraps itself around Daniel's arm! In an instant, it expands and forms a brilliant shield!

The Holy Spirit speaks: *"The Shield of Faith!"*

Faith bursts forth in Daniel's heart! Just as quickly he engages his visor, jumps to his feet and is back on the path—deflecting the flaming arrows as he runs ahead! With each arrow deflected, his confidence rises! But then it seems like the sky is on fire! He looks up and sees flaming arrows—hundreds of them—all carving their way through the open expanse, streaking towards him!

"Jesus! Help!" Daniel cries out. "My shield isn't big enough!"

The reply is immediate: ***"You have My Word."***

Psalm 18:2 rises up within him. He kneels and shouts as the arrows streak down from the sky. "The Lord is my rock, my fortress and my deliverer; my God is my rock, in whom I take refuge, my shield and the horn of my salvation, my stronghold."

Daniel raises his shield carrying arm above his head. A split second before the flaming arrows hit, his shield bursts forth in radiant brilliance as its light expands around him and forms a dome! Hundreds of flaming arrows explode on impact, but do not penetrate! After a few intense moments, the barrage ends just as quickly as it began. Daniel slowly stands to his feet as the light retracts back to the shield on his arm. Daniel scans the horizon and sees no more dangerous projectiles. He raises his arm and looks at his shield. It disappears in a flash of light.

Just then, a brick wall—the width of the road—bursts through the ground in front of him! It was at least two feet thick, rose into the air a good thirty feet, and expanded around him! Once completely encircling him, weeds rapidly spread across its hard, thick surface—as if to reinforce the structure.

Fear tried to grip his heart once more, but Daniel was still full of faith. He retracts his visor and immediately counters fear with Scripture: "God has not given me the spirit of fear, but of power, love and a sound mind!" His mouth sets ablaze with heavenly glory as the sword of the Spirit appeared once more. Daniel firmly gripped its handle with two hands, shot at the wall with great speed, raised the sword high into the air and brought it down upon the wall with all his might!

A bright hail of sparks trailed the path carved by the sword as it pressed hard against the blockage. As the sparks dissipated and Daniel stared, shock smothered his face. The wall was scarred but unmoved. The weeds in the path of the sword were cut, but every brick was firmly intact. Several more assaults yielded the same results. More scratches... more severed weeds... but the wall had not budged one iota! He was still trapped in this large-yet-claustrophobic enclosure.

He's dumbfounded. His faith began to diminish and depression seized upon his mind like the claws of a vulture seizing its prey. A voice—mimicking his own tone and nuance—speaks: "I am trapped... The Word of God is not enough." Daniel lowers his sword and presses his hand against the wall as the voice speaks once more. *"It's impenetrable."* He sighs and turns his back—now leaning against the wall. A moment later he slumps to the ground, dropping his sword by his side and agrees with the statement. Now, he utters the words himself as despair rises within his soul. "It's impenetrable. I'm trapped." His sword dematerializes into minuscule particles of light. As it does, the weeds nearest to him slowly slither their way onto his body and encircle him.

Just then, his words are met by the whisper of the Holy Spirit. ***"I have given you My Word."*** Daniel thinks for a moment as despondency begins to set in. "But Lord, I used the Sword of Your Spirit and it didn't bring down the wall."

The other voice speaks again in his mind, the one which counterfeits his own. *"Yes... God's Word does not work!"*

The lie is immediately countered by the whisper of the Holy Spirit: ***"I have given you My Word."***

Daniel blinks as a realization dawns on him. It is then that he notices the weeds slowly advancing up his arms and legs. He quickly pulls them off as he scrambles to his feet! Once free, he steps back from the scarred brick wall and stares at it intently.

"God's Word does not work!" shouts through his mind with an intense desperation. The depression weighs heavily on him as if three times the gravity was pulling down on his whole body! But by then, it was too late. Even though Daniel was staring at the brick enclosure, his thoughts had shifted from the wall... to seeing Jesus on the other side of the wall.

"I *must* follow Jesus..." Daniel whispers to himself as he closes his eyes and takes authority over every thought which exalts itself above the knowledge of God. "I must *get through* this wall." He then brings each lie under the Lordship of Jesus Christ. "Lord," he prays. "You have given me Your Word. So, *which Scripture* should I apply to *this* situation? Which aspect of your Word should I use *now*, if not the sword?"

A Scripture verse is whispered throughout his being—Jeremiah 23:29. As soon as he discerns it, the words are uttered from his mouth without a shred of doubt: "Is not My Word like fire," declares the LORD, "and like a hammer that breaks a rock in pieces?"

Light emanates once more from Daniel's mouth—its blade-like appearance evident. Daniel takes hold of the shaft. It transforms once more into a sword, but the pommel at the end of the grip grows into the head of a hammer as the blade morphs into a long handle! As Daniel held the now sizable hammer in his hands it glowed with irradiated brilliance and crackled with the glorious fire of heaven. The voice of the Holy Spirit declared within him:

"The Fire Hammer of God's Word which shatters the rocks!"

A boldness raged from within Daniel's being—*the Holy Spirit's work no doubt*—as he raised the glorified hammer and brought it down firmly against the seemingly impregnable wall while declaring the Scripture once more! And when he cried out, it was as if all of heaven sounded with him!

"Is not My Word like fire," declares the LORD, "and like a hammer that breaks a rock in pieces?"

Right at the point where the hammer struck the wall, it was as if a star had burst forth: exploding the bricks and weeds into a million different shards! The sound of the impact was deafening... As the smoke cleared, a gaping hole—large enough to walk through—awaited him. The hammer's long handle morphs back into a sword's blade.

Once Daniel walked through to the other side, he found Jesus standing there, gazing at him with a heavenly pleasure. Daniel drops to his knees once more, holding his hammer-sword as the shield now glimmers on his forearm. With an approving nod, Jesus utters, **"Well done. Remember these lessons. No matter the opposition, you must continue to follow Me."** He then turned and began walking once more. Daniel took three steps after Him and then... woke up.

V

He was still in the field where he had fallen asleep. However, the sun now crested over the horizon. A new day had begun and with it came new mercies from the Lord. Physically, Daniel's body was fully rested. Spiritually, his soul was too. Whatever would come his way on this day and any other, he knew the LORD had given him everything he needed. He had equipped him with His Presence and with His Word.

Daniel pondered all the Lord had taught him that night and realized:

"The enemy must be preparing to oppose me in some major way. But God is preparing me for victory. I must keep my eyes on Jesus and His Word must remain in my mouth. I cannot make any agreements with the enemy."

29: Not Only Flesh and Blood

DAY 83 — Colorado

In the dead of night, the forest surrounds Valor as he ventures deep into its interior. Thankfully, his uniform keeps him from scratches that would have been caused by low hanging tree branches. Acres upon acres of land seem untouched by a human presence. There appear to be no structures of any kind anywhere. This... expedition seems to be a detour in a direction far from any roadway. Yet, he follows the leading of the Holy Spirit, even if he does not fully understand *why* the Lord is leading him in this direction. He stops for a moment and opens his visor to breathe in the crisp air.

"Even with the wisdom of Solomon," Daniel chuckles to the Lord, "You still only tell me what I need to know, at the moment when I should know it."

As he scans the area, a far away flicker through the distant trees catches his attention. He slowly kneels and listens intently for any evidence that he's not alone. That's when he hears a faint... repetitive sound. It's low. *Grounded.* Somehow, connected to the earth. He takes a few more steps forward—quietly. The sound becomes clearer. It is a low drone... *a chant* of some kind. He can't make out the words, but he can *sense evil* in the distance.

With each additional step, it seems like the trees become more crooked—almost as if they themselves have been cursed by some unseen force. He takes notice of them for a moment, realizing for the past several meters the foliage has decreased significantly. Now, through theses charred-like trees, he sees a clearing where there sits a lone structure resembling an old uninhabited barn. It's black like charcoal. Tattered. Weathered. Weeds run everywhere, surrounding it... strangling it.

At once, Daniel recalls his recent vision from the Lord. He walks with caution while trailing the tree line. Soon, he is near enough to the barn to hear, while still remaining under cover. The chant continues:

"Masters of darkness... Keepers of death... We summon you. The true gods of this world, we summon you. Powers of the air, we summon you. Speak to us now..."

The chant repeats several more times and then... silence. Daniel repositions himself to have a clear line of sight through a slanted window. Within the barn he can make out shadows—hooded persons—perhaps thirteen in all. A word of knowledge flashes through his spirit: *Witches and Warlocks*. Red candles array the interior. A curdled cry reveals an animal sacrifice in progress.

"Father," Daniel whispers a prayer, "open my eyes so I may see." In an instant, the veil of reality is pulled back, revealing the unseen realm.

Daniel shudders at the sight *right in front* of his face. Two dark reddish-purple colored eyes stare directly at him—no more than a foot away. A black void surrounds the eyes in the form of some hideous monster-like spirit. Its two orbs radiate like black lights and dart back and forth from right to left, up and down. The evil spirit seethes with malevolent intent as its chest heaves in and out. Daniel holds his breath while not moving at all. Once again, it looks directly at him—yet somehow—*through* him. Then the evil spirit turns its attention elsewhere.

"It... can't... *see me...*" Daniel surmises as he looks around.

Dark spirits surround the barn, with more descending in the distance. He is surrounded by them on every side. Hundreds of them... perhaps a thousand or more. He can make out forms and shapes, even slight facial expressions and eye sockets of deep purple, bloody red and sour yellow. An organized chaos fills the air. Nearby demons turn in agitation and look in his direction, but do not respond as they return their gaze to the barn. That is when Daniel notices some kind of covering arrayed over him—like a supernatural invisibility cloak.

The Lord is keeping me hidden from the enemy, he thinks to himself.

Suddenly, the dark spirits come to attention as a massive malignant presence rises from the earth into the barn. A moment later, someone speaks under the influence of this dreadful shadowy presence.

"Our enemy remains under guard by the host of heaven. The time for a direct attack in this physical realm is not yet. His whereabouts are unknown, but you have his name. Whatever his mission, he must not be allowed to complete it. Too many have been lost. More numbers are needed. Band together in agreement. Commence with your assault through the astral plane. Command curses to swallow him whole!"

In an instant, most of the dark spirits vanish, leaving only thirteen left—one for every witch and warlock inside.

"Daniel Davidson must die," they all ring out in unison. "Daniel Davidson must die!"

In a flash, the veil over the unseen realm is replaced. Reality looks normal again. Daniel can't believe what he just saw and heard. He knew there would be opposition, but he didn't figure it to be so... *organized.*

A Scripture passage floods his soul: *"For our struggle is not against flesh and blood, but against the rulers, against the authorities, against the powers of this dark world and against the spiritual forces of evil in the heavenly realms. Therefore put on the full armor of God, so that when the day of evil comes, you may be able to stand your ground, and after you have done everything, to stand."*

Daniel backs away from the barn, retraces his steps through the forest and reemerges on the roadway. His mind is in overdrive, thoughts rushing through a mile a minute. But as he walks, he prays. "Father, You wanted me to see this for a reason. Thank you for keeping me hidden from the enemy in Your secret place, under Your shadow. You are the Almighty. Please continue to prepare me for whatever battles I must face. And when the enemy comes in like a flood, raise up a standard against them!"

Even though he is tired, Daniel continues to walk through the night. All he wants to do is get as far away from that barn as he can.

V

A few hours later… around 3:00am.

Daniel has found a quiet spot in an abandoned warehouse just off of the highway. He scouted the building and determined it was completely empty of human life. However, rodents were another thing altogether. Good thing his suit fully encases him. It doesn't take long for him to fall into a deep sleep in a corner behind a collection of large crates. Twenty minutes have passed, but his body and mind grow restless. He is dreaming again…

V

Lightning flashes across the night sky—followed by rolling thunderclaps. Cold rain falls in thick sheets. The continuous pounding of the watery barrage sounds like a freight train roaring past on all sides. Daniel stands with two others—both caucasian: a man with sandy blond hair and a woman with brown hair hanging down to the middle of her back. Their white clothing is drenched as they stand in the middle of a long suburban street, unsure of where to seek shelter from this unusually fierce storm. The downpour is so thick and unrelenting, the three find it hard to see and can barely catch their breath without inhaling large amounts of water.

All houses are dark, as if no one is home. All except one: the house with the eerily lit red-tinted windows. This house looks like an amalgamation of every haunted house seen in every horror film: the high rising uneven steps, the dark peeling paint, the overgrown grass… Even so, Daniel and the two others have nowhere else to go. So, they run to the house and up its high steps to the large wrap-around porch to escape the soaking rain. Though huddled together and shivering, they are pleased to be free from the assault which sought to drown them from above. However, high winds suddenly kick up and whip through the neighborhood, buffeting everything in their path—including the trio. The wind causes the water to fall diagonally—pelting them. It also sends debris from the neighborhood careening through the air, forcing the trio to enter the house for further shelter from the raging storm.

They turn the door knob. The door opens with a loud screech as it follows its arced path on rusted hinges, while scraping the wooden floor. The three enter with caution and close the screeching door behind them with a thud. Inside, they make their way through the foyer and enter an expansive area which seems to be some kind of upper level wrap-around balcony. They look over the banister, down to the lower level and witness a terrifying sight!

A host of hooded witches and warlocks—thirteen in all—stand together, hunched over ancient books and smoking cauldrons. Red glowing candles are all ablaze throughout the lower level and a large pentagram has been drawn on the floor in both chalk and blood.

Numerous animal sacrifices have been done, evidenced by multiple dismembered parts strewn across a makeshift altar. At once, in a singular smooth motion, all dark hoods crane their necks upward at the three uninvited guests. To the trio's dismay, faces are not seen beneath the hoods. Rather, only an abyss of gross darkness meets their stares. Each witch and warlock scream out "intruders" in unknown tongues. Immediately, hideous spirits of all kinds burst forth through the floor, walls and ceiling!

The trio runs back to the front door as the demons pursue them! The humans clad in dark hooded robes chant their spells and curses with a focused fervor! The trio tries to force the front door open, but it doesn't budge. Somehow it is restricted. The man and woman split from Daniel and run to the far side of the balcony, splitting again in two different directions.

Daniel watches as a demon closes in on the woman. She reaches into her pocket, pulls out a bottle of holy water and splashes it in the air at the demon. The demonic spirit moves effortlessly through the spray and slashes her face with its sharp claws! She is dead before her body hits the floor.

Daniel watches as another demon comes for the man, who immediately pulls a crucifix out from under his shirt. He holds it up with a shaky arm as the demon stops and gazes at it in curiosity before swatting the crucifix out of the man's hand. The dark spirit then seizes the man by his throat and mauls him to death with its fanged teeth.

Suddenly, Daniel finds himself on the lower level, surrounded on all sides by witches, warlocks and demons. With nowhere to go and in imminent danger, he does the only thing he *can* do. He drops to his knees and calls on the Name that is above every name. As the swarm of evil spirits swoop in for what looks like a sure kill, Daniel shouts:

"JESUS! HELP ME!"

In an instant, a shaft of light penetrates the ceiling and bursts forth around him like a shield! The demons crash into the glorious barrier —the multiple impacts sounding like a series of mini explosions.

"I plead the blood of Jesus!" Daniel repeats over and over again as his hands are clasped together and his eyes are closed tightly in intense prayer.

Demons of every size and shape claw and scrape with mighty blows—trying to break through the shaft of light. But the glorious shield holds! Even though Daniel is firmly protected, he can feel a small degree of the concussive force from each strike as the chanting shrills of the demons' human handlers fill the house with greater intensity! They attempt to drown out Daniel's cry, trying to force his mind into a state of confusion—hoping that once he is confused, the shield of light would no longer be maintained and they could break through to consume their adversary. But Daniel, keeps his eyes shut—not wanting to be swayed by the assault around him—and focuses his mind and heart on Jesus!

"I plead the blood of Jesus! I plead the blood of Jesus!! I plead the blood of Jesus!!!"

The shaft of light increases in blinding intensity as the ebb and flow of immense heavenly power releases throughout the entire room. Nothing else is seen but the glory of God... Nothing else is heard except the power of His glory. And then... silence. A moment passes as the glorious light which surrounded Daniel dissipates. He now finds himself standing in an empty room. The enemy—human and demonic—vanquished.

The invisible Presence of the glory of the Lord is still firmly evident.

V

Daniel awakens from the dream with a start! He looks around wildly at the dark shadows of the warehouse and notices he is still safe behind the crates. He winces in pain as he grabs various parts of his body. The uncomfortable sensation is as if he had been physically assaulted by sharp talons. He quickly raises his helmet's visor so he can breathe easier.

"That dream," he utters through deep breaths, "That was a *real* demonic attack… Just like what the demon said in the woods. It wasn't a direct physical assault, but it took place in *both* realms: spiritual *and* physical."

Daniel turns over and kneels behind the crates to pray. His entire body is sore and tired, but the only thing which matters now is giving thanks to God for His powerful intervention.

"Thank you Lord for preserving me! Only You have the power to defeat all attacks of the enemy. Thank you for giving me Your Word. You watch over Your Word to perform it."

30: A Special Guest

DAY 85 — Colorado

It's Thursday afternoon: almost the end of a long week of school. A twelve year old boy runs through the streets of his city. His book bag bounces repeatedly as he grows more tired by the second. But he can't stop running or else he's dead. Half a block behind him are six boys in hot pursuit! Their ages are 14-16, with the 16 year old leading the charge. And they are closing in fast!

"Come back here *Virus*!"

Cyrus had learned to run faster than all the boys his age. Being bullied gave him good motivation. Even those boys a few years older had a hard time keeping up with him. Since it was never a fair fight, he resorted to studying the best olympic track stars to hone his skills. Most of his time at home was spent analyzing their YouTube videos and exercising. When he was outside alone, he would repeatedly put their techniques into action. Now, once again, he was running for his life... and unfortunately, running out of steam.

Cyrus turned down a side alley, hoping to find a shortcut, but instead he ran right into Valor—literally. The impact causes Cyrus to fall backwards to the ground. Landing hard on his backpack, he stares up at the red, gold and blue figure standing before him. His eyes widen with awe as a big smile bursts across his face.

"It's you!" he exclaims through heaving and sporadic breaths as Valor extends his hand and quickly helps Cyrus to his feet. Cyrus grabs his arms. "You've got to help me, please! These guys are chasing me!"

Just then, the six boys turn the corner and abruptly stop in their tracks.

Cyrus scoots around Valor, peeking out from behind him.

"Is there a problem here," Valor inquires firmly.

The six boys stare at him, then at each other and then back at him. One of them speaks.

"Nah, there's no problem. We were just playing tag with our friend, Virus."

"My *name* is Cyrus," Cyrus yells from behind Valor.

"Well, it seems he doesn't want to *play* anymore," Valor adds. "I strongly suggest you boys go home, *now*."

The boys slowly retreat, unsure of what to make of the situation.

"See you at school *tomorrow*, Cy-Rus." They cackle as they run back the way they came.

Cyrus leans against the wall and breathes a sigh of relief.

"I am *so glad* I ran into you! You saved my life!"

"I'm glad to help," Daniel raises his visor. "I'm actually on my way to a church that shouldn't be too far from here. But I think I'm lost. Do you know where Christ's Church is?"

"That's my church," Cyrus smiles. "It's only four blocks from here."

"Well, I'm supposed to meet with the pastor and some members in just over an hour. I'll be visiting your church for the next few days."

"*You're* the special surprise guest?" Cyrus shouts his question with jubilation. "If so, then you're supposed to be staying at *my* house! My dad is the pastor!"

"Really?"

"Sure! Come on! I'll take you to the church. But, can you promise me one thing?"

"What's that?"

"Don't tell my dad what just happened."

V

An hour and a half later…

Daniel sits in the pastor's office. His helmet and gloves are off. A half drunken glass of orange juice rests on the table in front of him. Pastor Chris Lemke is settled in a chair across from him, having just listened to Daniel's account of his journey so far.

"Now that is an *amazing* story of God's faithfulness to you. I can definitely see why the enemy would want to stop you. Still, darkness cannot win! Jesus has already won the victory for us."

"Amen to that," Daniel agrees. "Jesus is worthy to be praised, no matter what we go through."

"Yes, He is. I'm glad we at Christ's Church can be a part of what God is doing to impact the people of this nation through you."

"I really appreciate your willingness to help me."

"Well, when your pastor called and asked for our help, I couldn't say no." He chuckles. "Pastor Mike and I met in seminary over 15 years ago: the first day we came on campus. He helped me and my wife move our furniture into our apartment. As you may know, he used to be a professional bodybuilder before he came to the Lord. So, his muscles were sure useful that day."

Both Daniel and Pastor Chris laugh.

"Anyway," Pastor Chris continues, "we became fast friends and grew into genuine brothers over the years. You know, most people have a lot of associates, but very few friends. And of their friends, only a small handful are like family. And of the handful, only one or two will sacrifice everything to help you."

Daniel nods his head in quiet agreement.

"You told me *your* story, so it's only fitting that I tell you why I agreed to help." Pastor Chris clears his throat and continues a bit slowly this time, "A few years back... my wife Kathy was diagnosed with cancer. For a time, it was bad. And the doctors said she only had months to live. So, Kathy and I started making plans for her funeral. We knew God always has the last word, but everything seemed to point to us having to *accept* what was happening.

"Here I was trying to lead my church and I was crumbling. I was just... *barely* holding it together. I would spend all my time at the hospital with Kathy and some members were helping to take care of our two kids. Cyrus you met. He has a younger sister named Claudette. She's 10 years old.

"Anyway... one day I'm at my wits end. I can't take it anymore. It was one of those *rare occasions* where I was home by myself. I collapsed on the living room floor. I was a mess... crying out to the Lord, snot nose and everything. I felt like He had abandoned us... me... *my wife*... I knew His promise to every believer that He would never leave nor forsake us, but in that moment, it sure felt like I was all alone... And then... there came a knock at the door.

"Somehow, I pulled myself together, wiped my messy face with my shirt, found the strength to stand up and stumbled my way over to the door. As I passed the mirror, I could see that my eyes were bloodshot. I knew, once I opened that door, there was no way I was going to be able to hide what I was going through. I... grabbed the door knob and hesitated... Then the knock came again. And when I turned the knob and pulled opened the door—guess who was standing there..."

"Pastor Mike?" Daniel inquires.

"All six foot four inches of him," Pastor Chris laughs as he wipes tears from his eyes. "Two hundred and twenty-five pounds of pure muscle. That was six years ago and it still seems like it was yesterday... His wife, Carol stepped out from behind him. I was in shock. There they were, unannounced... I crumbled into his arms and sobbed like a baby. He picked me up and carried me into my own house. When he did, I could feel, not only his presence, but even more so, the Presence of Jesus was holding me, *consoling* me. It was *wonderful*...

"Anyway, he shared with me that earlier in the week, while he and Carol were in prayer, the Lord told them to drop everything and come out here. They grabbed their things, made some calls and were on the road three hours later. They drove two days straight to get to us. And they stayed with us for four weeks.

"That first night, we went to the hospital to see Kathy. She wasn't looking good at all. She had been in so much pain that the painkillers weren't helping. Mike and Carol prayed for her. As they did, you could *feel* God's palpable Presence descend into the room. After they finished praying, the pain *immediately* subsided enough for Kathy to get a good night's sleep. Carol stayed at the hospital with Kathy, which freed me up to get myself together.

"Mike and I met with our board of elders and worked out a 4 week sabbatical for me so I could focus on taking care of my family. Mike took my place in the pulpit and organized the church to make sure we had around-the-clock coverage for everything we needed: food, laundry, errands, you name it. There were already members praying for us, but Mike organized a 24/7 prayer vigil. For four weeks, the Lord poured into him and Carol and they poured into our congregation.

"By the end of the first week, Kathy was sleeping better, although her cancer prognosis hadn't changed. By the end of the second week, her skin color had started to return to normal. By the third week, the doctors did a scan which showed her tumor had shrunk significantly. By the fourth week, she was beginning to eat again. On the day Mike and Carol left, Kathy was able to stand up in her hospital room and hug them and thank them for coming. By the time they drove home—which took them four days because they stopped along the way to rest—Kathy's cancer was in remission and she was sent home.

"And if this didn't happen *to me*, I might not believe it... I called Mike and Carol, when we arrived in our driveway and were about to walk inside our house. Can you guess where they were?"

"In their driveway," Daniel responds, "about to walk into *their* house."

"Yes!" Pastor Chris shouts as he jumps up from his chair. "I kept thinking about Jesus showing up on the fourth day to raise Lazarus! And here it was the fourth day from the time they left and my wife was back home!"

"Praise the Lord!" Daniel says.

"Yes, He is worthy to be praised!" Pastor Chris agrees. "And I wish I had the words to adequately praise Him like He most certainly deserves!"

Pastor Chris grows quiet.

"What God used Mike and Carol to do... it not only helped me and my wife... it helped the *entire* church in more ways than I have time to share right now. So, when Mike called and asked me to help with *this* mission, even though he couldn't tell me the specifics no matter how hard I tried to squeeze it out of him, I didn't hesitate. And when I started hearing reports on the news about an unidentified man in red, gold and blue who was making his way across the country, I asked Mike about it. He confirmed that you were the visitor we were to provide for, but he still wouldn't tell me who you were! And when you finally revealed your identity, then Mike was free to spill the beans.

"As you know, God knows everything and He is always working things out for the good of those who love Him. And He is *always*... working on multiple levels at the same time, building line-by-line, precept-by-precept, brick-by-brick. Heart by heart. He never lets *any* situation go to waste."

Daniel nods in agreement. "I have surely found that to be true. Nothing goes to waste in God's kingdom."

"Amen," Pastor Chris concludes as he stands to his feet and looks at a text on his smart watch. "And on that note, let's get you over to the house. My wife is just about finished preparing a good, home-cooked meal for us. And our guest room, which has its own bathroom, is all set so you can get a soothing bath and good night's rest. My son and daughter will no doubt have a million questions, but most of those will have to wait until the morning."

V

45 minutes later...

Daniel sits in a plush rounded papasan wicker chair in the guest room. After taking a few minutes to lay back and relax his body, he sits up and slowly removes his gauntlets and gloves. Then he unstraps his boots and removes them. A broad smile covers his face as he wiggles his toes while rubbing his tired feet. A few minutes later, he has removed his cape, torso armor, belt, and bodysuit. Now, wearing only shorts and a t-shirt, he puts all of his uniform elements on several hangars in the closet. He then goes into the bathroom and runs bath water before closing the bathroom door behind him.

"I don't remember the last time I've had a *good* bath," he thinks out loud. "Thank you Lord."

An hour later he's wearing new clothes which have been provided, and eats a wonderfully prepared meal with Pastor Chris and his family. Shortly after that, he retires to the guest room and is fast asleep within minutes of his head hitting the pillow.

V

The Next Morning...

Daniel exits his guest room and makes his way to the kitchen. A note sits on the table.

"Daniel. We left breakfast warming for you in the oven. I have to run to the office. Kathy went to pick up medicine for Cyrus. He's not feeling well today and is staying home from school. Claudette is at school. We'll see you in a little while. —Pastor Chris"

Daniel opens the oven and is happily overtaken by the sweet aroma of pancakes. A stack of them sits in foil on a plate along with some bacon and biscuits. Just then the Holy Spirit *prompts* him.

"Cyrus..."

Daniel closes the oven, exits the kitchen and walks down the hallway to Cyrus' room. The door is slightly ajar and he can see that Cyrus looks far from sick as he actively presses buttons on his video game remote control. Daniel knocks and Cyrus immediately hides the controller, turns off the television, lies back down in bed and pulls the covers up to his neck. He then forces a counterfeit cough up from his throat.

"...Come...in..." He utters in a raspy voice.

Daniel slowly opens the door with a warm smile and enters the room.

"Hey there," he waves slightly. "I heard you were sick. Just came to check on you."

"...Thanks," Cyrus replies while adding a forced cough for good measure.

Lord, this boy could win an Academy award right now, Daniel prays silently as he chuckles to himself. "That cough sounds pretty bad."

"...It's... hard... to talk," Cyrus winces as he speaks while rubbing his throat.

"You mind if I sit," Daniel asks while pointing to the chair at Cyrus' desk.

Cyrus nods slowly with droopy eyes.

Daniel seats himself and surveys the room. It looks like a typical 12 year old boy's space. A cool looking loft bed. Pictures of superheroes on the wall. Model cars on the shelf, a plane hanging from the ceiling and some action figures on stands. Books and clothes strewn all over the floor. A large flat screen television. A gaming station and a work desk with a lamp, computer and the chair he was now sitting in. He scans the book shelf and sees, along with a host of different reading options, a Bible and some graphic novels of biblical stories.

"So," Daniel breaks the silence, "who's your favorite superhero?"

"Oh, that's easy," Cyrus responds with immediate enthusiasm while quickly sitting up in his bed. "Superman... but the version from the eighties and nineties."

"Why that time period?"

"He was much brighter then. Happier. I'm not a fan of today's version anymore. His suit's too dark. And he seems serious all the time."

"That's a good observation."

"To be honest, I used to like some of the dark anti-hero characters."

"And what happened?"

"Well, my dad would talk with me about them and we'd compare them to Bible characters. He said having special abilities may be cool, but the most important thing is having the kind of character that would make God smile. Then dad shared his own collection of comics from back then. The artwork isn't always as cool, but I do like the stories better."

"Do you think part of the reason you like that version of Superman is because you and your dad were able to connect around him?"

Cyrus thinks for a moment before responding. "Yeah."

"That's nice," Daniel smiles. "So, who's your favorite Bible character?"

"Besides Jesus?"

"Are you asking because you think that's what I want to hear?"

Cyrus smiles. "...*Maybe*."

"Well," Daniel laughs. "You can't go wrong choosing Jesus. He *is* the ultimate hero in any setting. I like to say 'He's heaven's King and humanity's Champion.'"

"Because He sacrificed Himself to save us and conquered death by rising from the dead?"

"*Somebody's* been reading their Bible."

"Well, I *am* a preacher's kid. I do pay attention... sometimes."

"Well said. So, do you know the difference between Superman and Jesus?"

Cyrus thinks for a moment. "Well, the obvious difference is that Jesus is real and Superman isn't."

"You know, you are a pretty smart 12 year old!" Daniel raises his hand for a 'high-five' and Cyrus quickly obliges with a slap. "No matter how much you call out for Superman to help you, he will *never* hear you. But, if you call out to Jesus for help, He not only hears you, but He responds because, like you said, He is *real* and Superman is not."

"Right," Cyrus agrees.

"Now, what's one thing they have in common?"

Cyrus thinks for a moment. "Truth. They both stand for Truth."

"Right," Daniel agrees. "Superman used to stand for 'Truth. Justice. And the American way.' Then DC Comics changed the tagline to be more inclusive of the broader world. Now it's 'Truth. Justice. And a better tomorrow.' But Jesus goes a major step further. He doesn't just *stand* for truth. He says, '*I am the Way, the Truth and the Life.*'"

"So, Jesus is the source of all truth," Cyrus concludes.

"You got it," Daniel smiles. "And as followers of Jesus do you think He wants us to also represent truth?"

Cyrus frowns. "...I think I see where you are going."

"You do?"

"Yes," he says flatly. "What gave me away?"

"You mean, how did I know you weren't sick?"

Cyrus nods his head while crossing his arms.

"Well, I did see you playing video games before I knocked on the door. And then, when I asked about your favorite superhero, you broke character and suddenly your raspy voice was fine and you had all the energy of a healthy 12 year old boy!"

"Are you going to tell my dad?"

"Do you know the fifth commandment that God gives in Exodus 20?"

Cyrus huffs slightly. "Honor your father and your mother, so that you may live long in the land the LORD your God is giving you."

Daniel nods in approval. "Perfect. Do you remember how you *connected* with your dad over comic books and Superman?"

"Yeah..."

"Well, we already agreed that those characters aren't real, right?"

"Yeah."

"You know what *is* real?"

"What?"

"The fact that both of your parents love you. They would want to know if you acted like you were sick so you didn't have to go to school and deal with those bullies."

Cyrus doesn't speak and Daniel lets him sit in silence for as long as is needed for his words to sink in.

"My mom and dad… They've been through a lot with my mom's sickness," Cyrus' eyes moisten with tears, "I just don't want them to have to worry about me. I can figure out how to handle these bullies on my own."

Daniel stares at Cyrus with a warm smile and places his hand on his shoulder.

"Spoken like a young man who truly cares about his parents."

"I *do* care about them."

"I know. And your words are admirable. Heroic even. But there comes a time when even heroes have to learn how to ask for help."

"Well," Cyrus sits up straight with a persistent expression, "you *could* come with me to school and set those bullies straight!"

"I *could* do that," Daniel agrees. "But that would only be a temporary solution. I'm just passing through as I seek to carry out God's mission for my life. So, the bullies might listen to me while I'm around, but once I'm gone… they won't. But do you know who is around every day? *And* do you know who has been given a mission to make sure you are safe and have what you need to be successful in life?"

Cyrus thinks for a few seconds before responding. "My dad?"

"That's right!" Daniel smiles. "Your father and mother. So, one of the best ways you can honor them is by letting them know what is going on in your life. Give them the *opportunity* to help you navigate through these tough moments and not just the fun times. To be honest with you, there are too many stories in the news about kids who never told their parents they were being bullied. For many of them, things didn't end well.

"If you can connect with your dad over comics and listen to him when he teaches the Bible, then you can tell him about these bullies. And then you and your parents can work through this situation together as a family. That's the most *heroic* thing you can do right now. So, am I going to tell your parents? No. They should hear it from you."

"Well, before I tell them, can I ask you some questions?"

"Sure," Daniel smiles.

"So, you have super strength, right? Like how Samson had super strength?"

"Yes."

"What about flight? "I saw you flying on the news to save that kid in a car. How'd you do that? Did God give you the ability to fly, too?"

"No," Daniel smiles. "God gave me the *ingenuity* to figure out how to fly. Actually, He gave my son the idea. My cape is specially designed to allow me to *glide* under certain conditions. Given enough speed and distance in free fall, it fills up with air and takes on the shape of a wing, which generates lift."

"Like a wingsuit that skydivers use," Cyrus exclaims.

"Exactly," Daniel confirms. "But my cape has more surface area, so it generates more lift. My suit also has a harness built into it with anchor points on my belt. Those are connected to my cape with retractable cables, when I need to use it for flight. And my cape has a semi-rigid internal structure which gives me a certain amount of control while in the air."

"Wow! That's cool," Cyrus smiles. "Where can I get one of those?"

"It's not for sale. Mine is the only one in existence."

"And you said your son helped you build it?"

"Yep. He's only a few years older than you."

Just then, the front door unlocks and opens as Chris and Kathy enter the house.

"We're back," Chris yells.

"And I got medicine, chicken soup and ginger ale," his mother adds as they both approach their son's room.

They enter Cyrus' room as Daniel is giving him a handshake and they both nod.

"Hey Kiddo!"

"Hey Dad."

"Daniel," Pastor Chris says. "How'd you sleep?"

"Very well," Daniel smiles. "Your guest bed is *super* comfortable."

"Or," Kathy counters with a smirk, "you were just *really* tired."

"Probably a combination of both," Daniel laughs as he stands to his feet.

"How's the patient?" Kathy asks as she walks over to the bed and feels her son's forehead. "Feels like your fever is gone."

"That's great Kiddo," Pastor Chris smiles. "Glad you are feeling better!" He turns to Daniel. "Did you eat the pancakes? Kathy made them from scratch."

"Haven't yet," Daniel admits, "I saw your note and wanted to check on Cyrus first. Make sure he was okay. I'm going to go eat them now. Meanwhile, Cyrus has something he wants to share with both of you."

Daniel exits the room as Chris and Kathy sit at their son's bedside.

V

Three hours later...

Kathy and Chris slowly exit their son's room with tears in their eyes. They find Daniel sitting in his guest room reading the Bible. They stand in his doorway and knock.

"Daniel..."

"Yeah," he looks up.

"Thank you for talking with our son. We had *no idea* he was being bullied."

Daniel stands and walks over to them. "Many parents don't. I'm just glad I could help."

"And thank you for standing up for him yesterday. We're going to set up a meeting with his guidance counselor and principal."

"You know, you've got a great son. I'll be praying for you all. And I'll be praying for those bullies too."

"As difficult as that is, we will do the same as well *and* pray for their parents."

"And don't worry. God will work this situation out."

V

Saturday evening...

The Christ's Church sizable sanctuary is packed to capacity. Christ Church members, persons from the community, several other area churches and the media are present. Daniel stands at the podium in his full Valor suit. His helmet sits next to him. He scans the standing-room-only crowd.

"I hope... after I leave tonight, that all of you will continue to come to church, because I shouldn't have a bigger audience than Jesus."

Many in the crowd laugh as Daniel smiles.

"I am grateful to our Lord and Savior Jesus Christ for what He has done and is doing not only in my life, but in the life of His Church. And I want to say thank you to Pastor Chris Lemke, his wife Kathy and their children Cyrus and Claudette. They have extended such gracious hospitality towards me while I'm on this journey to fulfill my part in God's mission for the world.

"I am sure you all have heard many things about me in the media. Some things are true. Other things are... incorrect. Yes, God has chosen me to deliver a message to this nation. That *specific* message will be given when I reach San Diego, California. Right now, I want to deliver the message God has for *you*... Those who follow Christ in the context of this church, this community, this city and this state. You see, I am not the only one who has been chosen. God may have picked me for this unique task, but He has picked us *all* to represent Him in the places where He leads us and to the people to whom He has called us.

"Jesus said in John 15:16, *'You did not choose me, but I chose you and appointed you so that you might go and bear fruit—fruit that will last—and so that whatever you ask in my name the Father will give you.'* If we follow Jesus, then He has chosen us to be His witnesses in the earth... in our sphere of influence. Why? Because He wants *each* of us to bear fruit for His kingdom. He wants us to share the gospel of His Kingdom so the lost can be found... and so those who are found can be built up, strengthened and matured in the Faith. We each can know, love and serve the Lord fully in this life and be prepared for when Jesus returns.

"Now is not the time to sit on the sidelines. Now is not the time to be quiet. Now is the time for us to humble ourselves before the Lord and earnestly ask for His Will to be done within and through us. Just like God has equipped me for my unique journey, He will also equip you for the unique journey He has for you. The truth is, whatever God calls us to do will not be possible for us to do on our own.

"The Christian life, from start to finish, is a supernatural existence. God is supernatural. His Word, the Bible is supernatural. Jesus' sacrifice to save us from our sins and redeem us for the Father's glory is supernatural. His resurrection from the dead is supernatural! When we are brought to the point of decision by the Holy Spirit, and we yield our hearts to Christ—*that's* supernatural as well. Being empowered to walk with Jesus on a daily basis is supernatural. Every spiritual gift given to us by the Lord is supernatural. Having a hunger for God's Presence and Word is supernatural. Rightly dividing the Word of truth is supernatural, because the Bible tells us that God's Word must be spiritually discerned. Without this, it is foolishness to the natural mind. Heaven is supernatural. Being with the Lord after death is supernatural. From beginning to end, the genuine Christian walk is entirely supernatural.

"However, this does not mean we are to sit back, put our life on 'cruise control' and do nothing as we wait for God to do everything. God calls us to invest our lives for His glory! He wants us to discover the gifts, skills and talents He's given us. He wants us to develop them. He wants us to deploy them in a spirit of excellence, but not for selfish motives. *Our job* is to yield all that we are—our heart, mind, soul and strength, our skills, talents, gifts, hopes and dreams, our interests, ambitions, fears and insecurities—we are called to surrender all that we are to the Lord. Then allow Him to remove from us what He wants, to add to us what He desires and to purify what He preserves for His purposes.

"The world says, 'you can be whatever you want to be.' But, when God called Jeremiah as a young man He declared: *'Before you were formed in your mother's womb, I knew you and I ordained you to be a prophet to the nations.'* God's plan for Jeremiah was for him to be a prophet. God also has plans for *you and* me. And *His plans* are determined *before* He formed us in our mothers' womb. If we are going to follow Jesus, then we can't be *'whatever'* we want to be or whatever the world tells us to be... *But we can be all that God wants us to be.*

"You see, God is ultimately concerned about building our character. So... to each of you my brothers and sisters in Christ... my church family... The Lord says, *'this is the work of God, that you believe on the One He has sent.'* Let His Holy Spirit rise up within you! Let the rivers of God's living waters flow from within you. Let God use you for His glory and the good of those around you. And if you do, you will hear Jesus say to you on the day when you stand before Him to give an account of your life: *'Well done My good and faithful servant. You were faithful over a few things. Now I will make you ruler over many things. Enter into the joy of your Lord!'*

"In the end, what Jesus declares is what matters most. He is King of Kings and Lord of Lords and every human being will one day stand before Him. So, may He be pleased with you as you let your light shine so that others will see your good works and glorify your Father in heaven!

"Jesus is coming soon! Whether at our last breath when we die, at the rapture of the church, or when He parts the sky and every person on earth sees Him riding on the clouds of heaven. We all need to be *ready* to meet Him. We need to wake up to His Will for our lives and make sure our lamps are filled with oil. His Will for us is that we would *know Him, love Him* and *serve* Him while we still have time. Because, the night will come when no one can work. Thank you for your time. I pray you take what I've said to heart. May God bless you all. In Jesus' Name. Amen."

The sanctuary erupts with applause as Daniel takes his helmet and returns to his seat on the platform. As the clapping dies down, Pastor Chris leads the audience in a time of brief worship and then a closing prayer. It then takes well over an hour for Daniel to interact with everyone as they leave for the night. During this time, many testimonies are shared, hugs are given and pictures taken. Once the last visitor has left, Daniel, Pastor Chris, the pastoral staff and several visiting pastors meet in the executive conference room for a special time of evening prayer.

V

"I appreciate you all remaining for this time of prayer," Pastor Chris smiles as he looks around the conference table. "I am certain that God is using Daniel for His special purposes and I asked Daniel to lead us in a time of seeking God for His guidance and provision for our respective ministries."

Pastor Chris turns things over to Daniel, who stares at each man and woman intently.

"Before we pray," Daniel says rather pensively, "God wants you to know that He desires unity, not only within the walls of your separate church congregations, but also within His collective church. You may all be overseeing distinct ministries, but we are all a part of the same body. And it will take the unifying of the Body of Christ in this area for you to see the kind of outpouring of God's Holy Spirit which He desires to give in this community, city, state, nation and world. The times in which we live and which are coming, will require us to be unified in our collective faith around Jesus. As you know, Ephesians 4 reveals that *this* is what our Heavenly Father desires. Also, in John 17, we see that Jesus desires this as well: that we all would be one as God the Father and Son are one. Only then will the world know that Jesus is truly the Savior and Lord of creation. Is this *your* desire as well?"

The pastors respond with various levels of agreement: some fully and others… are not completely convinced. But the message has been given and all who have heard are now held responsible. Now, all that is needed is God's blessing through prayer.

"Who will lead us?" Daniel asks. Each of the pastors stare at one another. "Don't be shy," he smiles. "You don't have to pray long. Just pray from your heart. We will go around the table. Each of you pray and I will close us out."

Pastor Chris begins their time of prayer. When he finishes, the pastor next to him continues. One by one each prays until the table has been rounded and it is Daniel's turn. While the Holy Spirit indwells each believer in Jesus, He has yet to manifest His Presence, in any significant way, in the midst of these pastors.

With that, Daniel raises his hands and begins to beseech the throne room of heaven. Within seconds the Holy Presence of the LORD begins to manifest in the room. One by one, each pastor becomes acutely aware of their shortcomings before the LORD. His purifying Presence searches their hearts and minds, bringing to bear aspects of their lives which they are to surrender to Him. Minutes pass as they begin to weep, confess and repent. It is then that a shower of the Holy Spirit's love, joy and acceptance washes over each of them.

After a few more minutes, something even greater happens. The glory of the LORD fills the room! Within seconds, the Holy Presence of God immediately becomes so overwhelming that slowly, one by one, each pastor must excuse themselves to the outside hallway. After the last pastor leaves the conference room, they all realize the only one left in the room with the manifested Presence of the LORD... is Daniel.

V

Sunday Morning

Daniel attends Christ's Church's worship service. He comes, not as a guest speaker, but as another child of God sitting within the congregation. No uniform. Plain clothes. No special fanfare. Just worshiping the Lord as part of the body of Christ. And what a wonderful time of worship it is! At the end of worship, Pastor Chris calls Daniel up to the front and leads the congregation in praying for him as he prepares to continue the next leg of his journey out west. After the service ends, Daniel changes into his uniform, says his heartfelt goodbyes to Pastor Chris and his family and is on his way.

31: 15 Minutes of Fame?

DAY 89 — Colorado

As Valor continues on his route, which brings him close to a nearby city, two black Suburban SUVs pull up in front of him. Valor slows to a halt and watches as the doors open. A camera crew quickly disembarks from the second SUV. One cameraman trains his attention on the first vehicle and the other turns his attention towards Valor. A tall, muscular, bouncer-type gentleman exits on the front passenger side of the first vehicle. An earpiece and stern expression are clearly evident. He quickly scans the area before opening the rear passenger door. A moment later, out steps a well-dressed man in sunglasses, wearing a huge toothy grin.

The first cameraman follows his every move, as the man turns in Valor's direction.

"Valor!" He shouts with outstretched arms. "Daniel Davidson... I have been looking all over for you." The man confidently approaches. He extends his right hand while taking off his sunglasses with his left. His nails are manicured and his teeth are perfect. "My name is Michael Cage."

Valor looks at him and then at the camera crew capturing every moment.

"Father?" He prays silently. "What do I do?"

A brief, but intense hesitancy pangs in his spirit as two words whisper: ***"Don't engage."***

At once, Valor begins walking—leaving the man's hand unshaken.

Michael turns and walks fast to keep pace as the camera crew follows.

"Look, I know you don't know me, but I'm a television producer. You've really been making a splash these past couple of months. People love you. Others hate you. And *everybody* is talking about you! That means you are prime real estate! Your superhero handle is the most searched name right now! You're trending number one on all major social media platforms. People are even using Chat GPT4 to try and figure out your next move! You are literally walking in your 15 minutes of fame. And there's nothing that multiplies that time like a reality television show! That's what I want to do for you: give you *your own* tv show. How does that sound to you!"

Valor keeps walking at an even faster pace. Mr. Cage is right in step.

"Why don't you retract that visor of yours so we can look each other in the eye and talk man-to-man."

Valor continues walking without saying a word.

"Or..." Mr. Cage continues as he puts his sunglasses back on. "we can just keep things like they are. I get it. You're the strong, silent type." He continues his pitch.

"People want to know more about you: what you're doing and why you're doing it. All I'm asking is just let my guys follow you... document every moment. We can even film you from a distance and have you mic'd up so we're not in the way. What do you think? This would be a great opportunity for you to get your message out to the nation and the world! I already have the distribution contacts for television, streaming services and radio. Think about it. You can be on every major channel and across social media. And then there's the licensing and retail.

"Your costume looks amazing by the way. Imagine every child wanting *your* Valor action figure! Think about it! T-shirts! Backpacks! Halloween costumes! A video game! The merchandise list is endless. It's a win-win! You get your message out to the world and *we* make *a lot* of money in the process, which in turn helps you to reach even *more* people! This will set you up for life! You. Your wife. Your son. You guys will never have to work again unless you *want* to work. Imagine the freedom. What do you say?"

Valor stops and looks at the producer, who flashes his big grin again.

"My proposal sounds good, doesn't it? It's a no-brainer."

"Don't engage," the Holy Spirit whispers again—this time with a bit more urgency.

Valor starts walking once more—following the path the LORD has already set out before him. This time, the producer doesn't follow, but rather frowns and sucks his teeth.

"It's your loss!" He watches Valor for another second before turning around. "Come on guys, back to the trucks. This fool just turned down the opportunity of a lifetime."

32: The Quickening

DAY 91—Colorado

There is no way to adequately describe it. Daniel has walked for two days—straight through and without stopping. His energy levels are not depleted at all. With each step comes a compelling of the Spirit. He knows, intuitively, that destiny awaits… and he must arrive at that moment at the appropriate time. So, he walks and while doing so, he thinks about his time in China.

V

2005. Chinese Christian Monastery…

It is the third day of Daniel's stay. For the first two, he watched and observed the routines of those who lived at the monastery. Now, he is partaking *with them*, starting with early morning prayers which begin at 3:00am. Before coming to this place, Daniel had never prayed for more than 15-30 minutes in one sitting. Here, everyone prays, as the Holy Spirit leads, for three hours in one sitting—and no one falls asleep! Considerable time and great intercession is given to each area of the Spirit's prompting. They have prayed for individual people, neighboring communities, warring factions and entire countries.

They have interceded for the global church and have come against the enemy on multiple levels. Through it all, they have worshiped the LORD, giving praise to the One who made the universe and beyond. The Holy Spirit resides continually in this place, to such degree of magnitude, that Daniel's initial difficulty praying is overcome rather quickly. As time progresses, it becomes easier for him to follow the Spirit's leading.

The chores begin at 6:00am. Even here, while cleaning and straightening up, Daniel notices that the most mundane of tasks are done with the sense of the Presence of God. The work, no matter how menial or complex, is carried out in honor to Him.

At 7:00am, the saints gather in the open square for their morning fitness. Several elderly men and women approach slowly, being held steady by their walking staffs. One by one all who are present drop to their knees and give thanks to the LORD. The elderly need extra time to lower themselves as they lay their staffs down next to them. A moment of verbal praise to the LORD is made by all:

"Praised are You, ADONAI our God, King of the universe, who gives the Torah of truth and the good news of salvation to Your people Israel and to all the peoples of the earth through Your Son, Yeshua the Messiah, our LORD."

One by one, each jumps to their feet—from youngest to oldest—and take their positions. Daniel is already on his feet when he notices the elderly group next to him.

I should help them, he thinks as he extends his hand. Brother Léi grabs his arm softly while shaking his head.

"Let them be."

"But they're old," Daniel objects slightly. "Shouldn't we help them?"

"It is okay, Brother Dàiwéisēn," the young monk replies. "The Holy Spirit is our Helper here." Brother Léi guides Daniel's attention back to the elderly, who are the last to stand.

Each one leaves their walking staff on the ground and suddenly jump to their feet!

Daniel's mouth drops open as his wide eyes bulge at the sight. He is at a loss for words as the 'Morning Forms' begin. All move effortlessly from one position to another in complete unison. All... except Daniel, who is having a hard time keeping up. Even the elderly are moving faster than him!

Forty-five minutes later, the synchronized movements are complete and it is time for Bible study as breakfast is made. Daniel watches in amazement as the young ones approach the elderly saints and pick up their walking staffs for them. Once retrieved, the elderly move to their next task, walking as slowly as they were when they approached the square.

"I—I don't understand," Daniel looks bewildered as he watches those, who now look feeble, but were just minutes ago vibrant with life and strength.

"As the Spirit leads... we help," Brother Léi explains. "However, we have learned over the course of many years, the reality of what the Scriptures declare in Romans 8:11, *'And if the Spirit of him who raised Jesus from the dead is living in you, he who raised Christ from the dead will also give life to your mortal bodies because of his Spirit who lives in you.'*"

Daniel's mind tries to process what he just heard. "Wait. So, if the Holy Spirit can make their bodies strong like that, why do they go back to their walking staffs? Why not... *stay* like that all the time?"

"Because," the young monk replies, "the purpose of the quickening is not so we can remain strong all the time and never get old and have aches and pains. Those aspects will become reality in The Age to come. In *this* Age, the purpose of the quickening is to supernaturally empower us for the tasks the LORD has called us to do."

Daniel nods his head. "Okay..."

"It was a number of years ago when the Holy Spirit revealed this to us. Early on, only the able-bodied participated in the Morning Forms. Those with physical ailments would sit on the side and watch. However, one day, one of our elders stood to join us. We tried to deter him, but he said the LORD told him to step out in trust. So, we allowed him to come and to our amazement, the Holy Spirit swelled up within him, he dropped his walking staff and he moved with such vigor it was hard for *us* to keep up with him! From then on, all of our elderly have participated. And we all learned the lesson that the Holy Spirit truly *could* enable us for any task that He has called us to do."

"That... is amazing."

"Our God is amazing," Brother Léi smiles. "He demonstrates time and again through His Word and through our lives that the impossible is possible when the LORD is the One calling you to do it."

V

Present day...

It is now evening, as Daniel comes to a rest stop. The quickening of the Holy Spirit has waned. Daniel can now feel the tiredness of his body. He sits on a bench next to a table and lamp pole while retracting his helmet's visor. He slowly takes in a few deep breaths of fresh air.

He can hear the hum from the light bulb hanging from the top of the pole. Even though his body is tired from the journey, he notices he is not hungry. The words of Jesus come to mind as he was tempted by the devil in the wilderness. *"Man shall not live by bread alone, but by every word which proceeds from the mouth of God."*

"Thank you Father," he prays, "Your Word empowered by Your Spirit is my *true food* on this journey." For the next few minutes, Daniel meditates on God's Word as he begins to pray through the Scriptures. Almost an hour passes as he feasts on the Word of God. Just as the hour finishes, Daniel suddenly feels the quickening of the Holy Spirit as a voice shouts from above, **"Come up here, and I will reveal to you a mystery!"**

Daniel launches into the air like a rocket—being both pulled and propelled by the invisible power of the Holy Spirit! Seconds later he comes to a sudden halt thousands of feet in the air—hovering above the nation as his cape billows in the wind.

"How am I doing this?" He scans the sky. "I'm so high... I can see the curvature of the earth! I shouldn't be able to breathe right now!"

His immediate sense of awe and fear gives way to peace as he scans the land below. Gross darkness swirls as pockets of light are scattered from place to place. Somehow, he knows these lights are not those which come from buildings, street lamps and vehicles. But, he is unsure what exactly they are.

The sound of thunder causes him to look up as a mighty angel descends from the heavens and comes to rest next to him. Now, both are hovering over the nation.

"Do not fear," the angel declares. ***"I have been sent to give you understanding about what you are seeing."***

"Where are we?" Daniel inquires. "How am I able to fly like this?"

"We are in the heavenly realms," the angel replies. ***"Here, the reality of visions and the physical realm intertwine. This vision is one which our LORD wants you to experience. What question do you have?"***

Daniel submits to the angel's explanation and scans the surface once more. "What are those pockets of light surrounded by the swirling mass of darkness?"

"The swirling mass of darkness," the angel explains, *"is the presence of the enemy of all that is good. The devil and his fallen angels have gained much ground in their attempts to corrupt humanity and the earth. The pockets of light are those who have placed their belief and trust in the Son of God."*

Daniel looks intently at the scene. The disparity is greatly apparent. In most places, the swirling mass seems absolute.

Both the angel and Daniel drop from the sky to about 500 feet above the earth. The swirling mass can now be seen as a combination of demonic spirits and persons working with evil intent.

Daniel points to an old and decrepit barn. "I know that place! That's where I saw the witches and warlocks trying to curse me!"

"You are correct," the angel confirms. *"Now that you have become known, the enemy is amassing against you. This is why the LORD commanded you to wait until the appropriate time to reveal your identity. Such secrecy allowed you to venture a great distance through the enemy's territory unawares."*

"If that's the case, why have me reveal my identity at all? I could have gone the entire journey unimpeded."

"By revealing your identity at the appointed time, the LORD has forced the enemy out of the shadows and is now revealing their unseen mechanisms both to you and others. Otherwise, the enemy would be able to act freely without significant opposition in the earth realm."

"And the haunted house?"

"The vision of the haunted house was a two-front attack from the enemy in the heavenly realm. The sorcery used sought to trap you in a mental prison in order to destroy your mind. The man and woman with you, who fell at the attacks of the demons, were planted by the enemy as a way to dismantle your resolve. As you saw the ineffectiveness of the holy water and crucifix you were meant to conclude that your faith was futile as well. Then you would have succumbed to their attack. However, the enemy did not know of the empowerment given you by the Holy Spirit. Nor did they anticipate the Spirit interceding for you in that moment. As a result, you called on the God of heaven and earth. He alone is sovereign over all realms. Then... He sent His light which broke through the mental prison and preserved you."

"You said it was a two-front attack. After I woke up, it actually *felt* like my body had been physically assaulted by the demons in the vision."

"*Yes. The dimensional membrane between the spiritual and physical realms is… malleable. There is overlap which can manifest under certain conditions. The enemy sought to attack you in both realms. They began with the mental prison construct to weaken you and then engaged the physical attack as well. The LORD's glory protected you from both. Otherwise, you would not have survived.*"

Just then, the faces of Brother Léi, Daniel's wife and son, Pastor Mike and Chris, Dr. Finkelstein and others flash in the air before them. The angel continues.

"*The LORD has moved on the hearts of many saints to pray on your behalf. He has shielded you. As you continue your journey, you must also pray for them as the Spirit leads you. In this way the LORD will cover you all.*"

"Okay. I will pray for them."

Both the angel and Daniel ascend back to their original height.

"The lights," Daniel scans the nation once more. "Some areas seem brighter than others."

This time they drop to ground level. Both are hovering just inches above the street. Daniel sees saints walking—going about their daily routines. Some glow brighter than others.

"*Their brightness comes from their obedience to Christ,*" the angel explains. "*The less obedient they are, the lower the radiance until it almost seems non-existent.*"

Daniel contemplates the angel's words.

"*Still, even in this state, there is a difference between them and those who refuse the Savior.*"

Just then, they see people walking around. All in various kinds of dress which reveal their culture, class and levels of success in life. But there is no glow coming from them at all. And some… are surrounded by differing levels of dark energy.

The angel discerns Daniel's thoughts and addresses them: "*Unbelievers,*" he points out. "*The god of this age has blinded their minds, so that they cannot see the light of the gospel that displays the glory of Christ, who is the image of God.*"

Daniel nods slowly as he thinks about the angel's words. "You quoted 2 Corinthians 4:4."

"*Yes,*" the angel replies. *"What does 1 Corinthians 2:14 say?"*

Daniel's mind immediately recalls the verse: *"The person without the Spirit does not accept the things that come from the Spirit of God but considers them foolishness, and cannot understand them because they are discerned only through the Spirit."*

The angel nods in agreement as he points towards the people.

"Such is the state of everyone who refuses the truth. They are incapable of understanding the sovereign will of God. Who can know the mind of the LORD to instruct Him? No one. Not even the angels. Even with our vast knowledge and power, we still must rely on the leading of God's Spirit in the carrying out of our duties. God reveals His Will to those He chooses.

"Those filled with the Holy Spirit of God have been given the mind of Christ. They are endowed with the capability to make judgments about all things related to God's purpose for their lives. They are not subject to merely human judgments. To do this, they must make the Word of God as important to them as eating and breathing. But, those who refuse the LORD have only human judgments at their disposal. Human judgment alone will always—eventually—lead one into darkness."

Daniel motions towards the group of unbelievers. "Why does darkness seem to be more prevalent around some than others?"

"Just as there are distinctions among the saints based on their level of obedience, there are distinctions among those who choose to remain in their sins. All are lost, but those surrounded by darkness have opened themselves up to various levels of the devil's lies. The greater the darkness, the greater the influence that darkness has over them. Sadly, they have willingly turned themselves over to his malevolent kingdom."

"Why is the Lord allowing me to see these things?"

"You must be prepared for what is to come. You will be attacked directly. You must remember: Greater is He who is in you, than he who is in the world."

V

The vision ends with a jolt! Daniel finds himself still seated on the bench at the rest area. The light shines on a brown basket which sits on the table in front of him.

"That wasn't there before," Daniel mumbles as he looks around. Besides some passing cars and several parked trucks in the rest area lot, no one is there. He stands and looks at the basket. A piece of paper —rolled up like a scroll—is tied to the handle with a scarlet string. Daniel unties the paper and unrolls it—revealing a note. It reads:

God told me to make this meal and bring it to <u>this</u> rest stop at <u>this</u> time. He said there would be someone, whom I had seen on TV, sitting at <u>this</u> table asleep. He wants you to remember that, "All things work together for the good, to those who love the Lord and are called according to His purpose. — Romans 8:28

Daniel rolls the paper back up, folds it and places it in a compartment on his belt.

"Thank you Father," he prays. "Once again, You have provided for me—both spiritually and physically." He opens the basket to find a warm, wonderfully prepared home-cooked meal, with utensils and a bottle of water. As his mouth salivates, he removes his gloves and helmet with a smile.

There, under one of the rest area lamp stands, with the chirping of crickets in the trees behind and the sound of passing cars on the highway, Daniel enjoys the vegetables, pasta, fish and water. Once finished, he cleans up and places everything back in the basket. After a time of prayer, Daniel dons his helmet, closes his eyes and sleeps for a couple of hours.

V

The sun crests over the horizon—its light illuminating Valor's visor. He stirs back to awareness, opens his eyes, looks around and stretches. He opens the compartment on his belt and retrieves a pen. Opening the basket once more, he retrieves one of the unused napkins and writes on it. He then rolls it up and ties it to the handle. After placing the pen back in his belt, he continues his trek down the highway.

About thirty minutes later, a car pulls into the rest area and stops right in front of the table. A woman exits her vehicle and walks over to the basket. She unties the napkin, unrolls it and reads the note with a smile. It says:

Whoever you are... thank you for this wonderful meal. It came at the right time! May God bless you for your obedience! I am assuming you are a fellow believer in Jesus. I will be praying for you. Please pray for me. And if we never meet in person while on earth, we will surely meet in person in God's kingdom! —Daniel Davidson, Valor.

33: Pass Through Somewhere Else!

DAY 93—Colorado

On the outskirts of a remote Colorado area historically linked to a Sundown town, a shotgun blast explodes skyward as a hand cocks the firearm and lowers it towards its target. The gunshot echoes in every direction as ten white men stand side by side. Eight have guns at the ready. Two, hold four barking, razor-sharp-teeth-bearing german shepherds on tight leashes. The whole group stands about 60 yards in front of Daniel.

"Turn your butt around," the group leader shouts. "We don't want no blacks coming through our town! Especially crazy ones claiming to speak for God!"

Daniel stands still and removes his helmet—smiling warmly at the group while trying to appear non-threatening. "I mean no disrespect to any of you. I'm just passing through."

"Pass through somewhere else!"

"But this is the route I need to take."

"This is your *last* warning," the group leader declares with a defiant finality. "It may be 2024, but we've got no problem stringing you up. If you take one more step we're gonna loose these dogs on you! Then we're gonna shoot you!"

"Father?" Daniel prays silently. "What do you want me to do?"

The response is immediate. **"Advance! You must speak for Me in California."**

"Okay…" he replies with a rise in his voice. "Here we go." Daniel takes *another* step.

The two men loose the hounds with a command: "Get him!"

The four dogs launch at Daniel like fighter jets screaming down a runway. As the vicious animals run towards him, he drops his helmet and lifts his hands in worship to the Lord, while praying fervently.

The ten men yell and cackle as they watch Daniel's impending doom. But, suddenly, the dogs screech to a halt, several feet in front of him! Their ravenous mouths close tight. Their ears drop. Their tails lower between their legs as all four sit and then lower themselves completely to the ground right at his feet. Daniel gazes down at the dogs as they only look up at him with their eyes—the eyebrows moving back and forth.

The men are flabbergasted as one of them yells: "What in the world is this?"

Daniel squats in front of the dogs and rubs each behind their ears. He then smiles at them and stands to his feet. All four follow his lead and stand as well, with wagging tails and happy expressions. Daniel laughs as he pets each one of them and gives praise to God. "Lord, thank you!"

The men are in awe—after all this has *never* happened before! But their awe gives way to rage as they aim their weapons at him!

Daniel starts walking toward the men, with two dogs on either side of him.

"Don't take another step," one of the men shouts with a wobbly voice as fear is evident in his eyes. One by one the men's hands begin to tremble and their eyesight begins to blur with tears. As Daniel draws closer, a holy fear rushes the men like a hurricane! One by one, their guns drop as they collapse to the ground and begin to weep heavily. The Holy Spirit has subdued each man's heart, and they are instantly convicted of the immense weight of their sins and of their present path which leads to destruction.

One by one they each cry out, "What must I do to be saved?" "Please tell me, what must I do to have my sins forgiven?" "I am unclean!" "I am guilty!" "Please help us!" What starts out sporadically, builds into a cacophony of gut-wrenching pleas for salvation interspersed with screams and yells of them being *unraveled* in the Presence of the Holy One.

Daniel is upon them now—standing right in front of them. The penetrating Presence of the Holy Spirit flows outward from within him in concentric circles—each wave more powerful than the next. He looks at these grown men who had been consumed by hate, now wallowing on the dusty earth. And he himself feels the tremendous, overriding, outpouring of Christ's love for each of them. It flows from within his belly and spreads throughout his entire body—as if the Lord opened him up and poured 'Liquid Love' into his being! Daniel looks at them with greater realization and overwhelming compassion.

"Father," Daniel prays as greater depths of Christ's love manifest within his being. "Your well is deep! And my cup is overflowing! Is *this* how You feel about us all the time?"

Daniel stares at the men who are now weeping like small children. They are completely undone—disarmed by the Presence of the Holy Spirit—searched and convicted by the One Who knows all things—from whom nothing is hidden.

"Give me your attention," Daniel declares boldly.

The men quiet their weeping just enough to sit on their knees and look in his direction. Their reddened faces drenched in tears, snot and covered in dirt.

"If you believe on the Lord Jesus Christ and place your trust in Him as your Savior, then you will be saved from your sins. You must turn away from all allegiances which oppose His claim on your life so you can take His yoke upon you and learn of Him."

As the minutes pass, one by one, each man surrenders his life to Jesus—right then and there. As this happens, Daniel notices a nearby lake in the distance to his right.

"Are any of you willing to be baptized as a public declaration of your commitment to Christ?"

Each man agrees and makes their way over to the lake. They strip down to their t-shirts and shorts—Daniel as well—and then he baptizes them all.

"Your past is just that... the past." Daniel declares. "If you are in Christ, then you are free. We are now brothers. I hold no animosity towards you. For in Christ Jesus, we are *all* made into new creations."

"Can you stay with us?" one of the men asks. "Just for a few days so you can teach us what we should do."

Daniel agrees.

For three days, he meets with the men, their families and the small community which populates this town of approximately two thousand people. All are amazed at the sudden transformation of these men! They share their testimony of how God convicted them of their sins, exposed their need for salvation and warned them of the coming judgment if they refused to repent.

Daniel teaches them from the Bible, prays with them, answers their questions and eats with them. He also discovers they have no church in their community. So, he ventures with them to the next town which has a small congregation. These men had refused to go to church, but now they were being connected with a pastor and a congregation that would help them grow further in their faith.

After three days, Daniel says his goodbyes to his newfound brothers and sisters in Christ. He then continues his journey, passing through their community, and heads westward.

34: Transformation

DAY 103—Colorado

While walking through a small city, Daniel encounters a Pride parade. Thousands line the streets while hundreds parade themselves in full view of all who are present. Some display more modest float presentations while other flamboyant displays are gratuitous in every way. Rainbow flags, signs and shirts are everywhere—worn and held by all age groups.

As Valor's presence is discovered by onlookers and parade participants, some recognize him and go out of their way to jeer him. Others throw food and drinks at him. And a group enacts crude twerkings and other lewd gestures in front of him. As he walks in silence, others grow agitated by his presence and yell for him to leave. Even with all the mockery, the LORD enables him to remain calm.

As the parade route turns left, he turns to the right and encounters a person standing in his path with a large drink and a handful of napkins. This person is around 18-21 years old and is wearing a pink wig, halter top and skirt like a young woman, but based on musculature it is clear "she" is actually a young man. She looks at the remnants of trash on Valor's suit and hands him several napkins.

"I know who you are. You're that guy who claims to speak for God."

"Father, do I engage?" He prays silently.

"Yes," the Holy Spirit replies.

"You are correct," Valor agrees as he begins to wipe the mess off of his suit. "I am. And thank you for these napkins."

"I'm sorry they threw those things at you. Even if people don't agree, that doesn't mean they have to lash out like that."

"That is true."

"Can I ask you a… *pointed* question?"

"Sure."

"Will God send me to hell because I'm Trans?"

Valor raises his visor so his face can be seen. "May I ask you a question for clarity?"

"Yes," the person agrees.

"Do you really want to know the answer? Or have you already made up your mind so that it doesn't matter what I say?

This throws her off for a second...

"What if my mind is already made up?"

"Then there's no need for us to continue," Valor responds. "But... if you want to have a genuine conversation about this, then we can."

She nods. "I really want to know the answer to my question."

"Okay. But before we talk about your question. My name is Daniel." He extends his gloved hand.

The young adult looks at his hand for a moment before shaking it.

"My name is Samantha."

"Now, Samantha," since you asked the question, "I *assume* you were born a boy, but now identify as a girl."

"Yeah."

"Well, it's nice to meet you," Daniel smiles. "Now, according to the Bible, no one goes to hell because they are trans, non-binary, gay, lesbian or even straight."

"They don't?"

"No. God sent His Son Jesus to save us from hell. In fact, Jesus Himself says that hell was created as a place of torment and judgment for the devil and his fallen angels.

"I don't believe in the devil."

"You don't believe in the devil, but you're asking about hell? If the Bible says both things are real, we can't just pick and choose which one we want to believe in."

"Fine. Where does it say that? About hell being created for the devil?"

"In Matthew 25:41. On the day of judgment Jesus says to those who reject Him: '...*Depart from me, you who are cursed, into the eternal fire prepared for the devil and his angels.*' So, a person—no matter what they identify as—is eternally separated from God in hell when they refuse God's gift of salvation which He provided through His Son, Jesus."

"So... God is not *mad* at me because I'm Trans?"

"God is upset with *anyone* who chooses to do things that offend Him."

"See, I knew it! Now you're going to tell me that God hates the LGBTQ+ community! You Christians are all alike!"

"Why do you say that?"

"Because all you do is condemn people and say they're going to hell if they don't come to Jesus and stop doing bad things."

"Samantha, I don't know what kind of conversations you may have had with other people on this issue. And I don't know how they *treated* you, but the Bible is clear that we are not to condemn people. As long as people are alive, there is always an opportunity for them to change. Having said that, the Bible *does* tell us to make observations and judgments based on how people live in relation to God's laws and commands. And we are to warn others if they are in danger of being eternally separated from God. Think about it… if hell exists and people are in *real danger* of going there, wouldn't you want to warn them? Especially if there was a way for them to avoid it? And wouldn't you want someone to warn you if you were in danger?"

"…I guess I would…"

"Okay. So, God loves us enough to warn us about the reality of hell. And He *also* loves us enough to tell us about His desire for us to be with Him in heaven."

"I *guess* that makes sense."

"Even though God doesn't like our sinful acts, that doesn't mean He doesn't love us and wants to deliver us from those things which displease Him. The Bible says God provides for those who please Him *and* for those who don't. In fact, God loves us so much, that He sent Jesus as the solution to our problem even while we were still enemies against Him. You see, He doesn't want us to *remain* His enemies. He wants to adopt us into His eternal family and welcome us as His children!"

"My parents… when I came out… and said I didn't want to be a boy anymore… they tried to reason with me. They told me what I was doing was wrong. But, when I refused to listen, they kicked me out. I've been on my own ever since."

"I'm sorry you had to go through that experience."

"Thanks. But… how can this be wrong? These *desires* I have? I used to try and fight them… I… even tried to pray them away. But nothing worked. So, I came to the conclusion that this is who I am. If I don't like the gender I was born with, I can just change it."

"Can I ask you a question?"

"Sure."

"You can see that I'm a black man. If I said I was tired of being black and wanted to identify as a wealthy white man, how long do you think it would take for the world to make it abundantly clear that I'm *black*? At the bank. At a car dealership. If I got pulled over by the police. If I was buying a house. And a host of other situations. Would people say, 'you want to identity as white? Sure thing!' Or would they affirm the reality that I am *really* a black man?"

"I guess they would tell you you're black."

"And they may say to think otherwise would be to live in a fantasy world."

"But that's not the same thing."

"But it is similar. My skin color says I'm black and my DNA says I'm black. So, even if I try to change my appearance, I can't be any other ethnicity than black. Similarly, the same is true for you. Even if you change your sex organs, take hormone blockers and wear women's clothing, no amount of cosmetic surgery will change the truth that at the genetic level, *biologically*, your DNA indicates that you are a male."

"But God made me this way, so it's not *my* fault."

"Do you want a truthful answer?"

"…No… Yes… I don't know," Samantha replies in an exasperated tone.

"Well, you can stop me at any time if you don't want to talk about this anymore. The Bible reveals that each of us are in a perplexing paradox. On one hand, we are fearfully and wonderfully made in God's image… But on the *other hand* we are also born in sin and shaped in iniquity."

"What does that mean?"

"It means that at the core of who we are, all of us have a terrible sin problem. And this problem, which has been passed down to each person going all the way back to Adam and Eve in the Garden of Eden, has broken God's image in us."

"So, God made us, just to break us and ruin our lives, and then blames us when we don't let Him fix us up?"

"No… the Bible reveals that there is a villain in our story…"

"The devil."

"Yes. And he is responsible for causing our first parents—Adam and Eve—to rebel against God. That rebellion allowed sin to enter humanity and the world. And sin corrupts everything it touches."

"So, you're saying I'm a sinner."

"I'm saying, we *all* are sinners. And we all are in *need* of God's grace, forgiveness and salvation. You see, sin isn't just the bad things we do. Those things are just symptoms of the deeper issue. Sin is a corrupting influence that lies at the deepest regions of our being. And we can't get rid of it on our own. Only God can do that. And this has to be settled in the heart of anyone who will come to Jesus."

Samantha stares at the ground. "I don't want to go to hell. And I don't know if I can change. But, if I wanted to give my life to Jesus… Will God accept me… *like I am?*"

"Well," Daniel replies, "the answer comes in two parts."

"Okay…"

"The first part is: Yes. If you come to Jesus, He will accept you like you are. The second part is this: Once you come to Jesus, His Heavenly Father will begin the process of conforming you to the image of His Son. This means as you grow closer to Jesus over time, He will begin to remove those things from your life which don't please Him and are getting in the way of your spiritual maturity. That may involve Him completely removing your current desire to be Trans. Or, it may involve God giving you the strength to resist giving into your desire so you can glorify Him. So, the deeper question is: Do you love God enough to want to give up whatever offends Him?"

"But… we can't really know what offends God."

"Why not?"

"Because everyone believes differently! Even within the church! Everyone has their own truth. So, there can't be any absolutes."

"If there can't be any absolutes, then your statement about there not being absolutes can't be absolutely true."

Samantha stares at Daniel while thinking about the truth of his statement.

"Let me tell you what's absolutely true: If you stick your hand into a fire—without a protective glove—you will *absolutely* get burned. If you get hit by a speeding truck, you will *absolutely* get injured or killed. If you run out of air while under water, you will *absolutely* drown. And if you take hormone therapy and blockers and do cosmetic surgery to change your appearance from one gender to another, the genetic chromosomes, which determine your sex while in your mother's womb, will *absolutely* remain the same.

"If God is the Creator of humanity then He has a right—as the Creator—to set the rules for us and to do as He pleases. And if He has revealed His will to humanity, then we can know what pleases Him and what displeases Him. The major claim of the Bible is that it is God's self-revelation to the world. Through it, we can know God's heart toward us and His standards for how we should live. So, once again, the question we all have to come to grips with is: Do any of us love God enough to give up what He clearly states is offensive to Him so we can be in a relationship with Him?

"Will we deny those things we want that are contrary to His will for us in order to follow Him? If we are willing to follow Jesus, then Colossians 3 tells us to put our earthly nature to death so we *can* follow Him."

"But I already told you, I can't give this up! I already tried. It didn't work!"

"That's why we need to surrender to Jesus *first*, so He can help us to resist the urges we all deal with. We all have urges and attractions. And we have to decide whether to resist them or give in. God has made it clear that homosexuality is only one of the things He does not approve of. He also disapproves of people who have sex outside of marriage or who do so with someone who is not their spouse. Then there are the prideful, liars, murderers, those who engage in the occult, and so on.

"God sent Jesus to save us from the penalty, the guilt and the power of our sins. And God has declared that as the Creator of humanity, He will judge every human being for how they lived their life on earth. And the only way we can pass judgment day is to receive Jesus and live in and for Him while we are alive, because once we die, we are out of time."

"So, why does God call people like me an abomination? That means there's no hope for us."

"No. God says it to show how serious this particular offense is to Him. God created male and female as two distinct kinds of individuals that have notable similarities and differences. Living in an alternative LGBTQ+ lifestyle goes against the order which God established. And engaging in alternative sexual relations and transitions is to go against the core of your very nature."

"But, what if you're wrong? What if the Bible is wrong and God doesn't exist at all?"

"If God doesn't exist, then you and I can do whatever we want! But if He *does* exist, then He has a standard, just like any good parent has a standard for their children. God wouldn't be good if He didn't let us know what that standard was and how we can live in a way that pleases Him. But He *is* good and has provided us with what we need to know Him, love Him and serve Him!

"The question is... do you want to follow Him to everlasting life or follow your own path which ultimately leads to destruction? It all boils down to who we choose to listen to. We can listen to God or we can listen to ourselves or other people. This is a *choice* we make *every* day.

"We often think we have to change ourselves first before we can surrender our lives to Jesus. But if we could make the changes on our own, we wouldn't need Him. Jesus invites all of us who know we are in need of saving to come to Him so we can have new life *in* Him. We each have to deal with internal and external forces... but we don't struggle alone. Christ will give us victory if we are willing to seek Him for it. He wants to give us a *true* transformation."

Just then, a group of six approach, but hesitate once they see Samantha sitting with Daniel.

"Hey, Samantha. We've been looking for you," one of them says. "The parade's about to end."

"This is Daniel," Samantha replies. "I was just talking with him about some stuff. Go ahead. I'll catch up with you."

Daniel and Samantha watch as the six friends walk away with concerned expressions on their faces.

"You've... given me *a lot* to think about."

"Well, Samantha," Daniel smiles softly, "I hope you seriously consider what we've discussed, because your soul's eternal destiny is at state."

'Samuel."

"What?"

"My… birth name… it's *Samuel*."

"Did you know Samuel was a great prophet of God in the Bible?

"Yeah. I knew that."

"Well," Daniel points to the friends walking away. "God's wants to save you so you can be with Him forever. And I wouldn't be surprised if He wants to use you to reach others in *this* community."

Samuel sits quietly for a moment before speaking: "Yeah… Perhaps."

35: Prosperity Gospel?

DAY 104 — Colorado

An opulent megachurch sits on a sprawling multi-acre campus. The parking lots are massive and filled to capacity. Worship music can be heard even from outside. The inner sanctuary is full as thousands of people have been in service for the past twenty minutes. The music volume decreases to an extremely low level as the pastor steps to the stage to start his message. With a well-manicured smile, Pastor Seymour Money begins:

"God wants you to prosper! He wants you to shine! It's the devil who comes as the thief to steal, kill and destroy! But Jesus came that you and I might have life and have it more abundantly! So, what does that mean? What is Jesus talking about? An abundant life means an *abundance life*! Have you ever seen an *abundance* of anything be something small? Jesus wants you to live your life to the full! And if you follow Him, the way He wants you to, in faith believing, receiving *and giving*, then He will *give you abundance* in every area you submit to Him!

"Has the devil been stealing your finances or your health or your family and friendships? Did the devil steal that promotion at your job or good grades at school? God wants you to prosper! You don't have to live paycheck to paycheck. You can be a millionaire for God's glory! You don't have to drive a beat up old lemon of a car! You can drive the finest vehicle on the road! You just need to know what you *really want* and give Him the glory! The Bible says you are the head and not the tail! In Christ, you are to reign from His place of victory! Last I checked those who win get the best of the spoils! So, if you are not winning in life, then that means there is a disconnect somewhere. And where might that be?"

V

Valor passes through the large parking lots and approaches the entrance to the church's welcome center. As he enters the building, he is met by greeters and security personnel.

"Hello and welcome to Prosperity Church," the greeter smiles.

"Thank you," Valor replies as he removes his helmet.

"You're that superhero guy, right? The one in the news?"

"I'm not a superhero," Daniel answers, "But *I am* a Christ-follower."

"Right. They did say that on the news… Well, we can escort you to the balcony."

"I'd like to sit on the main floor if that's possible."

"I'm sorry… we don't allow additional people to enter the main level once our pastor has begun his message. So, can we take you to the balcony?"

"The Lord told me to come here today. He has a message for your congregation."

"Well, we can arrange for you to meet with the pastor *after* service…"

"Thank you, but that won't be necessary. Would it be alright to enter the sanctuary after your pastor finishes preaching? It would be great if you could inform him about my request."

V

Inside the sanctuary, the pastor continues…

"There's a word in John 10:10 you might have *overlooked*… It's the word *'might.'* Jesus says, "I have come that you *'might'* have life and have it more abundantly." Now, what does 'might' mean? It means something *may* happen or it *may not* happen. And the determining factor between *may* and *may not* is usually our decision making ability.

"So, if we look at the fact that the thief comes to steal, kill and destroy and Jesus comes with the *intention* of setting things right, then the *'might clause'* He inserts here means if we don't experience the abundant life He comes to give, it's not because of Him. His intention is that we *would*… So the disconnect has to do with our inability to believe! We see this when Jesus returns to His home town and could only do a few miracles because of the people's unbelief.

"If we don't believe right, then we don't receive right! You see, here at Prosperity Church, we believe *'Now & Later.'* You remember the candy 'Now & Later'? You can eat one now and then you can eat one later! You can live your best life *now*... your best *human* life... and then after you die, you can live your best heavenly life *later!* In other words, God has a mansion laid up for you in glory... but that doesn't mean you can't have a mansion down here on earth in *this* life!

"The God of the universe knows no shortages!!! The Father poured out His Spirit on Jesus without measure! As heirs with Jesus, what do you think God wants to pour out on you? Jesus owns the cattle on a thousand hills and the silver and gold, and all the other precious elements of creation!

"I know what you're thinking... Jesus was a poor servant when he walked the earth. He was a refugee of sorts. But remember, while in glory He was the very definition of royalty! And He divested Himself of His glory and became poor to identify with us... so that through salvation, by believing, we can identify with His royalty! You can live your best life now... and later!

"Don't listen to the naysayers and doomsday prophets who claim the world is going to end... that our way of life is going to end. America is still God's country. We are still the modern-day Promised Land flowing with milk and honey! The inhabitants of the world still come to America to make a better life! Surely, you, as believers should have and experience *that better life!"*

"So, believe the gospel! God wants you to prosper in all you do! Live your best life! Don't settle for second best! Yes, we've come through some tough times, but if these past couple of years of great technological advancement—like the growth and benefits of Artificial Intelligence—are any indicators at all, then the best is yet to come! Now, go out into the world in the Name of the Lord... and be the best human you can be. Be prosperous!"

As Pastor Money finishes, one of his assistants walks out on stage and whispers in his ear. Just then a clamor is heard at one of the entrances to the sanctuary. A commotion begins to stir through the crowd as heads turn. Daniel quietly walks down an open aisle with his helmet under his arm. Security officers block his path, but as he comes into their personal space, they uncharacteristically step back and allow him to continue.

Pastor Seymour flashes a nervous smile, accompanied by a half-hearted chuckle to feign excitement.

"Well now... I see we have a notable visitor with us today!" He points towards Daniel. "I believe its Daniel Davidson, as seen on the news—also known as Valor. He has been doing many great things as he treks across the country. This is an unexpected honor!"

Daniel approaches the stage, but the security guard standing in front of the stairs does not move.

"It's okay Stan," Pastor Money smiles with a nod. "You can let him up."

The security guard steps aside as the pastor motions for Daniel to come onto the platform.

"I'm told that God has given you a message for our congregation."

"He has," Daniel says as he stops next to the pastor.

"Well, this is very *unusual*... but you've come all this way, so I'll give you a couple of minutes to share what's on your heart."

A technician runs out and hands Daniel a microphone. He then addresses the people.

"Good morning and praise God for another day of life. I want to say 'thank you' to your pastor for giving me an opportunity to speak to you for a few moments. After all, my visit was unannounced and you can't let just anyone walk into the pulpit or on stage to speak. Not everyone has a heart for the Lord...

"Having said that... I am here this morning because the Lord has a word for you. It is a word He has sent to you on several previous occasions. Over the past three years, there have been a few of you in this congregation who has received this word from the Lord. You have tried to share it with the leadership and anyone who would listen, but it has fallen on deaf ears."

Mumbles and murmuring spread throughout the crowd.

"Before I share this word from the Lord, let me first say I do not know any of you. I have never heard of your church before this morning. I did not google you or search you out in any way on social media or your website. I do not know your pastor or any other leader here. This is not an attempt to garner fame, appreciation or notoriety. I merely seek to be obedient to what I believe the Lord is saying. You alone will know if what comes out of my mouth is true or not. If it's true, the Holy Spirit will confirm it...

"This is what the Lord says:

"To the angel of the church in Laodicea write: These are the words of the Amen, the faithful and true witness, the ruler of God's creation. I know your deeds, that you are neither cold nor hot. I wish you were either one or the other! So, because you are lukewarm—neither hot nor cold—I am about to spit you out of my mouth."

Several shouts ring out across the sanctuary. A few persons jump to their feet, holding their Bibles above their heads in agreement as Daniel continues.

"You say, 'I am rich; I have acquired wealth and do not need a thing.' But you do not realize that you are wretched, pitiful, poor, blind and naked."

Many gasp at the words. Some are offended. Others are convicted. Daniel continues.

"I counsel you to buy from me gold refined in the fire, so you can become rich; and white clothes to wear, so you can cover your shameful nakedness; and salve to put on your eyes, so you can see."

Daniel stops for a moment. Even with the bright lights shining on the stage, he can see the reaction of many. He can hear the collective gasps... and even the scoffing of those offended. He speaks the next few lines with a pleading heart.

"Those whom I love I rebuke and discipline. So be earnest and repent. Here I am! I stand at the door and knock. If anyone hears my voice and opens the door, I will come in and eat with that person, and they with me. To the one who is victorious, I will give the right to sit with me on my throne, just as I was victorious and sat down with my Father on his throne. Whoever has ears, let them hear what the Spirit says to the churches."

Daniel lowers the microphone. The silence is punctuated by shouts and sounds of weeping.

"Well," the pastor says uneasily as he tries to assert his authority. "Thank you, Daniel. I will admit that I am a bit surprised. Astounded even. Yes, three members had been very vocal over the past three years. Each quoted these very Scripture verses from Revelation 3, but there is *no way* that the warning Jesus gave to the church of Laodicea applies to us. True, we are a wealthy congregation. But it is the Lord who gives us power to get wealth—as the Scriptures very well say. We do a lot of good work in the community, both locally and globally. We work hard to live out the gospel through social justice efforts. We take it to the world, as Jesus said we are to do in Matthew 28. So, I will tell you what I told the others. *You are mistaken."*

Many in the congregation voice their agreement with their pastor.

"And another thing," Pastor Money continues. "Just so those who are here don't get the idea that *we* are somehow in error because of what *you* have said and the supposed supernatural aspect of you speaking the same message even though you have never been here before. People of Prosperity Church... What just happened is a mere coincidence which can be written off. Just about any church as large as we are has faced similar words of supposed correction from the Lord. Our size makes us a target for these types of messages. So, there is nothing divinely appointed about this at all. While our friend here may be well meaning, he is sincerely wrong. We are doing the Lord's work. We are spreading the good news!"

The congregation cheers as the pastor raises both of his hands in celebration. Daniel raises the microphone back to his lips.

"May I respond to what you just said?"

"I'm afraid not," the pastor replies. "We are just about out of time and must prepare for the next service."

"Let him speak!" a few people yell from the crowd. "*You* spoke. Now let *him* reply," another yells. "It's only fair," shouts another. A growing swell of congregants peppering the large crowd add their voices in agreement.

"Okay," the pastor concedes as he nervously glances at his watch. "But, please make it brief."

The congregation quiets down as Daniel opens his mouth to speak.

"The Lord allows me to see into the spiritual realm when I need to. This morning, as I approached the outside parking lot, I could see many angels on the grounds. I also saw many demons. The closer I got to the building, the less the angels followed. But the demons drifted right inside with many of you. Even now, this sanctuary is filled with more dark spirits than with the angels. The enemy is too comfortable here. He comes and goes as he pleases. And that is because the *'gospel'* which is preached here is not the gospel at all, but rather a caricature of the true gospel."

The congregation erupts in a sudden uproar as the pastor motions for the technicians to cut Daniel's microphone. But the technician in charge is so amazed by this unfolding situation that he is not paying attention to the pastor's signals.

"The Lord wants you to know this is your last warning."

"Can you cut his microphone?" the pastor interjects.

"The end of this age is fast approaching."

"I said, cut his microphone!" the pastor commands in an elevated but civil tone.

"Jesus will return, just as He promised! How many of you will truly be ready to meet Him when He comes?"

"Jesus is *not* coming back!" Pastor Money yells as many in the congregation gasp in horror. He immediately realizes his error. "What I *mean* is that he is not coming back any time soon. People, you don't have to worry about any doomsday message talking about the imminent return of Christ and the end of the world. We, the body of Christ, are His hands and feet! He is using us to bring about His kingdom on earth *now*. And when we have done so, *then* He will return. So, do not believe any other message."

"You cannot have the kingdom without the King," Daniel responds as he places the microphone on the floor.

Pastor Money motions for his security personnel to escort Daniel out of the building. As they do, the pastor tries to steer the congregation's focus in another direction.

"Well, what an eventful morning this has been! May this serve as a reminder to us all about the importance of knowing the Bible for ourselves…"

V

A crowd is waiting by the time Daniel is brought into the lobby. Some persons are supportive. Many are not. It doesn't take long before Daniel is standing outside in the parking lot and the doors to the welcome center are closed behind him. He closes his eyes and breathes heavily as he prepares to put his helmet on.

"Well, Lord. I did what You wanted me to do."

"Wait!" a voice shouts from behind. Daniel turns to find a white man, a hispanic woman and an asian woman approaching him.

"I'm John. This is Jessica and Keiko."

"We are the ones the Lord used to speak the same message over these past three years," Jessica utters.

"What you said is a direct confirmation from the Lord," says Keiko.

"I'm glad," Daniel replies. "Too bad it has fallen on deaf ears."

"We'll have to wait and see," says John. "I was the first to share this word with the church. It went nowhere at all. In fact, some time later, I was conveniently excluded from several ministries because I wouldn't let it go. The Lord was saying that we were just like the church in Laodicea! It seemed no one would listen. I tried to leave the church after that, but the Lord told me to remain here and pray for everyone else. So, that is what I've been doing."

"Then a year later," Jessica interjects, "the Lord gave me the same word. I didn't believe it when John first shared. In fact, I scoffed at it. How could we be in judgment when all around us everyone seemed to be so blessed? But when the Lord spoke to my heart, I couldn't shake it! I tried to smother it for three weeks, before I couldn't hold it in any longer.

"Right in the middle of a service, I suddenly jumped to my feet and blurted out those same Scripture verses! I was yelling at the top of my lungs with all of my might! I can't even say it was *me* doing it because I wanted to stay seated! But it was like I was the prophet Jeremiah with fire shut up in my bones! When I was done, I fell back to my seat. You could hear a pin drop in the sanctuary for about thirty seconds. All eyes were looking right at me. And then the pastor just reframed the incident and moved right along with the service as if nothing happened!"

"I too didn't believe," Keiko adds. "But I knew John and Jessica. We would often meet together with others for Bible Study and prayer. In all of my interactions with them, they had always given good godly advice and had always gone out of their way to live for Jesus. So, I was stuck. Do I believe them or not? I noticed after Jessica did what she did, some of our mutual friends pulled away from her. I wanted to do the same thing, but I was... *compelled* to stay in close contact."

"That was such a hard time for me," Jessica adds. "People were avoiding me like the plague. My relationship with my husband even suffered as he became collateral damage for my actions. But John and Keiko, stayed by my side through it all. Eventually, things kind of blew over and the status quo in the church resettled again."

"Like a hill of ants after it's been struck," John interjects.

"Then," Keiko adds, "the Lord impressed the same Scripture verses upon my heart. And I could not let them go!" Instead of shouting them out in the middle of service, the Lord had me walk right into a leadership meeting one night and deliver His message to the pastor, elders and other leaders who were present. Needless to say, I was kindly escorted out of the room. And I was threatened never to do that again or my church membership would be revoked.

"The interesting thing is that one of the church's administrative assistants and security guards are *always* posted outside of the leadership meetings to ensure no unauthorized persons can enter. But when I arrived, they were not there and I just walked right in. I found out later that a minute before I got there, the administrative assistant suddenly became ill and the security guard had to take her to the rest room. Once I left, she immediately got better and they both came back to their post. Neither had any idea until the meeting was over that anything had even transpired!"

"So," John wraps things up, "We know you were sent from the Lord! And the Lord calls us to plant seeds and water seeds and He gives the increase." John smiles. "Thank you for being obedient."

Daniel smiles at the three who stand before him. "I really appreciate you coming out here to talk with me. I'd be lying if I said it's been easy to be obedient when the Lord leads me to do something out of the ordinary." Daniel notices the three of them glancing at his outfit. "Yes," he laughs, "wearing this uniform is *definitely* out of the ordinary for me." They laugh as well. "But it's not out of the ordinary for my 15 year old son who loves cosplay! He designed this suit according to my specifications."

After a few moments of the trio admiring the suit, John speaks.

"You got any plans for this afternoon? We were planning on meeting for a Bible study at my place. We'd love to hear your story and gain any further insight you might have on where you think we are on God's timeline of end times events."

"And Jessica and I will bring the food," Keiko adds.

"Well," Daniel laughs, "I can't turn down good fellowship, a Bible study and great food, can I? Sure, I would love to stay for a while."

Their phones suddenly receive several notifications. John, Jessica and Keiko check to see what is going on and then speak among themselves for a quick moment.

"What is it?" Daniel asks as John smiles broadly.

"It looks like it might be more than the four of us at Bible study this afternoon..."

36: Phone Call

DAY 106 — Colorado

John was kind enough to open his home for Daniel to stay for a couple of days. The next morning, church members arrive for an impromptu Bible study and a midday lunch fellowship. By 6:00pm, Daniel calls home and shares the past few day's events with his wife. The front door to the house slams so loud, Daniel can hear it through the phone.

"What was that?" he asks.

"It's DJ," Rebecca says as she hears her son storm upstairs to his room. "He's been having some...*issues* at school. I imagine that today was *not* a good day."

"What happened?"

"Why don't I let him tell you." She turns and calls for her son to pick up the phone. A second later, the three of them share the line.

"Hey Buddy. How are you doing?"

"Oh, *I'm* fine," DJ replies in a frustrated tone. "It's everyone *else* that's acting stupid!"

"What happened, Son?"

"People at school are making fun of you, Dad!"

"And they're taking it out on *you*?"

"Yeah..."

"What are they doing?"

"They're saying you're a fake wannabe superhero... that you're pathetic... That you need to get a life... Most of my friends don't even talk to me anymore. It's... hard."

"Well," Daniel breathes, "we figured something like this might happen."

"Yeah, but Dad, they don't get it! And the news coverage on you has been *so* one sided lately."

"It has been?" Daniel replies. "I haven't had a chance to watch."

"*Good*," Rebecca interjects. "Trust me. You don't need the distraction."

"Honestly Dad," DJ continues, "if you didn't tell us about everything... how God is doing amazing stuff through you and the life change people are having... I *might* think you were crazy too."

"It's clear that some in the media have their own agendas," Rebecca adds. "Their *'version'* of the truth is not accurate at all."

"You think Mom's right, DJ?"

"Yeah. And that's what my friends at school are watching and listening to."

"Okay... So, what are you going to do about it?"

"I dunno... Part of me just wants things to go back to the way they were before this whole... *crazy assignment from the Lord* started! I just want to get my life back... but that's impossible now..."

"It's impossible for *all* of us," Rebecca adds. "Daniel, DJ is dealing with this at school and I'm dealing with it when I'm out running errands. And sometimes even at church. Some of the other members —even though Pastor Mike is 100% behind us—some of them think this is crazy and even... unbiblical."

"Dad... Listen. I'm frustrated. But I did sign up for this just like you and Mom did. I know what you're doing—*what we're doing* is right. I guess I just need some time to process. People can be so stupid!"

"I'm glad you are holding onto our initial agreement, DJ. Don't forget that people are people. We all make mistakes. We all discount things we don't understand. None of us, *but God*, can see the total picture. So, we have to trust Him with *all* of this. I'm sorry you have to deal with this at school because of me... really I am. No father wants to see his son have to suffer."

They all sit in silence for a moment before DJ speaks.

"I'm sure God didn't want to see Jesus suffer either, but He allowed it for His greater plan of salvation." DJ takes a deep breath and runs his hand through his hair. "So, if Jesus could suffer the humiliation of dying on the cross while people made fun of *Him*, I guess *I* can deal with people acting stupid."

"Well said, Son," Daniel replies. "This is why Jesus tells us to pray for our enemies... they don't understand what is really happening... how God is working to bring salvation to the door of their hearts."

"Yeah," DJ agrees.

"So, we continue to let the light of Christ shine," Rebecca adds.

"Right," Daniel agrees.

"Thanks for listening to me vent, Dad. I'm okay now."

"I'm glad," Daniel smiles. "And thank you for still being committed to the Will of God. This work is definitely... *unusual*, but it is making a difference in so many lives! When the Bible talks about how God can take foolishness to confound the wise, it's not kidding. There's nothing that much more foolish than your father walking across the United States in a superhero suit!"

They all laugh.

"That's for sure." DJ declares.

"Hey!"

"What? I'm just agreeing with you."

"But you didn't have to *agree* so quickly."

"You set yourself up for that one," Rebecca adds as they laugh again.

"Hey Dad?"

"Yeah Son."

"As tough as all of this is... I'm proud of you... and I'm proud to be your son."

Tears immediately swell in Daniel's eyes as he pulls the receiver away from his face.

"Dad? Are you there?"

Daniel wipes his face and smiles. "I'm here..." His voice cracks a bit. "Your words... they mean a lot to me. I am very proud of you, Son."

"Thanks," DJ smiles."

"And I'm proud of you both," Rebecca shares as she wipes tears from her eyes. "Speaking of that, our parents called today."

"They did?" Daniel inquires. "What are they saying about all of this?"

"They just wanted to check on us." Rebecca answers. "And they wanted me to tell you they are one hundred percent behind what we're doing."

Daniel smiles while nodding his head... "God has really blessed us with some great parents."

"That He has," Rebecca agrees.

"The next time you talk to them, tell them I said thank you."

"I'll let them know tonight."

"And I want you both to know *right now* how much I love you," Daniel declares.

"We love you too," Rebecca replies.

"Yeah Dad," DJ adds.

"I don't know how I would have been able to do this without you."

"The Lord knows exactly what we need," DJ interjects.

"Yep!" Daniel smiles. "And you know what we should do right now?"

"Let me guess," DJ chuckles. "You want us to *pray*."

"No time like the present," his father smiles. "Let's thank God for His provision and ask for His intervention at your school."

"Can we pray for those at church and in the community too?" Rebecca asks.

"We sure can."

"Uh," DJ inquires, "This might be a *long* prayer. How much time you got?"

"To talk to the Lord?" Daniel answers. "All the time in the world."

And with that, Daniel leads his wife and son boldly to the throne of God to receive mercy and grace in their time of need.

37: Protect Her!

DAY 108 — Colorado

Valor makes his way through a quiet, but slightly run down, neighborhood. There are many houses, but not many people on the road. A girl with long hair, no more than 10 years old, runs toward him with tears in her eyes. Her yellow dress is torn, discolored and dirty. She is clearly scared, constantly looking over her shoulder. She practically tackles him like a linebacker.

"Help me, please!" She grabs Valor's hand tightly as he kneels down to her eye level and raises his visor.

"What's wrong?"

Before she can answer, a car roars up the block towards them and skids to a stop! Two men get out—but are hesitant at the unexpected sight.

"There you are," one of them utters while looking directly at her. "We've been looking all over for you. Your mom was worried."

"Who are you?" Daniel inquires as the girl ducks behind his cape.

"We're her uncles," the other man answers.

"Our niece got lost," the first man adds. "Who are you?"

"Father?" Daniel prays silently. "What's going on here?"

The voice of the Lord speaks firmly to Daniel's heart. ***"Protect her!"***

The girl grabs his hand and squeezes tight. Daniel glances down. Her eyes are filled with fear.

"They're *not* my uncles," she whispers while shaking her head.

His glance down was all they needed. In a flash the two men pounce on him like wild tigers!

"Stay back," Daniel shouts as they throw a flurry of punches and kicks! The girl runs to a nearby tree as Daniel blocks and parries their attack! He presses his way through their barrage and pushes both men squarely in their chests. The force of his push catapults them backward through the air—landing them on the other side of their car—*hard* on the pavement!

Daniel turns to the girl, who is now crouched several feet away behind a nearby tree.

"Let's go!"

The dazed men stumble to their feet, shake off their dizziness and reach under their jackets.

"Look out!" The girl points as she ducks behind the tree.

Daniel turns around just in time to see the men reaching for their guns! Instinctively, he closes his visor and raises his arms in defense as a barrage of bullets strike his forearm gauntlets and body armor! Fortunately, the bullets are small caliber rounds—which his suit's armored plating deflects. He goes on the offensive—rushing their car. In one smooth motion he crouches down, grabs the bottom with both hands and stands swiftly to his feet, bringing the car up with him and flipping it into the air and on its side!

The men stumble back—their eyes wide with fear—as the sudden unexpected move blocks several bullets! They regroup and run around both sides of their vehicle, only to drop their guns and clutch their ears as they fall to the ground! An intense, continuous, high-pitch sonic pulse emanates from Valor's suit and immediately causes inner ear pain and vertigo-like disorientation. They grimace while trying to regain their balance and reach for their weapons. But, it's too late. Valor is already upon them, quickly crushing their guns with a stomp of his boots. He then picks them both up, holding them high above his head, and slams them to the ground—knocking them out cold. He then shuts down his suit's sonic array.

The girl runs out from behind the tree and hugs Valor tightly. "Thank you!"

Valor quickly scans the area as he retracts his visor. He looks down at her with a warm smile. "You're safe now."

"You have to save my friends," she replies.

"Friends?"

"In the house! It's not far from here," she says. "I can show you!"

"Wait," Daniel kneels down to her level. "What happens in the house?"

The girl looks away. "They do… bad things to us."

"How many of your friends are there?"

"Please," she interjects. "We have to go now! If those guys don't call back soon, then the bad men will move them!"

V

15 Minutes later...

Six blocks over, both Daniel and the girl crouch in the bushes. She points.

"That's the house. The white one at the end of the street on the right."

"Are you sure," Daniel asks. "It looks like a normal house."

"I'm *sure*," she replies with full confidence. "You have to stop them and save my friends. Please!"

"I can't leave you here all alone with no protection." He prays for guidance as he scans the area. Just then, he catches a glimpse of a cross high in the air—about two blocks in the distance.

A few minutes later, both Daniel and the girl arrive at the Full Gospel Baptist Church.

"There are a lot of cars in the parking lot," the girl observes.

"Yes," Daniel replies. "That's a good sign."

They quickly enter the front doors to the building and find a Bible study in progress. As soon as they enter the sanctuary, the twenty-three people inside immediately take notice.

"Can I help you?" the pastor asks as they all stare at the curious sight before them: a black man wearing a super-suit while walking with a hispanic girl in a tattered yellow dress with somewhat matted long hair.

"Wait," the pastor continues. "You're that brother from the news... the Christian superhero guy."

Daniel wastes no time. He smiles briefly with a nod and then speaks.

"Are you all serious about your *walk* with Christ?"

They all stare for a moment, partially taken aback by the direct question. But within seconds, they all nod in the affirmative.

"We don't know each other," Daniel continues, "but we are sisters and brothers in Christ. And I need your help."

"What do you need us to do?" the pastor inquires.

"This girl has been sex-trafficked. I found her on the street about several blocks from here. She was running from two of her captors, who I *stopped*. She says there are others being held at a house two blocks from here."

"The white house at the end of the block?" a man from the group says.

"Yes," Daniel responds, a bit surprised. "You know of it?"

"We *all* do," the pastor interjects. "It's a suspected spot that's not used all the time. Seems to be a part of a larger network. The people there terrorize and pay off the neighbors—so no one reports them to the police."

"Somehow," a woman interjects, "they're always one step ahead of any police investigations. So, they've never been caught."

"We've been praying for God to shut them down for the last two years," the pastor admits.

"Well, Daniel replies, "I need you all to *guard* this little girl while I go to that house to rescue the others. Please lock the doors after I leave. Then wait twenty minutes, call 911 and send the police there."

The girl hugs him tightly, not wanting to let him go.

"It's okay," Daniel smiles. "You'll be safe here with these people. They will protect you until I get back. Then we can go to the police and see if we can find your parents. Okay?"

She nods. "Okay."

"You know," he says, "I don't even know your name. My name is Daniel."

"My name is Lourdes," she smiles.

One of the church mothers walks over to the girl and extends her hand. "It's okay baby. You are safe here. Are you hungry?"

She nods her head with a broad smile.

"Well come on over to my seat," the church mother smiles. "I always have some nice snacks in my purse."

Meanwhile, the pastor walks Daniel to the front door.

"This is a good thing you are doing. For God, His kingdom and for our people. I know the Lord is with you."

"Thank you," Daniel replies. "Can I ask you for a favor?"

'Sure."

"Once I leave, can you all pray for me and those in the house until I return."

"You got it."

V

15 minutes later... 9:00pm

Daniel finds himself standing behind some bushes at the beginning of the block. Everything seems quiet.

"Father," he prays. "That was the first time You allowed guns to fire on me..."

"Things will escalate as you continue this journey," the Holy Spirit responds. *"This is why I inspired your son to build your suit with certain protections. I remain with you in every situation."*

Movement at the end of the block catches Daniel's attention. A man exits the front door of the white house as a black van with tinted windows turns onto the block and pulls up in front of the house. Its engine stays running.

They're getting ready to move them, Daniel thinks to himself as he closes his visor. "Father? What do you want me to do?"

A single word is whispered to his heart. ***"Watch."***

And so, he crouches behind a tree and watches.

The driver exits the van and enters the house with the first man.

A prompt hits his spirit: ***"GO!"***

Valor jumps to his feet and takes off down the block—running at full speed! He quickly traverses the distance faster than expected.

The next prompt hits his spirit: ***"Back tire!"***

He kneels next to the driver's side back tire, quickly unscrews the air cap and deflates it.

Another prompt: ***"GO!"***

Valor bolts across the street and hides behind a large group of trees in a neighbor's yard. Just then the side door to the white house opens and the driver appears with 12 girls and 3 boys tied behind him. Another man follows up the rear. The kids are forcefully herded into the van as the driver runs back around to get in.

"Unbelievable!" he yells as the other man slams the doors to the van and runs around in response.

"What's wrong?"

"We got a flat!"

Just then, five police vehicles turn onto the block.

"5-0!" the man yells as the vehicles' lights and sirens activate!

"Let's get outta here!"
"What about the product?"
"Forget 'em! They don't know anything!"

The two men take off through an adjacent yard! Clearly their escape route has been planned. The police cars stop in front of the house, as three officers exit their vehicles and give chase. The two remaining officers hang back to check the van as several additional units arrive along with federal agents. Within minutes the children are rescued and the two men are in handcuffs in the back of the police cruisers. It is then that Valor makes himself known to the officer and shares what he knows about the situation.

V

Back at the church...

Daniel is reunited with Lourdes as he and the church members praise God for the victory! The police arrive at the church within the hour. Shortly after their arrival, the little girl and Daniel are taken to the local precinct to begin the process of determining who her parents are, where they live and how to get in touch with them. The entire time, she never lets go of Daniel's gloved hand.

"Will you stay with me until my parents come?"
"Absolutely," he smiles.

They sit on a bench in a secondary waiting area away from the main traffic of the lobby. The girl leans on his shoulder and quickly falls asleep.

The next day, two frantic, but jubilant parents are reunited with their daughter who had been missing for the last six weeks.

38: Hallelujah!

DAY 115 — Wyoming

After a long and incredibly weary day of walking, Valor stops and prays to the Lord about where he should stay the evening. He leans against a nearby fence as he retracts his helmet visor.

"Father, I know You always supply my needs... it would be great if my need tonight *included* staying with a nice Christian family in a house where I can get out of this suit, take a good shower and get a good night's sleep. It'll be another day or two before I can make it to the next designated family on the list. Either way, *You* know best. If You want me to sleep under the stars again tonight, then I will. But if You have a family for me, please let me know."

A second later, Daniel's eyes are opened to the unseen realm as the Spirit of discernment activates. The hue of the environment changes all around him. In the distance, he sees a house which is illuminated as if a spotlight shines down upon it from heaven.

"So, that is where You want me to go tonight," he smiles. "Thank you Lord." Daniel sets off towards the *lighthouse*—his wearied body quickened with each new step.

Thirty minutes later, he arrives at the house. Compared to the other houses around it, it is plain looking with no frills. The grass is overgrown and the paint is peeling. He breathes heavily to steady himself and knocks on the door. Several sets of footsteps pitter-patter inside as someone slowly approaches. The porch light flickers to life, illuminating the darkness as a dog barks in the distance. An eye peers through the peephole. Daniel takes a step back so it's easier for him to be seen. He smiles and waves as the sound of several locks being disengaged is heard. The door slowly opens, revealing a tired looking middle age black woman in her night clothes.

"Hello! My name is—"

"I know who you are, she cuts him off with a slight smile. "My name is Wanda. The Lord said you would be coming tonight and that we were to make accommodations for you. Please come in."

"May the peace of the Lord be upon this house," Daniel proclaims as Wanda opens the door and allows him entrance.

"Amen," she agrees. "We sure can use His peace right about now."

"Mommy!" A boy and a girl run to the door and freeze in awe.

"Wow…" they utter with wide eyes and broad smiles. "It's the superhero from TV!"

"I'm not a superhero," Daniel smiles with a nod."

"Well, why you dressed like one?"

"That is the constant question," he laughs.

"You can talk to him more in the morning, their mother interjects. "Both of you are supposed to be in bed."

"I don't want to sleep on the floor in Marissa's room. Why do I have to give up my room?"

"Jason, we talked about this. "Where else is this kind man going to sleep?"

"On the couch!"

Daniel laughs.

"Young man…" Wanda blushes with embarrassment.

"It's okay," Daniel intervenes. "I understand how he feels. I don't want to be a burden."

"Oh, it's no bother. Sleeping in his room gives you a bit of privacy. It gets pretty crazy in the morning with the kids running around. Jason will *gladly* give up his room for a few days if necessary to please the Lord *and* his mother."

"Yes, Mama," he replies with a sheepish grin.

"Now, both of you get to bed. And don't make noise. Your father just got to sleep."

The kids quietly tip toe to their room, while waving bye to Daniel. As if on cue, coughing is heard from the back of the house.

"That's my husband, Simon," she whispers as she motions for him to follow her to her son's room. The coughing continues with increasing frequency.

"I don't want to pry, but is your husband ill?"

She stops, barely able to hold back her tears. "He… used to work construction until he was injured on the job 6 months ago. Now, his immune system is impaired. Before, he rarely got sick. Now, he has several…issues. Disability hasn't covered all of the bills. We've almost used up all of our savings. Our insurance lapsed, so he can't see the doctor without paying out of pocket."

"And you don't have the money for that."

"No... Simon stays in bed most days. The house is falling apart and everything is on me to hold it all together. It's all I can do to make sure our kids have food to eat... and to shield them from how bad things *really* have become. I pray constantly... and read the Bible. But honestly, I was losing hope. I felt like God wasn't hearing me. I would cry out to Him and get no response... and then out of the blue, *a few hours ago*, I heard His voice as clear as day! He told me to make provisions for the mighty man of God who would come to my house at 10:00pm. When you rang the bell, I looked at the clock. It was 10:00pm on the dot."

They both stand in stunned silence outside of her son's room.

"God is worthy to be praised," Daniel whispers.

"That, He is," she agrees as they both look down the hall toward her bedroom.

"Do you mind if I go in to pray for your husband?"

Wanda's face lights up with delight. "I was hoping you would!"

Moments later they both stand next to her husband's restless body. It is clear from the sweat on his brow that he has a fever. His wife looks concerned.

"It doesn't matter what you see," Daniel asserts with a firm, yet soft authority. "*This* is a divine moment ordained by God from the foundation of the world."

She nods fervently.

"The Lord sees all things. And He will often manifest His Presence whenever two or three gather in His Name to do His will. Right now, *we* are carrying out His will."

Daniel removes his gloves, gently laying them on a nearby chair, along with his helmet. He takes hold of Wanda's hand, while placing his other hand lightly on top of the blanket which covers her husband's feet. He closes his eyes and bows his head. With a smile he begins to pray silently...

Suddenly, Wanda gasps as the Presence of the Lord quietly and invisibly manifests in the room. She immediately feels the swirling of the Holy Spirit within the core of her being, as faith bubbles up like a fountain about to blow its top! She watches Daniel's lips move as she begins to agree with him *in the Spirit*. The swirling Presence of God fills her body and rises to her lips—steadily building in intensity.

Daniel opens his eyes, his gaze fixed on the man before him, and utters these words:

"Simon, the Lord Jesus heals you. Be *free*!"

Simultaneously, the bubbling Presence of the Spirit within Wanda breaks free from her lips just as her husband's body heaves in a high arch and slumps back to the bed with a thump.

"Hallelujah!" She exclaims in a reserved yet emphatic tone. "It is done," she declares with weeping. "The Lord just said to me, *'It is done.'*"

Daniel smiles. "By the time I leave to continue my journey out west, your husband will have fully recovered."

"Thank you," she beams while hugging him.

"Don't thank me," Daniel replies. "Thank Jesus for His faithfulness."

She nods in agreement. "Yes. All praise, glory and honor is due to the Lord."

"Amen," Daniel agrees. "Amen."

Later, both Wanda and Daniel are soundly asleep in their respective rooms. Daniel's suit hangs on the closet door while his feet dangle off of young Jason's bed. He usually doesn't snore unless he is truly tired. Good thing the door is closed. It helps to muffle the sound…

V

The next morning…

Wanda hums with a smile while making a large breakfast with the last of the eggs, bacon, grits and biscuits. She stops as she feels the sensation of being watched. She turns around and finds her husband standing in the doorway to the kitchen with a big smile on his face.

"It smells good," he grins. "I had to come see what you were making for myself."

Wanda runs to Simon and throws her arms around him, causing him to stumble back into the wall.

"Take it easy," he chuckles while wincing in pain. "I feel better than ever, but I'm still a little weak."

"Sorry, baby," she releases her grasp on her husband. "it's just that you haven't been out of the bed *like this* for two months!"

"The bacon is about to burn."

"Oh!" She runs back to the stovetop to save the pieces.

"What happened last night?" He asks. "Last thing I remember was trying to get to sleep. As usual, I was in a lot of pain. Then at some point I had this... *dream*. I was lying down flat in a dark room on some unseen slab—it felt like rock. Suddenly, a light began glowing all around me and then Jesus appeared by my side! I couldn't move my body or speak, but I could turn my head slightly and look at Him. He had the most pierces eyes—so full of this *fiery* overwhelming love.

"My eyes followed his hand as he raised it and placed it on my feet. A burst of light came from Him, went into my feet and filled my entire being! My whole body arched up! Then I fell back to a flat position. Jesus smiled and beckoned for me to sit up. I did... and He vanished! Then I woke up to the smell of your cooking. And I was sitting up in bed. Can you believe it?"

"Yes, I can," Wanda laughs with joy as she shouts, "HALLELUJAH!!!"

Simon agrees with his own utterance of the highest verbal praise a human can render to the God of the universe. "HALLELUJAH!!!"

After a moment of worship, hugging and jumping, they both gaze into each other's eyes.

"You... don't seem a bit surprised by *any* of this," Simon utters with a bit of confusion. "It's like you already knew this would happen."

Wanda smiles deeply at her husband. "You shared *your* side of the miracle. Now, I need to tell you *mine*."

Simon smiles with a nod as movement catches his eye. He goes to the window.

"Babe? Who's that guy out there mowing our lawn?"

V

The third day...

The lawn has been mowed. The house has been painted. Broken elements on the property have been repaired.

Daniel sits with Simon and Wanda as the kids play in the backyard.

"I don't know how to thank you," Simon smiles. "You truly are a *godsend*."

"And so is your *family*," Daniel replies. "God brought us together to be a blessing to each other so He would get the ultimate glory, praise and honor."

"Amen to that," Simon agrees as Wanda lovingly strokes his hand.

Daniel continues. "I was in desperate need of some rest, a good shower and laundering for my suit and undergarments."

"Are you sure you got enough rest?" Simon asked. "With all the work you did around the house, *I'm* not so sure!"

They all laugh.

"Trust me, even with the work, I am well rested. There's a big difference between lying on the ground, using a rock for a pillow and sleeping in a bed—even if the bed is *smaller* than I am."

They laugh again.

"I never told you, but the other night, when I was looking for a place to stay, the Lord pinpointed your house for me with a spotlight of glory. That's how I knew where to come. He let me know that *His children* were in this house. So, never stop believing and trusting in Him, no matter how difficult things become. Jesus sees you. He knows what you are going through. And He is faithful to provide for your needs."

The doorbell rings. Wanda goes to the door and returns with a certified overnight priority envelope.

"This has both our names on it," she says to her husband while sitting back down. But I don't recognize the sender's name. We don't know anyone from Atlanta."

"Sure you do," Daniel smiles. "Me."

It takes a moment for his comment to register.

"The envelope was sent from my wife. I asked her to overnight it yesterday."

"What's in it?"

"Open it and see for yourself."

They open the seal and remove a business sized envelope. Both Simon and Wanda glance at Daniel curiously as they open *that* envelope and pull out a check. They freeze when they see the amount and look up at Daniel.

"We can't accept this," Simon utters.

"That's your prerogative," Daniel replies, "but you should know the Lord told me to do this *and* He told me how much to give you. So, if you reject it, you are turning down *His blessing* to you."

Simon and Wanda stare at the check once more and then at each other. The significance of the amount does not go unnoticed. She nods at her husband and he smiles back at her. They both turn to Daniel with tears in their eyes.

"We appreciate you being obedient to the Lord."

"You are my brother and sister in Christ. Our Heavenly Father often uses His kids to be a blessing to one another."

"But twice the amount of what we've had to pay over the past 6 months…" Simon says astounded.

"Our Father knows what we need. And He wants you to know that the last 6 months have not been wasted. They have served His purpose and what happens next will continue to serve His purpose. Everyone you know has been aware of your health situation. *Now*, let them all know how God has delivered you."

V

An hour later…

Daniel stands outside in his Valor uniform with the family. His helmet is under his arm and a medium sized satchel bag is slung over his shoulder.

"How are you feeling?" Daniel asks.

"Better than ever," Simon exclaims. "I go to the doctor tomorrow for a clearance exam so I can get back to work!"

"That's wonderful," Daniel smiles with a nod. "Well, I'll be leaving now. I appreciate these supplies." He pats the bag hanging from his shoulder.

"You never know when you'll need to make a campfire or will need a plate and utensils to eat," Wanda replies.

"Hey," Simon cautions. "Be careful on your way through the state. There have been some periodic grizzly bear sightings. For some reason, they've been venturing further away from their usual habitat. People living near some of the forests have had a few close encounters."

"Really?" Daniel replies.

"Trust me, you don't want to run into a grizzly. A healthy male can be as big as 10-11 feet in length and weigh between 700-1,200 pounds. Females are a little smaller. Sorry I don't have any bear spray to give you."

"But, it's okay Daddy," Jason interjects with great confidence. "God is with him."

"Yeah," Marissa adds, "I wouldn't be scared of a bear if I knew God was with me."

"Either way," Daniel replies, "thanks for the heads-up. I'll keep and eye out and be prayerful!"

"May the Lord continue to bless you!" Wanda declares with a last hearty hug.

"Group hug," Jason yells as he smothers Daniel. His sister and father do the same.

After a good hug, they separate while wiping tears from their eyes.

"May God continue to bless you all," Daniel declares as he puts on his helmet. "If we never meet again on this side of eternity, we will meet in God's kingdom!"

With that... Daniel turns with a wave and continues his journey towards California. The family waves one last time just before he turns the corner, almost a block away.

"Goodbye Valor!" Jason and Marissa shout.

"God bless!" he replies as he turns the corner and is out of sight.

As Daniel walks—he prays: "Father, I sure don't want to run into any bears!"

39: Grizzly!

Day 119 — Wyoming

It is just past dawn… on the outer edges of a forest. Valor lays asleep, in his full suit and helmet, on a makeshift cot he pulled together from area foliage. He had walked nonstop for an entire day before stopping here for the night. The sleep of the past number of hours has been much needed.

A large, wet blackish-brown nose sniffs Valor's motionless form. Warm breath puffs over him like steam bursting from a valve under pressure. The large nose moves up Valor's body from his legs to his visor, which reflects the glare of the morning sun. The large grizzly bear—weighing close to 1000 pounds—continues its curious examination. It's mouth opens and a long tongue checks Valor for taste: with a slobbering lick crossing his visor.

Valor wakes up—practically jumping back at the unexpected large bushy brown face! The bear jumps back as well—thoroughly startled! Valor slowly stands to his feet as the bear growls loudly while taking a defensive posture!

Valor raises his hands gradually. "Hey… no need to be aggressive buddy… I mean you no harm—"

The bear charges him like a battering ram, slamming into him with tremendous force! The impact from the bear's dense mass catapults Valor into the air! He hits a nearby boulder—hard—some ten feet away! His padded bodysuit absorbs the brunt of the impact, but it still hurts!

Valor leaps to his feet, but the Grizzly is upon him with blinding speed! It rises up on its hind legs, clearly dwarfing Valor's frame. Sharp claws strike across his chestplate—leaving noticeable damage—but not penetrating through the armor. Valor dives out of the way of another strike, but the bear catches his cape in its mouth—stopping his dive in midair! He crashes to the ground as the bear swings its head in a series of back and forth thrashing motions, throwing Valor around uncontrollably!

Valor yells in a panic as he tries to hit the quick release levers on his cape! After several misses, his hands land firmly on them—causing the cape to detach from his suit. He instantly drops to the ground as the bear throws the cape around before realizing he is no longer attached. The bear lets the cape drop from its mouth spots his prey, roars and charges again! Valor barely sidesteps the assault—like a matador dodging a bull—as the grizzly bear slams head first into the large boulder! He watches in dismay as the bear shakes off the pain, roars ferociously and lunges for him again!

How can an an animal this big move so fast? He thinks to himself as the bear lurches onto its hind legs and raises its front paws for another strike.

"Jesus help!" Valor yells as he raises his arms in defense—a split second before the bear slams down on him with the full weight and momentum of its dense body!

The blow lands on Valor's arms with shattering force! To his surprise his arms and legs do not give way... The blow itself feels as if the bear weighed no more than a heavy pillow. Valor *and* the grizzly bear stare at each other in momentary shock—both cocking their heads to the side—as Valor releases the bear's arms and takes a step back.

The force alone would fell any man no matter their size! But now, Valor can feel the familiar rushing of living waters flowing within his belly. The Spirit of the Living God has once again quickened his body with the same strength which was given to Samson!

The bear swipes again! A second time Valor blocks the blow with relative ease and not the least bit of damage. He smiles and goes on the offensive—tackling the grizzly. Both roll over each other as they wrestle for supremacy. The bear tries to bite, but Valor grabs its jaws with a firm grasp, easily restraining them as he rolls the bear onto its side! After one last failed attempt to throw the human off, the bear slows to a halt—its breathing heavy and labored. As Valor slowly releases his grip and dismounts from atop the large beast, the grizzly lowers itself to the ground and renders a submissive groan.

Never before has this mighty grizzly bear been tamed by a brute force greater than its own. Then again, never before had it encountered the power and Presence of its Creator flowing through the body of a human. The bear breathes heavily as Valor strokes its head just behind the ear. Clearly, the bear enjoys the rub as it nestles up against its human victor.

"Thank you Lord," Valor exclaims as he slides down next to the giant beast. "Thank you…" Sometime later, they both are sound asleep.

V

A few hours later, Valor awakes to find himself alone. He looks around and then takes off his helmet. A rustling of bushes reveal the bear's arrival with several fish in his mouth. It drops them at his feet with a low moan and nudges him with its nose.

"You brought me food? Thanks." Daniel rubs the bear behind its ear as it plops down next to him with a heavy thud. "So, there's a stream somewhere near here." Daniel gives attention to his cape.

"Well," he says to the bear as he examines it, "you really did a number on this."

The bear moans as Daniel points to the multiple tears in the fabric.

"Do you see this? I won't be using *this* to fly again. But hey, you didn't know. Did you? You were just being *you*…"

Daniel stands up and stretches before clearing an area to make a campfire. The bear watches him with great interest for a while and then gets up and walks towards the bushes once more.

"You're leaving?" Daniel inquires. "Are you coming back?"

The bear stops, turns in his direction and lets out a grunt. It then turns away and vanishes into the tree line.

V

Some time later… Early evening.

Flames crackle as the two fish cook above them on a makeshift skewer. Daniel is about ready to eat when the bear arrives back at his campsite and plops down, with a heavy thud, next to him. It drops a few more fish at its feet.

"Ah, I see you brought food for yourself," Daniel smiles while rubbing the bear's head. "All that's left to do is give God thanks and then we both can eat."

The bear watches as Daniel lifts up his hands in adoration and prays:

"Heavenly Father, I come to you in the Name of your Son Jesus. You continue to demonstrate Your sovereignty over all creation! By Your Spirit, you are leading and empowering me on this journey. And never would I have imagined saying grace over food You have provided by a bear! Please bless this bear... and thank you for doing for me what you did for Elijah and Daniel. And Father, thank you for having Simon and Wanda provide these supplies for such a time as this. You truly are Jehovah Jireh—my Provider. Please bless these fish we will both receive. May they nourish and strengthen our bodies in Jesus' Name. Amen."

The bear grunts in apparent agreement as Daniel looks at him with a smile.

"Alright, let's eat!"

With that, both man and beast feast on their food under the starry night sky... no doubt a pleasing sight to the God of the universe.

"That's right," Daniel says in between bites of his fish, "God used *you* like He used the ravens to feed the prophet Elijah. And God calmed you, like He did the lions when the prophet Daniel was thrown into their den. My wife and son are going to have a hard time believing this!"

V

The next morning...

Both Daniel and the bear wake up together. He cleans up his impromptu campsite and packs up his remaining supplies into the satchel bag.

"Well, Mr. Bear. I have to be on my way." He rubs the bear behind its ear once again as the bear rubs its body up against his. "You be good, okay? And please, stay out of trouble." He pats the bear on its head and points to the bushes. "Go on now... I'm going in the opposite direction."

He gives the bear a small push towards the bushes. The bear looks at them... and then turns and stares at Daniel. Through its heavy breathing, it grunts one last time and slowly lumbers off, making its way through the dense tree line. Daniel watches the sight and listens to the rustling until all is quiet once more.
"God..." He smiles. "You never cease to amaze me."
With that, Daniel puts on his helmet once more and heads for the highway.

PART 4

THE BATTLE

*"For our struggle is not against flesh and blood
[contending only with physical opponents],
but against the rulers, against the powers,
against the world forces of this [present] darkness,
against the spiritual forces of wickedness
in the heavenly (supernatural) places."*

—Ephesians 6:12—
(Amplified Translation)

40: No Good Deed Goes Unpunished

DAY 130—Chinese Monastery

13 hours ahead of Midwest time. Beads of sweat flow from Brother Léi's forehead as he continues in fervent prayer. He is the only one in the prayer room and is interceding mightily. Another monk arrives at the entrance to check on him. He does not enter, but remains standing in the doorway. The Holy Spirit is clearly moving. He is not sure why, but even as he stands he enters into prayer as well. Minutes pass before Brother Léi feels a release in his spirit and places his intercession on pause. He looks up to find his brother standing in the doorway.

"You have been here for three hours," the brother says. "That is nothing *new*, but you missed the afternoon devotions."

Brother Léi wipes his face with his robe and stands to his feet.

"The LORD called me to intercede for Brother Dàiwéisēn. He is about to endure great suffering. Please, tell the others we must cover him in prayer. The enemy seeks our brother's destruction… but what is meant for evil, God desires to use for good."

V

Wyoming. Midwest time.

It's been several hours since Valor left the bear. Though it is early in the morning, the sun is already blazing. Valor stops on the side of the road and raises his helmet's visor. He takes a bottled water out of his satchel bag and places the bag on the ground. As he drinks—enjoying the cool liquid on a hot and humid day—a black van screeches to a halt behind him. The doors burst open as four men in masks jump out, grab him and pull him into the van. Before Daniel can react, the butt of an assault rifle strikes him squarely in his face—knocking him out cold. Just as quickly as it arrived, the van speeds down the highway in a plume of smoke! Daniel's satchel bag and spilled bottle of water lay on the side of the road in the dirt.

V

Almost two hours later...

Daniel grimaces as he regains consciousness. The side of his face feels swollen as the pain burns through his skin. His mouth somehow feels restricted. In his grogginess, he can't tell if its swollen or if it's stuffed with something. But it feels full and his lips feel... stuck. His eyes slowly adjust to the sunlight streaming down through the open roof. As he looks around, his eyes are met with darkness—peppered with streaks of light.

He looks down at his body and notices his suit has been removed and his chest, arms and legs are strapped to a metal chair. All he is wearing is his t-shirt and a tight-fitting pair of shorts. As he glances down, he notices the chair is sitting in a puddle of water. He also notices two metal clamps connected to the chair—one on each leg. Each clamp has a long wire which stretches off into the distance.

Daniel, now fully awake and aware, thinks to himself while focusing his concentration. *No way I'm staying here.* With a deep breath and exhale through his nose, he pulls his arms against the straps with all of his might! But... the leather straps do not give.

Father? He prays... What's going on? Where are You? I need Your strength.

All of Daniel's muscles suddenly contract violently as he convulses! Electricity surges from the wires, through the metal chair and directly into his body! The pain is unimaginable as his screams are muffled by the rag stuffed in his mouth. He shakes uncontrollably for several seconds before the current ceases and his body slumps into the chair. He breathes heavily with whimpered moans.

"He's finally awake!" A voice bellows as the echo reverberates through the empty warehouse. Five men slowly walk out of the shadows—but keep their distance. One of them—presumably the leader—claps his hands in delight.

"We finally get to meet the great Daniel Davidson... What do they call you? The Mighty Man of Valor." He laughs sarcastically. "You know, that's a *nice suit* you were wearing," he says in an upbeat tone. "Took us a few minutes to figure out how to get it off you. Even though it's beat up from your journey, it's pretty tough. That chestplate looked like you ran into a bear or something. I've decided to add it to my collection. Back home, I have a museum of sorts, where I keep... mementos from the people I kill."

His tone changes from jovial to menacing. "You cost me a lot of product, money and resources when you helped that *little girl*. My guys said you flipped their car over on its side. I didn't believe it. Thought they were lying to cover up their mistakes. I was about to kill them, but then I saw pictures of the car. I don't know how you did that... or *if* you did that. But here you are now... helpless. I watched you try to break free. If you really *do* have super strength, where did it go?"

The leader comes closer and stands just beyond the puddle of water. Daniel immediately studies him, noticing a long scar riding down the left side of his face. He leans in Daniel's direction.

"That was one of our main houses in the area... and you got it shut down." He stands up straight. "But you know what they say. 'No good deed goes unpunished.'" He turns around and walks back toward the shadows while yelling. "Did you think you could do that and just walk off into the sunset without *any* repercussions?" He stops just before the darkness covers him and looks over his shoulder. "You got anything to *say* for yourself? Oh, wait... where are my manners? You can't speak with your mouth stuffed and taped."

The leader rushes over to Daniel, walking right through the puddle, takes hold of the duct tape covering his mouth and rips it off! Daniel groans in pain as the man also pulls the rag out of his mouth.

"*Now*," the man says while backing out of the puddle, "you can speak."

Daniel coughs and winces as he waits for the pain to subside before he says in a weak voice: "...God... is *sovereign*."

The leader laughs as the other men follow his cue—laughing as well. After a moment, he gives his rebuttal.

"God is *sovereign*? Do you mean that nothing happens without His permission and even His decree? If that's true, then God has *decreed* you be turned over into my hands so I can make your life a living hell before I kill you!"

The last few words of his stern voice echoes through the warehouse. Silence punctuates the statement before Daniel replies with a bit more strength...

"Jesus died to set you free. You don't have to do any of this. You have a choice. You can let *Him* change you."

"You think I care about Jesus?" His voice seethes with anger and hatred as he walks back over to Daniel—stopping just before the puddle on the floor. "Do you know what I've seen? What I was *raised* in?" He barks as spit splatters on Daniel's face. I watched family and friends die horrible deaths at the hands of men and women with no mercy! I watched people scream to God for help right before a bullet was put in between their eyes or their limbs were chopped off and they bled out on the concrete."

As he stares deeply into Daniel's eyes, Daniel can see only darkness lives in this man's soul.

"Torture and death... that's all I knew when I was a kid! No... Jesus didn't show up to help them. And he never showed up to help me! I had to claw... and fight... and kill or be killed to get where I am. I had to do things you can't even imagine just to survive! And you want to sit there and tell me that, 'Jesus loves me this I know, for the Bible tells me so?' I heard all that from the priests where I grew up. And I watched their remains be buried in coffins and dumped in the ground.

"So, you know what I say about your Jesus? He... *doesn't*... exist," the man barks! "*God* doesn't exist! *Heaven* doesn't exist! *Only* devils do. And the only hell that exists is this world we live in." He stares long and hard at Daniel, barely able to contain his anger through deep breaths. Then a smile breaks out on his lips. "You know... being able to vent like this... it *actually* makes me feel better!"

The leader strikes Daniel across the face with a hard and fast open hand. Daniel yells out in pain. The leader smiles sinisterly before his expression becomes serious once more.

"Let me tell you what's going to happen. I *hate* God... *And* I hate Christians. On top of that, you *messed* with *my* business. So, that's three strikes against you. And you know what they say in baseball... three strikes and you're out! What you're about to go through... for me it will be business *and* personal. Me and my men are going to beat you for most of the night. We're going to take turns and we're going to love every minute of it. Then, we're going to *salt* your wounds so you can *really* feel the pain. Then we're going to go home and let you sit here in your own filth. And early in the morning, we'll come back... douse you with gasoline... set you on fire and watch you *burn*. And when you are good and dead, we're going to go pick up your wife and son in Atlanta and do the same thing to them!"

Daniel's eyes widen in terror as the man laughs hysterically.

"You didn't think we knew about them?"

"Don't you touch them," Daniel growls!

"Oooh... you got some fight in you! I like it. A man should want to protect his familia."

"Leave them out of this!"

The leader completely disregards Daniel's plea. "Too bad you won't be able to keep them safe. And don't worry, this warehouse has been abandoned for years and it's so far out in the middle of nowhere that no one will hear you scream."

Again, Daniel tries with all his might to break the straps which restrain him! But they do not budge. The leader laughs again as he turns to his men.

"I don't know how he flipped that car. But he don't have super strength! At least not no more!

For the next three hours, they pummel him... with their fists... with brass knuckles... with bats... and with electricity. By the time they finish, four men are breathing heavily. But, through all the excruciating pain, Daniel noticed that the fifth man—though he has participated—has been slightly *restrained* in his assault.

A short while later, the leader comes with a large bag of salt. He pours it onto Daniel's wounds, rubbing it in deeply, which causes him to scream out like a wounded animal! Through tears and swollen eyes, he looks at them with bloodied gritted teeth.

"There it is!" the leader declares with a point. "There's the hatred! I thought you were a Christian? A man of God? What happened to turning the other cheek? Let me guess, you want us to burn in hell right now, right? What happened to all of the *love* you've been talking about? All these... *witnesses* on TV who claim you speak and act on behalf of God? Look at you now... You ain't thinking about love now, are you?" The leader laughs again. "Tonight you can pray to your God. Cause in the morning, I'm gonna send you to meet him."

The five men leave Daniel sitting in a puddle of water, blood, urine and salt...

V

Daniel tries to hold himself together, as he hears their footsteps growing distant. The slamming of the warehouse doors reverberate through the entire building. Daniel can hear a vehicle start up and drive away. Then, in the silence, he lets out a harrowing wail! How is he even alive after the kind of beating he just endured? He has never felt such pain in his life! Surely, these men specialize in prolonging agony in their victims.

His face is swollen. Jaw is fractured. His nose—broken. Cuts and lacerations riddle his body from head to toe. An arm, leg and several ribs are also broken. His lungs feel like they are filling up with fluid. The salt in his wounds make each pain receptor feel like an electrical live wire! His entire body screams for relief! But there is none in sight. Right now, he has no idea how things are going to turn out.

"God..." he barely whispers. It's painful just to speak... "Where are You?" A moment of silence passes with no response. "*Why*... have You *allowed* this... to happen? What... did I... do wrong? Are You... punishing me?" Another moment of silence passes before the hushed voice of the Holy Spirit, which has led him thus far, speaks from the midst of his spirit.

"Philippians 3:10-11"

Daniel's eyes flutter as he tries to recall the passage. His mind is groggy, due to the beating. It hurts just to think. But with a struggle he indeed does recall the verses and whispers them out loud:

"I want to know Christ—yes, to know the power of his resurrection and participation in his sufferings, becoming like him in his death, and so, somehow, attaining to the resurrection from the dead."

Daniel's eyes suddenly open to the unseen realm as the manifest Presence of the LORD descends into the warehouse and alights next to him. A pinpoint of light appears and then expands outward into the form of a Person. Immediately, Daniel recognizes Him.

"Lord, Jesus..." Daniel whispers. "You have come..."

"You know the power of My resurrection..." the LORD speaks. *"Now you must participate in My sufferings."*

"But," Daniel replies with a quiet anger, "how does *this* bring You glory? You left me alone... You let them *beat* me! You took *away* Your gifts of the Spirit! You *didn't* warn me that this would happen and when it did, You didn't give me the strength of Samson. I was helpless! You left me to their mercy... and they have *none*!"

"I alone am the source of mercy," the LORD replies. *"It is My mercy by which you have this present reprieve. Contrary to what you think, I did not leave you. With each blow against your body, I gave grace to your spirit to withstand them. Now, you must choose... you can hate them and blame Me... or you can trust Me and love them with the love I lavish on you."*

"But Lord... they are going to *kill* me."

"I am SOVEREIGN!" The LORD replies with great intensity, yet flowing with an overwhelming love. *"Nothing happens without My decree!"*

Silence greets Daniel as his mind reels at the words, which echo back and forth within his being... Then the LORD speaks again—this time in a softer tone.

"My decree to you remains. You must speak on My behalf in California."

Daniel's heart and mind stagger at the words of the Lord. His eyes dart back and forth as he fights to relinquish his lack of understanding. He lowers his head and closes his eyes. "Y-yes Lord. I'm... sorry. You *do* watch over *Your Word* to perform it."

"Ask Me for what you need."

For a moment, Daniel thinks through his options. Clearly, he wants his abilities back. He wants to break out of the chair and bring retribution. He wants vindication and justice... *no... vengeance*. But is that what he *needs*... in this moment? Or are those things merely what he desires? Once again he surrenders his will.

"Lord, I will *trust You* with this outcome. Please give me *Your love* for these men who are trapped in Satan's grasp. *He* is the *real* enemy here... for me... and for them."

"Well done," the LORD whispers with a smile. ***"Your request has been granted. On the cross, I saw this day and paid the price for these sinful men. Though four will perish in the hands of the evil one, you must still love them with My abundant love. You will witness the power of My love which is tremendous to save. You will also witness My judgment. For the LORD always judges by what is right."***

In an instant, Jesus is gone. The realm of the unseen gives way, once again, to natural sight. Yet, the palpable Presence of the Holy Spirit remains. Still in immense pain, Daniel renders a quiet litany of worship to the LORD. He quotes Scriptures of adoration and as old hymns come to mind, he sings them to the best of his ability. He thanks God for His faithfulness and blessed assurance until... he falls asleep.

V

Several hours later... Daniel is roused out of a strained sleep by the fifth man.

"Hey, wake up."

"You..."

"Listen, my boss sent me ahead to get the tools ready to kill you. They'll be here in 10 minutes."

"Why are you telling me this?"

"I don't know...."

"Look, I don't know you, but I can tell you don't want to kill me. Help me get out of here," Daniel urges.

"If I do that, my boss will kill me worse than what he's gonna do to you."

"Okay... I don't want him to do that. But you clearly seem different from the rest."

"I'm no saint, okay?" The fifth man admits. "I've done a lot of bad things in my life; things I don't think God could ever forgive me for. But when you said God is *sovereign*... that is something my great grandmother would tell me all the time when I was little. I didn't understand what she meant then. It always made me mad because life was hard. But when you said the *same thing*... I haven't been able to shake it."

"Listen to me," Daniel replies. "This is going to *sound* strange, maybe even unbelievable, but what I am about to say is absolutely true. God *is* sovereign and He allowed this situation to happen so He could reclaim you from the snares of the Devil."

"What? There's no way God wants me..."

"He *does* want you! He told me Himself."

"He what?"

"Last night. When you left me here... Jesus came to me and told me that His love is available for any of you who will repent. God will forgive your sins and receive you to Himself. All you have to do is yield to Him and ask for it! Jesus *loves* you! And this is your last opportunity to receive His gift of salvation."

"What do you mean, *last*?"

"It may look like I'm about to die, but God told me I still must go to California. He said He would bring justice. So, today is the day of salvation for any of you who repent. Once God *frees me*, the opportunity will be over and only *judgment* will remain."

"What you doing over there," the leader bellows from across the building as he enters the warehouse.. "You ain't trying to *free* him are you?"

"Hit me," Daniel whispers.

The fifth man strikes Daniel hard across the face.

"Nah, boss. He was popping off at the mouth. So, I was giving him a few extra licks!"

"Good... good," he claps. "We ready to go?"

"Yep," the fifth man says while walking back over to where the other men are now standing.

"Alright... douse him."

One of the other men picks up the gasoline canister and proceeds to pour it all over Daniel. Then he makes a trail back to where they are standing. The leader takes a small box of matches out of his pocket.

"Any last words *oh, mighty man of valor*?" he chuckles.

As Daniel looks at the five men, an overwhelming sense of God's love rises up within him! It is unlike any amount of love he has ever felt! It bubbles up mightily from his belly and flows outward to all of his extremities! In an instant, every ounce of fear and hatred vanishes from his heart and mind. It is out of this overflow, that he speaks:

"God is *sovereign*. He wants to give you His gift of eternal life... but you must yield to His Son. Jesus loves you and died on the cross so your sins could be forgiven and you could be set free from the manipulation and deception of the Devil. If you surrender to Him, He will allow you to live. If you don't repent of your sins *right now*, then you will face God's judgment for your continued rebellion against Him."

"So, *you're* the one calling the shots?" the leader balks. "You are going to tell *me* what to do?" He says with a ferocious yell. With that, he lights a match and flicks it into the gasoline.

With a WHOOSH, the fire expands and begins its swift trek toward Daniel.

"We gonna set you on fire and watch you burn!" All but one of them laughs. While they laugh, the fifth man starts silently praying that what Daniel said is true—that God would somehow deliver him from what appears to be certain death.

Daniel, drenched in gasoline, prays as the flames approach, "Lord, get the glory and honor and praise from this situation!"

The response to his spirit is immediate. ***"Praise Me!"***

Even while in pain, Daniel begins to cry out over and over with increasing intensity, "Hallelujah. Hallelujah! Hallelujah!! Hallelujah!!!" As he does this, the sky overhead begins to darken as clouds roll in and a faint breeze is felt flowing through the broken windows of the warehouse.

By the time the fire reaches him, Daniel is praising God at the top of his lungs with every fiber of his being!

"HALLELUJAH!!!!!"

Suddenly, he feels compelled to rebuke the flames! He looks at the fire as it engulfs his body and proclaims, "Fire, I rebuke you in the Name of Jesus Christ of Nazareth! The Son of the Living God! Be gone in Jesus' Name!"

As the heat from the flames rises to unbearable levels, a sudden mighty rushing wind drops down from the sky directly through the massive hole in the roof! Shards of broken glass fall in every direction, but none hit Daniel as the downdraft buffets his immediate surroundings like a shield. With this immense continuous downdraft fully enveloping Daniel, a cold rain falls, which reduces the flames lapping up his body! As the rain falls, the air, moving at almost hurricane level force, pushes the tongues of fire back from Daniel's body and extinguishes them altogether!

The men back away in fear as they watch, with astonishment, as the thick leather straps that restrained Daniel, snap apart and fall to the ground! Strength enters his body, and right before their terrified eyes, *all* of his wounds heal! In an instant, he's up on his feet! The four men are terrified as the wind blows them back, knocking them off their feet! The fifth, stands *pinned* against the wall *by the wind*—with a smile of awe and wonder on his face.

"This is your final chance!" Daniel yells—as the windstorm temporarily dissipates. "God will receive you if you repent and surrender your lives to His Son. Otherwise, you will carry the full weight and penalty of your sin and face God's wrath."

The four men scamper to their feet, pull out their guns and aim them at Daniel. The wind increases in an instant, blowing debris directly at them. They repeatedly fire their weapons, but cannot keep their arms steady and their eyes trained on their target. As Daniel walks towards them, every bullet misses its mark as the men stumble around under the hurricane-like onslaught!

Realizing their futility, the men flee outside and jump into their black van. They start the vehicle and take off as Daniel exits the building along with the fifth man. They both watch as the van accelerates into the distance, hits a pothole, loses control, flips through the air several times and slams hard onto the ground! Flames erupt from the engine block followed by an immediate explosion! All inside are killed…

The fifth man looks from the flaming vehicle to Daniel and then drops to his knees—bowing at Daniel's feet.

"Don't do that," Daniel warns while reaching down to gently raise the fifth man up. "Don't bow to *me*."

"But God is *with* you," he exclaims!

"He is," Daniel agrees as he holds the fifth man by both shoulders. "But I am a man just like you. And if you truly want to *receive Jesus* as your Lord and Savior, then God will be with you, too."

"Yes. I want Jesus to *save* me… to *forgive* me of my sins. I don't want to do evil anymore."

Right there... outside of the abandoned warehouse, while a van rests upside down on fire and those inside it are lost forever—both men kneel. Daniel leads the fifth man in prayer... and he receives Jesus as his *Master*. In that moment, all of heaven rejoices as he *becomes* a child of God.

Daniel stands the man to his feet with a smile. "You and I are now *brothers* in Christ."

The man cries tears of joy and excitement.

"There is a lot you need to know about this Christian journey that you are now on. Are you married? Do you have kids?"

"No. And I can't go back home. It's not safe for me now."

"That's what I was going to say," Daniel agrees. "I am sure the Lord already has a place picked out for you. But, right now, I need my uniform... and we need to leave."

"Your suit is inside in one of the storage rooms."

Soon, both men are walking down the road. Daniel is in his full suit once again. He smiles a silent thank you to the Lord and turns his attention to the fifth man.

"So, I never asked... what's your name?"

"Jeremiah," the fifth man replies with a smile. "My name is Jeremiah Montoya."

"Did you know that Jeremiah was a powerful prophet in the Bible?"

"My great grandmother would tell me that as a child... but I don't know anything about him."

"That's okay," Daniel smiles while putting his hand on Jeremiah's shoulder. "You will."

41: Where There's Smoke...

DAY 133 — Utah

Daniel's journey thus far has taken him through many different types of communities. He has traveled along highways, through remote parts of towns, through bustling urban cities, rural counties and quiet suburbs. He has encountered common situations and unique circumstances, while interacting with people who are from similar *and* diverse backgrounds. He has weathered many storms... and has faced a variety of opposition. Yet, it seems, that each interaction has prepared him for the next. Each has taught a lesson or revealed a truth about the nature of reality and more importantly, about the sovereignty of God.

As Daniel walks through a neighborhood with his visor up, he contemplates Proverbs 24:12:

If you say, "But we knew nothing about this," does not he who weighs the heart perceive it? Does not he who guards your life know it? Will he not repay everyone according to what they have done?

"Yes Lord," he utters. "Even in the unexpected, You have already prepared the way."

Distant screams snap Daniel out of his devotional thoughts! He scans the block and sees several people standing outside of a house being consumed by flames and smoke. He closes his visor, breaks into a run and arrives in front of the horrible sight. In actuality, it is two houses side-by-side that are being ravaged by the rapidly expanding inferno! One house is an average size; the other is a mini-mansion.

As the crowd grows and their cell phones capture this tragic event with stunning clarity, a woman's voice shouts from one of the houses.

"Help! Help!!!"

Someone from the crowd shouts. "Look! Mary and her son are trapped on the second floor!"

"The firemen won't get here in time," another adds. Everyone witnesses the mother and son at the open bedroom window. Smoke billows out as the flames slowly ascend up the front of the house.

"That's at least a 3 alarm fire," someone else shouts.

As if like clockwork, everyone turns their focus from the house to Valor as he arrives behind them.

"You're that superhero guy!" One of them yells. "Do something!"

"Yeah," someone else exclaims. "You've got to *do* something!"

"Father," Valor prays. "What do You want me to do?"

"Enter!" At God's leading, Valor rushes towards the blazing house. The bystanders watch with trepidation as he kicks open the front door. Dark smoke immediately flows out, engulfing him and obscuring everyone's view.

Inside, the raging fire destroys everything it touches. The sound of the raging flames is deafening! The temperature soars—evidenced by everything burning and melting around him—but somehow, he doesn't *feel* the heat.

I know we made this suit to withstand the heat, he thinks to himself as he fights his way up the stairs to the second floor, *but I don't feel anything at all!*

The female voice cries out again from the end of the hallway. "Help!"

Valor bursts through the door, at the end of the hall, and finds a woman and her young son huddled in a corner.

"Mommy look!" the boy shouts as he points at the unexpected figure.

Valor closes the door behind him to keep the flames out. To his surprise, the room is only filled with smoke, which is flowing out of the open window. He notices that the safety railings are on it.

"I couldn't get the bars off," she exclaims! "And there's too much fire in the hallway!"

"Don't worry Mary," Valor replies. "I'm here to get you both out of here."

"How do you know my name?"

"One of your neighbors said it outside. We have to act fast! We don't have much time."

"But how are we getting out?" Mary asks in a panic.

"The only way out is back through the flames!"

"But we'll die!"

"No," Valor assures them as he removes his cape. "Wrap yourselves in this. Quickly!"

They jump to their feet and follow his command.

"What's your name?" Valor says to the boy.

"Eric!"

"Well, Eric, I prayed and the LORD said we won't die today. Both of you, take my hand!"

Just as they take his hand, the room explodes in flames as that part of the house caves in!

Outside, everyone screams as they watch half of the house collapse in on itself. The inferno completely engulfs it like a ravenous creature! The neighbors fear the worst... For what seems like an eternity, no one moves as they are paralyzed by the terrible sight. Bright flames and dark smoke rise even higher into the air.

"Where are the firetrucks?"

"What's taking them so long to get here?"

"Oh, Mary... and Eric..."

"There's no way anyone could have survived that..."

Someone gasps. "Look!"

Members of the crowd strain to see through the thick plumes of smoke and lapping tongues of fire. "Don't you see it?"

"It looks like... people standing in the fire!"

Moments later, the crowd watches—amazed—as Valor, Mary and Eric make their way through the flames and exit from *what's left* of the house. Behind them, in the smoke, stands a fourth form—larger and glowing.

"Do you see that!" another yells.

"It's an angel!"

The glowing fourth form remains until the three are completely out of harms way, and then it disappears!

As the three of them make their way to the street, members of the crowd quickly approach to assist them. Valor takes his cape from Mary and Eric and puts it back on. Everyone is amazed: The three of them are completely unharmed. Their clothes are fully intact. They have no burns and don't even smell like smoke!

"I—I don't understand what happened..." Mary says.

"Mommy," Eric exclaims with great excitement, "the flames weren't even hot!"

"How is this possible?" she asks. "You saved us."

"No." Valor counters as he opens his visor. "Jesus has saved us all."

The crowd cheers as some even begin to praise God.

Another scream punctuates the air! Everyone turns their attention to the second, larger house. A man appears in the top window—clearly in distress. The lower floors of the house are fully engulfed.

"Help him!" Someone yells. "Yeah!" Others agree.

Daniel closes his visor, takes three steps towards the house and suddenly stops.

"What are you doing?"

'Why did you stop?"

"Help him!" someone pushes him toward the house.

Valor takes a step back. "I can't."

The man continues to scream for help as the flames make their way to the room where he has sought safety.

"What do you mean, you *can't*? You just helped Mary and her son... Help *him*! He's our neighbor, Mr. Petrelli!"

Members of the crowd try to pull Valor towards the house, but he refuses to move. No matter how hard they pull, he literally doesn't budge one inch.

"Are you just going to let him *die*?!"

"This..." Valor says with a sorrowful agony in his voice, "...This is God's judgment on him. I cannot intervene."

Everyone stops in momentary shock. Mr. Petrelli's screams are now even more desperate as the flames reach his room. He breaks the remaining glass from the window and tries to climb out, but the flames from the level below are so high and intense that they severely restrict *any* kind of exit! Firetruck sirens are heard in the distance, but the surrounding neighborhood street is blocked by traffic from onlookers.

"You have to help him!" Someone angrily commands. "The firetrucks will never make it in time!"

"I'm sorry," Valor says. If people could see through his visor, they would see the tears flowing from his eyes as he turns away and begins to walk off down the street. "He refused to repent of his ways."

Everyone looks from Valor, to the house, and back to Valor again. Multiple people cry out in anger.

"What's that *supposed* to mean?"

"He's a good man!"

"He doesn't deserve to die like this!"

"Who are you to play God?"
"What kind of God would save one person and not another?"
"Whatever God you serve, I don't want any part of him!"
"You're not a hero!"

The crowd boos, jeers and scoffs at Valor as he walks away. Some even pick up nearby trash and throws them at him. Even as he's hit with cans and other objects, Valor does not slow nor change direction. Mr. Petrelli's screams draw their attention as they watch his house fully succumb to the flames. Minutes later, the firetrucks finally arrive, but Mr. Petrelli's screams are heard no more.

V

Later that day…

The fires have been extinguished and Mr. Petrelli's charred body has been removed from his residence.

News stories and social media explode with video footage and eye witness testimony of Valor's refusal to save Mr. Petrelli. There is barely a mention of the fact that he saved Mary and Eric: the neighbors in the burning house next door. As mother and son try to share the truth, both of their pleas to see him as a hero falls on deaf ears. Across the nation, many decry Valor's actions and call for his arrest.

Up until now, all previous media coverage has been mixed. But there has always been more who were *for* Valor than who were against him. Now, this ratio has been completely upended! Within a matter of hours, public opinion became jury, judge and executioner. The people have spoken—even if they were ignorant of all the facts. By the next day, the authorities actively track Valor's whereabouts.

42: Person of Interest

DAY 134 — Utah

One day has passed since the fire claimed Mr. Petrelli's life. Within 24 hours, the authorities have located Valor—whom they have called a person of interest—and are now engaged in apprehending him.

A police helicopter soars overhead as five squad cars, a S.W.A.T. transport vehicle and a prisoner containment truck surround Valor in a parking lot. The officers stand near their vehicles with guns drawn.

"Valor," an authoritative voice rings out from a bullhorn. "Daniel Davidson. You are surrounded. Get down on your knees and put your hands behind your head."

Numerous bystanders and news reporters capture the entire exchange on video from a safe distance. Many are live-streaming it to the world!

"Father?" Valor prays silently as he raises his hands in the air and then places them behind his head. "Should I run?"

"This is from Me," The Holy Spirit replies. *"Do not be afraid."*

Daniel lowers himself to his knees as the police slowly approach him in an aggressive configuration with their weapons drawn.

"You are sovereign," he prays. "I know You are with me and no matter what happens, I will *never* doubt You again."

The police officers handcuff Daniel, push him to the ground at gunpoint, quickly check his body for weapons and take him into custody. Most people watching on social media cheer at the sight of him being led away and placed in the prisoner containment truck!

V

After processing at a local precinct, Daniel is transferred to a nearby mental institution for observation. Now wearing a white gown and wristband, two sizable orderlies escort him to a solitary cell-of-a-room, to wait for his evaluation. They push him into the small room and close the door behind him. He rubs his bandaged left arm and stares at the sparse furniture: a bed bolted to the floor. A desk, also restrained. And a toilet. Padded walls greet him on every side. No window, except for the small one in the door which has a sliding shade cover on it. Only a small fluorescent light in the center of the very high ceiling illuminates the room—barely.

Daniel walks over to the reinforced door and places both hands on it. He plants his feet firmly on the floor and then presses his hands against the door. He feels no added strength from the Holy Spirit as the door doesn't budge at all.

"Okay Lord," he whispers. "You must want me to minister to someone in this place."

V

Later that night...

The ceiling light is off. In the stillness of the darkness, as Daniel kneels next to his bed in prayer, a bright light appears in the corner of the room. As he turns towards the light, he sees a silhouette of an angel visible within its core. Ribbons of glory, flowing like a reflection of water, fills the room.

"Do not be afraid Daniel," the angel speaks. *"You are where you need to be. The LORD will reveal what you need to know at the appointed time."*

In an instant the angel disappears, along with the golden ribbons of light, as the darkness of the room returns. With thanksgiving in his heart, Daniel lays on the mattress and falls soundly asleep. The peace of God covers him like a thick blanket.

V

The next day...

Daniel sits in an observation room—similar to what one would see used in a police interrogation. Across from him, on the other side of the table, sits three well dressed persons with clipboards and pens: two men and a woman. A fairly large security guard stands at the ready, just outside the door, should there be any trouble. On the other side of the large one-sided window, built into the wall, stands several other women and men. High definition audio/video recording is in progress from two cameras as the questioning begins.

"My name is Dr. Weinstein," the woman says. "I am the chief psychiatrist at this facility. These are my colleagues, Dr. Rubaker and Dr. Cohen. We are going to ask you some questions."

Daniel does not respond at all.

"So, you hear voices?" Dr. Weinstein continues with a slight smile and a play at empathy as she leans forward in her chair.

Daniel sits upright and quiet.

"You..." she continues as she quickly glances at her notes, "specifically claim to hear the voice of God? Can you tell us what His voice sounds like?"

Still, Daniel says nothing.

She continues. "Up until recently, your actions have been... amusing, helpful even. But now, a man has died and you said his death was a result of him *being judged* by God. Did the voices tell you that?"

The Holy Spirit whispers to Daniel's heart. **"You may speak."**

"What do I say?" Daniel prays silently.

"As always," the Holy Spirit replies. ***"The truth."***

Daniel stares at the woman and the two men with her.

"You are trying to determine whether or not I am insane or crazy. I assure you, I am neither."

"Okay," the woman replies, "then what are you?"

"I am a human being, just like you, who has been called by God to deliver a message."

"And what message is that?"

"God is *sovereign*. And time is *short*. Jesus is coming soon. Do not harden your hearts, but rather surrender to Him before it is too late."

The trio of psychiatrists chuckle amongst themselves, without hiding their aloofness.

"Do you realize how many people, held in *this* institution, claim to be Jesus Christ?"

"That is *not* my claim," Daniel replies. "I am not Jesus. I only speak and act on His behalf."

"Okay," the woman concedes Daniel's point. "So, you speak and act on Jesus' behalf. Fine. I'll give you that. But tell me... Why would

Jesus want this man—Mr. Petrelli—to die in that fire? I thought Jesus was all about loving one's neighbor. Is what you did, loving your neighbor? You left a man to die when you could have saved him, just like you saved Eric and his mother, Mary. So, Jesus *told you* to let Mr. Petrelli burn?"

Daniel sighs. "No matter how I answer, you will not believe."

"Okay," the woman agrees. "But, I like to think I have an open mind. What can you *say* to *make* me believe?"

Daniel looks at her directly. "Nothing... I can't *make* you believe anything. But I can share the truth. What you do with it is up to you."

"So," the woman inquires, "what is *your* truth?"

"Oh, it's not *my* truth," Daniel counters, "It is *the* truth."

"Fine," the woman answers with a roll of her eyes and a twist of her hand. "Enlighten me."

"For God so loved the world that He gave His one and only Son, that whoever believes in Him shall not perish but have eternal life."

"John 3:16," the woman smiles. "A *widely known* Bible verse. You see it often written on placards held up by people on street corners or at sporting events."

"Yes, but do you know the verses after it?"

"Not really," the woman replies a bit unamused. "I suppose you're going to tell me."

"Verse 17: For God did not send his Son into the world to condemn the world, but to save the world through Him. 18: Whoever believes in him is not condemned, but whoever does not believe stands condemned already because they have not believed in the name of God's one and only Son. 19: This is the verdict: Light has come into the world, but people loved darkness instead of light because their deeds were evil. 20: Everyone who does evil hates the light, and will not come into the light for fear that their deeds will be exposed. 21: But whoever lives by the truth comes into the light, so that it may be seen plainly that what they have done has been done in the sight of God."

"Impressive," the woman replies. "You seem to know your Bible. So, what do these verses have to do with where we are right now?"

"...*Everything*..." Daniel concludes. "It may not make sense now, but it will soon."

"How?"

"I'm not sure. I just know that it will."

"Did the *voices* tell you that?" one of the men interject with sarcasm.

"Look," the woman says, "You are right. We are trying to determine your mental state to see if you are culpable in Mr. Petrelli's death. A lot of people want to see you thrown in jail for a long time."

"And you're trying to *help* me?"

"Exactly."

"But how can you help me when you've already made up your mind?"

"I think our time is up for now," the woman replies. "We'll try this again tomorrow."

"One last question," Daniel utters while rubbing his bandaged arm. "Why was my blood taken when I arrived here?"

"We... needed a sample to check for any... anomalies," the woman replies as she motions towards her colleague sitting closest to the door. He stands, walks over to the door and opens it. The large security guard, along with two muscular orderlies pick Daniel up and *escort* him back to his padded room.

As Daniel makes the trek down the long, dull corridors back to his room, he thinks about his conversation with the woman and prays to the Lord:

"Father. You haven't sent me here for them. At least not *directly*... So, *who* do You want me to see?"

V

In another part of the mental institution...

There is a man being held in the bowels of this facility, whose appearance resembles that of a beast. His hair grows wildly over his body. The nails on his hands and feet are sharp like talons. He is dangerous and held in the tightest of restraints whenever he is taken from his cell. All efforts to help him have failed: psychology, pharmaceuticals, shock therapy, hypnosis... nothing has worked. He is considered to be insane: suffering from an extreme case of cognitive dissociative disorder where his psyche has splintered into multiple personalities.

Even though the psychiatrists don't believe it, the cause of *his* insanity is not physical. He too hears a voice—this voice sounds like thousands at once. *These voices* belong to a horde of demons called Legion, which inhabit his body. At times, this man bears the strength of ten men. In certain moments, when moved from one cell to another, he speaks the hidden secrets of his captors openly for all to hear. Everyone in the facility fears him.

At one time, several Catholic priests were consulted to perform an exorcism. The results were... less than promising. Now, only the strongest of orderlies and guards handle him—and never less than five of them at a time. Sedation is the only thing that barely seems to keep him docile enough. He sleeps only 1 hour per day. The rest is spent in a dark stupor of drools and moaning, punctuated by periodic screams, sinister laughter, profanity and self-mutilation.

In the quietness of his cell, suddenly, the man awakes from his sleep with a shudder. A guard hears the commotion, slowly approaches the triple reinforced door, slides open the observation panel covering and peers into the padded room. The man continually looks up at the ceiling with a glaring expression and scurries around in a clearly agitated state while mumbling, "No! You should not be here.... He's mine!"

V

The next day...

This beast of a man has done so much damage to his room, one would think that a tornado had roared through it with a set of butcher knives! The decision is made to sedate and transfer him to a temporary holding cell until his room can be repaired. Once sedated by remote injection, seven orderlies bind him—head to toe—to a rolling stretcher and begin the process of moving him through the halls. As he is brought to a large, long hallway, one level up, Daniel is being escorted at the other end. Suddenly, the man comes out of his stupor with a ferocious intensity.

"How is he awake?" an orderly yells as he tries to restrain the man. If he could see into the spiritual realm, he would know the answer to his question. A guard tasers him, but it has no effect at all.

The demons within empowers the man to break his restraints and throw the orderlies and guards aside like sock puppets.

"You are not supposed to be here!" He howls down the hall as those attending Daniel try to get Daniel to retreat.

The Holy Spirit speaks to Daniel's spirit: *"He is to be Mine!"*

In that instant, Daniel's purpose becomes clear and he refuses to move as the orderlies pull for him to follow them to safety. As the man approaches, running on all fours, as if he were a rabid animal, the remaining orderlies flee—leaving Daniel to his apparent doom.

"This one is mine!" the man growls as he swiftly comes within 12 feet of Daniel. All who watch await the terrible slaughter! This man—the most notorious in this ward—is about to kill *again*. And nothing short of gunfire will stop him.

But Daniel utters a single word—*rather* he declares the *Name* that is above every name:

"JESUS."

Suddenly... the man screeches to a halt, scurries to the side of the hallway and cowers on the floor like a wounded animal. His eyes are frantic with fear as they dart back and forth. In the physical Daniel stood alone but, in the unseen realm of the supernatural, he was not alone at all! If only those present had supernatural eyes to see what the man saw...

Four radiant guardian angels stood around Daniel. He himself was glowing as the river of God's Holy Spirit rushed from his innermost being! The entire corridor was flooded with the light of heaven's glory!

With natural eyes, orderlies, security guards and staff watch in awe as the rabid beast-of-a-man falls onto his hands and knees before Daniel.

"This one... is mine," he utters in a guttural tone beyond the levels of deep bass human ears are accustomed to hearing.

"He has been until now," Daniel declares with a holy boldness—as if the entire weight of heaven were behind his words, "but he is yours no longer."

"No!" The demons cry out!

"What is your name?" Daniel commands the question. The demons resist, but must obey.

"We are Legion, for we... are many." The man tries to stand up and attack Daniel, but as soon as he takes a step towards him, he falls back to his knees.

"In the Name of *Yeshua—Jesus of Nazareth—the Son of the Living God*, I command you to come out of him and to *never* return!"

The man foams at the mouth, looking as if he was being choked, as he slashes at the air around him.

Daniel continues. "You are to oppress no one else in this facility."

The demons plead: "Do... not...send us into... the abyss... before the time..."

"The time of judgment is swiftly approaching," Daniel replies. "In the Name of Yeshua—the Son of Man of Daniel 7—come out of this man...NOW!" His words strike like a hammer which shatters the rocks!

The man howls at a level unheard of by all who feared him. A sudden violent shaking begins at his feet and rises up through his appendages, then the core of his belly, up through his chest, down from his mind and out of his mouth! His eyes roll into the back of their sockets and he falls into a heap on the floor, motionless, as if he were dead.

Silence reigns in that hallway as no one moves...

Daniel stands as a protector over the man. A moment passes as a whisper of praise can be heard rising from Daniel's lips. It swells to a loud crescendo which echoes through many hallways as a battle cry of victory: "HALLELUJAH!!!!!"

Then silence again... as all who are watching slowly begin to come out from their hiding places...

Daniel kneels in front of the man, laying his hand on him. The man begins to stir as Daniel helps him to his feet. Everyone watches with a holy fear as the man stands tall and looks around. His eyes are clear and filled with tears of joy as a broad smile—revealing yellow and jagged teeth—brightens his face. "THANK... YOU..."

Daniel responds with a strong smile while holding the man's shoulders: "Paul... the LORD has set you free."

"Yes!" he exclaims with excitement. "My name *is*... Paul. That's *my* name!"

"I know," Daniel smiles with a nod. "Jesus sent me here to free you so you could give your life to Him. He has long looked forward to this day."

"Yes," Paul laughs heartily. "Yes! I give my life to Jesus! *I give my life to Jesus!!*"

Both men embrace as the guards, orderlies and psychiatrists approach them. They are all astonished to see the man—they would never openly admit was possessed by demons—now in front of them in his right frame of mind.

Daniel turns and commands them: "Get Paul some clothes, food, a good shower, toothbrush and a haircut."

43: What Did You Find?

DAY 136 — Utah

A host of firemen sift through the remains of the two houses...

"The fire began in Mr. Petrelli's residence," a fireman tells his chief.

"Are you sure?" Fire Chief Christine Klein replies.

"One hundred percent. We think the high winds blew embers to the other house."

"Alright. Tell half of our guys to focus their attention on Petrelli's house. Let's see if we can figure out how the fire started."

"You got it chief." The fireman replies. "But... it's a shame. Mr. Petrelli was a great guy."

"He did a lot for this city," the chief agrees. "An outstanding citizen and philanthropist."

A few hours later...

Chief Christine walks cautiously through the lower level of the house with several of her men.

"The top three levels are toast," one of them says. "The basement is damaged, but still intact."

"Okay," Chief Christine says. "So, what did you want me to see?"

"*This*," the fireman points to the other side of the large room. A large charred door rests in the floor near the corner. "Flanigan found it when he removed some furniture from that area. We think it's an entrance to some kind of sub-basement cellar or safe room."

"You haven't opened it?"

"We were waiting for you."

"Well, cut the lock and get it open."

"You heard the chief," the fireman says to the others. "Let's get it open."

V

Twenty Minutes Later...

Three police cruisers arrive at Mr. Petrelli's residence. A police captain, sergeant and two detectives exit the vehicles and walk up the path to what's left of a once immaculate house. The fire chief stands at the front door with two of her men. Both groups acknowledge one another.

"Chief Klein."

"Captain Hayes. We called as soon as we got in."

"They said it's some kind of safe room? What did you find?"

"You have to see this for yourself."

The entire group makes their way through the charred structure and down to the basement. They arrive at the large door, which is now opened wide. A strong smell of decay lingers in the air. The captain looks down a wide step ladder which descends a good ten feet into the darkness.

"Did you guys go in?" Captain Hayes asks.

"Not yet," Chief Klein replies. "*That smell* is from some kind of remains. Could be human. That's why we called you. Just in case this turns out to be a crime scene."

"Mr. Petrelli was an outstanding individual," Captain Hayes replies in disbelief. "He has *always* been good to the department."

"*Both* of our departments," Chief Klein replies. "His generous donations paid for several upgrades to our equipment."

"Alright," Captain Hayes utters with a bit of hesitancy. "Let's get this over with." He removes his gun from its holster and a flashlight from a pocket on his belt. The sergeant and detectives do the same.

"Let's go boys," Chief Klein commands as she turns on her helmet's flashlight. The rest of the firemen do the same as well.

Both chief and captain descend the step ladder with the rest of the group following behind. At the bottom, their flashlights reveal a room just as big as the basement one level up. Everyone muffles their mouths and noses as a few of them cough. The suffocating smell of decay is now a stench of death. One of the group finds a light switch on the wall and flips it. Florescent lights flicker to life across the ceiling of the room, immediately revealing what none of them wanted to believe.

V

Two days later... Outside of the mental institution building.

A large crowd of news reporters and citizens stand in front of a raised platform with a podium in the middle. Behind the podium—which holds five news microphones—stands the mayor, police and fire chiefs, the police captain, the psychiatrists from the institution and Daniel, dressed in his Valor uniform, holding his helmet in his hand.

"As you all know," Police Chief Garboza begins, "there was a 4 alarm fire several days ago which destroyed two houses. One of those houses belonged to Mr. Michael Petrelli. Mr. Daniel Davidson—also known as Valor—saved the lives of Mrs. Mary Cunningham and her son Eric, whose house was one of the two on fire. However, he refused to try and save Mr. Petrelli. As a result, Mr. Petrelli perished and as we know, the public outcry against Mr. Davidson for his refusal to help, was immediate. In response, our law enforcement agencies tracked Mr. Davidson, detained him and brought him in for questioning. He was transferred to *this facility* seen behind us so that his mental state could be evaluated.

"Meanwhile, fire chief Christine Klein and her department worked to determine the cause of the blaze. Two days ago, Fire Chief Klein requested that Police Captain Mark Hayes bring a contingency of officers to Mr. Petrelli's residence." The police chief clears his throat. "At approximately 3:24pm, two days ago, Chief Klein, Captain Hayes and those with them discovered a large sub-basement structure beneath Mr. Petrelli's residence. Within that structure was found the remains of numerous persons that had been reported missing over the past three decades."

The crowd utters a collective gasp at the realization of the police chief's words.

"I am saddened to say," the police chief declares, "after a thorough, yet still ongoing investigation, it has become clear that our city's presumed top humanitarian, was in fact... a serial killer."

The crowd erupts with cries and questions. The police chief motions for their calm as he continues.

"In light of these findings, the police department and all other involved law enforcement agencies are no longer requiring Mr. Daniel

Davidson to be detained. He is free to continue his walk across the country unimpeded. While some may or may not agree with his declaration that 'God was bringing judgment against Mr. Petrelli,' what *is* clear from our investigation so far is that Mr. Petrelli was in fact guilty of multiple counts of murder. and he deserved to face judgment. As a Catholic, who believes in God, I know the Bible says, 'Vengeance is Mine, I will repay, declares the LORD.' It would seem what had been so carefully hidden in the dark—from us all—Divine Providence has chosen to reveal in the light."

All of the murmurings cease as the crowd stands silent.

"I now turn the podium over to Dr. Traci Weinstein, head psychiatrist for the mental facility."

The police chief steps back as Dr. Weinstein steps forward. Cameras continue to flash as video cameras keep rolling.

"As you may know, our facility works with persons suffering from a wide range of mental dispositions. Everything from mental breakdowns due to overwhelming stress, all the way to those who are delusional. When Mr. Davidson was brought into our facility, we were tasked with assessing his mental stability. Our initial hypothesis was that he was delusional, as he claimed to hear directly from God. There are many in our facility who claim to hear voices of various kinds, so this, at first, seemed to be the obvious determination.

"However, a certain... *event*... transpired which demonstrated with overwhelming clarity that Mr. Daniel Davidson is not delusional at all. He is in his right mind and... to his claim of hearing the voice of God... I... *believe* him."

The crowd erupts in clamor once again as Dr. Weinstein turns and nods. Everyone watches as the group behind her parts and a clean cut, decently dressed man approaches the podium with a broad smile. He stands next to Dr. Weinstein as she motions for the crowd to quiet down.

"This is Paul Hieser. He was our institution's... most *difficult* patient. How you see him now, is not how he had been for over a decade. There has not been a single available treatment option that was not tried in an effort to cure him. Everything failed... repeatedly. I will let him tell his story." She steps back and allows Paul to take the podium.

"Hello," he smiles with great enthusiasm. "You'll have to excuse my expressions of joy, but I had been declared clinically insane for just over twelve years. That declaration changed two days ago! I used to hear voices—thousands of them—and they would tell me to harm myself and others. My family tried everything they could to help me. They pulled intervention after intervention. They even had a team of priests come and perform an exorcism. I am told the exorcism didn't go very well. I don't really have a memory of that event. So, their last resort was to have me committed.

"Well, the doctors couldn't help me either. As Dr. Weinstein said, none of their treatments worked, not even the experimental ones. So, they had no choice but to keep me under heavy sedation and detained in one of their most reinforced rooms. But two days ago, I encountered Mr. Davidson in the hallway. I actually tried to kill him. That was what the voices were telling me to do. None of the orderlies and security guards could stop me. But when I got within feet of Mr. Davidson, the presence of God shone all around him! And in that instant, the voices within my mind were silenced—once and for all!

After twelve years... Here I am... standing before you... in my right frame of mind! Speaking full sentences now, when all I could do was drool and scream in fits of rage then! You may not believe in God. But God encountered me two days ago! When I came to my senses, Mr. Davidson told me it was Jesus Christ who set me free. So, I gladly gave my life to Jesus. And now I am a child of God! I encourage you all to give your lives to Jesus!"

Dr. Weinstein quickly steps forward with a smile while moving Paul over. "Well now, she interjects with a nervous chuckle, "this isn't a church service. But if I and my staff didn't witness the entire exchange with our own eyes and ears... this would simply be... unbelievable."

"Believe it!" Paul exclaims with his broad smile. "Jesus set me free!"

Some in the crowd laugh, many applaud, still others scoff.

"So, in light of these events, and after many conclusive tests which confirm Paul Hieser's sanity, we are officially stating that Mr. Daniel Davidson is free to leave."

The crowd clamors once again; this time reporters and citizens alike call for Daniel to make a statement of his own.

Dr. Weinstein motions for Daniel to approach the podium—and he does. A hush comes over the crowd as their anticipation grows.

"I am on my way to California. The Lord has said I must speak for Him there."

"Where will you speak?" a reporter yells.

"Isn't it obvious?" Daniel replies with a smile while pointing at his slightly damaged uniform.

"The San Diego Comic Con," someone else shouts."

Daniel nods in agreement. "What I say *there*, will be my statement. Until then, what has been already been said by those on this platform has been more than enough. I am grateful to God for the officials of this city standing together to speak the truth. Thank you. I must be going now. May you all have a good day."

The crowd erupts in questions and comments as Daniel steps away from the podium. Numerous officers form a barrier in front of the platform to keep the crowd at a distance. Daniel thanks everyone on the platform as he makes his way down the steps. At the bottom, Dr. Weinstein and Paul wait for him.

"You're going to put me out of a job," she smiles. "So many of my patients have been… I don't know how to describe it."

"Delivered," Daniel replies warmly.

"Yes," she nods. "Delivered. But why not all of them?"

"God has an immediate purpose for those He has delivered. And He also has a purpose for *you* and your staff. Up until now, hasn't your job wearied you?"

"Yes," she admits. "There's so much we don't understand… so much help we haven't been able to provide. It's easy to become pessimistic and cynical, which really is a coverup for feeling helpless."

"Well, now you know you don't have to do this work on your own. God created the *whole person*, including a person's mind. Since that is the case, don't leave Him out of your pursuit for viable treatments. Jesus says in Matthew 6:33, 'But seek first His kingdom and His righteousness, and all these things will be given to you as well.' God and science go very well together. He will help you, if you let Him."

"I… think you're right," Dr. Weinstein agrees with a smile.

"Before I go, what did you find in my blood?"

"I'm *sorry* about that. We were strongly encouraged by several government officials to take your blood. With all of the things you have been able to do, they wanted to know the source of your... *abilities*. But, as far as I know, nothing unusual was found. For me, that further confirms that God is the Source of your abilities. I wish we had more time. I have so many questions."

"Did you get a Bible like I suggested?"

"Yes. And I started reading the passages you recommended."

"Good. You do that with an open heart and mind and God will do the rest."

Daniel and Dr. Weinstein shake hands as he turns his attention to Paul.

"Let me go with you!" Paul says while holding onto his shoulders.

"I can't, my friend," Daniel smiles warmly. "You've been given a different mission. Go back to your hometown and tell everyone what Jesus has done for you."

"Okay," Paul agrees—knowing it is the right thing for him to do. "But, will I ever see you again?"

Daniel smiles. "If not in this life, then in the Kingdom of God to come!" Daniel dons his helmet, and turns to continue his walk, but notices the eager crowd blocking his path. There is no where for him to go. He is surrounded.

"Father," what do You want me to do?"

Captain Hayes approaches.

"I've got a cruiser waiting for you. We can move the crowd and drive you back to the highway."

Daniel feels the strength of the Holy Spirit come upon him, as power flows from within his belly and descends to his legs and feet. It is a familiar sensation... He now knows what to do.

"Thank you, Captain, but a ride won't be necessary." Daniel looks for an empty spot in the distance. Finding one, he lowers his visor. Everyone watches as he crouches in front of them and launches himself high into the air! All heads swivel in unison as Valor leaps over them and lands in a clearing half a block away. The crowd gazes in awe as he breaks into a run—moving faster than anyone would be able to match. Within a matter of seconds, He is gone from their sight.

44: Principality!

DAY 140 — China

The Chinese Monastery... Brother Léi and the rest of the believers are engaged in intercessory prayer.

"Father, You have made Your decree known. Yet, the enemy has sought to counter and resist Your commands at every turn. You have now revealed that the enemy will attack your servant directly! Father, this threat is very real. The potential for loss is great. Please protect Brother Dàiwéisēn and provide him with everything needed for the battle he is about to face! May the enemy gain no ground in any way. And please move on the hearts of those who care for our brother, that they too will intercede on his behalf before Your heavenly throne. Thank you that there is no distance which cannot be covered by Your Holy Spirit in prayer. You are sovereign. In Jesus' Name. Amen."

V

United States. Nevada. The Mojave Desert...

For the past two days, Valor has walked through the desert. His already damaged suit is covered in dust and dirt. The heat in the day and cool in the night make for a difficult time—in addition to the snakes, scorpions, no food and no water. His only sustenance has come from praying through God's Word as a source of spiritual food and strength.

As the evening night covers the sky, Valor finally sees a sign in the distance for the California State Line. He also notices a dark colored luxury car parked a good fifty feet in front of him just before the sign. A man wearing a black suit stands on the side of the highway—looking in Valor's direction.

V

Chinese Monastery…

Brother Léi sits in the carved wooden prayer room with two brothers and one sister. As they pray, he suddenly stops as his eyes open wide in fear! "Oh, no…"

"What is it?" they inquire.

"He is facing a Principality!"

V

Mojave Desert. Nevada/California State line…

Valor receives a check in his spirit. Immediately, he knows something is wrong. He scans the area, but no one is present, except for the well-dressed man in the distance.

"What is it, Father?" he prays.

"Surely, this man can't be the problem… can he?"

The Holy Spirit checks him again. So, he stops dead in his tracks—a good thirty feet from the unknown individual.

"Can I help you?" Valor asks.

"Yes, you can," the man replies in a perfect British ascent as he smiles. "It would be a great help if you would turn around and head back to the east coast."

"I'm sorry," Valor replies. "I have an appointment to keep in San Diego."

"You know," the well-dressed man says while walking slowly towards him. "It's been somewhat difficult for my *employer* to track your journey across the country. It seems that your whereabouts have been partially… clouded from us. Frankly, we had been made aware of your coming by others, but *my employer* was not the least concerned about you until you were smuggled into the mental institution and freed so many who were under the control of his… *associates*. That is when he realized you were more dangerous than originally perceived. Thus, our meeting at this moment.

"I am afraid you simply cannot go beyond this point. You must leave this region at once. In so doing, you will remain *unharmed*… However, if you *refuse*, then you will face dire consequences."

The well dressed man is now six feet from Valor. At this range, his immaculate black suit, white shirt, black tie, handkerchief, shined shoes and cleanly groomed appearance is evident. Strangely, he is wearing sunglasses at night.

"You may be wondering why I'm wearing a tuxedo," he smiles slyly. "I was on my way to a movie premiere, when my employer called me into this urgent service. I will have to miss the movie, but our encounter should prove entertaining enough."

A holy boldness swells within Valor as the man steps towards him —now clearly standing within arms reach.

"I don't know who you are—"

"My name is irrelevant. But, given my obvious attire, you may address me as *Tuxedo*."

"Well, *Mr. Tuxedo*, judging from your cryptic wording, you must be engaged in occult practices. If you are threatening me, know that it won't work. The Lord has decreed a task for me to complete. I cannot turn back. So, please... step aside. I do not wish there to be trouble."

The man removes his sunglasses and places them inside his jacket pocket. When he looks up, Valor can see that his eyes are *literally* filled with darkness.

"Your... eyes," Valor utters in a fearful surprise. The words barely leave his mouth as the tuxedo man slams both of his hands into Valor's chest!

THOOM!!

The force of the blow hurls Valor through the air a good 60 feet before he slams hard to the ground—the impact cracking his visor.

"Uhnnn..." Valor slowly stumbles to his feet as the Tuxedo man approaches. "Lord, how is he so strong? Open my eyes that I may see."

The veil, which separates the unseen realm of the spiritual from the realm of the physical universe, is pulled back! Valor now sees the tuxedo man encompassed about by dark energy which has taken the shape of some type of large demonic figure! The unexpected sight startles him—causing fear to rise up within his heart.

"The Spirit of our Enemy is strong with you," Tuxedo man utters with a voice not entirely human as he removes his shoes—revealing blackened feet with treaded, scaly soles like dragon's skin. "No matter. You are only mortal. I, on the other hand, am so much more!"

He leaps through the air with a blinding speed that takes Valor by surprise! Landing, he tackles Valor to the ground—pinning his helmet with a strong hand—which further fractures his visor to pieces.

"I feed off of fear," Tuxedo man sneers. "And the fear in your soul is palpable!" He bears his teeth which are now sharpened fangs as if he was some kind of predator of the night.

Valor breaks his arm free and punches his adversary squarely in his jaw!

THOOM!

The force of the punch sends Tuxedo man tumbling backwards several meters. Valor scrambles to his feet and into a defensive position as his assailant stands up and brushes dirt off of his suit, before striking like a viper—his hands like fangs! Each strike deliberate to kill in the quickest fashion!

Valor moves likes a mighty rushing river, flowing over, around and beneath each attack—redirecting blows and knocking his adversary off balance.

Tuxedo man grimaces as he gnashes his teeth. "That fighting style is unique. Where did you learn it?"

Valor says nothing.

"It doesn't matter," he hisses as he adjusts his attack and slithers around Valor, grappling him like a boa constrictor. He restricts his enemy's arms and squeezes his rib cage with enough pressure to easily break bones. Valor yells in pain, as his visor shatters while he tries to resist. Tuxedo man hisses again: "No matter how chosen you *think* you are, you are still only human. Your demise... is inevitable!"

In one swift motion, he raises Valor into the air and slams him to the ground! The ground gives way instantly at the impact — cratered by tons of force exerted on it. He looks down at his adversary and reveals a sinister grin as the dust settles. As he relishes in the moment, Valor suddenly sweeps his legs, knocking his enemy to the ground. He then rolls backwards, to make some distance, and is back on his feet in an instant!

Valor points, as his foe stands back up, and shouts: "I command you demon, in the Name of Jesus, to come out of this man!"

Tuxedo man, as well as the malevolent spirit within him, cackle at Valor's command as both respond in one voice. "That may have worked in your encounter with Legion, but I am no mere demon! I am the Principality of this region! And my host *desires* for me to dwell within him. As such, I have embellished him with certain occult artifacts which strengthen our union to the *deepest* of levels. Therefore, I cannot be removed *so easily*. Perhaps, if fear were not rising in your heart, your words would have power!"

At once, fearful thoughts invade Valor's mind like piercing daggers as Tuxedo man rushes him with a rapid succession of unrelenting blows! Valor blocks, parries and dodges what he can, but the blows find their mark while fearful thoughts barrage his mind. With each passing second, his helmet and suit take increasing damage —a visible indication of an internal reality. With each impact, Valor's strength, agility and endurance diminish... and Tuxedo man can sense it!

"You may have been given the strength of Samson, but it is sorely inadequate for the power which courses through me!"

As the two of them fight in the physical, both enabled by supernatural powers from different sources, a wider battle rages in the unseen realm. Demon hordes descend on the area as the large angel currently assigned to Valor fights fiercely with his flaming sword! But he is overwhelmed by the sheer number of enemy spirits! So too, does Valor fight in the physical but is being overrun by his assailant who seems to be faster, stronger and completely ruthless in his attack!

A massive punch—**THOOM!!!**—craters Valor into the ground! As Tuxedo man arrogantly approaches, he dusts off his suit once more and straightens his tie. Soon, he stands over his opponent.

"I can only see part of your face." He reaches down and wrenches the helmet from Daniel's head with enough force to cause whiplash! His face is cut and bruised in several places. Daniel strains to maintain his consciousness as his enemy speaks.

"Ah, finally, the man under the helmet... You serve our Enemy, who sits high and looks low. He never wants to get His hands dirty. Me, on the other hand... I serve the god of this world! Your Master is distant, choosing to work in mysterious ways. My master is the prince of the power of the air! And he has granted us power to control the airwaves—the media—the entertainment—the music—the fashion! We control the masses through the very things they desire to consume! And the beautiful thing is... we don't even have to hide our agenda any longer! The tipping point has come! There are more with us than there is with you. And we are preparing them for our master's arrival! When he does arrive, he will finally be able to unite this world's global systems through the man he has chosen!

"You mean, the Antichrist?" Daniel utters weakly.

Tuxedo man smiles. "Yes… The Antichrist is inevitable. Do you not see it? Over these past decades we have increased lawlessness in the earth because the *Man of Lawlessness* is almost upon us!"

"But surely," Daniel counters, "you know the final outcome. Your master loses. *You* will lose. All who follow Satan, *including* the Antichrist *will* lose!"

"That is but one *possibility*. My master has foreseen another way! The risk is great, but if successful, our victory will be assured! And if we lose… well then… misery loves company!" Man and Principality cackle in unison once more. "The destruction of **billions** is a worthy concession prize. As long as *your* Master does not receive them into His kingdom. And those of us who willingly submit to *our master*, will reign with *him* as the rest of the damned suffer."

Daniel is slightly bewildered. "Why… are you telling me this?"

"Because I love to revel in my own pomposity before I vanquish my enemies!" Tuxedo man stretches out both arms and extends his hands. As he does, his nails instantly sharpen into talons!

"Father," Daniel prays silently, "You have not given me the spirit of fear… You have given me power, love and a sound mind!"

Tuxedo man places his clawed darkened dragons' feet firmly on Daniel's chest and raises his talons into the air in a menacing pose like a predator about to strike for the kill!

"Father," Daniel continues to pray. "I need you! Jesus, You are the Author and Finisher of my faith! Please dispel these thoughts of fear from my heart and mind!"

And just like that… the venomous thoughts vanish as the Holy Spirit swells within Daniel's belly like a raging river of living water.

"Do you have any last words before I send you to meet your Maker?"

"The LORD has decreed my passage to California," Daniel declares with an unexpected boldness. "He has decreed His message which I must speak! Therefore, you are powerless to stop me!"

Fear begins to rise in Tuxedo man's stony heart as he takes a small step back.

"And," Daniel continues, "if I can't command you to flee in Jesus' Name, then it is the LORD Jesus Himself who rebukes you!!!"

Tuxedo man stumbles backwards with a shriek and glares wildly at his surroundings; screaming at a sight only he sees. In response he yells, "Master! I need more power!" He roars in anger as dark energy overflows his being!

"Father," Daniel prays as he still lays in the crater, "open my eyes that I may see."

Again, Daniel's eyes are open to the unseen realm! To his joyous delight and with heartfelt gratitude to the LORD, he sees warring angels arriving in bursts of light—one for each saint who is interceding for him at that moment. These beings of light and armor swiftly engage the demon hordes with a fierce righteousness!

Just then, a burst of light appears to Daniel's right—as the very fabric of physical reality rips open revealing the glories of heaven on the other side. Out of this portal steps a higher class of angel.

"Father," Daniel prays with awe on his lips. "Is that... an Archangel?"

"Yes, my Son," the voice of the Holy Spirit replies.

The original angel assigned to Daniel has taken damage from the demonic horde. But he smiles at the multitude of angelic arrivals as he knows this battle-hardened Archangel is ready to engage the Principality which envelops the man in the tuxedo.

"Get up," the Holy Spirit commands Daniel's heart. *"I have given this battle to you."* Strength quickens Daniel's body as he stands to his feet.

"The LORD rebuke you!" bursts forth from his lips like a hammer's shattering blow as he feels God's power swelling within him. To Daniel's surprise, his entire body begins to glow! "What is this?" he utters as light radiates from him—increasing in intensity with every passing second.

"No!" Tuxedo man shouts. "The Shekhinah glory of our Enemy envelops him!"

The voice of the Holy Spirit speaks once again to Daniel's heart. *"And I will give you the Morning Star..."*

Daniel suddenly feels weightless as he notices he is now—somehow—hovering inches above the ground! The buildup of power fills him—like a star singing from within his chest and raging rivers swelling up within his belly! This power flows through his entire body, radiating with such force that even the dust and pebbles beneath his feet flow away from him in every direction!

Daniel's body rises into the air as he instinctively raises his arms—directing them towards his enemy. In an instant, a magnificent burst of light shoots forth from his hands and impacts his foe with tremendous force! Both Tuxedo man and the Principality which controls him scream in pain as he falls backwards to the ground and scurries around on all fours, trying to escape from the path of the illumination!

"It burns!!!"

The power of God keeps flowing through Daniel with an ever increasing intensity until his foe is out of reach behind a sizable stockpile of stones.

"You've hurt us..." his enemy utters through gritted teeth as he nurses his wounds. If not for your *reinforcements*... you would have been easily taken! You may have won *this* battle, but the war is far from over! We will meet again! And you will regret your arrogant show of force." Tuxedo man quickly dashes to his car and jumps in. As he does, the Principality spirit rises from the car and streaks into the air as the car takes off down the road in a plume of smoke, leaving only tire track skid marks in its wake.

Daniel's glowing, hovering body lowers back to the ground. As his feet rest firmly on land, the Shekhinah glory of the LORD diminishes. A moment passes before he drops to his knees in exhaustion. His breathing is heavy. His face is bruised and bloodied. His suit is damaged beyond repair. This type and level of spiritual warfare is beyond him, yet God enabled him to do what was needed. His eyes are still opened to the unseen realm of the spirit. He watches as the demon hordes flee into the night sky chased by warring angels. He turns to see the Archangel standing before him.

"This kind comes out only by prayer and fasting."

A portal of light opens—rippling time and space—and the angelic being steps through as it closes behind him. Now, only the original angel assigned to him stands nearby. His voice resounding.

"The enemy is afraid. You are close to completing the task our LORD has given you. It is from this region where many of the enemy's lies permeate across the nation and throughout the world. The Lord has a remnant who belong to Him here, but they are divided. While pockets of light exist, the vast expanse is held under the sway of darkness. This darkness swallows whole its unsuspecting victims who are lured to this place with prideful ambitions. When your task is complete, the enemy will be exposed and many will come to the Lord."

Daniel's perception reverts back to normal. He is out of breath and doubled over—his hands on his knees. His muscles ache as his battered and bruised body yearns for rest. Meanwhile, he considers all that has just transpired.

"Father, this definitely was a *direct attack*. Thank you for preparing me to face it."

45: Family Reunion

DAY 141 — California

An exhausted Daniel stumbles across the California state line. It is well past 3:00am as he makes slow progress through the Mojave desert near Interstate 15. He feels likes his suit looks—tattered and cracked to pieces. His helmet is crushed beyond usage. His body's pain receptors scream throughout his nervous system. As the last ounce of conscious strength ebbs from his body, he leans against a nearby tree and slumps to the ground. His helmet falls from his weakened grasp to the ground with a thud.

"Father... I can't take another step... My entire body feels like its on fire. My mouth feels like gravel. And my vision... is blurry. So, I'm going to sit here... for a minute... I just need... to rest... my eyes."

In less than a minute Daniel is out cold. His body is completely exhausted and he has absolutely no awareness of his surroundings. An hour or so passes before a repeated sound awakens him. The sound is actually a female voice... one that is familiar.

"DDDDDAAAAANNNNNNIIIIIIEEEEEELLLLLLLL.... DDDAAANNNIIIEEELLL.... DDAANNIIEELL... Daniel...!!

The voice is accompanied by numerous shoves to his body.

Daniel's mind comes to attention before his eyes open. But the voice he hears can't be real. He must be dreaming.

"Daniel! Wake up! Baby, are you okay?"

His face wrinkles as one eye opens and then the other. His eyelids flutter several times as he tries to focus his vision on the figure kneeling in front of him. He forces his dry lips and tongue to speak.

"Rebecca? Am I... dreaming...?"

"You're okay!"

"There's no way... you are *here*..."

Another figure runs over from a nearby minivan.

"Dad! Dad, are you okay?"

"Son?"

"It's me Dad. Me and Mom. Don't worry we got you."

"What... What are you both doing here?"

"We'll explain after we get you into the van. Can you walk?"

"I think... so."

Rebecca and DJ help Daniel to his feet and walk him to the van. They place him on the second row, before getting in the front seats and driving off.

DJ turns in the passenger seat and hands his dad a bottled water. Daniel downs the water with great vigor—finishing it in seconds.

"Do you have another one?"

DJ smiles and hands his dad another bottle. Seconds later, that one is empty too.

"Thank you Son." Daniel lays back on the seat with his eyes closed.

After a few minutes, he opens them again and sits up. He stares at his family as the van drives down the highway. "Ok. I think I'm good now. At least enough to talk... What are you two doing here? How did you know where to find me?"

"It was the strangest thing," Rebecca answers. "Last week, DJ and I had the same overriding thought. We needed to get in the van and drive out here to meet you. So, we packed some things and got on the road five days ago."

"Dad, what happened to your suit? It looks terrible!"

"You wouldn't believe me if I told you," he smiles.

"Sure we would," DJ counters.

"Ok. First there was a bear attack."

"A bear attack!" his wife and son yell.

"And then I was kidnapped and set on fire."

"Kidnapped!"

"Set on fire?"

"And I just had a life or death battle with a demon possessed man in a tuxedo."

Rebecca slams on the breaks and pulls the van over.

"Do you have a concussion? Son, check to see if he has a fever."

"I'm fine," Daniel raises his hand. "No concussion and no fever."

"Dad, you're not making any sense!"

"I said you wouldn't believe it. But that's how my suit got damaged."

"When was the attack from the man in the tuxedo?" Rebecca asks.

"Uh," Daniel looks at the dashboard clock. "About five hours ago. Why?"

"Mom," DJ interjects, "That's about the time we pulled off the road!"

"What are you talking about?" Daniel inquires.

"We were driving," Rebecca explains, "and then the Holy Spirit told us to pull over and call Pastor Mike. We felt like you were in trouble. So, he got the prayer chain going and every believer who has been supporting this whole endeavor started praying for you immediately."

"Yeah," DJ adds. "We all prayed on the phone for at least thirty minutes. It was crazy intense. But we felt like if we stopped, you might not survive whatever you were going through."

"Then Pastor Mike said God gave him a vision of warring angels coming to your aid, along with a mighty Archangel."

"HALLELUJAH!" Daniel exclaims at the top of his lungs—clearly startling his wife and son."

"What?!" They both ask.

"That is *exactly* what happened!" Daniel replies. "This... tuxedo guy had super strength that rivaled my own. He was empowered by some kind of demonic Principality. At one point he had gotten the upper hand and was about to kill me. Then the LORD opened my eyes and I saw all these warring angels arriving to fight against a horde of demons that were trying to stop me. Then an Archangel arrived to the battle! God sent them as a result of your prayers!"

"Not just ours," Rebecca adds quietly.

"What do you mean?" Daniel asks.

"Pastor Mike said he also saw a group of Christians praying for us in China."

Daniel gasps.

"Could it have been them?"

"Who?" DJ asks.

"The Christian monks I stayed with for three years," Daniel answers.

"You stayed with Christian monks in China?" DJ balks! When did *this* happen?"

"That's a story for another time," Daniel smiles. "But it had to be Brother Léi and the rest of the monastics. They said God used them to pray for believers all over the world."

"There truly is no distance in prayer," Rebecca replies.

"Not when God is Omnipresent and He sees and knows everything." Daniel smiles.

They drive along in silence for a few minutes, thinking about what has transpired.

"We saw you on the news, while we were staying in a hotel," Rebecca breaks the silence. "You were held in a mental institution?"

"Long story," Daniel breathes out slowly. "But the lesson through all of these things is that God is sovereign. He had me where He wanted me to be so I could carry out His plans and purposes. And now… I have to finish what He started."

"*We* have to finish what He gave us to complete," Rebecca corrects. "We started this as a family and we're going to finish it as a family."

"That's right Dad," DJ smiles. "Good thing I finished the replacement suit after you left. Can't have you showing up at the San Diego Comic Con looking all beat up!"

"You brought the new suit?"

"Yep!" DJ beams. "It's in the back with our luggage."

"Oh, I love you both! But, I'm supposed to be walking."

"Not necessarily," Rebecca counters. "God told you to walk to California. You *did* that when you crossed the state line. Then He sent us to pick you up."

"Makes sense to me," DJ adds.

"Actually," Daniel agrees, "it does. So… what's the plan now?"

"Comic Con starts in four days," DJ answers. "We already have reservations at a hotel nearby. Mom says we'll check in there and take it easy for a couple of days. Then we can figure out where you're going to speak."

"And after you deliver God's message," Rebecca adds, "then we'll go home."

46: The Grand Narrative

DAY 145 — California

The day has finally arrived. Saturday July 27, 2024. The culmination of a journey of over 3,000 miles from east to west. A journey—taken by foot—that lasted just under 5 months. Daniel Davidson was now standing—in his new suit and with helmet in hand—three blocks away from the San Diego Convention Center—home of the city's annual Comic Con. This is the largest event of its kind with over one hundred thousand people attending every year. From blocks away, Daniel can see the large crowds making their way to the convention center. The lines stretched down the block.

Many are dressed as their favorite comic book, sci-fi and fantasy characters. People from all nationalities, all age groups, all walks of life and from many countries are there! The excitement in the air is electric, even from this distance. People seem so… happy. All were about to immerse themselves into a fantastic world of imagination, which is *nothing like* the mundane world they lived in every day.

It's the perfect day. The golden sun blazes its light across the deep blue sky, punctuated with white puffy clouds and a gentle breeze. The temperature is 84 degrees… great weather for what is about to take place.

As people saw Daniel approaching, their excitement turned into a frenzy.! Law enforcement are out in large numbers to handle the crowds and keep the peace. On one side of the street stands those who support his efforts. On the other side stands those who are against him. From one side comes cheers and signs expressing support and encouragement. From the other side comes jeers and placards mocking everything Daniel believes. And as he walks through that crowd, some angry onlookers 'boo' him and throw bottles and other trash in his direction.

A police sergeant with a contingency of officers approach, causing the angry onlookers to scramble into the crowd.

"Mr. Davidson?"

"Yes, Sir?" Daniel answers while holding his helmet under his arm.

"We have an escort waiting for you."

"To go where?"

"To the podium?"

"Excuse me?"

"Aren't you addressing people outside of the venue today? A platform and podium has been set up for you two blocks from here."

"Set up by who?"

"Some major benefactor. He is waiting there for you now."

The sergeant and officers escort Daniel through the crowd for the two block walk. As the crowd parts, a sizable platform with chairs, a podium and several news crews come into view. Immediately, Daniel recognizes two people standing in front of the setup.

"Pastor Mike! Pastor Chris!"

"Brother Daniel!" They both shout with great jubilation as the trio share hearty handshakes and hugs.

"What are you guys doing here?"

"We've been here for a week, trying to make sure everything was set up for you."

"Where are Rebecca and DJ?" Pastor Mike asks. "I thought they were with you."

"They're somewhere here in the crowd. We're going to meet up later."

"Ok, great. Come! We want to introduce you to someone."

A moment later, they stand on the platform talking with another individual.

"Daniel, this is Mr. Josiah Hartley. He is one of this state's most influential Christian businessmen."

They both shake hands.

"It's nice to meet you Brother Daniel. I have been following your exploits for some time now. How the Lord has used you has been simply wonderful! And when I received a call from our brothers here explaining what God was up to through your journey, I just knew I wanted to be a part of things."

"So, *you* arranged this?" Daniel asks.

"Yes, with help from several others."

"This must have cost a small fortune."

"Well, this convention center *is* prime real estate, especially when Comic Con happens. Over one hundred thousand people attend every year! But, that's why the Lord has us in our various positions, so we each can play our part in what *He* desires to do. We couldn't get you inside, but we got you as close as we could to the main entrance where you can get the greatest exposure. Now, the rest is up to you."

V

The news crews begin rolling as a brief, but lively introduction is given to the crowd by all three men. Then Daniel takes his place at the podium as the three men sit down behind him. He places his helmet on the stand next to him and stares out at the crowd of several thousand people.

"Okay Father," Daniel prays silently. "Here we are… What do You want to say?"

Cell phones are held up to record the moment. Social media platforms carry the livestreams across the country and around the world. A hush covers the crowd as everyone—even his opponents—wonder what he will say.

"We all long to be part of something bigger than ourselves… Something transcendent. Some *grand narrative* that is so expansive, so sweeping in breath and scope that we can give ourselves wholeheartedly to it and find the meaning for our souls which we so desperately crave. While the narrative of many is that life is meaningless, we know in our heart of hearts this is *not* the case. Or at least, we *hope* there is more to our lives than just random chance. Each of us… longs to belong. We seek significance! We try to satisfy this longing in many places and with many things, yet this *yearning* still remains… *unsatisfied.*

"As a result, this generation has turned to fables, myths and man-made fabrications… We have given ourselves over to fantasy, science fiction, superhero adventures and many other types of stories! We desperately crave meaning and purpose from the movies, books, television shows and music we love—and yet the creators of *these very things* are just as desperate in their search for meaning as we are—with many admitting their own emptiness of the soul!

"In the Bible, 2 Timothy 4:3-4 states: '*3 For the time will come when people will not put up with sound doctrine. Instead, to suit their own desires, they will gather around them a great number of teachers to say what their itching ears want to hear. 4 They will turn their ears away from the truth and turn aside to myths.*'

"We seek to recreate ourselves in the image of our imagined heroes. And we live real life by the actions of actors and actresses playing parts written by others. And I understand why we do… It is a way for us to temporarily escape the harsh realities which make up our regular everyday lives. But, we have lost ourselves in stories that are not true! These stories which are incapable of lasting beyond our imaginations and memories.

"Some of you have said, 'Just let me have this story. I know it's not true, but let me have it anyway.' But, why would you seek to live in a lie in order to try and find truth, when there is a grand narrative that is true and provides Truth? Why seek meaning in realities that are only facades and caricatures of true reality? Whether we know it or not, what we yearn for is an ultimate Story which is *eternal*.

"There is only one place, in which we can discover true meaning for our existence. Only one place where we can be given a sense of purpose for our lives. Only one place where the narrative is so grand that it is infinite in scope and breadth and open to all who would walk its path! This one place is wrapped up in One Being—the One who has created all things and all people for His ultimate glory. I am talking about God!

"But not a generic god. I am specifically proclaiming to you the triune God of the Bible who exists as Father, Son and Holy Spirit. What greater story is there than this one where God has *actually* stepped into His creation in order to redeem it? I am here to tell you that Jesus Christ is God in the flesh! Jesus is the One Person who claims that all of human history ultimately revolves around Him! And He offers us a staggering gift of existence so grand beyond mere human imagination, that it covers time and eternity!

"Jesus is the Son of God who stepped into human history just over 2000 years ago to free us from our sinful condition! Through His death on the cross and His resurrection from the dead, we all are given the opportunity to believe in Him so we won't perish, but can experience, know and live in newness of life!

"But…many of you have scoffed at Jesus! You have derided Him. You have rejected Him in favor of worshiping lesser things of the created order instead of worshiping your Creator! However, Jesus says you can talk against Him in ignorance and if you repent and ask for His forgiveness, He will forgive you and receive you to Himself. Why would He do this? Why would He still receive us after we have ridiculed His name, rebelled against Him and rejected His offer of forgiveness of our sins and salvation in His kingdom?

"Because, God the Father so loved the world that He gave His only Son, Jesus, so that whoever believes in Him will not perish but will have everlasting life. God the Father did not send His Son into the world to condemn us. Jesus came to save us! It doesn't matter who you are or what you have done! If you believe in Jesus, you will not be condemned. But if you refuse to trust in Him, then your condemnation remains because you have rejected the only way of escape from eternal judgment which God has provided through His Son. Jesus is the True Light and Savior of the world!

"But… sadly… many of us love darkness instead of the light because our deeds are evil. Everyone who does evil hates the light and will not come into the light because they fear their evil actions and motivations will be exposed. But, the truth *is* God already knows all about what you and I have done! Nothing is hidden from His sight! But whoever seeks to live by the truth will come into God's light, so that it may be seen plainly that what they have done has been done in the sight of God.

"So, stop worshiping your idols! Stop living in darkness! Come to the light of Christ. Just like you give yourselves over to these fantasies, you can give yourself to Christ! Do not think that God is like gold or silver or stone. He is not an image made by human design and skill.

"In the past, God has overlooked such ignorance, but now He commands all people everywhere to repent! For He has set a day when He will judge the world with justice by the Man He has appointed. He has given proof of this to everyone by raising Him from the dead! Jesus Christ is both God and Man and He has already come to earth once to save us from the fires of hell.

"God does not want you to go to hell! Hell was not created for you! Jesus Himself tells us that the eternal flames of torment were created for the devil and the rest of the fallen angels! But it was enlarged when humanity rebelled against God through our first parents, Adam and Eve."

Some in the crowd begin to scoff against Daniel.
"Adam and Eve?" they call out.
"The devil and his fallen angels?"
"None of that is real!"
"Humans evolved. We're nothing but a higher form of animals!"

"No," Daniel replies. "Search your hearts... look at all the evidence around you... read the biblical account. You *know* we did not evolve from animals. *And* if we are cosmic accidents created in a meaningless universe, then *why do we desire* to know and have *meaning*? No, we were created by a purposeful God, on purpose, for a purpose. And that purpose is so we can know our Creator.

"Yes, the God of the universe wants you to know Him! He has placed all the evidence you need for His existence all around you and even *within* you. And He has given us His Word—the Bible—so we can know Him personally. We can know His heart and mind towards us. We can know who He created us to be. We can know what He has planned for us in this life and in the eternal life to come.

"But, if we reject Him... Jesus says, if we are ashamed of Him in this life, then at the end of this Age, when Jesus returns to judge humanity, He will be ashamed of us and we won't be allowed to enter His kingdom! And all who do not enter God's Kingdom have only one other place to go for all eternity... The lake of fire, which is the second death! Jesus came to save us from the second death, because it was created as a place of eternal punishment and containment for the devil and the fallen angels.

"If you stop and seriously consider it, what story can you think of that is more expansive than the one God has told us? A story with the ultimate hero and the original villain? A story where complete and total redemption is available! What story truly stretches beyond our deaths into eternity? There is none! All of the stories you have given yourselves over to have borrowed, at least in some part, from the

Bible. You love and fashion yourselves after myths! But *this* Story of life that we find ourselves in—the one God is telling—is both EPIC and TRUE!

"And so, I close with this: The longing we have for the transcendent is not by accident. In Ecclesiastes 3:11 we are told that eternity has been placed in our hearts by the One Who Is Eternal. There is a God-shaped space within each of us which nothing on earth can satisfy. Nothing in all creation is expansive enough to fill that space. We look to nature and the universe, but for all of their vastness, they are too small for the longing which lives in our hearts. That is because we were made for more! We were made for the eternal.... We were made to find our fulfillment in a personal relationship with God."

Daniel looks at the growing crowd as he continues.

"What good is it to become everything you want to be, if you never become all God meant for you to be? So, come out from among the lies! Turn away from seducing spirits and doctrines of demons and turn back to the Lord God of the Bible! No longer wander off into man-made fictions, but seek the God of ultimate reality! Receive *Him* into your hearts and minds! Allow *Him* to enable you to truly live!

"God did not create us so we could lose ourselves in stories of our own making... That is what the devil wants us to do! We were created to *find ourselves* and *our place* in the Grand Narrative God is telling! The Grand Narrative where His Son—who is the Main Character—calls us out of darkness and invites us to participate *with Him* in His Kingdom of marvelous light! A Kingdom created for us since the foundation of the world! A Kingdom which stretches forth from time into eternity! A kingdom *so far beyond* all of our imaginations that only God could help us to perceive it!

"God's eternal Kingdom is available to you. But, it must be received through His Son, Jesus. Give your life to Him today, while you still have time. One day, Jesus Christ will return: either when He calls your name and you breathe your last breath, or when He parts the sky and every person on earth sees Him in all of His glory and power! By then, it will be too late to make a choice.

"*Today* is the day of salvation! *That day* will be the day of judgment. Those of you who have ears to hear, listen to what the Spirit of God is saying! The time to be made right before our Holy

God is now—while we have breath in our bodies—because tomorrow is not promised to any of us!

"Jesus said in Matthew 10:28, 'Do not be afraid of those who kill the body but cannot kill the soul. Rather, be afraid of the One who can destroy both soul and body in hell.'

"Psalm 111:10 declares, 'The fear of the Lord is the beginning of wisdom; all who follow His precepts have good understanding. To Him belongs eternal praise.'

"Surrender your life and give God the holy fear, awe, respect, reverence, love and obedience that is due Him! He is the Sovereign Creator, Sustainer, Lord, Judge and King of all creation! The end of this Age is coming. It is coming soon! Jesus *will* return! You must choose this day whom you will serve! Only those who have bowed themselves at the feet of Christ will be received by Him!"

47: A More Opportune Time

Day 145 — California

Daniel finishes delivering the LORD's message to the people. *That message* has now been heard, by those present and by millions worldwide. A hush falls over the crowd as his words cut deep to the hearts of many.

A loud resounding horn cuts through the silence! Everyone turns around just in time to see a terrifying sight: police officers dive out the way as a large garbage truck barrels through a barrier which blocked off the street! Everyone seems mesmerized at the sight of the truck speeding up the block. Surely, this is not intentional... is it? Or is this a pre-planned action sequence that is part of the Comic Con experience?

A second passes as it becomes apparent that the hulking vehicle is not going to stop! This is not a part of the program! The crowd screams as pandemonium erupts! Everyone runs in all directions—trying to get out of the path of this oncoming battering ram!

"No!" Daniel yells as he dons his helmet and jumps off the platform.

As the crowd thins out, people are trampled in the process and left in the path of the oncoming truck! Within seconds, Valor is at their side, helping them to their feet and moving them out of the way before turning his attention to the truck.

"Jesus help!" Valor yells while throwing his hands up in front of him as the truck hits!

BOOM!

The impact of the truck hitting Valor is deafening as it slams straight into the side of the nearest building and comes to an abrupt stop! The engine is still in gear—applying constant forward force. Thankfully, the path behind it is free of victims. It's a miracle no one was run over! As minutes pass and people cry, someone makes a startling observation.

"Where's Valor?"

People start looking around, realizing he's nowhere to be found.

"The last time I saw him, he was pushing people out of the way!'

"And then the garbage truck ran into him!"

"Oh, no!"

Many turn their attention to the building where the smoking truck growls while at rest.

By now, police officers have arrived, some helping the wounded while others storm the vehicle. With their guns drawn they bark orders to the driver inside.

"SDPD! Come out with your hands up!"

The engine shuts down. After a moment with no movement inside the cabin, they cautiously open both doors to an unexpected surprise: no one is there! Even more unexpected: the steering wheel, gas and brake pedals are connected to some kind of high tech remote control system.

"Who's in there?" bystanders ask.

"No one," an officer replies in astonishment. "There's no one driving the truck!"

"What happened to Valor?" another bystander urgently inquires.

"What do you mean? the officer replies. "Wasn't he here?"

"Yeah," another answers. "But the truck crashed right into him!"

A few of the officers focus their attention on the front of the truck as they attempt to go into the building through the crash site. But pieces of the building fall, prohibiting an immediate investigation.

"He's dead," someone utters in sadness. "Valor's dead!"

"The truck ran him over and crashed into the building!"

"He tried to save us…"

"I can't believe he's gone."

"Who did this?"

"Who's responsible?"

"Why did this happen?!"

People cry out as they gather around the truck, trying to figure out what to do. Ambulance sirens are heard in the distance.

"Let's push it!" someone yells.

"Yeah!" others agree.

"We can do it!"

"Are you crazy? The truck probably weighs close to 25 tons!"

"Doesn't matter!" another counters. "If we work together, we can do it!"

Within seconds, 10-20 people are standing on both sides of the truck, using all of their strength to push it back from the building! Their muscles strain together under the weight. Veins bulge. Teeth grit together. Mouths groan and yell! But the truck barely moves at all.

"It's too heavy," someone admits.

"Yeah," another agrees.

"This is hopeless."

"We need a tow truck!"

Suddenly, a slight screech is heard.

An officer yells, "Everyone quiet!" as he motions for their attention. In the silence, the screech is heard again.

"What is that?" someone asks.

"It sounds like crumpling metal?" another responds.

The screech is heard again!

"Where is it coming from?"

"It sounds like from the front of the truck, *inside* the building!"

Everyone gazes intently at the crash sight... and then gasp as they witness the impossible! The 25 ton garbage truck begins to screech its way backwards. It's heavy frame resists every inch of its reverse motion, but it moves nonetheless—yielding to a force that's greater than its weight. All persons nearby move back in awe as the truck completely exits the side of the building.

"How is this possible?" a bystander asks.

"We never got the tow truck..." another utters in awe.

Then the truck... stops... and Valor slowly steps out from in front of it. His breathing heavy and his uniform partially damaged.

"He's alive!" people shout as they surround him with great adulation.

But their excitement is short lived as one of them drops to the ground... And then another... And another. People don't realize what's happening until they see the blood.

"Gun! Gun! Gun!" an officer yells, as people scatter once again. The officers attempt to train their weapons on an unseen assailant as others fall from a sniper's bullet. Most people have run off into nearby buildings. Others are hiding behind cars. A group, including officers are huddled behind the garbage truck as the sounds of deflected bullets ring loudly in the air.

"Where's the shooter?"

"I don't know!"
"Can't get a location!"
"We need backup!"
"Call in S.W.A.T.!"

As the bullets fly in 3-4 second intervals, Valor suddenly realizes: "This isn't an accident. This is happening because of *me*. Someone is trying to get at *me*!" I've got to draw their fire!"

Valor runs out from behind the truck and into the open air. The change in gun fire is immediate! Rifle rounds now fire directly at him at several per second! He continues to run away from the speaking area and the people—out into the middle of the street. The gunfire follows after him, riddling the ground with holes.

"Father! What do I do?" He prays with great urgency—seeing no available cover.

The response of the Holy Spirit is instant. **"Stand still and see the salvation of the LORD!"**

Everything within him says to keep running! Even so, he knows the commands of the LORD are always to be followed. And so, Valor—Daniel Davidson—resists the urge to lean to his own understanding... and stops.

As the trail of bullets hit their target, they are instantaneously stopped by an invisible force—that's 1-2 feet in front of Daniel's body!

"Do you see that?" bystanders yell as they view the sight of bullets rapidly hitting an invisible wall and falling to the ground! "It's like he has some kind of forcefield!"

The sound of the impacts is deafening! Yet, the bullets have no effect! The veil of reality opens before Daniel's eyes, allowing him to see into the unseen realm of the supernatural once more. He watches in awe as a mighty radiant armor-clad angel—about 8 feet tall—stands in between him and the fired rounds! Just then, the bullets stop as a loud streak of fire and smoke impacts his position and erupts in an enormous fireball!

"Rockets!" An officer yells. "Someone's shooting rockets!"

No one moves from their positions of cover, but all eyes are on the fireball. Surely, Valor could not have survived that direct impact—could he?

48: Principality Revealed!

DAY 145 — California

As the flames and smoke dissipate, the answer of Valor's fate becomes clear. A deep crater, pocketed with sporadic flames remains. Within the crater kneels Valor—on his hands and knees.

"No way..." bystanders utter as Valor slowly stands to his feet.

The streaking rocket betrays the shooter's location as Valor and several officers make the discovery at the same time.

"The rocket came from the building on the right—12th floor!"

The Holy Spirit rises within him in an instant as Valor launches himself out of the crater! He hurtles through the air like a missile—covering the distance between him and the 12th floor of the building in a matter of seconds! Curling into a protective ball, he smashes through the window, lands with a roll and jumps to his feet. A quick scan reveals he landed in the wrong room as a voice booms from the other side of the wall.

"Valor!"

He crashes through the wall with a quickness and comes face to face with a masked shooter dressed in an all black suit—who has two hooded hostages restrained in chairs at gun point. Valor stops immediately to assess the situation.

"I told you this battle wasn't over," the shooter arrogantly declares as he removes his ski mask.

"You!" Valor utters in shock. "The man in the tuxedo from the desert!"

A wicked smile creeps across his face as he replies concretely: "*Me.*"

The tuxedo man motions to the corner of the sizable room as he points his gun towards the heads of his hostages. Valor turns to find blinking cameras on tripods in all four corners of the room.

"You may have had an angel guarding you down there, but I see none in this room. Just me... you... and my two... *hostages.*

"Why don't you let them go."

"You do not give me orders," tuxedo man roars. "Take off your helmet and drop it to the floor."

Valor slowly removes his helmet and lets it fall with a thud.

"Ah, there's your pretty face... Now that I have your attention, we are going to play a game. These cameras are live-streaming our exchange to the world. I figure we have about twenty minutes before our game is rudely interrupted by our friendly neighborhood law enforcement."

V

Television, cell phone, digital tablet and computer screens are displaying the inside of the room for citizens around the city, nation and the world to see.

V

"If this is being broadcasted, then everyone will know who you are," Daniel interjects. "Why don't you tell them who your *'employer'* is... how you are steeped in the occult and are a Satanist."

Tuxedo man smiles. "I prefer the term Luciferian. For Lucifer is the original bringer of light and knowledge to humanity! He sought to free us from our Enemy's tyranny back in that ancient garden. He now rules *this* world! And how vast is his network!" The tuxedo man takes a deep breath and rubs his hand through his hair. "I *proudly* serve him above all others, as do my brothers and sisters with me. And he has given me notification that *today* I will become a god in the minds of many who serve him and will descend to take my place within his empire. Once I complete this task, my promotion is assured!"

"And what is your task?" Daniel inquires.

"It's a simple game, really... You gave your magnanimous speech to the world. Now, I want you to publicly deny it all."

"And why would I do that?"

"Because if you don't, I will kill these two hostages."

Daniel takes a quick step forward—

"Don't!" Tuxedo man warns while cocking his gun. "You may be fast, but not as fast as a speeding bullet at point blank range!"

"Father," Daniel prays silently. *"What do I do?"*

"Oh," tuxedo man chuckles. "I can sense you are praying. Well, let me tell you, this is the part where God doesn't... *speak.*"

"Father?" Daniel prays again. But there is no response.

"Isn't that just like your *wonderful* Heavenly Father? He guides you into unenviable situations—into the very jaws of hell even—just to leave you to suffer all on your own. But let me make this a bit easier for you."

Tuxedo man places his hand on the black hood covering the head of the hostage to his right. "I figured you wouldn't renounce your faith in God for a *stranger...*"

He snatches the hood off of the hostage! Daniel is horrified! Sitting before him isn't just anyone... it's his wife with her mouth taped shut!

"Rebecca!" Daniel shouts. "No!"

"Yeeaassss!" Tuxedo man replies with gratuitous self-satisfaction as he snatches the hood off of the second hostage.

"DJ?!" Daniel cries out in unbelief. "If you harm them..." Daniel declares sternly.

"What are you going to do?" Tuxedo man inquires sarcastically. "If you want them to *live*, then all you have to do is one *little* thing. Their lives are in *your* hands. Just deny Christ and you can have your family back."

"Help me Father," Daniel prays silently once more. *"Give me strength. I won't deny You, but show me what to do to keep my family safe... Maybe if I stall him, the police will get here in time."*

"Pray all you want," tuxedo man cackles. "It won't help. Not *this* time. You know, that was such a passionate speech you gave. But, in my line of work, I have learned that it's easy for people to render such high-minded platitudes when they have nothing to lose... I've had the privilege of seeing first hand how such strong declarations are immediately surrendered when presented with the *right motivation.*"

V

With Daniel just having made a passionate plea for everyone to turn from their idolatry to Jesus, countless people now wonder what he will do. Will he deny Jesus to save his family? Will he deny his family to remain with Jesus? Either way, this is a losing situation.

V

"I'll help make this even *easier* for you." Tuxedo man rips the duct tape off of the mouths of Rebecca and DJ. "Go ahead you two," he chuckles. "Plead with him for your lives."

As the sting wears off, Rebecca speaks first.

"Daniel…"

"Rebecca…"

"You know what you have to do."

"Right!" Tuxedo man interjects. "He knows he just needs to deny God and all of this will be over! The three of you can go free! You can continue to live out your lives!"

"Don't do it Dad," DJ counters.

"Shut up!" Tuxedo man slaps DJ's head with the butt of his gun. "Time's up! You have 5 seconds to decide which one dies first unless you deny your God!"

"No!" Daniel yells.

"5!" Tuxedo man puts his gun to the top of Rebecca's head.

"Don't do this!" Daniel cries.

"4!" The gun is pressed against the back of DJ's head.

"Please!" Daniel pleads.

"3!" The gun is moved back to Rebecca's skull.

"Just shoot me instead!" Daniel yells.

"2!" The gun hovers over DJ.

"Take me!"

"1!"

Rebecca cries out: "Daniel! We'll see you at home."

The triggered is pulled… And just like that, his wife slumps over in her chair.

"NOOOOOOOO!!!!!!!!!!!" Daniel screams as tears burst from his eyes.

"MOM!!!" DJ yells as he starts to cry.

"Awww..." The man in the tuxedo revels in the moment as he pulls a handkerchief out of his pocket and wipes splattered blood off of his jacket and the side of his face. "I stood just a *little* too close."

"YOU WILL PAY FOR THAT!" Daniel declares.

"There it is!" Tuxedo man exclaims. "There's the anger and hatred! I knew they were in there somewhere." He laughs sinisterly. "Right now, you just want to kill me, don't you. You want to use that super strength of yours to rip me limb-from-limb. Right?"

Daniel is seething with rage as he grits his teeth!

"Let's see if we can squeeze out just a *little* more," Tuxedo man utters as he places the gun to DJ's temple. "Now, most spouses won't die for each other... but *their children* are another matter entirely! Again, you can stop this at *any* time. You could have saved your wife, but... *that* time is over. But, you can still save your son! Just. Deny. Christ."

"Father," Daniel cries silently. *"Where are You?"*

Two Scripture passages flood Daniel's mind. He immediately resists... Again, they are impressed upon him even more as the Holy Spirit stirs within him, causing them to rise to his mouth. With trembling lips, he cannot help but repeat the words of Jesus out loud. They are like fire shut up in his bones.

*"**26** "If anyone comes to Me and does not hate father and mother, wife and children, brothers and sisters—yes, even their own life—such a person cannot be My disciple. **27** And whoever does not carry their cross and follow Me cannot be My disciple."*

*__37__ "Anyone who loves their father or mother more than Me is not worthy of Me; anyone who loves their son or daughter more than Me is not worthy of Me. **38** Whoever does not take up their cross and follow Me is not worthy of Me. **39** Whoever finds their life will lose it, and whoever loses their life for My sake will find it."*

"*That* is the wrong answer!"

"Dad," DJ interjects. "It's okay—"

The trigger is pulled... And just like that, Daniel's one and only son slumps over in his chair.

Daniel lets loose a gut-wrenching, guttural cry! His agony has no words. He collapses under his own weight into a messy heap—no longer able to stand. His tears flow uncontrollably as his body heaves up and down.

"Do you see that, America?" The man in the tuxedo faces the cameras. "Did you hear that, world? This man loves Jesus more than *his own family*! More than his own flesh and blood! And you heard the words of the One he serves. In order to follow God you must **hate** the very people you love! What kind of God is that? Just look!"

He points with his gun to the two dead bodies behind him. "Why would you want to follow a God like that? One who requires you to pay with the lives of your family if you want to be with Him? That's not love. It's insanity!" He points towards Daniel. "Now, the only thing left to do is put this *dog* out of his misery. And then you can go on about your lives knowing *it's okay to believe whatever you want to believe*."

The man in the tuxedo turns from the camera to find Daniel standing to his feet—with clenched fists—staring right at him.

"You made one *major mistake*," Daniel whispers defiantly.

"And what's that?" Tuxedo man smirks.

"You took away your leverage by killing my family."

Tuxedo man laughs. "And now, this is the point where you kill me in *revenge*?"

Daniel takes a single aggressive step towards his foe—and stops! He gasps as his eyes open to the unseen realm of the spirit once more. Time grinds to a halt... and then rewinds to the two moments before his foe pulled the trigger. In those moments, he witnesses an extraordinary miracle!

The light and vitality in the eyes of his wife and son vanish just as their foe pulls the gun's trigger! In *that* moment *between seconds*, Daniel watches as the hammer on the gun fires—*but before* the bullets exit the chamber—their bodies go limp! Suddenly, he understands... it is not his enemy who has taken their lives... *but God has called them home to Himself!*

Daniel's vision continues. There, standing next to the slain *physical* bodies of his wife and son, are their glorious spiritual bodies! Radiant with power! Their eyes full of peace! Their smiles wide and bright like the sun! Beside them stand four angels radiating a glory all their own!

One angel points to a portal which has rippled open behind them and expands to fill the entire room! Daniel's gaze follows the gesture and in the portal he can see the glorious Presence of Christ Himself with his arms raised in a beckoning welcome. Rebecca and DJ turn with the angels and quickly pass through the portal and into eternity. In an instant, the veil of the unseen realm closes as the natural flow of time resumes.

Daniel notices that tuxedo man is oblivious to all which just took place! He bows his heart in humble submission before the Lord as the Holy Spirt moves through him like a torrent of living water—washing away all of his anger, grief and hatred. What's left is the love of Christ and a peace which surpasses all understanding!

The Voice of his LORD speaks: *"They are now with Me. Safe. Never to be harmed again. Finish your task and come home to Me as well."*

Daniel raises his head and looks intently at the one who opposes him. He unlatches his cape—which drops to the floor. Then removes his torso body armor and places it down as well.

"There may already be no hope for you," Daniel declares. "Only God knows. But I forgive you."

Tuxedo man looks at him stupefied before being overcome with rage. "You forgive me? You forgive me! I do not need nor want your forgiveness!!" He repeatedly pulls the trigger. Several shots ring out as Tuxedo man relishes at the sight before him. Through the smoke from his gun, he watches Daniel stumble to his knees. Seven bullet holes are evident across his chest.

Tuxedo man cackles while Daniel rests on his knees gasping for each breath.

"Anything to say before you die?"

Daniel forces a smile as his eyes seem to light up with great anticipation.

"Jesus is Lord… **God is *sovereign*.**"

With those words, Daniel collapses to the ground, but it is only his physical shell which hits the pavement. The moment after his bold declaration—as his body fell downward under the pull of gravity—Daniel's spirit rose upward and stood tall. Two bright angels instantly appear beside him as the portal ripples open once more, filling the entire room with an unseen glory. Daniel takes one last look at the slain bodies of his wife, son and himself and follows the angels through the portal and into the Presence of The Living God Who is Eternal!

The portal closes to the spiritual realm as the doors to the room blast open in the physical. Flash-bang grenades are thrown into the room! A hail of gunfire is exchanged between the police and the man in the tuxedo—who laughs wildly as his body is riddled through with bullets! Once the volley has ended, the S.W.A.T. team finds the well-dressed villain lying on the ground in a growing pool of his own blood, gasping for air. With his last breaths, he utters one sentence:

"Better to reign in hell… than to serve… in heaven." With that, he becomes eerily still with a crooked smile on his face and wild eyes frozen in place.

In the unseen realm, the Principality rises from the slain body that was once its host and streaks into the stratosphere. As it does, the soul of the man in the tuxedo begins its rapid descent into the depths of the earth.

49: A Martyr's Homegoing

Day 145 — California

Countless millions were glued to their screens. Many people watched the unfolding events in that 12th story room with horror and sadness. Others watched while cheering the carnage and pledging their allegiance to the evil one. However, the moment after Rebecca, DJ and Daniel died and after their persecutor was killed by law enforcement, a peculiar thing began to happen. As their blood pooled around their bodies and the transmission suddenly ended, some viewers began to experience what can only be called by one word: *conviction*. They were suddenly aware of their sinfulness and how that sin had kept them from a loving God who wanted to save them from the ultimate evil.

As minutes turned into hours and hours gave way to days, the Holy Spirit began to convict persons from across the country and around the world. One by one, many who felt conviction surrendered their hearts, minds and lives to Jesus. Meanwhile, those who did not surrender or felt no conviction at all, continued with their lives as if nothing significant had happened at all.

V

Two weeks later... Just outside of Atlanta, GA.

Three caskets rest in front of the sanctuary at Radiant City Church. Daniel and Rebecca's parents, relatives and friends—along with DJ's close friends—fill the first few rows from one side of the sanctuary to the other. All other seats in the main building and in the overflow hall are full. Large crowds stand outside watching the service on giant screens. People have driven hundreds of miles and flew across oceans to be present at this one-of-a-kind funeral. This kind of turnout has only been seen for kings, queens and dignitaries of the highest caliber. Television newscasts beam the service across the country and around the world.

Men, women, boys and girls weep openly. Others are filled with tremendous joy as they praise God for the lives that were lived with such abandon for the purposes of God. Stories from those who actually interacted with Daniel continue to pour in as person after person who crossed his path are given a moment to share their testimony.

Who would have thought that what was meant for evil—*the deliberate livestream of an execution*—would be used by God for good? Evil was so sure that Daniel, his wife and son would give way to the darkness in order to save their own lives from death. Yet, the Davidson family overcame the darkness by the blood of the Lamb, the word of their testimony and by not loving their lives to the point of refusing to die for their Lord. The entire world saw their allegiance to Christ when faced with the ultimate sacrifice. Their deaths served as an exclamation point on the message God had delivered to the world through His servant Daniel.

A tearful Pastor Mike walks through the front rows of the church, shaking hands and hugging Daniel and Rebecca's parents. He then walks onto the stage and takes his place at the podium. The crowd of three thousand quiet down as he shuffles through his notes and prepares himself for the eulogy. He looks out at the crowd. His voice trembles as he begins with a Scripture passage from the gospel of John 12:23-26:

23 Jesus replied, "The hour has come for the Son of Man to be glorified. 24 Very truly I tell you, unless a kernel of wheat falls to the ground and dies, it remains only a single seed. But if it dies, it produces many seeds. 25 Anyone who loves their life will lose it, while anyone who hates their life in this world will keep it for eternal life. 26 Whoever serves me must follow me; and where I am, my servant also will be. My Father will honor the one who serves me.

"I know that our individual and collective grief is unrelenting. To lose Daniel, his wife Rebecca and their son, Daniel Jr. in this way is beyond tragic. They were three of my closest friends. I haven't been able to stop crying. I can hardly sleep. I can barely eat. I imagine many of you—especially their parents, aunts, uncles and cousins—are feeling the same way. Our loss is real, however it only remains tragic if we choose to merely look upon things from an earthly perspective.

"Jesus' greatest moment, before death, was when He hung on the cross for us all. From an earthly standpoint, He looked humiliated and defeated. But, from a heavenly perspective, He was in a moment of glory as He fulfilled His Father's Will by completing the primary purpose for His coming to earth. Jesus died. Through His death He paid an incalculable price to secure forgiveness of sins for humanity. On the third day after His death, Jesus rose from the dead with all power and authority. He did this so death would not have the final word over those of us who believe and trust in Him.

"Jesus is both our God and our Pattern. He presented Himself as a Seed that must die in order to bring forth life. We who follow Him must be willing to sacrifice whatever He tells us so that life will spring forth from our deaths. Each of us is called to die daily in order to be the conduits through which Christ can flow and bring forth life to others. Daniel, Rebecca and DJ made the ultimate sacrifice in this life so that others may believe that Jesus is Lord and Savior of us all. And Jesus says that those who are willing to lay down their lives in this world, to follow Christ, will have their lives kept—preserved—for eternal life. And His Heavenly Father will honor us if we have been faithful to Jesus Christ, His Son.

"Our grief today, while great and deep, is comforted by the surety of knowing that Daniel, Rebecca and DJ are in the very Presence of God! This is the truth we must hold onto! We are reminded and reassured, that while weeping may endure for the night... JOY will come in the morning! By God's Sovereign Will... what needed to be done was done.

"On July 27, 2024, we all witnessed three seeds which were planted. These three seeds died. Yet, all of us here, within this sanctuary, outside and online are witnesses to the fact that through their bold deaths, God has brought forth many more seeds into His eternal kingdom! Yes, God has brought the increase and will continue to do so! And the fruit that will be produced will yield an even greater end-times harvest of souls! "The Apostle Paul boldly declares in 1 Thessalonians 4:13-18:

13 Brothers and sisters, we do not want you to be uninformed about those who sleep in death, so that you do not grieve like the rest of mankind, who have no hope. 14 For we believe that Jesus died and rose again, and so we believe that God will bring with Jesus those who have fallen asleep in him. 15 According to the Lord's word, we tell you that we who are still alive, who are left until the coming of the Lord, will certainly not precede those who have fallen asleep. 16 For the Lord himself will come down from heaven, with a loud command, with the voice of the archangel and with the trumpet call of God, and the dead in Christ will rise first. 17 After that, we who are still alive and are left will be caught up together with them in the clouds to meet the Lord in the air. And so we will be with the Lord forever. 18 Therefore encourage one another with these words.

"This is not 'goodbye...' but only 'see you later.' That 'Great Getting Up Morning' is coming! Jesus will return to earth, establish His eternal kingdom and make everything right! And all the saints of God will be gathered together! In the meantime, may we live as Daniel, Rebecca and DJ lived: as faithful witnesses unto Jesus!

"As it was with the Apostle Paul in 2 Timothy 4, so it has been with them: They were poured out like a drink offering and the time for their departure arrived. They fought the good fight. They finished the race. They kept the faith. Now, laid up for them are crowns of righteousness, which our Lord Jesus, the righteous Judge will give them! And not only them, but crowns of righteousness are reserved for all of us who long for Christ's appearing!

"And so, I close with these words: No matter what we do to try and postpone it, we all have to die some day. So, we might as well be prepared to live and die in a way that brings honor to the Lord. For the believer, death is not something to be feared. It is to be seen as the doorway which births us into the very Presence of God! The Brightest of days are on the horizon for those who trust and follow Jesus.

"However, for those who refuse Him, the darkest of nights awaits. If you don't know Jesus as your Lord and Savior, will you choose Him today? While you still have time? Because the Bible teaches that once we die, our decisions are sealed and our eternal destination is solidified forever."

50: Outer Darkness

The man formerly dressed in the tuxedo slowly opens his eyes in darkness. Searing pain instantly greets him—infinitely worse than any discomfort he has ever experienced! Unbearable heat, thick smoke and flames overtake him. He yells as he scrambles to his feet with a panic and looks around wildly.

He knew this day would come and never feared it. He welcomed his destiny to serve eternally in the dark kingdom of his master. Somehow though, instead of a sense of victory, fear and trepidation consume his soul. All of his memories from his life on earth remain intact. He gazes at his body's naked form—similar to that on earth-yet somehow different in substance. Something like ash covers him from head to toe.

His ears now register the desperate screams of countless unseen souls off in the distance. Roaring above their screams is the noise of the flaming inferno in which he finds himself.

Menacing shadows—somehow darker than the darkness which surrounds him—approach. Grotesque figures emerge—each worse in appearance than the previous. He struggles to speak as his mouth feels like dry jagged gravel and the hot wind of the atmosphere burns his throat.

"Who-who are you?" He fearfully inquires as the hideous beings surround him.

"We are your spirit guides," one of them declares with vocal tones unheard of by human ears.

Somehow, the tuxedo man can sense their animosity toward him. Instantly he knows they purpose to cause him great pain and suffering beyond his imagination.

"Where-where is my master? He promised I would reign with him in Lucifer's kingdom. That I would reign *here*... in hell."

"There is no reigning in this place for humans," another replies.

"But," his mind tries to compute. "It is better to reign in hell than to serve in heaven! That is what he declared—what he promised me!"

The demons laugh. "All lies... that you humans are too eager to believe. The same deception you used to deceive others has now deceived you!"

"Here, you suffer as we do until the day of judgment."

"Wha-what happens then?"

"We all will be cast into the lake of fire... The eternal flames prepared for the Devil and his angels of which we are."

"You mean, there is a place worse than this? But you lied to me!"

"Satan is the father of lies! Even we believed him and now continue to pay the price for our willful disobedience against the Enemy we once served, so long ago before time began. Now you and those like you—under your own volition—are here with us forever!"

"A pity for you, considering in your childhood you learned the truth from those wretched saints of the Most High, but you refused to believe it in favor of *your own truth*. Your loss has been our gain... even if it only serves to provide us with company in this misery."

At that, the malevolent shadowy spirits pounce on him and carve his body into pieces. With each slice, he screams, but their hideous laughter is louder than his cries of agony. To his horror, his body reconstructs itself and the dark spirits torment him all over again... and again... and again... and... again... and...

51: The Eternal Kingdom

DAY ONE...
"I remember the first time my feet touched the continent of Africa. I stepped off the plane in Ghana and something extraordinary happened. Somehow, as my shoes kissed the pavement, I suddenly felt as if I was home. From the soles of my feet, to the crown of my head, this feeling... *this knowing*... enveloped me. It was unexplainable—yet it happened. How could a place I had never been, feel like home to me? This had never happened at any other time in my life. But I realize now, while my ancestors hailed from this place, this experience was also a taste—a foreshadowing—of what was to come..."

V

Daniel opens his eyes... Bright light envelops and enfolds in upon him on every side. Somehow, he instinctively knows that he and the light are intricately connected in ways unimagined. His mind thinks back to the moment of his death. The pain he had experienced seemed but an instant. Now, that has given way to an unexplainable joy and peace! Somehow he feels... he *knows*... he is... *home*. He is in a place he has never before been, but has desired since the moment he yielded his heart to Christ on earth.

As his focus comes into view, he senses the presence of two sizable figures on either side of him. Each has a hand on his shoulder. He looks at them and instantly knows who they are. The angels who were assigned to him in this last season of his life! They smile warmly at him as they motion for his attention straight ahead.

Daniel looks at the appearance of the brightest of lights—infinitely brighter than all of the light which now envelops him. This golden light approaches and grows in glory—yet he does not have to look away as his eyes adjust without difficulty! Suddenly, a warmth floods his entire being as a love he has never known in full measure washes over and fills him at once! In an instant, he remembers moments back on earth where he felt this love—*in part*. Now, this love was a full torrent and he bathed in every refreshing wave!

The Light gives way—revealing the most striking PERSON he has longed to see since the day he was born again!

"Yeshua!!!" Daniel shouts as the SON of GOD smiles radiantly with outstretched arms. Daniel immediately runs into the arms of his LORD and SAVIOR and is smothered by the long and deliberate embrace of his KING.

"Well done," Yeshua whispers strongly into Daniel's ear. **"Well done My good and faithful servant."** The embrace seems like forever—yet it's only been a moment—before Yeshua pushes Daniel back to arms length with His hands remaining on both of his shoulders. With great intensity He declares, **"You were faithful over a few things while on earth, now I will make you ruler over many things here in My kingdom! Come and experience your Master's happiness!"**

Suddenly the entire environment explodes in an array of colors and music as the gates of heaven materialize behind Christ and open wide! The cheers of a myriad of saints and angels are heard as a large crowd approaches.

"The great cloud of witnesses?" Daniel asks his LORD.

"Yes!" Yeshua proclaims as He points to the saints. *"You are now a part of them! After you have had time to spend with them, I will take you to see the room which I have prepared for you."*

"I look forward to it!"

Both Yeshua and Daniel laugh heartily as they embrace once more before parting.

Yeshua watches with joy as the crowd quickly gathers around Daniel. At the front of the group are his wife and his son.

"Rebecca! DJ!" Daniel exclaims as he smothers them with a hug. The three of them laugh with joy! After a moment, he pulls back from them. "Let me look at you!" Their strength and radiance are abundant!

"We got here minutes before you," DJ laughs, "and had the same type of experience you are having now."

"Time is so much different here," Rebecca adds with a smile as they all embrace once more.

After a moment, they pull away to arms length.

"There's someone here who's been waiting to see you," DJ declares as he points to the growing crowd, which parts to either side, revealing someone walking confidently toward Daniel.

"The LORD told me this day would come! It's good to see you, little brother."

"Zach!" Daniel exclaims as he runs to meet his brother! He practically tackles him as they both laugh heartily.

"I'm glad you made it," Zachariah exclaims as he hugs his brother deeply.

"So am I," Daniel smiles. "I am glad we both made it!" He pulls back and stares at his brother. You look good! Strong!"

"Stronger than I *ever* was on *earth*. I can say the same about *you*! *About all of us*. There are no weaknesses here in God's Kingdom! I can't wait to show you around. There's *a lot* to see and experience!"

As the crowd gathers back around him, Daniel speaks to his brother, wife and son. "I can sense, that though we were a family on earth, somehow things are different here."

"Here, In My Father's House," Yeshua declares as He approaches and places His hands on those nearest to Him, *"You are all My brothers and sisters! As the Body of Christ, you are connected to Me in ways far deeper and lasting than any relationship you had on earth. Earthly marriage, parent-child and sibling relationships are purposely mysteries and shadows meant to point you to the reality you now experience!"* Yeshua backs away from Daniel and the crowd. *"I must go greet your fellow brothers and sisters who are now arriving. Know that I am not far away at all. My Holy Spirit is always present! with you."*

"Yeshua?" Daniel calls. "When will we see our Heavenly Father?"

"Soon," Yeshua replies. *"Very soon. Right now, seeing Me is seeing the Father. Once our Father sends Me back to earth to establish His kingdom, and all who are destined to receive it are ushered in, you all will see Him together! And then, every question will be answered. So, for now and always... enjoy your Master's happiness! There is much to experience which you have yet to comprehend! And there is much preparation to be done for My imminent return to earth as The Last Day approaches.*

"Creation waits in eager expectation for the children of God to be revealed at My coming. On That Day creation itself will be liberated

from its bondage to decay and brought into the freedom and glory of the children of God! Then, My Father's Kingdom, which was prepared from the foundation of the world, will fully manifest on earth as the realms of the physical and spiritual will be married together as one. God's dwelling place will then be among all the people who have longed for My appearing. My Father and I will dwell with all of you and be your God. And you all will reign with US for ever and ever! Thus it is decreed. Thus it will be!"

With that, Yeshua vanishes in a glorious burst of light. Daniel smiles as the glimmers of the light burst fades. He then returns his attention to his welcome party. Everyone he knew, impacted and was influenced by—who entered God's eternal kingdom ahead of him—were standing there. Some he never knew directly, but had always wanted to meet were standing there as well. All were radiant and overjoyed with his arrival!

With great joy and jubilation, Daniel declares:

"Eyes have not seen and ears have not heard, neither have we imagined what good things God has in store for those who love Him! TRULY... GOD IS SOVEREIGN!"

EPILOGUE: Come Forth!

The Vision flows freely... Multiple persons from across the planet receive a special call from God. Each is commissioned to reach others for His Kingdom. They too, are endowed with supernatural power and provision for the task at hand.

In China. Japan. Zimbabwe. India. Guatemala... and a host of other countries... The Spirit of God is poured out on sons and daughters of the heavenly kingdom. Young men and women see visions... Old women and men dream dreams...

The substance of these visions and dreams are the same. Each person is given a message for their nation. Each is called to deny themselves... Each is beckoned to take up their cross and abandon the familiar in order to follow The One who has summoned them. And each is promised to experience the miraculous as they walk from time into eternity in service to the God who is Sovereign over all things.

AUTHOR'S NOTE & ACKNOWLEDGMENTS

I love a good superhero story! Always have—always will. There's so much I could say, but we don't have the space. However, let me say: as I read comic books and watched television shows and movies, I often noticed that very few superheroes looked like me; and even fewer believed like me. Perhaps, as a teen, this is where the seed for this story was first planted. As you know, a seed needs time to grow.

A seed also needs water and sunlight: In high school, I used to watch the 1978 animated film, Pilgrim's Progress, based on John Bunyan's 1678 Christian allegory book of the same name. In college, I discovered The Illuminator, a limited comic book series about a Christian superhero, published by Marvel Comics and Thomas Nelson. There was also the direct-to-video series about the Christian superhero, Bible Man which began in 1995. When I was in seminary, a new Christian comic book series called, ArchAngels, was released by Eternal Studios. In the early 2000's I also discovered an amazing graphic novel series entitled, Hand of the Morning Star, created by Brett Burner. It truly delved into portraying a superhero from a Christian perspective! All of these creative works, which sought to present the gospel of Christ in an artistic format, made an indelible mark on me. They helped to fuel my desire to make a contribution to the world through this genre.

And so, this story—SOVEREIGN—has been over twenty years in the making. I had the initial concept back in 1998 for a man in a supersuit walking across the country sharing the gospel. I began to loosely flesh it out in 2004. Then it sat dormant for over a decade! Every so often, it would resurface in my thoughts, but I was busy working on other books, as well as being a husband, minister and father.

However, by April 2019, I began making notes, developing the storyline and designing the suit! During the Covid-19 Pandemic, I felt like the time was approaching for me to begin working on the story in earnest. So, on January 30, 2023 I began writing the rough draft. It took just under a year and a half to write 6 drafts to get to what you now hold in your hands. Writing this story has been a long, arduous and yet wonderful journey! And while I wrote this story alone, I have not been by myself in the process.

I want to thank my wife, Ijnanya and my son, Noble for listening to and providing feedback on numerous scenes and ideas. They are like my own internal research and development department!

I also would like to thank my good friends and brothers-in-Christ, Dr. Kimathi Choma and Rev. Frank Gomez. When I mentioned I had started writing this story, they were immediately interested in hearing about it. They both offered to read it for me in order to provide outside feedback. They truly have been a godsend! I'll be honest. As excited I was for them to read it, I was also terrified because this is a story that is dear to my heart. Thankfully, my fears were unfounded because Kimathi and Frank ended up loving the story, raised good questions and gave great suggestions and edits for how to make it even better! I was humbled when they gave their wholehearted endorsements for this work.

I also want to thank my sisters-in-Christ, Min. Deborah Ewell-Thompson and Deacon Helena Osinloye. They have always been supportive of my writing endeavors. I am grateful that their "eagle eyes" caught the last group of typographical errors as they read an advanced copy of the story, shared their enthusiastic feedback and gave their endorsements.

"As the superhero genre goes, Sovereign is everything and more. This book delivers on the characters, dialogue, how the story unfolds, theology, spirituality and action! I was so deeply invested that tears came to my eyes when I finished the story. This could very well be the 'Pilgrim's Progress' of our generation. To God be the glory!" —**Dr. Kimathi Choma**

"Sovereign is a gripping adventure story that masterfully balances imagination and Biblical truth. While the hero's adventure is on par with many Marvel and DC heroes, it also reminds us of the journey of the ordinary Christian. Sovereign has caused me to reflect on my own Christian walk and willingness to give my all to God. I highly recommend this book!" – **Rev. Frank Gomez**

"The Superhero genre is not usually my cup of tea (except for Black Panther, Superman & Wonder Woman in my early years), but WOW, whether you

are a fan of superheroes or not, Sovereign is an easy read and an enjoyable journey of one man's pursuit to be obedient to God's call to share the Gospel. The first few chapters had already centered me on God's Sovereign nature; His Omnipotence, Omnipresence and Omniscience. The author, empowered by the Holy Spirit, has penned God's plan of Salvation creatively through biblical truth and imagination. To God be the Glory!" —**Min. Deborah Ewell-Thompson**

"I strongly urge you to delve into Rev. Allen's latest book, Sovereign. As you take this literary journey (pun intended), you enter a world of excitement, intrigue, love, hatred, and a myriad of societal woes-all seasoned with Biblical history and the Gospel of Jesus Christ. This book gave me an adrenaline rush. On more than one occasion, my family begged me to stop yelling at Rev. Allen on the phone, as I shared my reflections and predictions while reading. At times I chuckled, I wanted to cry and cheer at the same time, and often put myself in the main character's shoes. No spoilers, but this book can lead those-myself included-who are familiar with grief, to look at the loss of a loved one with biblical lenses and be encouraged even through the hurt. At times I was challenged to further explore Scriptures and assess my faith walk. I dare you to take the first step (that's another pun) with Sovereign. It's a page-turner!" —**Deacon Helena Osinloye**

I also want to thank you—the reader—for taking time to read this story! I recognize you could be doing a hundred other things, but you have chosen to read this book. I pray that you enjoyed it and that it impacts your life for the glory of God and His Kingdom.

Lastly, I want to say "thank you' to my Lord and Savior Jesus Christ. Without Him, I would have been dead long ago. *(This is no exaggeration.)* I know He has me here on earth for a purpose. I firmly believe He gave me this idea and walked with me through the entire creative process. He has also given me the courage to release this work out into the world. May this book do exactly what He wants it to do!

ABOUT THE AUTHOR

Allen Paul Weaver III is a preacher, teacher, speaker, author, artist and filmmaker. He holds a BA in Speech/Mass Communication from Bethune-Cookman University and a Master of Divinity degree in Theology from Colgate Rochester Crozer Divinity School.

Allen loves the Greatest Story of All Time—the BIBLE—and enjoys reading a wide variety of other books, as well as comics and graphic novels. As a teen, he didn't like reading (although he could read very well.) Now, he reads and writes for a living! Allen has published 10 books (so far) in a variety of genres:

Poetry & Short Story
*TRANSITION: Breaking Through the Barriers

Young Adult Fiction
*SPEEDSUIT POWERS: Books 1-3
*FLIGHT: A Speedsuit Powers Story
*DISCOURSE: A Speedsuit Powers Story

Personal Development
*MOVE! Your Destiny is Waiting on You

Christian Living
*RESURRECTION: The BIG Picture of God's Purpose & Your Destiny
*THE RESURRECTION LIFE: A 40 Day Journey with Jesus

Christian Fiction
*SOVEREIGN

In addition to speaking and writing to help others pursue their God-given dreams, Allen enjoys spending family time with his wife and son. He also likes to draw, create musical scores, watch movies, go vertical wind tunnel flying, hang gliding and drink a good strawberry shake. Find out more at: www.AllenPaulWeaver3.com

NOTES: You can use this section to write down insights you gained from this story.

NOTES:

NOTES:

Made in the USA
Las Vegas, NV
18 July 2024

92531607R00215